THE BLACK BOX

MORE WILDSIDE CLASSICS

Please see www.wildsidepress.com for a complete list!

THE BLACK BOX

E. PHILLIPS OPPENHEIM

WILDSIDE PRESS

THE BLACK BOX

This edition published 2005 by Wildside Press, LLC.
www.wildsidepress.com

CHAPTER I

SANFORD QUEST, CRIMINOLOGIST

The young man from the west had arrived in New York only that afternoon, and his cousin, town born and bred, had already embarked upon the task of showing him the great city. They occupied a table in a somewhat insignificant corner of one of New York's most famous roof-garden restaurants. The place was crowded with diners. There were many notabilities to be pointed out. The town young man was very busy.

"See that bunch of girls on the right?" he asked. "They are all from the chorus in the new musical comedy—opens tomorrow. They've been rehearsing every day for a month. Some show it's going to be, too. I don't know whether I'll be able to get you a seat, but I'll try. I've had mine for a month. The fair girl who is leaning back, laughing, now, is Elsie Havers. She's the star…. You see the old fellow with the girl, just in a line behind? That's Dudley Worth, the multimillionaire, and at the next table there is Mrs. Atkinson—you remember her divorce case?"

It was all vastly interesting to the young man from the west, and he looked from table to table with ever-increasing interest.

"Say, it's fine to be here!" he declared. "We have this sort of thing back home, but we are only twelve stories up and there is nothing to look at. Makes you kind of giddy here to look past the people, down at the city."

The New Yorker glanced almost indifferently at the one sight which to a stranger is perhaps the most impressive in the new world. Twenty-five stories below, the cable cars clanging and clashing their way through the narrowed streets seemed like little fire-flies, children's toys pulled by an invisible string of fire. Further afield, the flare of the city painted the murky sky. The line of the river scintillated with rising and falling stars. The tall buildings stabbed the blackness, fingers of fire. Here, midway to the clouds, was another world, a world of luxury, of brilliant toilettes, of light laughter, the popping of corks, the joy of living, with everywhere the vague perfume and flavour of femininity.

The young man from the country touched his cousin's arm suddenly.

"Tell me," he enquired, "who is the man at a table by himself? The waiters speak to him as though he were a little god. Is he a millionaire, or a judge, or what?"

The New Yorker turned his head. For the first time his own face showed some signs of interest. His voice dropped a little. He himself was impressed.

"You're in luck, Alfred," he declared. "That's the most interesting man in New York—one of the most interesting in the world. That's Sanford Quest."

"Who's he?"

"You haven't heard of Sanford Quest?"

"Never in my life."

The young man whose privilege it was to have been born and lived all his days in New York, drank half a glassful of wine and leaned back in his chair. Words, for a few moments, were an impossibility.

"Sanford Quest," he pronounced at last, "is the greatest master in criminology the world has ever known. He is a magician, a scientist, the Pierpont Morgan of his profession."

"Say, do you mean that he is a detective?"

The New Yorker steadied himself with an effort. Such ignorance was hard to realise—harder still to deal with.

"Yes," he said simply, "you could call him that—just in the same way you could call Napoleon a soldier or Lincoln a statesman. He is a detective, if you like to call him that, the master detective of the world. He has a great house in one of the backwater squares of New York, for his office. He has wireless telegraphy, private chemists, a little troop of spies, private telegraph and cable, and agents in every city of the world. If he moves against any gang, they break up. No one can really understand him. Sometimes he seems to be on the side of the law, sometimes on the side of the criminal. He takes just what cases he pleases, and a million dollars wouldn't tempt him to touch one he doesn't care about. Watch him go out. They say that you can almost tell the lives of the people he passes, from the way they look at him. There isn't a crook here or in the street who doesn't know that if Sanford Quest chose, his career would be ended."

The country cousin was impressed at last. With staring eyes and opened mouth, he watched the man who had been sitting only a few tables away from them push back the plate on which lay his bill and rise to his feet. One of the chief maîtres d'hôtel handed him his straw hat and cane, two waiters stood behind his chair, the manager hurried forward to see that the way was clear for him. Yet there was nothing about the appearance of the man himself which seemed to suggest his demanding any of these things. He was of little over medium height, broad-shouldered, but with a body somewhat loosely built. He wore quiet grey clothes with a black tie, a pearl pin, and a neat coloured shirt. His complexion was a little pale, his features well-defined, his eyes dark and penetrating but hidden underneath rather bushy eyebrows. His deportment was quite unassuming, and he left the place as though entirely ignorant of the impression he created. The little cluster of chorus girls looked at him almost with awe. Only one of them ventured to laugh into his face as though anxious to attract his notice. Another dropped her veil significantly as he drew near. The millionaire seemed to become a smaller man as he glanced over his shoulder. The lady who had been recently divorced bent over her plate. A group of noisy young fellows talking together about a Stock Exchange deal, suddenly ceased their clamour of voices as he passed. A man sitting alone, with a drawn face, deliberately concealed himself behind a newspaper, and an aldermanic-looking gentleman who was entertaining a fluffy-haired young lady from a well-known typewriting office, looked for a moment like an errant schoolboy. Not one of these people did Sanford Quest seem to see. He passed out to the elevator, tipped the man who sycophantly took him the whole of the way down without a stop, walked through the crowded hall of the hotel and entered a closed motor-car without having exchanged greetings with a soul. Yet there was scarcely a person there who could feel absolutely sure that he had not been noticed.

Sanford Quest descended, about ten minutes later, before a large and gloomy-looking house in Georgia Square. The neighbourhood was, in its way, unique. The roar and hubbub of the city broke like a restless sea only a block or so away. On every side, this square of dark, silent houses seemed to be assailed by the clamour of the encroaching city. For some reason or other, however, it remained a little oasis of old-fashioned buildings, residences, most of them, of a generation passed away. Sanford Quest entered the house with a latch-key. He glanced into two of the rooms on the ground-floor, in which telegraph and telephone operators sat at their instruments. Then, by means of a small elevator, he ascended to the top story and, using another key, entered a large apartment wrapped in gloom until, as he crossed the threshold, he touched the switches of the electric lights. One realised then that this was a man of taste. The furniture and appointments of the room were of dark oak. The panelled walls were hung with a few choice engravings. There were books and papers about, a piano in the corner. A door at the further end led into what seemed to be a sleeping-apartment. Quest drew up an easy-chair to the wide-flung window, touching a bell as he crossed the room. In a few moments the door was opened and closed noiselessly. A young woman entered with a little bundle of papers in her hand.

"Anything for me, Laura?" he asked.

"I don't believe you will think so, Mr. Quest," she answered calmly.

She drew a small table and a reading lamp to his side and stood quietly waiting. Her eyes followed Quest's as he glanced through the letters, her expression matched his. She was tall, dark, good-looking in a massive way, with a splendid, almost unfeminine strength in her firm, shapely mouth and brilliant eyes. Her manner was a little brusque but her voice pleasant. She was one of those who had learnt the art of silence.

The criminologist glanced through the papers quickly and sorted them into two little heaps.

"Send these," he directed, "to the police-station. There is nothing in them which calls for outside intervention. They are all matters which had better take their normal course. To the others simply reply that the matter they refer to does not interest me. No further enquiries?"

"Nothing, Mr. Quest."

She left the room almost noiselessly. Quest took down a volume from the swinging book-case by his side, and drew the reading lamp a little closer to his right shoulder. Before he opened the volume, however, he looked for a few moments steadfastly out across the sea of roofs, the network of telephone and telegraph wires, to where the lights of Broadway seemed to eat their way into the sky. Around him, the night life of the great city spread itself out in waves of gilded vice and black and sordid crime. Its many voices fell upon deaf ears. Until long past midnight, he sat engrossed in a scientific volume.

CHAPTER II

THE APARTMENT-HOUSE MYSTERY

1.

"This habit of becoming late for breakfast," Lady Ashleigh remarked, as she set down the coffee-pot, "is growing upon your father."

Ella glanced up from a pile of correspondence through which she had been looking a little negligently.

"When he comes," she said, "I shall tell him what Clyde says in his new play—that unpunctuality for breakfast and overpunctuality for dinner are two of the signs of advancing age."

"I shouldn't," her mother advised. "He hates anything that sounds like an epigram, and I noticed that he avoided any allusion to his birthday last month. Any news, dear?"

"None at all, mother. My correspondence is just the usual sort of rubbish—invitations and gossip. Such a lot of invitations, by-the-bye."

"At your age," Lady Ashleigh declared, "that is the sort of correspondence which you should find interesting."

Ella shook her head. She was a very beautiful young woman, but her expression was a little more serious than her twenty-two years warranted.

"You know I am not like that, mother," she protested. "I have found one thing in life which interests me more than all this frivolous business of amusing oneself. I shall never be happy—not really happy—until I have settled down to study hard. My music is really the only part of life which absolutely appeals to me."

Lady Ashleigh sighed.

"It seems so unnecessary," she murmured. "Since Esther was married you are practically an only daughter, you are quite well off, and there are so many young men who want to marry you."

Ella laughed gaily.

"That sort of thing may come later on, mother," she declared,—"I suppose I am only human like the rest of us—but to me the greatest thing in the whole world just now is music, my music. It is a little wonderful, isn't it, to have a gift, a real gift, and to know it? Oh, why doesn't Delarey make up his mind and let father know, as he promised!... Here comes daddy, mum. Bother! He's going to shoot, and I hoped he'd play golf with me."

Lord Ashleigh, who had stepped through some French windows at the farther end of the terrace, paused for a few minutes to look around him. There was certainly some excuse for his momentary absorption. The morning, although it was late September, was perfectly fine and warm. The cattle in the park which surrounded the house were already gathered under the trees. In the far distance, the stubble fields stretched like patches of gold to ridges of pine-topped hills, and beyond to the distant sea. The breakfast table at which his wife and daughter were seated was arranged on the broad grey stone terrace, and, as he slowly approached, it seemed like an oasis of flowers and fruit and silver. A footman stood discreetly in the background. Half a dozen dogs of various breeds came trotting forward to meet him. His wife, still beautiful notwithstanding her forty-five years, had turned her pleasant face towards him, and Ella, whom a great many Society papers had singled out as being one of the most beautiful débutantes of the season, was welcoming him with her usual lazy but wholly good-humoured smile.

"Daddy, your habits are getting positively disgraceful!" she exclaimed. "Mother and I have nearly finished—and our share of the post-bag is most uninteresting. Please come and sit down, tell us where you are going to shoot, and whether you've had any letters this morning?"

Lord Ashleigh loitered for a moment to raise the covers from the dishes upon a side table. Afterwards he seated himself in the chair which the servant was holding for him.

"I am going out for an hour or two with Fitzgerald," he announced. "Partridges are scarcely worth shooting yet but he has arranged a few drives over the hills. As for my being late—well, that has something to do with you, young lady."

Ella looked at him with a sudden seriousness in her great eyes.

"Daddy, you've heard something!"

Lord Ashleigh pulled a bundle of letters from his pocket.

"I have," he admitted.

"Quick!" Ella begged. "Tell us all about it? Don't sit there, dad, looking so stolid. Can't you see I am dying to hear? Quick, please!"

Her father smiled, glanced for a moment at the plate which had been passed to him from the side table, approved of it and stretched out his hand for his cup.

"I heard this morning," he said, "from your friend Delarey. He went into the matter very fully. You shall read his letter presently. The sum and substance of it all, however, is that for the first year of your musical training he advises—where do you think?"

"Dresden," Lady Ashleigh suggested.

"Munich? Paris?" Ella put in breathlessly.

"All wrong," Lord Ashleigh declared. "New York!"

There was a momentary silence. Ella's eyes were sparkling. Her mother's face had fallen.

"New York!" Ella murmured. "There is wonderful music there,

and Mr. Delarey knows it so well."

Lord Ashleigh nodded portentously.

"I have not finished yet. Mr. Delarey wound up his letter by promising to cable me his final decision in the course of a few days. This cablegram," he went on, drawing a little slip of blue paper from his pocket, "was brought to me this morning whilst I was shaving. I found it a most inconvenient time, as the lather—"

"Oh, bother the lather, father!" Ella exclaimed. "Read the cablegram, or let me."

Her father smoothed it out before him and read—

"To Lord Ashleigh, Hamblin House, Dorset, England.

"I find a magnificent programme arranged for at Metropolitan Opera House this year. Have taken box for your daughter, engaged the best professor in the world, and secured an apartment at the Leeland, our most select and comfortable residential hotel. Understand your brother is still in South America, returning early spring, but will do our best to make your daughter's year of study as pleasant as possible. Advise her sail on Saturday by Mauretania."

"On Saturday?" Ella almost screamed.

"New York!" Lady Ashleigh murmured disconsolately. "How impossible, George!"

Her husband handed over the letter and cablegram, which Ella at once pounced upon. He then unfolded the local newspaper and proceeded to make an excellent breakfast. When he had quite finished, he lit a cigarette and rose a little abruptly to his feet as a car glided out of the stable yard and slowly approached the front door.

"I shall now," he said, "leave you to talk over and discuss this matter for the rest of the day. I believe you said, dear," he added, turning to his wife, "that we were dining alone tonight?"

"Quite alone, George," Lady Ashleigh admitted. "We were to have gone to Annerley Castle, but the Duke is laid up somewhere in Scotland."

"I remember," her husband assented. "Very well, then, at dinnertime tonight you can tell me your decision, or rather we will discuss it together. James," he added, turning to the footman, "tell Robert I want my sixteen-bore guns put in the car, and tell him to be very careful about the cartridges."

He disappeared through the French windows. Lady Ashleigh was studying the letter stretched out before her, her brows a little knitted, her expression distressed. Ella had turned and was looking out westwards across the park, towards the sea. For a moment she dreamed of all the wonderful things that lay on the other side of that silver streak. She saw inside the crowded Opera House. She felt the tense hush, the thrill of excitement. She heard the low sobbing of the violins, she saw the stage-setting, she heard the low notes of music creeping and growing till every pulse in her body thrilled with her one great enthusiasm. When she turned back to the table, her eyes were bright and there was a little flush upon her cheeks.

"You're not sorry, mother?" she exclaimed.

"Not really, dear," Lady Ashleigh answered resignedly.

2.

Lord Ashleigh, who in many respects was a typical Englishman of his class, had a constitutional affection for small ceremonies, an affection nurtured by his position as Chairman of the County Magistrates and President of the local Unionist Association. After dinner that evening, a meal which was served in the smaller library, he cleared his throat and filled his glass with wine. His manner, as he addressed his wife and daughter, was almost official.

"I am to take it, I believe," he began, "that you have finally decided, Ella, to embrace our friend Delarey's suggestion and to leave us on Saturday for New York?"

"If you please," Ella murmured, with glowing eyes. "I can't tell you how grateful I am to you both for letting me go."

"It is naturally a wrench to us," Lord Ashleigh confessed, "especially as circumstances which you already know of prevent either your mother or myself from being with you during the first few months of your stay there. You have very many friends in New York, however, and your mother tells me that there will be no difficulty about your chaperonage at the various social functions to which you will, of course, be bidden."

"I think that will be all right, dad," Ella ventured.

"You will take your own maid with you, of course," Lord Ashleigh continued. "Lenora is a good girl and I am sure she will look after you quite well, but I have decided, although it is a somewhat unusual step, to supplement Lenora's surveillance over your comfort by sending with you, also, as a sort of courier and general attendant—whom do you think? Well, Macdougal."

Lady Ashleigh looked across the table with knitted brows.

"Macdougal, George? Why, however will you spare him?"

"We can easily," Lord Ashleigh declared, "find a temporary butler. Macdougal has lived in New York for some years, and you will doubtless find this a great advantage, Ella. I hope that my suggestion pleases you?"

Ella glanced over her shoulder at the two servants who were standing discreetly in the background. Her eyes rested upon the pale, expressionless face of the man who during the last few years had enjoyed her father's absolute confidence. Like many others of his class, there seemed to be so little upon which to comment in his appearance, so little room for surmise or analysis in his quiet, negative features, his studiously low voice, his unexceptionable deportment. Yet for a moment a queer sense of apprehension troubled her. Was it true, she wondered, that she did not like the man? She banished the thought almost as soon as it was conceived. The very idea was absurd! His manner towards her had always been perfectly respectful. He seemed equally devoid of sex or character. She withdrew her gaze and turned once more towards her father.

"Do you think that you can really spare him, daddy," she asked, "and that it will be necessary?"

"Not altogether necessary, I dare say," Lord Ashleigh admitted. "On the other hand, I feel sure that you will find him a comfort, and it would be rather a relief to me to know that there is some one in touch with you all the time in whom I place absolute confidence. I dare say I shall be very glad to see him back again at the end of the year, but that is neither here nor there. Mr. Delarey has sent me the name of some bankers in New York who will honour your cheques for whatever money you may require."

"You are spoiling me, daddy," Ella sighed.

Lord Ashleigh smiled. His hand had disappeared into the pocket of his dinner-coat.

"If you think so now," he remarked, "I do not know what you will say to me presently. What I am doing now, Ella, I am doing with your mother's sanction, and you must associate her with the gift which I am going to place in your keeping."

The hand was slowly withdrawn from his pocket. He laid upon the table a very familiar morocco case, stamped with a coronet. Even before he touched the spring and the top flew open, Ella knew what was coming.

"Our diamonds!" she exclaimed. "The Ashleigh diamonds!"

The necklace lay exposed to view, the wonderful stones flashing in the subdued light. Ella gazed at it, speechless.

"In New York," Lord Ashleigh continued, "it is the custom to wear jewellery in public more, even, than in this country. The family pearls, which I myself should have thought more suitable, went, as you know, to your elder sister upon her marriage. I am not rich enough to invest large sums of money in the purchase of precious stones, yet, on the other hand, your mother and I feel that if you are to wear jewels at all, we should like you to wear something of historic value, jewels which are associated with the history of your own house. Allow me!"

He leaned forward. With long, capable fingers he fastened the necklace around his daughter's neck. It fell upon her bosom, sparkling, a little circular stream of fire against the background of her smooth, white skin. Ella could scarcely speak. Her fingers caressed the jewels.

"It is our farewell present to you," Lord Ashleigh declared. "I need not beg you to take care of them. I do not wish to dwell upon their value. Money means, naturally, little to you, and when I tell you that a firm in London offered me sixty thousand pounds for them for an American client, I only mention it so that you may understand that they are likely to be appreciated in the country to which you are going."

She clasped his hands.

"Father," she cried, "you are too good to me! It is all too wonderful. I shall be afraid to wear them."

Lord Ashleigh smiled reassuringly.

"My dear," he said, "you will be quite safe. I should advise you to keep them, as a rule, in the strong box which you will doubtless find in the hotel to which you are going. But for all ordinary occasions you need feel, I am convinced, no apprehension. You can understand now, I dare say, another reason why I am sending Macdougal with you as well as Lenora."

Ella, impelled by some curious impulse which she could not quite understand, glanced quickly around to where the man-servant was standing. For once she had caught him unawares. For once she saw something besides the perfect automaton. His eyes, instead of being fixed at the back of his master's chair, were simply riveted upon the stones. His mouth was a little indrawn. To her there was a curious change in his expression. His cheekbones seemed to have become higher. The pupils of his eyes had narrowed. Even while she looked at him, he moistened a little his dry lips with the tip of his tongue. Then, as though conscious of her observation, all these things vanished. He advanced to the table, respectfully refilled his master's glass from the decanter of port, and retreated again. Ella withdrew her eyes. A queer little feeling of uneasiness disturbed her for the moment. It passed, however, as in glancing away her attention was once more attracted by the sparkle of the jewels upon her bosom. Lord Ashleigh raised his glass.

"Our love to you, dear," he said. "Take care of the jewels, but take more care of yourself. Your mother and I will come to New York as soon as we can. In the meantime, don't forget us amidst the hosts of your new friends and the joy of your new life."

She gave them each a hand. She stooped first to one side and then to the other, kissing them both tenderly.

"I shall never forget!" she exclaimed, her voice breaking a little. "There could never be any one else in the world like you two—and please may I go to the looking-glass?"

3.

The streets of New York were covered with a thin, powdery snow as the very luxurious car of Mrs. Delarey drew up outside the front of the Leeland Hotel, a little after midnight. Ella leaned over and kissed her hostess.

"Thank you, dear, ever so much for your delightful dinner," she exclaimed, "and for bringing me home. As for the music, well, I can't talk about it. I am just going upstairs into my room to sit and think."

"Don't sit up too late and spoil your pretty colour, dear," Mrs. Delarey advised. "Good-bye! Don't forget I am coming in to lunch with you tomorrow."

The car rolled off. Ella, a large umbrella held over her head by the door-keeper, stepped up the little strip of drugget which led into the softly-warmed hall of the Leeland. Behind her came her maid, Lenora, and Macdougal, who had been riding on the box with the chauffeur. He paused for a moment to wipe the snow from his clothes as Ella crossed the hall to the lift. Lenora turned towards him. He whispered something in her ear. For a moment she shook. Then she turned away and followed her mistress upstairs.

Arrived in her apartment, Ella threw herself with a little sigh of content into a big easy-chair before the fire. Her sitting-room was the last word in comfort and luxury. A great bowl of pink roses, arrived during her absence, stood on the small table by her side. Lenora had just brought her chocolate and was busy making preparations in the bedroom adjoining. Ella gave herself up for a few moments to reverie. The magic of the music was still in her blood. She had made progress. That very afternoon her master, Van Haydn, had spoken to her of her progress—Van Haydn, who had never flattered a pupil in his life. In a few weeks' time her mother and father were coming out to her. Meanwhile, she had made hosts of pleasant friends. Attentions of all sorts had been showered upon her. She curled herself up in her chair. It was good to be alive!

A log stirred upon the fire. She leaned forward lazily to replace it and then stopped short. Exactly opposite to her was a door which opened on to a back hall. It was used only by the servants connected with the hotel, and was usually kept locked. Just as she was in the act of leaning forward, Ella became conscious of a curious hallucination. She sat looking at the handle with fascinated eyes. Then she called aloud to Lenora.

"Lenora, come here at once."

The maid hurried in from the next room. Ella pointed to the door.

"Lenora, look outside. See if any one is on that landing. I fancied that the door opened."

The maid shook her head incredulously.

"I don't think so, my lady," she said. "No one but the waiter and the chambermaid who comes in to clean the apartment, ever comes that way."

She crossed the room and tried the handle. Then she turned towards her mistress in triumph.

"It is locked, my lady," she reported.

Ella rose to her feet and herself tried the handle. It was as the maid had reported. She, however, was not altogether reassured. She was a young woman whose nerves were in a thoroughly healthy state, and by no means given to imaginative fears. She stood a little away, looking at the handle. It was almost impossible that she could have been mistaken. Her hands clasped for a moment the necklace which hung from her neck. A queer presentiment of evil crept like a grey shadow over her.

She looked at herself in the glass—the colour had left her cheeks. She tried to laugh at her self.

"This is absurd!" she exclaimed. "Lenora, go down and ask Macdougal to come up for a minute. I am going to have this thing explained. Hurry, there's a good girl."

"You are sure your ladyship doesn't mind being left?" the maid asked, a little doubtfully.

"Of course not!" Ella replied, with a laugh which was not altogether natural. "Hurry along, there's a good girl. I'll drink my chocolate while you are gone, and get ready for bed, but I must see Macdougal before I undress."

Something of her mistress's agitation seemed to have become communicated to Lenora. Her voice shook a little as she stepped into the elevator.

"Where are you off to, young lady?" the boy enquired.

"I want to go round to our quarters," Lenora explained. "Her ladyship wants to speak to Mr. Macdougal."

"He's gone out, sure," the elevator boy remarked. "Shall I wait for you, Miss Lenora?" he asked, as they descended into the hall.

"Do," she begged. "I sha'n't be more than a minute or two."

She walked quickly to the back part of the hotel and ascended in another elevator to the wing in which the servants' quarters were situated. Here she made her way along a corridor until she reached Macdougal's room. She knocked, and knocked again. There was no answer. She tried the door and found it was locked. Then she returned to the elevator and descended once more to the floor upon which her mistress's apartments were situated. She opened the door of the suite without knocking and turned at once to the sitting-room.

"I am sorry, my lady," she began—

Then she stopped short. The elevator boy, who had had a little trouble with his starting apparatus and had not as yet descended, heard the scream which broke from her lips, and a fireman in an adjacent corridor came running up almost at the same moment. Lenora was on her knees by her mistress's side. Ella was still lying in the easy-chair in which she had been seated, but her head was thrown back in an unnatural fashion. There was a red mark just across her throat. The small table by her side had been overturned, and the chocolate was running in a little stream across the floor. The elevator boy was the first to speak.

"Holy shakes!" he exclaimed. "What's happened?"

"Can't you see?" Lenora shrieked. "She's fainted! And the diamonds—the diamonds have gone!"

The fireman was already at the telephone. In less than a minute one of the managers from the office came running in. Lenora was dashing water into Ella's still, cold face.

"She's fainted!" she shrieked. "Fetch a doctor, some one. The diamonds have gone!"

The young man was already at the telephone. His hand shook as he took up the receiver. He turned to the elevator boy.

"Run across to number seventy-three—Doctor Morton's," he ordered. "Don't you let any one come in, fireman. Don't either of you say a word about this. Here, Exchange, urgent call. Give me the police-station—yes, police-station!... Don't be a fool, girl," he added under his breath. "You won't do any good throwing water on her like that. Let her alone for a moment.... Yes! Manager, Leeland Hotel, speaking. A murder and robbery have taken place in this hotel, suite number forty-three. I am there now. Nothing shall be touched. Send round this moment."

The young man hung up the receiver. Lenora was filling the room with her shrieks. He took her by the shoulder and pushed her back into a chair.

"Shut up, you fool!" he exclaimed. "You can't do any good making a noise like that."

"She said she saw the door handle turn," Lenora sobbed. "I went to fetch Macdougal. He'd gone out. When I came back she was there—like that!"

"What door handle?" the manager asked.

Lenora pointed. The young man crossed the room. The lock was still in its place, the door refused to yield. As he turned around the doctor arrived. He hurried at once to Ella's side.

"Hands still warm," he muttered, as he felt them.... "My God! It's the double knot strangle!"

He bent over Ella for several moments. Then he rose to his feet.

The door from outside had been opened once more. A police inspector, followed by a detective, had entered.

"This is your affair, gentlemen, not mine," the doctor said gravely. "The young lady is dead. She has been cruelly strangled within the last five or ten minutes."

The Inspector turned around.

"Lock the outside door," he ordered his man. "Has any one left the room, Mr. Marsham?"

"No one," the manager declared.

"Who discovered her?"

"The maid."

Lenora rose to her feet. She seemed a little calmer but the healthy colour had all gone from her cheeks and her lips were twitching.

"Her ladyship had just come in from the Opera," she said. "She was sitting in her easy-chair. I was in the bedroom. She looked toward the handle of that door. She thought it moved. She called me. I tried it and found it fast locked. She sent for Mr. Macdougal."

"Macdougal," Mr. Marsham explained, "is a confidential servant of Lord Ashleigh's. He was sent over here with Lady Ella."

The Inspector nodded.

"Go on."

"I found Mr. Macdougal's door locked. He must have gone out. When I came back here, I found this!"

The Inspector made a careful examination of the room.

"Tell me," he enquired, "is this the young lady who owned the wonderful Ashleigh diamonds?"

"They've gone!" Lenora shrieked. "They've been stolen! She was wearing them when I left the room!"

The Inspector turned to the telephone.

"Mr. Marsham," he said, "I am afraid this will be a difficult affair. I am going to take the liberty of calling in an expert. Hello. I want Number One, New York City—Mr. Sanford Quest."

4.

There seemed to be nothing at all original in the methods pursued by the great criminologist when confronted with this tableau of death and robbery. His remarks to the Inspector were few and perfunctory. He asked only a few languid questions of Macdougal and Lenora, who were summoned to his presence.

"You had left the hotel, I understand, at the time when the crime occurred?" he asked the latter.

Macdougal, grave and respectful, made his answers with difficulty. His voice was choked with emotion.

"I brought my mistress home from the Opera, sir. I rode on the box with Mrs. Delarey's chauffeur. After I had seen her safely in the hotel, I went up to my room for two minutes and left the hotel by the back entrance."

"Any one see you go?"

"The door-keeper, sir, and I passed a page upon the stairs."

"Wasn't it rather late for you to go out?"

"My days are a little dull here, sir," Macdougal replied, "and my attendance is not required early in the morning. I have made some friends in the city and I usually go out to a restaurant and have some supper."

"Quite natural," Mr. Quest agreed. "That will do, thanks."

Macdougal turned towards the door. Lenora was about to follow him but Quest signed to her to remain.

"I should like to have a little conversation with you about your mistress," he said to her pleasantly. "If you don't mind, I will ask you to accompany me in my car. I will send the man back with you."

For a moment the girl stood quite still. Her face was already ghastly pale. Her eyes alone seemed to indicate some fresh fear.

"I will go to my rooms and put on my hat," she said.

Quest pointed through the half open door.

"That will be your hat and coat upon the bed there, won't it?" he remarked. "I am sorry to hurry you off but I have another appointment. You will send, of course, for the young lady's friends," he added, turning to Mr. Marsham, "and cable her people."

"There is nothing more you can do, Mr. Quest?" the hotel manager asked, a little querulously. "This affair must be cleared up for the credit of my hotel."

Quest shrugged his shoulders. He glanced through the open door to where Lenora was arranging her coat with trembling fingers.

"There will be very little difficulty about that," he said calmly. "If you are quite ready, Miss Lenora. Is that your name?"

"Lenora is my name, sir," the girl replied.

They descended in the elevator together and Quest handed the girl into his car. They drove quickly through the silent streets. The snow had ceased to fall and the stars were shining brightly. Lenora shivered as she leaned back in her corner.

"You are cold, I am afraid," Quest remarked. "Never mind, there will be a good fire in my study. I shall only keep you for a few moments. I dare not be away long just now, as I have a very important case on."

"There is nothing more that I can tell you," Lenora ventured, a little fearfully. "Can't you ask me what you want to, now, as we go along?"

"We have already arrived," Quest told her. "Do you mind following me?"

She crossed the pavement and passed through the front door, which Quest was holding open for her. They stepped into the little elevator, and a moment or two later Lenora was installed in an easy-chair in Quest's sitting-room, in front of a roaring fire.

"Lean back and make yourself comfortable," Quest invited, as he took a chair opposite to her. "I must just look through these papers."

The girl did as she was told. She opened her coat. The room was delightfully warm, almost overheated. A sense of rest crept over her. For the first moment since the awful shock, her nerves seemed quieter. Gradually she began to feel almost as though she were passing into sleep. She started up, but sank back again almost immediately. She was conscious that Quest had laid down the letters which he had been pretending to read. His eyes were fixed upon her. There was a queer new look in them, a strange new feeling creeping through her veins. Was she going to sleep?...

Quest's voice broke an unnatural silence.

"You are anxious to telephone some one," he said.

"You looked at both of the booths as we came through the hotel. Then you remembered, I think, that he would not be there yet. Telephone now. The telephone is at your right hand. You know the number."

She obeyed almost at once. She took the receiver from the instrument by her side.

"Number 700, New York City."

"You will ask," Quest continued, "whether he is all right, whether the jewels are safe."

There was a brief silence, then the girl's voice.

"Are you there, James?... Yes, I am Lenora. Are you safe? Have you the jewels?... Where?... You are sure that you are safe.... No, nothing fresh has happened."

"You are at the hotel," Quest said softly. "You are going to him."

"I cannot sleep," she continued. "I am coming to you."

She set down the receiver. Quest leaned a little more closely over her.

"You know where the jewels are hidden," he said. "Tell me where?"

Her lips quivered. She made no answer. She turned uneasily in her chair.

"Tell me the place?" Quest persisted.

There was still no response from the girl. There were drops of perspiration on her forehead. Quest shrugged his shoulders slightly.

"Very good," he concluded. "You need not tell me. Only remember this! At nine o'clock tomorrow morning you will bring those jewels to this apartment.... Rest quietly now. I want you to go to sleep."

She obeyed without hesitation. Quest watched, for a moment, her regular breathing. Then he touched a bell by his side. Laura entered almost at once.

"Open the laboratory," Quest ordered. "Then come back."

Without a word or a glance towards the sleeping figure, she obeyed him. It was a matter of seconds before she returned. Together they lifted and carried the sleeping girl out of the room, across the landing, into a larger apartment, the contents of which were wrapped in gloom and mystery. A single electric light was burning on the top of a square mirror fixed upon an easel. Towards this they carried the girl and laid her in an easy-chair almost opposite to it.

"The battery is just on the left," Laura whispered.

Quest nodded.

"Give me the band."

She turned away for a moment and disappeared in the shadows. When she returned, she carried a curved band of flexible steel. Quest took it from her, attached it by means of a coil of wire to the battery, and with firm, soft fingers slipped it on to Lenora's forehead. Then he stepped back. A rare emotion quivered in his tone.

"She's a subject, Laura—I'm sure of it! Now for our great experiment!"

They watched Lenora intently. Her face twitched uneasily, but she did not open her eyes and her breathing continued regular. Quest bent over her.

"Lenora," he said, slowly and firmly, "your mind is full of one subject. You see your mistress in her chair by the fireside. She is toying with her diamonds. Look again. She lies there dead! Who was it entered the room, Lenora? Look! Look! Gaze into that mirror. What do you see there?"

The girl's eyes had opened. They were fixed now upon the mirror—distended, full of unholy things. Quest wiped a drop of perspiration from his forehead.

"Try harder, Lenora," he muttered, his own breath labouring. "It is there in your brain! Look!"

Laura for the first time showed signs of emotion. She pointed towards the mirror. Quest was suddenly silent. He seemed to have turned into a figure of stone. For a single second the smooth surface of the mirror was obscured. A room crept dimly like a picture into being, a fire upon the hearth, a girl leaning back in her chair. A door in the background opened. A man stole out. He crept nearer to the girl—his eyes fixed upon the diamonds, a thin, silken cord twisted round his wrist. Suddenly she saw him—too late! His hand was upon her lips,—his face seemed to start almost from the mirror—then blackness!

Lenora opened her eyes. She was still in the easy-chair before the fire.

"Mr. Quest!" she faltered.

He looked up from some letters which he had been studying.

"I am so sorry," he said politely. "I really had forgotten that you were here. But you know—that you have been to sleep?"

She half rose to her feet. She was perplexed, uneasy.

"Asleep?" she murmured. "Have I? And I dreamed a horrible dream!... Have I been ringing anyone up on the telephone?"

"Not that I know of," Quest assured her. "As a matter of fact, I was called downstairs to see one of my men soon after we got here."

"Can I go now?" she asked.

"Certainly," Quest replied. "To tell you the truth, I find that I shall not need to ask you those questions, after all. A messenger from the police-station has been here. He says they have come to the conclusion that a very well-known gang of New York criminals are in this thing. We know how to track them down all right."

"I may go now, then?" she repeated, with immense relief.

Quest escorted the girl downstairs, opened the front door, blew his whistle and his car pulled up at the door.

"Take this young lady," he ordered, "wherever she wishes. Good night!"

The girl drove off. Quest watched the car disappear around the corner. Then he turned slowly back and made preparations for his adventure....

"Number 700, New York," he muttered, half an hour later, as he left his house. "Beyond Fourteenth Street—a tough neighbourhood."

He hesitated for a moment, feeling the articles in his overcoat pocket—a revolver in one, a small piece of hard substance in the other. Then he stepped into his car, which had just returned.

"Where did you leave the young lady?" he asked the chauffeur.

"In Broadway, sir. She left me and boarded a cross-town car."

Quest nodded approvingly.

"No finesse," he sighed.

5.

Sanford Quest was naturally a person unaffected by presentiments or nervous fears of any sort, yet, having advanced a couple of yards along the hallway of the house which he had just entered without difficulty, he came to a standstill, oppressed with the sense of impending danger. With his electric torch he carefully surveyed the dilapidated staircase in front of him, the walls from which the paper hung down in depressing-looking strips. The house was, to all appearances, uninhabited. The door had yielded easily to his master-key. Yet this was the house connected with Number 700, New York, the house to which Lenora had come. Furthermore, from the street outside he had seen a light upon the first floor, instantly extinguished as he had climbed the steps.

"Any one here?" he asked, raising his voice a little.

There was no direct response, yet from somewhere upstairs he heard the half smothered cry of a woman. He gripped his revolver in his fingers. He was a fatalist, and although for a moment he regretted having come single-handed to such an obvious trap, he prepared for his task. He took a quick step forward. The ground seemed to slip from beneath his feet. He staggered wildly to recover himself, and failed. The floor had given from beneath him. He was falling into blackness....

The fall itself was scarcely a dozen feet. He picked himself up, his shoulder bruised, his head swimming a little. His electric torch was broken to pieces upon the stone floor. He was simply in a black gulf of darkness. Suddenly a gleam of light shone down. A trap-door above his head was slid a few inches back. The flare of an electric torch shone upon his face, a man's mocking voice addressed him.

"Not the great Sanford Quest? This surely cannot be the greatest detective in the world walking so easily into the spider's web!"

"Any chance of getting out?" Quest asked laconically.

"None!" was the bitter reply. "You've done enough mischief. You're there to rot!"

"Why this animus against me, my friend Macdougal?" Quest demanded. "You and I have never come up against one another before. I didn't like the life you led in New York ten years ago, or your friends, but you've suffered nothing through me."

"If I let you go," once more came the man's voice, "I know very well in what chair I shall be sitting before a month has passed. I am James Macdougal, Mr. Sanford Quest, and I have got the Ashleigh diamonds, and I have settled an old grudge, if not of my own, of one greater than you. That's all. A pleasant night to you!"

The door went down with a bang. Faintly, as though, indeed, the footsteps belonged to some other world, Sanford Quest heard the two leave the house. Then silence.

"A perfect oubliette," he remarked to himself, as he held a match over his head a moment or two later, "built for the purpose. It must be the house we failed to find which Bill Taylor used to keep before he was shot. Smooth brick walls, smooth brick floor, only exit twelve feet above one's head. Human means, apparently, are useless. Science, you have been my mistress all my days. You must save my life now or lose an earnest disciple."

He felt in his overcoat pocket and drew out the small, hard pellet. He gripped it in his fingers, stood as nearly as possible underneath the spot from which he had been projected, coolly swung his arm back, and flung the black pebble against the sliding door. The explosion which followed shook the very ground under his feet. The walls cracked about him. Blue fire seemed to be playing around the blackness. He jumped on one side, barely in time to escape a shower of bricks. For minutes afterwards everything around him seemed to rock. He struck another match. The whole of the roof of the place was gone. By building a few bricks together, he was easily able to climb high enough to swing himself on to the fragments of the hallway. Even as he accomplished this, the door was thrown open and a crowd of people rushed in. Sanford Quest emerged, dusty but unhurt, and touched a constable on his arm.

"Arrest me," he ordered. "I am Sanford Quest. I must be taken at once to headquarters."

"That so, Mr. Quest? Stand on one side, you loafers," the man ordered, pushing his way out.

"We'll have a taxicab," Quest decided.

"Is there any one else in the house?" the policeman asked.

"Not a soul," Quest answered.

They found a cab without much difficulty. It was five o'clock when they reached the central police-station. Inspector French happened to be just going off duty. He recognized Quest with a little exclamation.

"Got your man to bring me here," Quest explained, "so as to get away from the mob."

"Say, you've been in trouble!" the Inspector remarked, leading the way into his room.

"Bit of an explosion, that's all," Quest replied. "I shall be all right when you've lent me a clothes-brush."

"The Ashleigh diamonds, eh?" the Inspector asked eagerly.

"I shall have them at nine o'clock this morning," Sanford Quest promised, "and hand you over the murderer somewhere around midnight."

The Inspector scratched his chin.

"From what I can hear about the young lady's friends," he said, "it's the murderer they are most anxious to see nabbed."

"They'll have him," Quest promised. "Come round about half past nine and I'll hand over the diamonds to start with."

Quest slept for a couple of hours, had a bath and made a leisurely toilet. At a quarter to nine he sat down to breakfast in his rooms.

"At nine o'clock," he told his servant, "a young lady will call. Bring her up."

The door was suddenly opened. Lenora walked in. Quest glanced in surprise at the clock.

"My fault!" he exclaimed. "We are slow. Good morning, Miss Lenora!"

She came straight to the table. The servant, at a sign from Quest, disappeared. There were black rims around her eyes; she seemed exhausted. She laid a little packet upon the table. Quest opened it coolly. The Ashleigh diamonds flashed up at him. He led Lenora to a chair and rang the bell.

"Prepare a bedroom upstairs," he ordered. "Ask Miss Roche to come here. Laura," he added, as his secretary entered, "will you look after this young lady? She is in a state of nervous exhaustion."

The girl nodded. She understood. She led Lenora from the room. Quest resumed his breakfast. A few minutes later, Inspector French was announced. Quest nodded in friendly manner.

"Some coffee, Inspector?"

"I'd rather have those diamonds!" the Inspector replied.

Quest threw them lightly across the table.

"Catch hold, then."

The Inspector whistled.

"Say, that's bright work," he acknowledged. "I believe I could have laid my hands on the man, but it was the jewels that I was afraid of losing."

"Just so," Quest remarked. "And now, French, will you be here, please, at midnight with three men, armed."

"Here?" the Inspector repeated.

Quest nodded.

"Our friend," he said, "is going to be mad enough to walk into hell, even, when he finds out what he thinks has happened."

"It wasn't any of Jimmy's lot?" the Inspector asked.

Sanford Quest shook his head.

"French," he said, "keep mum, but it was the elderly family retainer, Macdougal. I felt restless about him. He has lost the girl—he was married to her, by-the-bye—and the jewels. No fear of his slipping away. I shall have him here at the time I told you."

"You've a way of your own of doing these things, Mr. Quest," the Inspector admitted grudgingly.

"Mostly luck," Quest replied. "Take a cigar, and so long, Inspector. They want me to talk to Chicago on another little piece of business."

It was a few minutes before midnight when Quest parted the curtains of a room on the ground floor of his house in Georgia Square, and looked out into the snow-white street. Then he turned around and addressed the figure lying as though asleep upon the sofa by the fire.

"Lenora," he said, "I am going out. Stay here, if you please, until I return."

He left the room. For a few moments there was a profound silence. Then a white face was pressed against the window. There was a crash of glass. A man, covered with snow, sprang into the apartment. He moved swiftly to the sofa, and something black and ugly swayed in his hand.

"So you've deceived me, have you?" he panted. "Handed over the jewels, chucked me, and given me the double cross! Anything to say?"

A piece of coal fell on to the grate. Not a sound came from the sofa. Macdougal leaned forward, his white face distorted with passion. The life-preserver bent and quivered behind him, cut the air with a swish and crashed full upon the head.

The man staggered back. The weapon fell from his fingers. For a moment he was paralysed. There was no blood upon his hand, no cry—silence inhuman, unnatural! He looked again. Then the lights flashed out all around him. There were two detectives in the doorway, their revolvers covering him,—Sanford Quest, with Lenora in the background. In the sudden illumination, Macdougal's horror turned almost to hysterical rage. He had wasted his fury upon a dummy! It was sawdust, not blood, which littered the couch!

"Take him, men," Quest ordered. "Hands up, Macdougal. Your number's up. Better take it quietly."

The handcuffs were upon him before he could move. He was trying to speak, but the words somehow choked in his mouth.

"You can send a wireless to Lord Ashleigh," Quest continued, turning to French. "Tell him that the diamonds have been recovered and that his daughter's murderer is arrested."

"What about the young woman?" the Inspector asked.

Lenora stood in an attitude of despair, her head downcast. She had turned a little away from Macdougal. Her hands were outstretched. It was as though she were expecting the handcuffs.

"You can let her alone," Sanford Quest said quietly. "A wife cannot give evidence against her husband, and besides, I need her. She is going to work for me."

Macdougal was already at the door, between the two detectives. He swung around. His voice was calm, almost clear—calm with the concentration of hatred.

"You are a wonderful man, Mr. Sanford Quest," he said. "Make the most of your triumph. Your time is nearly up."

"Keep him for a moment," Sanford Quest ordered. "You have friends, then, Macdougal, who will avenge you, eh?"

"I have no friends," Macdougal replied, "but there is one coming whose wit and cunning, science and skill are all-conquering. He will brush you away, Sanford Quest, like a fly. Wait a few weeks."

"You interest me," Quest murmured. "Tell me some more about this great master?"

"I shall tell you nothing," Macdougal replied. "You will hear nothing, you will know nothing. Suddenly you will find yourself opposed. You will struggle—and then the end. It is certain."

They led him away. Only Lenora remained, sobbing. Quest went up to her, laid his hand upon her shoulder.

"You've had a rough time, Lenora," he said, with strange gentleness. "Perhaps the brighter days are coming."

CHAPTER III

THE HIDDEN HANDS

1.

Sanford Quest and Lenora stood side by side upon the steps of the Courthouse, waiting for the automobile which had become momentarily entangled in a string of vehicles. A little crowd of people were elbowing their way out on to the sidewalk. The faces of most of them were still shadowed by the three hours of tense drama from which they had just emerged. Quest, who had lit a cigar, watched them curiously.

"No need to go into Court," he remarked. "I could have told you, from the look of these people, that Macdougal had escaped the death sentence. They have paid their money—or rather their time, and they have been cheated of the one supreme thrill."

"Imprisonment for life seems terrible enough," Lenora whispered, shuddering.

"Can't see the sense of keeping such a man alive myself," Quest declared, with purposeful brutality. "It was a cruel murder, fiendishly committed."

Lenora shivered. Quest laid his fingers for a moment upon her wrist. His voice, though still firm, became almost kind.

"Never be afraid, Lenora," he said, "to admit the truth. Come, we have finished with Macdougal now. Imprisonment for life will keep him from crossing your path again."

Lenora sighed. She was almost ashamed of her feeling of immense relief.

"I am very sorry for him," she murmured. "I wish there were something one could do."

"There is nothing," Quest replied shortly, "and if there were, you would not be allowed to undertake it. You didn't happen to notice the way he looked at you once or twice, did you?"

Once more the terror shone out of Lenora's eyes.

"You are right," she faltered. "I had forgotten."

They were on the point of crossing the pavement towards the automobile when Quest felt a touch upon his shoulder. He turned and found Lord Ashleigh standing by his side. Quest glanced towards Lenora.

"Run and get in the car," he whispered. "I will be there in a moment."

She dropped her veil and hastened across the pavement. The Englishman's face grew sterner as he watched her.

"Macdougal's accomplice," he muttered. "We used to trust that girl, too."

"She had nothing whatever to do with the actual crime, believe me," Quest assured him. "Besides, you must remember that it was really through her that the man was brought to justice."

"I harbour no ill-feelings towards the girl," Lord Ashleigh replied. "Nevertheless, the sight of her for a moment was disconcerting.... I would not have stopped you just now, Mr. Quest, but my brother is very anxious to renew his acquaintance with you. I think you met years ago."

Sanford Quest held out his hand to the man who had been standing a little in the background. Lord Ashleigh turned towards him.

"This is Mr. Quest, Edgar. You may remember my brother—Professor Ashleigh—as a man of science, Quest? He has just returned from South America."

The two shook hands, curiously diverse in type, in expression, in all the appurtenances of manhood. Quest was dark, with no sign of greyness in his closely-trimmed black hair. His face was an epitome of forcefulness, his lips hard, his eyes brilliant. He was dressed with the utmost care. His manner was self-possessed almost to a fault. The Professor, on the other hand, though his shoulders were broad, lost much of his height and presence through a very pronounced stoop. His face was pale, his mouth sensitive, his smile almost womanly in its sweetness. His clothes, and a general air of abstraction, seemed rather to indicate the clerical profession. His forehead, however, disclosed as he lifted his hat, was the forehead of a scholar.

"I am very proud to make your acquaintance again, Professor," Quest said. "Glad to know, too, that you hadn't quite forgotten me."

"My dear sir," the Professor declared, as he released the other's hand with seeming reluctance, "I have thought about you many times. Your doings have always been of interest to me. Though I have been lost to the world of civilisation for so long, I have correspondents here in New York to keep me in touch with all that is interesting. You have made a great name for yourself, Mr. Quest. You are one of those who have made science your handmaiden in a wonderful profession."

"You are very kind, Professor," Quest observed, flicking the ash from his cigar.

"Not at all," the other insisted. "Not at all. I have the greatest admiration for your methods."

"I am sorry," Quest remarked, "that our first meeting here should be under such distressing circumstances."

The Professor nodded gravely. He glanced towards his brother, who was talking to an acquaintance a few feet away.

"It has been a most melancholy occasion," he admitted, his voice shaking with emotion. "Still, I felt it my duty to support my brother through the trial. Apart from that, you know, Mr. Quest, a scene such as we have just witnessed has a peculiar—I might almost say fascination for me," the Professor continued, with a little glint in his eyes. "You, as a man of science, can realise, I am sure, that the criminal side of human nature is always of interest to an anthropologist."

"That must be so, of course," Quest agreed, glancing towards the automobile in which Lenora was seated. "If you'll excuse me, Professor, I think I must be getting along. We shall meet again, I trust."

"One moment," the Professor begged eagerly. "Tell me, Mr. Quest—I want your honest opinion. What do you think of my ape?"

"Of your what?" Quest enquired dubiously.

"Of my anthropoid ape which I have just sent to the museum. You know my claim? But perhaps you would prefer to postpone your final decision until after you have examined the skeleton itself."

A light broke in upon the criminologist.

"Of course!" he exclaimed. "For the moment, Professor, I couldn't follow you. You are talking about the skeleton of the ape which you brought home from South America, and which you have presented to the museum here?"

"Naturally," the Professor assented, with mild surprise. "To what else? I am stating my case, Mr. Quest, in the *North American Review next month. I may tell you, however, as a fellow scientist, the great and absolute truth. My claim is incontestable. My skeleton will prove to the world, without a doubt, the absolute truth of Darwin's great theory.*"

"That so?"

"You must go and see it," the Professor insisted, keeping by Quest's side as the latter moved towards the automobile. "You must go and see it, Mr. Quest. It will be on view to the public next week, but in the meantime I will telephone to the curator. You must mention my name. You shall be permitted a special examination."

"Very kind of you," Quest murmured.

"We shall meet again soon, I hope," the Professor concluded cordially. "Good morning, Mr. Quest!"

The two men shook hands, and Quest took his seat by Lenora's side in the automobile. The Professor rejoined his brother.

"George," he exclaimed, as they walked off together, "I am disappointed in Mr. Quest! I am very disappointed indeed. You will not believe what I am going to tell you, but it is the truth. He could not conceal it from me. He takes no interest whatever in my anthropoid ape."

"Neither do I," the other replied grimly.

The Professor sighed as he hailed a taxicab.

"You, my dear fellow," he said gravely, "are naturally not in the frame of mind for the consideration of these great subjects. Besides, you have no scientific tendencies. But in Sanford Quest I am disappointed. I expected his enthusiasm—I may say that I counted upon it."

"I don't think that Quest has much of that quality to spare," his brother remarked, "for anything outside his own criminal hunting."

They entered the taxicab and were driven almost in silence to the Professor's home—a large, rambling old house, situated in somewhat extensive but ill-kept grounds on the outskirts of New York. The Englishman glanced around him, as they passed up the drive, with an expression of disapproval.

"A more untidy-looking place than yours, Edgar, I never saw," he declared. "Your grounds have become a jungle. Don't you keep any gardeners?"

The Professor smiled.

"I keep other things," he said serenely. "There is something in my garden which would terrify your nice Scotch gardeners into fits, if they found their way here to do a little tidying up. Come into the library and I'll give you one of my choice cigars. Here's Craig waiting to let us in. Any news, Craig?"

The man-servant in plain clothes who admitted them shook his head.

"Nothing has happened, sir," he replied. "The telephone is ringing in the study now, though."

"I will answer it myself," the Professor declared, bustling off.

He hurried across the bare landing and into an apartment which seemed to be half museum, half library. There were skeletons leaning in unexpected corners, strange charts upon the walls, a wilderness of books and pamphlets in all manner of unexpected places, mingled with quaintly-carved curios, gods from West African temples, implements of savage warfare, butterfly nets. It was a room which Lord Ashleigh was never able to enter without a shudder.

The Professor took up the receiver from the telephone. His "Hello" was mild and enquiring. He had no doubt that the call was from some admiring disciple. The change in his face as he listened, however, was amazing. His lips began to twitch. An expression of horrified dismay overspread his features. His first reply was almost incoherent. He held the receiver away from him and turned towards his brother.

"George," he gasped, "the greatest tragedy in the world has happened! My ape is stolen!"

His brother looked at him blankly.

"Your ape is stolen?" he repeated.

"The skeleton of my anthropoid ape," the Professor continued, his voice growing alike in sadness and firmness. "It is the curator of the museum who is speaking. They have just opened the box. It has lain for two days in an anteroom. It is empty!"

Lord Ashleigh muttered something a little vague. The theft of a skeleton scarcely appeared to his unscientific mind to be a realisable thing. The Professor turned back to the telephone.

"Mr. Francis," he said, "I cannot talk to you. I can say nothing. I shall come to you at once. I am on the point of starting. Your news has overwhelmed me."

He laid down the receiver. He looked around him like a man in a nightmare.

"The taxicab is still waiting, sir," Craig reminded him.

"That is most fortunate," the Professor pronounced. "I remember now that I had no change with which to pay him. I must go back. Look after my brother. And, Craig, telephone at once to Mr. Sanford Quest. Ask him to meet me at the museum in twenty minutes. Tell him that nothing must stand in the way. Do you hear?"

The man hesitated. There was protest in his face.

"Mr. Sanford Quest, sir?" he muttered, as he followed his master down the hall.

"The great criminologist," the Professor explained eagerly. "Certainly! Why do you hesitate?"

"I was wondering, sir," Craig began.

The Professor waved his servant on one side.

"Do as you are told," he ordered. "Do as you are told, Craig. You others—you do not realise. You cannot understand what this means. Tell the taxi man to drive to the museum. I am overcome."

The taxicab man drove off, glad enough to have a return fare. In about half an hour's time the Professor strode up the steps of the museum and hurried into the office. There was a little crowd of officials there whom the curator at once dismissed. He rose slowly to his feet. His manner was grave but bewildered.

"Professor," he said, "we will waste no time in words. Look here."

He threw open the door of an anteroom behind his office. The apartment was unfurnished except for one or two chairs. In the middle of the uncarpeted floor was a long wooden box from which the lid had just been pried.

"Yesterday, as you know from my note," the curator proceeded, "I was away. I gave orders that your case should be placed here and I myself should enjoy the distinction of opening it. An hour ago I commenced the task. That is what I found."

The Professor gazed blankly at the empty box.

"Nothing left except the smell," a voice from the open doorway remarked.

They glanced around. Quest was standing there, and behind him Lenora. The Professor welcomed them eagerly.

"This is Mr. Quest, the great criminologist," he explained to the curator. "Come in, Mr. Quest. Let me introduce you to Mr. Francis, the curator of the museum. Ask him what questions you will. Mr. Quest, you have the opportunity of earning the undying gratitude of a brother scientist. If my skeleton cannot be recovered, the work of years is undone."

Quest strolled thoughtfully around the room, glancing out of each of the windows in turn. He kept close to the wall, and when he had finished he drew out a magnifying-glass from his pocket and made a brief examination of the box. Then he asked a few questions of the curator, pointed out one of the windows to Lenora and whispered a few directions to her. She at once produced what seemed to be a foot-rule from the bag which she was carrying, and hurried into the garden.

"A little invention of my own for measuring foot-prints," Quest explained. "Not much use here, I am afraid."

"What do you think of the affair so far, Mr. Quest?" the Professor asked eagerly.

The criminologist shook his head.

"Incomprehensible," he confessed. "Can you think, by-the-bye, of any other motive for the theft besides scientific jealousy?"

"There could be no other," the Professor declared sadly, "and it is, alas! too prevalent. I have had to suffer from it all my life."

Quest stood over the box for a moment or two and looked once more out of the window. Presently Lenora returned. She carried in her hand a small object, which she brought silently to Quest. He glanced at it in perplexity. The Professor peered over his shoulder.

"It is the little finger!" he cried,—"the little finger of my ape!"

Quest held it away from him critically.

"From which hand?" he asked.

"The right hand."

Quest examined the fastenings of the window before which he had paused during his previous examination. He turned away with a shrug of the shoulders.

"See you later, Mr. Ashleigh," he concluded laconically. "Nothing more to be done at present."

The Professor followed him to the door.

"Mr. Quest," he said, his voice broken with emotion, "it is the work of my lifetime of which I am being robbed. You will use your best efforts, you will spare no expense? I am rich. Your fee you shall name yourself."

"I shall do my best," Quest promised, "to find the skeleton. Come, Lenora. Good morning, gentlemen!"

With his new assistant, Quest walked slowly from the museum and turned towards his home.

"Make anything of this, Lenora?" he asked her.

She smiled.

"Of course not," she answered. "It looks as though the skeleton had been taken away through that window."

Quest nodded.

"Marvellous!" he murmured.

"You are making fun of me," she protested.

"Not I! But you see, my young friend, the point is this. Who in their senses would want to steal an anthropoid skeleton except a scientific man, and if a scientific man stole it out of sheer jealousy, why in thunder couldn't he be content with just mutilating it, which would have destroyed its value just as well—What's that?"

He stopped short. A newsboy thrust the paper at them. Quest glanced at the headlines. Lenora clutched at his arm. Together they read in great black type—

ESCAPE OF CONVICTED PRISONER!

MACDOUGAL, ON HIS WAY TO PRISON, GRAPPLES WITH SHERIFF AND JUMPS FROM TRAIN! STILL AT LARGE THOUGH SEARCHED FOR BY POSSE OF POLICE

2.

The windows of Mrs. Rheinholdt's town house were ablaze with light. A crimson drugget stretched down the steps to the curbstone. A long row of automobiles stood waiting. Through the wide-flung doors was visible a pleasant impression of flowers and light and luxury. In the nearer of the two large reception rooms Mrs. Rheinholdt herself, a woman dark, handsome, and in the prime of life, was standing receiving her guests. By her side was her son, whose twenty-first birthday was being celebrated.

"I wonder whether that professor of yours will come," she remarked, as the stream of incoming guests slackened for a moment. "I'd love to have him here, if it were only for a moment. Every one's talking about him and his work in South America."

"He hates receptions," the boy replied, "but he promised he'd come. I never thought, when he used to drill science into us at the lectures, that he was going to be such a tremendous big pot."

Mrs. Rheinholdt's plump fingers toyed for a moment complacently with the diamonds which hung from her neck.

"You can never tell, in a world like this," she murmured. "That's why I make a point of being civil to everybody. Your laundry woman may become a multimillionaire, or your singing master a Caruso, and then, just while their month's on, every one is crazy to meet them. It's the Professor's month just now."

"Here he is, mother!" the young man exclaimed suddenly. "Good old boy! I thought he'd keep his word."

Mrs. Rheinholdt assumed her most encouraging and condescending smile as she held out both hands to the Professor. He came towards her, stooping a little more than usual. His mouth had drooped a little and there were signs of fatigue in his face. Nevertheless, his answering smile was as delightful as ever.

"This is perfectly sweet of you, Professor," Mrs. Rheinholdt declared. "We scarcely ventured to hope that you would break through your rule, but Philip was so looking forward to have you come. You were his favourite master at lectures, you know, and now—well, of course, you have the scientific world at your feet. Later on in the evening, Professor," she added, watching some very important newcomers, "you will tell me all about your anthropoid ape, won't you? Philip, look after Mr. Ashleigh. Don't let him go far away."

Mrs. Rheinholdt breathed a sigh of relief as she greeted her new arrivals.

"Professor Ashleigh, brother of Lord Ashleigh, you know," she explained. "This is the first house he has been to since his return from South America. You've heard all about those wonderful discoveries, of course...."

The Professor made himself universally agreeable in a mild way, and his presence created even more than the sensation which Mrs. Rheinholdt had hoped for. In her desire to show him ample honour, she seldom left his side.

"I am going to take you into my husband's study," she suggested, later on in the evening. "He has some specimens of beetles—"

"Beetles," the Professor declared, with some excitement, "occupied precisely two months of my time while abroad. By all means, Mrs. Rheinholdt!"

"We shall have to go quite to the back of the house," she explained, as she led him along the darkened passage.

The Professor smiled acquiescently. His eyes rested for a moment upon her necklace.

"You must really permit me, Mrs. Rheinholdt," he exclaimed, "to admire your wonderful stones! I am a judge of diamonds, and those three or four in the centre are, I should imagine, unique."

She held them out to him. The Professor laid the end of the necklace gently in the palm of his hand and examined them through a horn-rimmed eyeglass.

"They are wonderful," he murmured,—"wonderful! Why—"

He turned away a little abruptly. They had reached the back of the house and a door from the outside had just been opened. A man had crossed the threshold with a coat over his arm, and was standing now looking at them.

"How extraordinary!" the Professor remarked. "Is that you, Craig?"

For a moment there was no answer. The servant was standing in the gloom of an unlit portion of the passage. His eyes were fixed curiously upon the diamonds which the Professor had just been examining. He seemed paler, even, than usual.

"Yes, sir!" he replied. "There is a rain storm, so I ventured to bring your mackintosh."

"Very thoughtful," the Professor murmured approvingly. "I have a weakness," he went on, turning to his hostess, "for always walking home after an evening like this. In the daytime I am content to ride. At night I have the fancy always to walk."

"We don't walk half enough." Mrs. Rheinholdt sighed, glancing down at her somewhat portly figure. "Dixon," she added, turning to the footman who had admitted Craig, "take Professor Ashleigh's servant into the kitchen and see that he has something before he leaves for home. Now, Professor, if you will come this way."

They reached a little room in the far corner of the house. Mrs. Rheinholdt apologised as she switched on the electric lights.

"It is a queer little place to bring you to," she said, "but my husband used to spend many hours here, and he would never allow anything to be moved. You see, the specimens are in these cases."

The Professor nodded. His general attitude towards the forthcoming exhibition was merely one of politeness. As the first case was opened, however, his manner completely changed. Without taking the slightest further notice of his hostess, he adjusted a pair of horn-rimmed spectacles and commenced to mumble eagerly to himself. Mrs. Rheinholdt, who did not understand a word, strolled around the apartment, yawned, and finally interrupted a little stream of eulogies, not a word of which she understood, concerning a green beetle with yellow spots.

"I am so glad you are interested, Professor," she said. "If you don't mind, I will rejoin my guests. You will find a shorter way back if you keep along the passage straight ahead and come through the conservatory."

"Certainly! With pleasure!" the Professor agreed, without glancing up.

His hostess sighed as she turned to leave the room. She left the door ajar. The Professor's face was almost touching the glass case in which reposed the green beetle with yellow spots.

Mrs. Rheinholdt's reception, notwithstanding the temporary absence of its presiding spirit, was without doubt an unqualified success. In one of the distant rooms the younger people were dancing. There were bridge tables, all of which were occupied, and for those who preferred the more old-fashioned pastime of conversation amongst luxurious surroundings, there was still ample space and opportunity. Philip Rheinholdt, with a pretty young débutante upon his arm, came out from the dancing room and looked around amongst the little knots of people.

"I wonder where mother is," he remarked.

"Looking after some guests somewhere, for certain," the girl replied. "Your mother is so wonderful at entertaining, Philip."

"It's the hobby of her life," he declared. "Never so happy as when she can get hold of somebody every one's talking about, and show him off. Can't think what she's done with herself now, though. She told me—"

The young man broke off in the middle of his sentence. He, too, like many others in the room, felt a sudden thrill almost of horror at the sound which rang without warning upon their ears—a woman's cry, a cry of fear and horror, repeated again and again. There was a little rush towards the curtained space which led into the conservatories. Before even, however, the quickest could reach the spot, the curtains were thrown back and Mrs. Rheinholdt, her hands clasping her neck, her splendid composure a thing of the past, a panic-stricken, terrified woman, stumbled into the room. She seemed on the point of collapse. Somehow or other, they got her into an easy-chair.

"My jewels!" she cried. "My diamonds!"

"What do you mean, mother?" Philip Rheinholdt asked quickly. "Have you lost them?"

"Stolen!" Mrs. Rheinholdt shrieked. "Stolen there in the conservatory!"

They gazed at her open-mouthed, incredulous. Then a still, quiet voice from the outside of the little circle intervened.

"Instruct your servants, Mr. Rheinholdt, to lock and bar all the doors of the house," the Professor suggested. "No one must leave it until we have heard your mother's story."

The young man obeyed almost mechanically. There was a general exodus of servants from the room. Some one had brought Mrs. Rheinholdt a glass of champagne. She sipped it and gradually recovered her voice.

"I had just taken the Professor into the little room my husband used to call the museum," she explained, her voice still shaking with agitation. "I left him there to examine some specimens of beetles. I thought that I would come back through the conservatory, which is the quickest way. I was about halfway across it when suddenly I heard the switch go behind me and all the electric lights were turned out. I couldn't imagine what had happened. While I hesitated, I saw—I saw—"

She broke down again. There was no doubt about the genuineness of her terror. She seemed somehow to have shrunken into the semblance of a smaller woman. The pupils of her eyes were distended, she was white almost to the lips. When she recommenced her story, her voice was fainter.

"I saw a pair of hands—just hands—no arms—nothing but hands—come out of the darkness! They gripped me by the throat. I suppose it was just for a second. I think—I lost consciousness for a moment, although I was still standing up. The next thing I remember is that I found myself shrieking and running here—and the jewels had gone!"

"You saw no one?" her son asked incredulously. "You heard nothing?"

"I heard no footsteps. I saw no one," Mrs. Rheinholdt repeated.

The Professor turned away.

"If you will allow me," he begged, "I am going to telephone to my friend Mr. Sanford Quest, the criminologist. An affair so unusual as this might attract him. You will excuse me."

The Professor hurried from the room. They brought Mrs. Rheinholdt more champagne and she gradually struggled back to something like her normal self. The dancing had stopped. Every one was standing about in little groups, discussing the affair. The men had trooped towards the conservatory, but the Professor met them on the portals.

"I suggest," he said courteously, "that we leave the conservatory exactly as it is until the arrival of Mr. Sanford Quest. It will doubtless aid him in his investigations if nothing is disturbed. All the remaining doors are locked, so that no one can escape if by any chance they should be hiding."

They all agreed without dissent, and there was a general movement towards the buffet to pass the time until the coming of Mr. Sanford Quest. The Professor met the great criminologist and his assistant in the hall upon their arrival. He took the former at once by the arm.

"Mr. Quest," he began, "in a sense I must apologise for my peremptory message. I am well aware that an ordinary jewel robbery does not interest you, but in this case the circumstances are extraordinary. I ventured, therefore, to summon your aid."

Sanford Quest nodded shortly.

"As a rule," he said, "I do not care to take up one affair until I have a clean slate. There's your skeleton still bothering me, Professor. However, where's the lady who was robbed?"

"I will take you to her," the Professor replied. Mrs. Rheinholdt's story, by frequent repetition, had become a little more coherent, a trifle more circumstantial, the perfection of simplicity and utterly incomprehensible. Quest listened to it without remark and finally made his way to the conservatory. He requested Mrs. Rheinholdt to walk with him through the door by which she had entered, and stop at the precise spot where the assault had been made upon her. There were one or two plants knocked down from the tiers on the right-hand side, and some disturbance in the mould where some large palms were growing. Quest and Lenora together made a close investigation of the spot. Afterwards, Quest walked several times to each of the doors leading into the gardens.

"There are four entrances altogether," he remarked, as he lit a cigar and glanced around the place. "Two lead into the gardens—one is locked and the other isn't—one connects with the back of the house—the one through which you came, Mrs. Rheinholdt, and the other leads into your reception room, into which you passed after the assault. I shall now be glad if you will permit me to examine the gardens outside for a few minutes, alone with my assistant, if you please."

For almost a quarter of an hour, Quest and Lenora disappeared. They all looked eagerly at the criminologist on his return, but his face was sphinxlike. He turned to Mrs. Rheinholdt, who with her son, the butler, and the Professor were the only occupants of the conservatory.

"It seems to me," he remarked, "that from the back part of the house the quickest way to reach Mayton Avenue would be through this conservatory and out of that door. There is a path leading from just outside straight to a gate in the wall. Does any one that you know of use this means of exit?"

Mrs. Rheinholdt shook her head.

"The servants might occasionally," she remarked doubtfully, "but not on nights when I am receiving."

The butler stepped forward. He was looking a little grave.

"I ought, perhaps, to inform you, madam, and Mr. Quest," he said, "that I did, only a short time ago, suggest to the Professor's servant—the man who brought your mackintosh, sir," he added, turning to the Professor—"that he could, if he chose, make use of this means of leaving the house. Mr. Craig is a personal friend of mine, and a member of a very select little club we have for social purposes."

"Did he follow your suggestion?" Sanford Quest asked.

"Of that I am not aware, sir," the butler replied. "I left Mr. Craig with some refreshment, expecting that he would remain until my return, but a few minutes later I discovered that he had left. I will enquire in the kitchen if anything is known as to his movements."

He hurried off. Quest turned to the Professor.

"Has he been with you long, this man Craig, Professor?" he asked.

The Professor's smile was illuminating, his manner simple but convincing.

"Craig," he asserted, "is the best servant, the most honest mortal who ever breathed. He would go any distance out of his way to avoid harming a fly. I cannot even trust him to procure for me the simplest specimens of insect or animal life. Apart from this, he is a man of some property which he has no idea what to do with. He is, I think I may say, too devoted to me to dream of ever leaving my service."

"You think it would be out of the question, then," Quest asked, "to associate him with the crime?"

The Professor's confidence was sublime.

"I could more readily associate you, myself, or young Mr. Rheinholdt here with the affair," he declared.

His words carried weight. The little breath of suspicion against the Professor's servant faded away. In a moment or two the butler returned.

"It appears, madam," he announced, "that Mr. Craig left when there was only one person in the kitchen. He said good-night and closed the door behind him. It is impossible to say, therefore, by which exit he left the house, but personally I am convinced that, knowing of the reception here tonight, he would not think of using the conservatory."

"Most unlikely, I should say," the Professor murmured. "Craig is a very shy man. He is at all times at your disposal, Mr. Quest, if you should desire to question him."

Quest nodded absently.

"My assistant and I," he announced, "would be glad to make a further examination of the conservatory, if you will kindly leave us alone."

They obeyed without demur. Quest took a seat and smoked calmly, with his eyes fixed upon the roof. Lenora went back to her examination of the overturned plants, the mould, and the whole ground within the immediate environs of the assault. She abandoned the search at last, however, and came back to Quest's side. He threw away his cigar and rose.

"Nothing there?" he asked laconically.

"Not a thing," Lenora admitted.

Quest led the way towards the door.

"Lenora," he decided, "we are up against something big. There's a new hand at work somewhere."

"No theories yet, Mr. Quest?" she asked, smiling.

"Not the ghost of one," he admitted gloomily.

Along the rain-swept causeway of Mayton Avenue, keeping close to the shelter of the houses, his mackintosh turned up to his ears, his hands buried in his pockets, a man walked swiftly along. At every block he hesitated and looked around him. His manner was cautious, almost furtive. Once the glare of an electric light fell upon his face, a face pallid with fear, almost hopeless with despair. He walked quickly, yet he seemed to have little idea as to his direction. Suddenly he paused. He was passing a great building, brilliantly lit. For a moment he thought that it was some place of entertainment. The thought of entering seemed to occur to him. Then he felt a firm touch upon his arm, a man in uniform spoke to him.

"Step inside, brother," he invited earnestly, almost eagerly, notwithstanding his monotonous nasal twang. "Step inside and find peace. Step inside and the Lord will help you. Throw your burden away on the threshold."

The man's first impulse at being addressed had seemed to be one of terror. Then he recognised the uniform and hesitated. The light which streamed out from the building seemed warm and pleasant. The rain was coming down in sheets. They were singing a hymn, unmusical, unaccompanied, yet something in the unison of those human voices, one quality—the quality of earnestness, of faith—seemed to make an irresistible appeal to the terrified wanderer. Slowly he moved towards the steps. The man took him by the arm and led him in. There were the best part of a hundred people taking their places after the singing of the hymn. A girl was standing up before them on a platform. She was commencing to speak but suddenly broke off. She held out her arms towards where the Professor's confidential servant stood hesitating.

"Come and tell us your sins," she called out. "Come and have them forgiven. Come and start a new life in a new world. There is no one here who thinks of the past. Come and seek forgiveness."

For a moment this waif from the rain-swamped world hesitated. The light of an infinite desire flashed in his eyes. Then he dropped his head. These things might be for others. For him there was no hope. He shook his head to the girl but sank into the nearest seat and on to his knees.

"He repents!" the girl called out. "Some day he will come! Brothers and sisters, we will pray for him."

The rain dashed against the windows. The only other sound from outside was the clanging of the street cars. The girl's voice, frenzied, exhorting, almost hysterical, pealed out to the roof. At every pause, the little gathering of men and women groaned in sympathy. The man's frame was shaken with sobs.

CHAPTER IV

THE POCKET WIRELESS

1.

Mr. Sanford Quest sat in his favourite easy-chair, his cigar inclined towards the left hand corner of his mouth, his attention riveted upon a small instrument which he was supporting upon his knee. So far as his immobile features were capable of expression, they betrayed now, in the slight parting of his lips and the added brightness of his eyes, symptoms of a lively satisfaction. He glanced across the room to where Lenora was bending over her desk.

"We've done it this time, young woman," he declared triumphantly. "It's all O.K., working like a little peach."

Lenora rose and came towards him. She glanced at the instrument which Quest was fitting into a small leather case.

"Is that the pocket wireless?"

He nodded.

"I've had Morrison out at Harlem all the morning to test it," he told her. "I've sent him at least half a dozen messages from this easy-chair, and got the replies. How are you getting on with the code?"

"Not so badly for a stupid person," Lenora replied. "I'm not nearly so quick as Laura, of course, but I could make a message out if I took time over it."

Laura, who had been busy with some papers at the further end of the room, came over and joined them.

"Say, it's a dandy little affair, that, Mr. Quest," she exclaimed. "I had a try with it, a day or so ago. Jim spoke to me from Fifth Avenue."

"We've got it tuned to a shade now," Quest declared. "Equipped with this simple little device, you can speak to me from anywhere up to ten or a dozen miles. What are you working on this morning, Laura?"

"Same old stunt," the girl replied. "I have been reading up the records of the savants of New York. From what I can make out about them, it doesn't seem to me that there's one amongst the whole bunch likely to have pluck enough to tamper with the Professor's skeleton."

Quest frowned a little gloomily. He rose to his feet and moved restlessly about the room.

"Say, girls," he confessed, "this is the first time in my life I have been in a fix like this. Two cases on hand and nothing doing with either of them. Criminologist, indeed! I guess I'd better go over to England and take a job at Scotland Yard. That's about what I'm fit for. Whose box is this?"

Quest had paused suddenly in front of an oak sideboard which stood against the wall. Occupying a position upon it of some prominence was a small black box, whose presence there seemed to him unfamiliar. Laura came over to his side and looked at it also in puzzled fashion.

"Never saw it before in my life," she answered. "Say, kid, is this yours?" she added, turning to Lenora.

Lenora shook her head. She, too, examined it a little wonderingly.

"It wasn't there a short time ago. I brought a duster and went over the sideboard myself."

Quest grunted.

"H'm! No one else has been in the room, and it hasn't been empty for more than ten minutes," he remarked. "Well, let's see what's inside, any way."

"Just be careful, Mr. Quest," Laura advised. "I don't get that box at all."

Quest pushed it with his forefinger.

"No bomb inside, any way," he remarked. "Here goes!"

He lifted off the lid. There was nothing in the interior but a sheet of paper folded up. Quest smoothed it out with his hand. They all leaned over and read the following words, written in an obviously disguised hand:

"You have embarked on a new study—anthropology. What characteristic strikes you most forcibly in connection with it? Cunning? The necklace might be where the skeleton is. Why not begin at the beginning?"

The note was unsigned, but in the spot where a signature might have been there was a rough pen drawing of two hands, with fingers extended, talon fashion, menacingly, as though poised to strike at some unseen enemy. Quest, after their first moment of stupefaction, whistled softly.

"The hands!" he muttered.

"What hands?" Lenora asked.

"The hands that gripped Mrs. Rheinholdt by the throat," he reminded them. "Don't you remember? Hands without any arms?"

There was another brief, almost stupefied silence. Then Laura broke into speech.

"What I want to know is," she demanded, "who brought the thing here?"

"A most daring exploit, any way," Quest declared. "If we could answer your question, Laura, we could solve the whole riddle. We are up against something, and no mistake."

Lenora shivered a little. The mystery of the thing terrified her, the mystery which only stimulated her two companions.

"The hand which placed that box here," Quest continued slowly, "is capable of even more wonderful things. We must be cautious. Hello!"

The door had opened. The Professor stood upon the threshold. He carried his soft felt hat in his hand. He bowed to the two young women courteously.

"I trust that I have done right in coming up?" he enquired.

"Quite right, Professor," Quest assured him. "They know well enough downstairs that I am always at liberty to you. Come in."

"I am so anxious to learn," the Professor continued eagerly, "whether there is any news—of my skeleton."

"Not yet, Professor, I am sorry to say," Quest replied. "Come in and shut the door."

The Professor was obviously struggling with his disappointment. He did not, however, at once close the door.

"There is a young lady here," he said, "who caught me up upon the landing. She, too, I believe, wishes to see you. My manners suffered, I fear, from my eagerness to hear from your own lips if there was anything fresh. I should have allowed her to precede me."

He threw open the door and stood on one side. A young woman came a little hesitatingly into the room. Her hair was plainly brushed back, and she wore the severe dress of the Salvation Army. Nothing, however, could conceal the fact that she was a remarkably sweet and attractive-looking young person.

"Want to see me, young lady?" Quest asked.

She held out a book.

"My name is Miss Quigg," she said. "I want to ask you for a subscription to our funds."

Quest frowned a little.

"I don't care about this house-to-house visitation," he remarked.

"It is only once a year that we come," the girl pleaded, "and we only go to people who we know can afford to help us, and who we believe can appreciate our work. You know so much of the darker side of New York, Mr. Quest. Wherever you go you must find signs of our labours. Even if I put on one side, for a moment, the bare religious question, think how much we do for the good and the welfare of the poor people."

Quest nodded.

"That's all right," he admitted. "You reach the outcasts all right. There's many a one you save whom you had better leave to die, but here and there, no doubt, you set one of them on their legs again who's had bad luck. Very well, Miss Quigg. You shall have a donation. I am busy today, but call at the same hour tomorrow and my secretary here shall have a cheque ready for you."

The girl smiled her gratitude.

"You are very kind indeed, Mr. Quest," she said simply. "I will be here."

The Professor laid his hand upon her arm as she passed. He had been watching her with curious intentness.

"Young lady," he observed, "you seem very much in earnest about your work."

"It is only the people in earnest, sir," she answered, "who can do any good in the world. My work is worth being in earnest about."

"Will you forgive an old man's question?" the Professor continued. "I am one of the men of the world who are in earnest. My life is dedicated to science. Science is at once my religion and my life. It seems to me that you and I have something in common. You, too, move in the unusual ways. Your life is dedicated to doing good amongst the unworthy of your sex. Whether my brain approves of your efforts or not, you compel my admiration—my most respectful admiration. May I, too, be permitted?"

He drew out a pocket-book and passed over towards her a little wad of notes. She took them without a moment's hesitation. Her eyes, as she thanked him, were filled with gratitude.

"It is so kind of you," she murmured. "We never have any hesitation in accepting money. May I know your name?"

"It is not necessary," the Professor answered. "You can enter me," he added, as he held open the door for her, "as a friend—or would you prefer a pseudonym?"

"A pseudonym, if you please," she begged. "We have so many who send us sums of money as friends. Anything will do."

The Professor glanced around the room.

"What pseudonym shall I adopt?" he ruminated. "Shall I say that an oak sideboard gives you five hundred dollars? Or a Chippendale sofa? Or," he added, his eyes resting for a moment upon the little box, "a black box?"

The two girls from the other side of the table started. Even Quest swung suddenly around. The Professor, as though pleased with his fancy, nodded as his fingers played with the lid.

"Yes, that will do very nicely," he decided. "Put me down—'Black Box,' five hundred dollars."

The girl took out her book and began to write. The Professor, with a little farewell bow, crossed the room towards Quest. Lenora moved towards the door.

"Let me see you out," she said to the girl pleasantly. "Don't you find this collecting sometimes very hard work?"

"Days like today," the girl replied, "atone for everything. When I think of the good that five hundred dollars will do, I feel perfectly happy."

Lenora opened the door. Both girls started. Only a few feet away

Craig was standing, his head a little thrust forward. For a moment the quiet self-respect of his manner seemed to have deserted him. He seemed at a loss for words.

"What do you want?" Lenora demanded.

Craig hesitated. His eyes were fixed upon the Salvation Army girl. The changes in his face were remarkable. She, however, beyond smiling pleasantly at him, gave no sign of any recognition.

"I was waiting for my master," Craig explained.

"Why not downstairs?" Lenora asked suspiciously. "You did not come up with him."

"I am driving the Professor in his automobile," Craig explained. "It occurred to me that if he were going to be long here, I should have time to go and order another tire. It is of no consequence, though. I will go down and wait in the car."

Lenora stood at the top of the stairs and watched him disappear. Then she went thoughtfully back to her work. The Professor and Quest were talking at the farther end of the room.

"I was in hopes, in great hopes," the Professor admitted, "that you might have heard something. I promised to call at Mrs. Rheinholdt's this afternoon."

Quest shook his head.

"There is nothing to report at present, Mr. Ashleigh," he announced.

"Dear me," the Professor murmured, "this is very disappointing. Is there no clue, Mr. Quest—no clue at all?"

"Not the ghost of one," Quest acknowledged. "I am as far from solving the mystery of the disappearance of your skeleton and Mrs. Rheinholdt's necklace, as I have ever been."

The Professor failed entirely to conceal his disappointment. His tone, in fact, was almost peevish.

"I should have expected this from the regular officials of the law, Mr. Quest," he admitted, "but I must say that in your hands I had hoped—but there, there! Excuse me! I am an old man, Mr. Quest. I am getting a little irritable. Disappointments affect me quickly. I must be patient. I will be patient."

"There are certain evidences," Quest remarked, with his eyes upon the black box, "which seem to point to a new arrival in the criminal world of New York. More than that I cannot tell you. I will simply ask you to believe that I am doing my best."

"And with that, Mr. Quest, I will be content," the Professor promised. "I will now pay my promised call upon Mrs. Rheinholdt. I shall convey to her your assurance that everything that is possible is being done. Good morning, young ladies," he concluded. "Good morning, Mr. Quest."

He took a courteous leave of them all and departed. Lenora crossed the room to where Quest was seated at the table.

"Mr. Quest," she asked, "do you believe in inspiration?"

"I attribute a large amount of my success," Quest replied, "to my profound belief in it."

"Then let me tell you," Lenora continued, "that I have one and a very strong one. Do you know that when I went to the door a few minutes ago, the Professor's servant, Craig, was there, listening?"

"Craig?" Quest repeated. "Let me see, that was the man who was at the Rheinholdts' house the night of the robbery, and who might have left through the conservatory."

"He did leave by it," Lenora declared. "He is in a state of panic at the present moment. What else do you suppose he was out there listening for?"

"The Professor speaks very highly of him," Quest reminded her.

"The Professor is just one of those amiable old idiots, absorbed in his mouldy old work, who would never notice anything," Lenora persisted. "He is just the man to be completely hoodwinked by a clever servant."

"There is some sense in what the kid says," Laura remarked, strolling up. "The fact remains that Craig was one of the few men who could have got at the necklace that night, and he is also one of the few who knew about the skeleton."

Quest sighed as he lit a cigar.

"It is a miserably obvious solution," he said. "To tell you the truth, girls, our friend Inspector French has had his men watching Craig ever since the night of the robbery. What's that? Answer the telephone, Lenora."

Lenora obeyed.

"It's Inspector French," she announced. "He wants to speak to you."

Quest nodded, and held out his hand for the receiver.

"Hullo, French," he exclaimed. "Anything fresh?"

"Nothing much!" was the answer. "One of my men, though, who has been up Mayton Avenue way, brought in something I found rather interesting this morning. I want you to come round and see it."

"Go right ahead and tell me about it," Quest invited.

"You know we've been shadowing Craig," the Inspector continued. "Not much luck up till now. Fellow seems never to leave his master's side. We have had a couple of men up there, though, and one of them brought in a curious-looking object he picked up just outside the back of the Professor's grounds. It's an untidy sort of neighbourhood, you know—kind of waste ground they commenced to build over, and then the real estate man who had it in hand, went smash."

"What is the thing?" Quest asked.

"Well, I want to see whether you agree with me," French went on. "If you can't come round, I'll come to you."

"No necessity," Quest replied. "We've got over little difficulties of that sort. Laura, just tack on the phototelesme," he added, holding the receiver away for a moment. "One moment, French. There, that's right," he added, as Laura, with deft fingers, arranged what seemed to be a sensitised mirror to the instrument. "Now, French, hold up the article just in front of the receiver."

French's reply was a little brusque.

"What are you getting at, Quest?" he demanded. "You are not going to pretend that you can see from your room into this, are you?"

"If you'll hold the object where I told you," Quest replied, "I can see it. I promise you that. There, that's right. Hold it steady. I've got the focus of it now. Say, French, where did you say that was found?"

"Just outside the Professor's back gates," French grunted, "but you're not kidding me—"

"It's a finger from the Professor's skeleton you've got there," Quest interrupted.

"How the blazes did you guess that?" the Inspector demanded.

"I'm not kidding," Quest assured him. "I've got a phototelesme at work here. I've seen the bone all right. French, this is interesting. I must think it over."

Quest hung up the receiver and rang off. Then he turned towards his two assistants.

"Another finger from the Professor's skeleton," he announced, "has been found just outside his grounds. What do you suppose that means?"

"Craig," Lenora declared confidently.

"Craig on your life," Laura echoed. "Say, Mr. Quest, I've got an idea."

Quest nodded.

"Get right ahead with it."

"Didn't the butler at Mrs. Rheinholdt's say that Craig belonged to a servants' club up town? I know the place well. Let me go and see if I can't join and pick up a little information about the man. He must have a night out sometimes. Let's find out what he does. How's that?"

"Capital!" Quest agreed. "Get along, Laura. And you, Lenora," he added, "put on your hat. We'll take a ride towards Mayton Avenue."

2.

The exact spot where the bone of the missing skeleton was discovered, was easily located. It was about twenty yards from a gate which led into the back part of the Professor's grounds. The neighbourhood was dreary in the extreme. There were half finished houses, little piles of building materials, heaps of stones, a watchman's shed, and all the dreary paraphernalia of an abandoned building enterprise. Quest wasted very little time before arriving at a decision.

"The discovery of the bone so near the Professor's house," he decided, "cannot be coincidence only. We will waste no time out here, Lenora. We will search the grounds. Come on."

They advanced towards the gate but found it locked. The wall was unusually high as though to obscure a view of anything that lay on the other side. Quest noticed with interest that, in places where it had shown signs of crumbling away, it had been repaired. He contemplated the lock thoughtfully and drew a little instrument from his pocket, an instrument which had the appearance of a many-sided key.

"Looks like storming the fortress, eh?" he remarked. "Here goes, any way."

The gate swung open with a single turn of the wrist. Quest glanced for a moment at the lock and replaced the instrument in his pocket.

"The Professor's not looking for visitors," he muttered. "Gee! What a wilderness!"

It was hard to know which way to turn. Every path was choked with tangled weeds and bushes. Here and there remained one or two wonderful old trees, but the vegetation for the greater part consisted of laurel and other shrubs, which from lack of attention had grown almost into a jungle. They wandered about almost aimlessly for nearly half an hour. Then Quest came to a sudden standstill. Lenora gripped his arm. They had both heard the same sound—a queer, crooning little cry, half plaintive, half angry. Quest looked over his right shoulder along a narrow, overgrown path which seemed to end abruptly in an evergreen hedge.

"What's that?" he exclaimed.

Lenora still clung to his arm.

"I hate this place," she whispered. "It terrifies me. What are we looking for, Mr. Quest?"

"Can't say that I know exactly," the latter answered, "but I guess we'll find out where that cry came from. Sounded to me uncommonly like a human effort."

They made their way up as far as the hedge, which they skirted for a few yards until they found an opening. Then Quest gave vent to a little exclamation. Immediately in front of them was a small hut, built apparently of sticks and bamboos, with a stronger framework behind. The sloping roof was grass-grown and entwined with rushes. The only apology for a window was a queer little hole set quite close to the roof.

"The sort of place where the Professor might keep some of his pets," Quest observed thoughtfully. "We'll have a look inside, any way."

There was a rude-looking door, but Quest, on trying it, found it locked. They walked around the place but found no other opening. All the time from inside they could hear queer, scuffling sounds. Lenora's cheeks grew paler.

"Must we stay?" she murmured. "I don't think I want to see what's inside. Mr. Quest! Mr. Quest!"

She clung to his arm. They were opposite the little aperture which served as a window, and at that moment it suddenly framed the face of a creature, human in features, diabolical in expression. Long hair drooped over one cheek, the close-set eyes were filled with fury, the white teeth gleamed menacingly. Quest felt in his pocket for his revolver.

"Say, that's some face!" he remarked. "I'd hate to spoil it."

Even as he spoke, it disappeared. Quest took out the little gate opening apparatus from his pocket.

"We've got to get inside there, Lenora," he announced, stepping forward.

She followed him silently. A few turns of the wrist and the door yielded. Keeping Lenora a little behind him, Quest gazed around eagerly. Exactly in front of him, clad only in a loin cloth, with hunched-up shoulders, a necklace around his neck, with blazing eyes and ugly gleaming teeth, crouched some unrecognisable creature, human yet inhuman, a monkey and yet a man. There were a couple of monkeys swinging by their tails from a bar, and a leopard chained to a staple in the ground, walking round and round in the far corner, snapping and snarling every time he glanced towards the newcomers. The creature in front of him stretched out a hairy hand towards a club, and gripped it. Quest drew a long breath. His eyes were set hard.

"Drop that club," he ordered.

The creature suddenly sprang up. The club was waved around his head.

"Drop it," Quest repeated firmly. "You will sit down in your corner. You will take no more notice of us. Do you hear? You will drop the club. You will sit down in your corner. You will sleep."

The club slipped from the hairy fingers. The tense frame, which had been already crouched for the spring, was suddenly relaxed. The knees trembled.

"Back to that corner," Quest ordered, pointing.

Slowly and dejectedly, the ape-man crept to where he had been ordered and sat there with dull, non-comprehending stare. It was a new force, this, a note of which he had felt—the superman raising the voice of authority. Quest touched his forehead and found it damp. The strain of those few seconds had been intolerable.

"I don't think these other animals will hurt," he said. "Let's have a look around the place."

The search took only a few moments. The monkeys ran and jumped around them, gibbering as though with pleasure. The leopard watched them always with a snarl and an evil light in his eye. They found nothing unusual until they came to the distant corner, where a huge piano box lay on its side with the opening turned to the wall.

"This is where the brute sleeps, I suppose," Quest remarked. "We'll turn it round, any way."

They dragged it a few feet away from the wall, so that the opening faced them. Then Lenora gave a little cry and Quest stood suddenly still.

"The skeleton!" Lenora shrieked. "It's the skeleton!"

Quest stooped down and drew away the matting which concealed some portion of this strange-looking object. It was a skeleton so old that the bones had turned to a dull grey. Yet so far as regards its limbs, it was almost complete. Quest glanced towards the hands.

"Little fingers both missing," he muttered. "That's the skeleton all right, Lenora."

"Remember the message!" she exclaimed. "'Where the skeleton is, the necklace may be also.'"

Quest nodded shortly.

"We'll search."

They turned over everything in the place fruitlessly. There was no sign of the necklace. At last they gave it up.

"You get outside, Lenora," Quest directed. "I'll just bring this beast round again and then we'll tackle the Professor."

Lenora stepped back into the fresh air with a little murmur of relief. Quest turned towards the creature which crouched still huddled up in its corner, its eyes half closed, rolling a little from side to side.

"Look at me," he ordered.

The creature obeyed. Once more its frame seemed to grow more virile and natural.

"You need sleep no longer," Quest said. "Wake up and be yourself."

The effect of his words was instantaneous. Almost as he spoke, the creature crouched for a spring. There was wild hatred in its close-set eyes, the snarl of something fiendlike in its contorted mouth. Quest slipped quickly through the door.

"Any one may have that for a pet!" he remarked grimly. "Come, Lenora, there's a word or two to be said to the Professor. There's something here will need a little explanation."

He lit a cigar as they struggled back along the path. Presently they reached the untidy-looking avenue, and a few minutes later arrived at the house. Quest looked around him in something like bewilderment.

"Say, fancy keeping a big place like this, all overgrown and like a wilderness!" he exclaimed. "If the Professor can't afford a few gardeners, why doesn't he take a comfortable flat down town."

"I think it's a horrible place," Lenora agreed. "I hope I never come here again."

"Pretty well obsessed, these scientific men get," Quest muttered. "I suppose this is the front door."

They passed under the portico and knocked. There was no reply. Quest searched in vain for a bell. They walked round the piazza. There were no signs of any human life. The windows were curtainless and displayed vistas of rooms practically devoid of furniture. They came back to the front door. Quest tried the handle and found it open. They passed into the hall.

"Hospitable sort of place, any way," he remarked. "We'll go in and wait, Lenora."

They found their way to the study, which seemed to be the only habitable room. Lenora glanced around at its strange contents with an expression almost of awe.

"Fancy a man living in a muddle like this!" she exclaimed. "Not a picture, scarcely a carpet, uncomfortable chairs—nothing but bones and skeletons and mummies and dried-up animals. A man with tastes like this, Mr. Quest, must have a very different outlook upon life from ordinary human beings."

Quest nodded.

"He generally has," he admitted. "Here comes our host, any way."

A small motor-car passed the window, driven by Craig. The Professor descended. A moment or two later he entered the room. He gazed from Quest to Lenora at first in blank surprise. Then he held out his hands.

"You have good news for me, my friends!" he exclaimed. "I am sure of it. How unfortunate that I was not at home to receive you! Tell me—don't keep me in suspense, if you please—you have discovered my skeleton?"

"We have found the skeleton," Quest announced.

For a single moment the new-comer stood as though turned to stone. There was a silence which was not without its curious dramatic significance. Then a light broke across the Professor's face. He gave a great gulp of relief.

"My skeleton!" he murmured. "Mr. Quest, I knew it. You are the greatest man alive. Now tell me quickly—I want to know everything, but this first of all.—Where did you find the skeleton? Who was the thief?"

"We found the skeleton, Professor," Quest replied, "within a hundred yards of this house."

The Professor's mouth was wide open. He looked like a bewildered child. It was several seconds before he spoke.

"Within a hundred yards of this house? Then it wasn't stolen by one of my rivals?"

"I should say not," Quest admitted.

"Where? Where exactly did you find it?" the other insisted.

Quest was standing very still, his manner more reserved even than usual, his eyes studying the Professor, weighing every spoken word.

"I found it in a hut," he said, "hidden in a piano box. I found there, also, a creature—a human being, I must call him—in a state of captivity."

"Hidden in a piano box?" the Professor repeated wonderingly. "Why, you mean in Hartoo's sleeping box, then?"

"If Mr. Hartoo is the gentleman who tried to club me, you are right," Quest admitted. "Mr. Ashleigh, before we go any further I must ask you for an explanation as to the presence of that person in your grounds!"

The Professor hesitated for a moment. Then he slowly crossed the room, opened the drawer of a small escritoire, and drew out a letter.

"You have heard of Sir William Raysmore, the President of the Royal Society?" he asked.

Quest nodded.

"This letter is from him," the Professor continued. "You had better read it."

The criminologist read it aloud. Lenora looked over his shoulder:—

"To Professor Edgar Ashleigh, New York.

"My dear Professor,

"Your communication gratifies and amazes me. I can say no more. It fell to your lot to discover the skeleton of the anthropoid, a marvellous thing, in its way, and needing only its corollary to form the greatest discovery since the dark ages. Now you tell me that in the person of Hartoo, the last of the Inyamo Race of South America, you have found that corollary. You have supplied the missing link. You are in a position to give to the world a definite and logical explanation of the evolution of man. Let me give you one word of warning, Professor, before I write you at greater length on this matter. Anthropologists are afflicted more, even, than any other race of scientific men, with jealousy. Guard your secret well, lest the honour of this discovery should be stolen from you.

"William Raysmore."

The Professor nodded deliberately as Quest finished the letter.

"Now, perhaps, you can understand," he said, "why it was necessary to keep Hartoo absolutely hidden. In a month's time my papers will be ready. Then I shall electrify the world. I shall write not a new page but a new volume across the history of science. I shall—"

The door was suddenly thrown open. Craig sprang in, no longer the self-contained, perfect man-servant, but with the face of some wild creature. His shout was one almost of agony.

"The hut, Professor! The hut is on fire!" he cried.

His appearance on the threshold was like a flash. They heard his flying feet down the hall, and without a moment's hesitation they all followed. The Professor led the way down a narrow and concealed path, but when they reached the little clearing in which the hut was situated, they were unable to approach any nearer. The place was a whirlwind of flame. The smell of kerosene was almost overpowering. The wild yell of the leopard rose above the strange, half human gibbering of the monkeys and the hoarse, bass calling of another voice, at the sound of which Lenora and even Quest shuddered. Then, as they came, breathless, to a standstill, they saw a strange thing. One side of the hut fell in, and almost immediately the leopard with a mighty spring, leapt from the place and ran howling into the undergrowth. The monkeys followed but they came straight for the Professor, wringing their hands. They fawned at his feet as though trying to show him their scorched bodies. Then for a single moment they saw the form of the ape-man as he struggled to follow the others. His strength failed him, however. He fell backwards into the burning chasm.

The Professor bade them farewell, an hour later, on the steps of the house. He seemed suddenly to have aged.

"You have done your best, Mr. Quest," he said, "but Fate has been too strong. Remember this, though. It is quite true that the cunning of Hartoo may have made it possible for him to have stolen the skeleton and to have brought it back to its hiding-place, but it was jealousy—cruel, brutal, foul jealousy which smeared the walls of that hut with kerosene and set a light to it. The work of a lifetime, my dreams of scientific immortality, have vanished in those flames."

He turned slowly away from them and re-entered the house. Quest and Lenora made their way down the avenue and entered the automobile which was waiting for them, almost in silence. The latter glanced towards his companion as they drove off.

"Say, this has been a bit tough for you," he remarked. "I'll have to call somewhere and get you a glass of wine."

She tried to smile but her strength was almost gone. They drove to a restaurant and sat there for a some little time. Lenora soon recovered her colour. She even had courage to speak of the events of the afternoon when they re-entered the automobile.

"Mr. Quest," she murmured, "who do you suppose burned the hut down?"

"If I don't say Craig, I suppose you will," he remarked. "I wonder whether Laura's had any luck."

They were greeted, as they entered Quest's room, by a familiar little ticking. Quest smiled with pleasure.

"It's the pocket wireless," he declared. "Let me take down the message."

He spelt it out to Lenora, who stood by his side:

"Have joined Servants' Club disguised as your butler. Craig frequent visitor here ten years ago, comes now occasionally. Thursday evenings most likely time. Shall wait here on chance of seeing him."

"Good girl, that," Quest remarked. "She's a rare sticker, too."

He turned away from the instrument and was crossing the room towards his cigar cabinet. Suddenly he stopped. He looked intently towards the sideboard.

"What is it?" Lenora asked.

He did not answer. She followed the direction of his gaze. Exactly in the same spot as before reposed another but somewhat larger black box, of the same shape and material as the previous one.

"Say, who put that there?" he demanded.

Lenora shook her head.

"I locked the door when we went out," she assured him.

Quest took the box into his hands and removed the lid. It seemed half full of cotton-wool. On the top were a few lines of writing and beneath them the signature of the parted hands. He read the form out slowly:

"Drop all investigation. The hands that return these jewels command it."

Quest raised the cotton-wool. Beneath lay Mrs. Rheinholdt's necklace!

CHAPTER V

AN OLD GRUDGE

1.

Sanford Quest was smoking his after breakfast cigar with a relish somewhat affected by the measure of his perplexities. Early though it was, Lenora was already in her place, bending over her desk, and Laura, who had just arrived, was busy divesting herself of her coat and hat. Quest watched the latter impatiently.

"Well?" he asked.

Laura came forward, straightening her hair with her hands.

"No go," she answered. "I spent the evening in the club and I talked with two men who knew Craig, but I couldn't get on to anything. From all I could hear of the man, respectability is his middle name."

"That's the Professor's own idea," Quest remarked grimly. "I merely ventured to drop a hint that Craig might not be quite so immaculate as he seemed, and I never saw a man so horrified in my life. He assured me that Craig was seldom out of his sight, that he hadn't a friend in the world nor a single vicious taste."

"We're fairly up against it, boss," Laura sighed. "The best thing we can do is to get on to another job. The Rheinholdt woman has got her jewels back, or will have at noon today. I bet she won't worry about the thief. Then the Professor's mouldy old skeleton was returned to him, even if it was burnt up afterwards. I should take on something fresh."

"Can't be done," Quest replied shortly. "Look here, girls, your average intellects are often apt to hit upon the truth, when a man who sees too far ahead goes wrong. Rule Craig out. Any other possible person occur to you?—Speak out, Lenora. You've something on your mind, I can see."

The girl swung around in her chair. There was a vague look of trouble upon her face.

"I'm afraid you'll laugh at me," she began tentatively.

"Won't hurt you if I do," Quest replied.

"I can't help thinking of Macdougal," Lenora continued falteringly. "He has never been recaptured, and I don't know whether he's dead or alive. He had a perfect passion for jewels. If he is alive, he would be desperate and would attempt anything."

Quest smoked in silence for a moment.

"I guess the return of the jewels squelches the Macdougal theory," he remarked. "He wouldn't be likely to part with the stuff when he'd once got his hands on it. However, I always meant, when we had a moment's spare time, to look into that fellow's whereabouts. We'll take it on straight away. Can't do any harm."

"I know the section boss on the railway at the spot where he disappeared," Laura announced.

"Then just take the train down to Mountways—that's the nearest spot—and get busy with him," Quest directed. "Try and persuade him to loan us the gang's hand-car to go down the line. Lenora and I will come on in the automobile."

"Take you longer," Lenora remarked, as she moved off to put on her jacket. "The cars do it in half an hour."

"Can't help that," Quest replied. "Mrs. Rheinholdt's coming here to identify her jewels at twelve o'clock, and I can't run any risk of there being no train back. You'd better be making good with the section boss. Take plenty of bills with you."

"Sure! That's easy enough," Laura promised him. "I'll be waiting for you."

She hurried off and Quest commenced his own preparations. From his safe he took one of the small black lumps of explosive to which he had once before owed his life, and fitted it carefully in a small case with a coil of wire and an electric lighter. He looked at his revolver and recharged it. Finally he rang the bell for his confidential valet.

"Ross," he asked, "who else is here today besides you?"

"No one today, sir."

"Just as well, perhaps," Quest observed. "Listen, Ross. I am going out now for an hour or two, but I shall be back at mid-day. Remember that. Mrs. Rheinholdt and Inspector French are to be here at twelve o'clock. If by any chance I should be a few moments late, ask them to wait. And, Ross, a young woman from the Salvation Army will call too. You can give her this cheque."

Ross Brown, who was Quest's secretary-valet and general factotum, accepted the slip of paper and placed it in an envelope.

"There are no other instructions, sir?" he enquired.

"None," Quest replied. "You'll look out for the wireless, and you had better switch the through cable and telegraph communication on to headquarters. Come along, Lenora."

They left the house, entered the waiting automobile, and drove rapidly towards the confines of the city. Quest was unusually thoughtful. Lenora, on the other hand, seemed to have lost a great deal of her usual self composure. She seldom sat still for more than a moment or two together. She was obviously nervous and excited.

"What's got hold of you, Lenora?" Quest asked her once. "You seem all fidgets."

She glanced at him apologetically.

"I can't help it," she confessed. "If you knew of the many sleepless nights I have had, of how I have racked my brain wondering what could have become of James, you wouldn't really wonder that I am excited now that there is some chance of really finding out. Often I have been too terrified to sleep."

"We very likely shan't find out a thing," Quest reminded her. "French and his lot have had a try and come to grief."

"Inspector French isn't like you, Mr. Quest," Lenora ventured.

Quest laughed bitterly.

"Just now, at any rate, we don't seem to be any great shakes," he remarked. "However, I'm glad we're on this job. Much better to find out what has become of the fellow really, if we can."

Lenora's voice suddenly grew steady. She turned round in her place and faced her companion.

"Mr. Quest," she said, "I like my work with you. You saved me from despair. Sometimes it seems to me that life now opens out an entirely new vista. Yet since this matter has been mentioned between us, let me tell you one thing. I have known no rest, night or day, since we heard of—of James's escape. I live in terror. If I have concealed it, it has been at the expense of my nerves and my strength. I think that very soon I could have gone on no longer."

Quest's only reply was a little nod. Yet, notwithstanding his imperturbability of expression, that little nod was wonderfully sympathetic. Lenora leaned back in her place well satisfied. She felt that she was understood.

By Quest's directions, the automobile was brought to a stand-still at a point where it skirted the main railway line, and close to the section house which he had appointed for his rendezvous with Laura. She had apparently seen their approach and she came out to meet them at once, accompanied by a short, thick-set man whom she introduced as Mr. Horan.

"This is Mr. Horan, the section boss," she explained.

Mr. Horan shook hands.

"Say, I've heard of you, Mr. Quest," he announced. "The young lady tells me you are some interested in that prisoner they lost off the cars near here."

"That's so," Quest admitted. "We'd like to go to the spot if we could."

"That's dead easy," the boss replied. "I'll take you along in the hand car. I've been expecting you, Mr. Quest, some time ago."

"How's that?" the criminologist asked.

Mr. Horan expelled a fragment of chewing tobacco and held out his hand for the cigar which Quest was offering.

"They've been going the wrong way to work, these New York police," he declared. "Just because there was a train on the other track moving slowly, they got it into their heads that Macdougal had boarded it and was back in New York somewhere. That ain't my theory. If I were looking for James Macdougal, I'd search the hillsides there. I'll show you what I mean when we get alongside."

"You may be right," Quest admitted. "Anyway, we'll start on the job."

The section boss turned around and whistled. From a little side track two men jumped on to a hand-car, and brought it round to where they were standing. A few yards away, the man who was propelling it—a great red-headed Irishman—suddenly ceased his efforts. Leaning over his pole, he gazed at Quest. A sudden ferocity darkened his coarse face. He gripped his mate by the arm.

"See that bloke there?" he asked, pointing at Quest.

"The guy with the linen collar?" the other answered. "I see him."

"That's Quest, the detective," the Irishman went on hoarsely. "That's the man who got me five years in the pen, the beast. That's the man I've been looking for. You're my mate, Jim, eh?"

"I guess so," the other grunted. "Are you going to try and do him in?"

"You wait!"

"Now, then, you fellows," Horan shouted. "What are you hanging about there for, Red Gallagher? Bring the carriage up. You fellows can go and have a smoke for an hour. I'm going to take her down the line a bit."

The two men obeyed and disappeared in the direction of the section house. Quest looked after them curiously.

"That's a big fellow," he remarked. "What did you call him? Red Gallagher? I seem to have seen him before."

"He was the most troublesome fellow on the line once, although he was the biggest worker," the boss replied. "He got five years in the penitentiary and that seems to have taken the spirit out of him."

"I believe I was in the case," Quest observed carelessly.

"That so! Now then, young ladies," Mr. Horan advised, "hold tight, and here goes!"

They ambled down the line for about half a mile. Then Horan brought them to a standstill.

"This is the spot," he declared. "Now, if you want my impressions, you are welcome to them. All the search has been made on the right-hand side here, and in New York. I've had my eye on that hill for a long time. My impression is that he hid there."

"I'll take your advice," Quest decided. "We'll spread out and take a little exercise in hill climbing."

"Good luck to you!" the boss exclaimed. "You'll excuse my waiting? It ain't a quarter of a mile back by the road, and I'm going a bit farther on, inspecting."

Quest slipped something into his hand and the little party left the track, crossed the road, scrambled down a bank and spread out. In front of them was a slope some hundreds of feet high, closely overgrown with dwarf trees and mountain shrubs. It was waste land, uncultivated and uninhabited. Quest made a careful search of the shrubs and ground close to the spot which Horan had indicated. He pointed out to his two companions the spot where the grass was beaten down, and a few yards farther off where a twig had been broken off from some overhanging trees, as though a man had pushed his way through.

"This may have been done by the police search," he remarked, "or it may not. Don't spread out too far, girls, and go slowly. If we find any trace of James Macdougal on this hill-side, we are going to find it within fifty yards of this spot."

They searched carefully and deliberately for more than half an hour. Then Lenora suddenly called out. They looked around to find only her head visible. She scrambled up, muddy and with wet leaves clinging to her skirt.

"Say, that guy of a section boss told me to look out for caves. I've been in one, sure enough! Just saved myself."

They hurried to where she was. Quest peered into the declivity down which she had slipped. Suddenly he gave vent to a little exclamation. At the same time Laura called out. An inch or two of tweed was clearly visible through the strewn leaves. Quest, flat on his stomach, crawled a little way down, took out his electric torch from his pocket and brushed the stuff away. Then he clambered to his feet.

"Our search is over," he declared gravely, "and your troubles, Lenora. That is Macdougal's body. He may have slipped in as you did, Laura, or he may have crept there to hide, and starved. Anyhow, it is he."

Lenora's face sank into her hands for a moment. Quest stood on one side while Laura passed her arm around the other girl's waist. Presently he returned.

"We can do no more," he pointed out; "we must send for help to bring the body up."

"I shall stay here, please," Lenora begged. "Don't think I'm foolish, please. I can't pretend I am sorry, but I'll stay till some one comes and takes—it away."

"She is quite right," Laura declared, "and I will stay with her."

Quest glanced at his watch.

"That's all right," he declared. "I'll have to get, but I'll send some one along. Cheer up, Lenora," he added kindly. "Look after her, Laura."

"You bet!" that young woman declared brusquely.

Quest hastened along the road to the spot where he had left the car. The chauffeur, who saw him coming, started up and climbed to his seat. Quest took his place.

"Drive to the office," he ordered.

The man slipped in his clutch. They were in the act of gliding off when there was a tremendous report. They stopped short. The man jumped down and looked at the back tire.

"Blow-out," he remarked laconically.

Quest frowned.

"How long will it take?"

"Four minutes," the man replied. "I've got another wheel ready. That's the queerest blow-out I ever saw, though."

The two men leaned over the tire. Suddenly Quest's expression changed. His hand stole into his hip pocket.

"Tom," he explained, "that wasn't a blow-out at all. Look here!"

He pointed to the small level hole. Almost at once he stood back and the sunshine flashed upon the revolver clutched in his right hand.

"That was a bullet," he continued. "Some one fired at that tire. Tom, there's trouble about."

The man looked nervously around.

"That's a rifle bullet, sure," he muttered.

The car was drawn up by the side of the road, a few yards past the section house. A little way farther up was the tool shed, and beyond, the tower house. There was no one in sight at either of these places. On the other side of the road were clumps of bushes, any one of which would prove sufficient for a man in hiding.

"Get on the wheel as quick as you can," Quest directed. "Here, I'll give you a hand."

He stooped down to unfasten the straps which held the spare wheel. It was one of his rare lapses, realised a moment too late. Almost in his ears came the hoarse cry:

"Hands up, guvnor! Hands up this second or I'll blow you to hell!"

Quest glanced over his shoulder and looked into the face of Red Gallagher, raised a little above the level of the road. He had evidently been hiding at the foot of the perpendicular bank which divided the road from the track level. A very ugly little revolver was pointed directly at Quest's heart.

"My mate's got you covered on the other side of the road, too. Hands up, both of you, or we'll make a quick job of it."

Quest shrugged his shoulders, threw his revolver into the road and obeyed. As he did so, the other man stole out from behind a bush and sprang for the chauffeur, who under cover of the car was stealing off. There was a brief struggle, then the dull thud of the railway man's rifle falling on the former's head. The chauffeur rolled over and lay in the road.

"Pitch him off in the bushes," Red Gallagher ordered. "You don't want any one who comes by to see. Now lend me a hand with this chap."

"What do you propose to do with me?" Quest asked.

"You'll know soon enough," Red Gallagher answered. "A matter of five minutes' talk, to start with. You see that hand-car house?"

"Perfectly well," Quest assented. "My eyesight is quite normal."

"Get there, then. I'm a yard behind you and my revolver's pointing for the middle of your back."

Quest looked at it anxiously.

"You have the air, my red friend," he remarked, "of being unaccustomed to those delicate weapons. Do keep your fingers off the trigger. I will walk to the hand-car house and talk to you, with pleasure."

He sprang lightly down from the road, crossed the few intervening yards and stepped into the hand-car house.

Gallagher and his mate followed close behind. Quest paused on the threshold.

"It's a filthy dirty hole," he remarked. "Can't we have our little chat out here? Is it money you want?"

Gallagher glanced around. Then with an ugly push of the shoulder he sent Quest reeling into the shed. His great form blocked the doorway.

"No," he cried fiercely, "it's not money I want this time. Quest, you brute, you dirty bloodhound! You sent me to the pen for five years—you with your cursed prying into other people's affairs. Don't you remember me, eh? Red Gallagher?"

"Of course I do," Quest replied coolly. "You garrotted and robbed an old man and had the spree of your life. The old man happened to be a friend of mine, so I took the trouble to see that you paid for it. Well?"

"Five years of hell, that's what I had," the man continued, his eyes flashing, his face twitching with anger. "Well, you're going to have a little bit more than five years. This shed's been burnt down twice—sparks from passing engines. It's going to be burnt down for the third time."

"Going to make a bonfire of me, eh?" Quest remarked.

"You can sneer, my fine friend," the man growled. "You've had a good many comfortable years of wearing fine clothes and smoking twenty-five-cent cigars, swaggering about and hunting poor guys that never did you any harm. This is where we are going to get a bit of our own back. See here! We are locking this door—like that. It's a lonely bit of the line. The man in the tower never takes his eyes off the signals and there ain't a soul in sight. Me and my mate are off to the section house. Two minutes will see us there and back. We're going to bring a can of oil and an armful of waste. Can you tell what for, eh? We're going to burn the place to a cinder in less than three minutes, and if you're alive when the walls come down, we'll try a little rifle practise at you, see?"

"Sounds remarkably unpleasant," Quest admitted. "You'd better hurry or the boss will be back."

Gallagher finally slammed the door. Quest heard the heavy footsteps of the two men as they turned towards the section house. He drew a little case from his coat pocket.

"Just as well, perhaps," he said softly to himself, "that I perfected this instrument. It's rather close quarters here."

He opened what seemed to be a little mahogany box, looked at the ball of black substance inside, closed it up, placed it against the far wall, untwisted the coil, stood back near the door and pressed the button. The result was extraordinary. The whole of the far wall was blown out and for some distance in front the ground was furrowed up by the explosion. Quest replaced the instrument in his pocket, sprang through the opening and ran for the tower house. Behind him, on its way to New York, he could see a freight train coming along. He could hear, too, Red Gallagher's roar of anger. It was less than fifty yards, yet already, as he reached the shelter of the tower, the thunder of the freight sounded in Quest's ears. He glanced around. Red Gallagher and his mate were racing almost beside it towards him. He rushed up the narrow stairs into the signal room, tearing open his coat to show his official badge.

"Stop the freight," he shouted to the operator. "Quick! I'm Sanford Quest, detective—special powers from the chief commissioner."

The man moved to the signal. Another voice thundered in his ears. He turned swiftly around. The Irishman's red head had appeared at the top of the staircase.

"Drop that signal and I'll blow you into bits!" he shouted.

The operator hesitated, dazed.

"Walk towards me," Gallagher shouted. "Look here, you guy, this'll show you whether I'm in earnest or not!"

A bullet passed within a few inches of the operator's head. He came slowly across the room. Below they could hear the roar of the freight.

"This ain't your job," the Irishman continued savagely. "We want the cop, and we're going to have him."

Quest had stolen a yard or two nearer during this brief colloquy. Gallagher's mate from behind shouted out a warning just a second too late. With a sudden kick, Quest sent the revolver flying across the room, and before the Irishman could recover, he struck him full in the face. Notwithstanding his huge size and strength, Gallagher reeled. The operator, who had just begun to realize what was happening, flung himself bodily against the two thugs. A shot from the tangled mass of struggling limbs whistled past Quest's head as he sprang to the window which overlooked the track. The freight had already almost passed. Quest steadied himself for a supreme effort, crawled out on to the little steel bridge and poised himself for a moment. The last car was just beneath. The gap between it and the previous one was slipping by. He set his teeth and jumped on to the smooth top. For several seconds he struggled madly to keep his balance. He felt himself slipping every minute down to the ground which was spinning by. Then his right heel caught a bare ledge, scarcely an inch high. It checked his fall. He set his teeth, carefully stretched out his hand and gripped the back of the car. Then his knee touched something—a chain. He caught it with his other hand. He lay there, crouching, gripping wherever he could, his fingernails breaking, an intolerable pain in his knee, death spinning on either side of him....

Back behind the tower, Red Gallagher and his mate bent with horrified faces over the body of the signalman.

"What the hell did you want to plug him for?" the latter muttered. "He ain't in the show at all. You've done us, Red! He's cooked!"

Red Gallagher staggered to his feet. Already the horror of the murderer was in his eyes as he glanced furtively around.

"I never meant to drop him," he muttered. "I got mad at seeing Quest get off. That man's a devil."

"What are we going to do?" the other demanded hoarsely. "It's a quiet spot this, but there'll be some one round before long. There goes the damned signals already!" he exclaimed, as the gong sounded in the tower.

"There's the auto," Gallagher shouted. "Come on. Come on, man! I can fix the tire. If we've got to swing for this job, we'll have something of our own back first."

They crawled to the side of the road. Gallagher's rough, hairy fingers were still trembling, but they knew their job. In a few minutes the tire was fixed. Clumsily but successfully, the great Irishman turned the car round away from the city.

"She's a hummer," he muttered. "I'll make her go when we get the hang of it. Sit tight!"

They drove clumsily off, gathering speed at every yard. Behind, in the shadow of the tower, the signalman lay dead. Quest, half way to New York, stretched flat on his stomach, was struggling for life with knees and hands and feet.

2.

Mrs. Rheinholdt welcomed the Inspector with a beaming smile as he stepped out of his office and approached her automobile.

"How nice of you to be so punctual, Mr. French," she exclaimed, making room for him by her side. "Will you tell the man to drive to Mr. Quest's house in Georgia Square?"

The Inspector obeyed and took his place in the luxurious limousine.

"How beautifully punctual we are!" she continued, glancing at the clock. "Inspector, I am so excited at the idea of getting my jewels back. Isn't Mr. Quest a wonderful man?"

"He's a clever chap, all right," the Inspector admitted. "All the same, I'm rather sorry he wasn't able to lay his hands on the thief."

"That's your point of view, of course," Mrs. Rheinholdt remarked. "I can think of nothing but having my diamonds back. I feel I ought to go and thank the Professor for recommending Mr. Quest."

The Inspector made no reply. Mrs. Rheinholdt was suddenly aware that she was becoming a little tactless.

"Of course," she sighed, "it is disappointing not to be able to lay your hands upon the thief. That is where I suppose you must find the interference of an amateur like Mr. Quest a little troublesome sometimes. He gets back the property, which is what the private individual wants, but he doesn't secure the thief, which is, of course, the real end of the case from your point of view."

"It's a queer affair about these jewels," the Inspector remarked. "Quest hasn't told me the whole story yet. Here we are on the stroke of time!"

The car drew up outside Quest's house. The Inspector assisted his companion to alight and rang the bell at the front door. There was a somewhat prolonged pause. He rang again.

"Never knew this to happen before," he remarked. "That sort of secretary-valet of Mr. Quest's—Ross Brown, I think he calls him—is always on the spot."

They waited for some time. There was still no answer to their summons. The Inspector placed his ear to the keyhole. There was not a sound to be heard. He drew back, a little puzzled. At that moment his attention was caught by the fluttering of a little piece of white material caught in the door. He pulled it out. It was a fragment of white embroidery, and on it were several small stains. The Inspector looked at them and looked at his fingers. His face grew suddenly grave.

"Seems to me," he muttered, "that there's been some trouble here. I shall have to take a liberty. If you'll excuse me, Mrs. Rheinholdt, I think it would be better if you waited in the car until I send out for you."

"You don't think the jewels have been stolen again?" she gasped.

The Inspector made no reply. He had drawn from his pocket a little pass-key and was fitting it into the lock. The door swung open. Once more they were both conscious of that peculiar silence, which seemed to have in it some unnamable quality. He moved to the foot of the stairs and shouted.

"Hello! Any one there?"

There was no reply. He opened the doors of the two rooms on the right hand side, where Quest, when he was engaged in any widespread affair, kept a stenographer and a telegraph operator. Both rooms were empty. Then he turned towards Quest's study on the left hand side. French was a man of iron nerve. He had served his time in the roughest quarters of New York. He had found himself face to face with every sort of crime, yet as he opened that door, he seemed to feel some premonition of what was to come. He stepped across the threshold. No power on earth could have kept back the cry which broke from his lips.

The curtains of the window which looked out on to the street, were drawn, and the light was none too good. It was sufficient for him, however, to see without difficulty the details of a ghastly tragedy. A few feet away from the door was stretched the body of the secretary-valet. On the other side of the room, lying as though she had slipped from the sofa, her head fallen on one side in hideous fashion, was the body of Miss Quigg, the Salvation Army young woman. French set his teeth and drew back the curtains. In the clearer light, the disorder of the room was fully revealed. There had been a terrible struggle. Between whom? How?

There was suddenly a piercing shriek. The Inspector turned quickly around. Mrs. Rheinholdt, who had disregarded his advice, was standing on the threshold.

"Inspector!" she cried. "What has happened? Oh, my God!"

She covered her face with her hands. French gripped her by the arm. At that moment there was the sound of an automobile stopping outside.

"Keep quiet for a moment," the Inspector whispered in her ear. "Pull yourself together, madam. Go to the other end of the room. Don't look. Stay there for a few moments and then get home as quick as you can."

She obeyed him mutely, pressing her hands to her eyes, shivering in every limb. French stood back inside the room. He heard the front door open, he heard Quest's voice outside.

"Ross! Where the devil are you, Ross?"

There was no reply. The door was pushed open. Quest entered, followed by the Professor and Craig. The Inspector stood watching their faces. Quest came to a standstill before he had passed the threshold. He looked upon the floor and he looked across to the sofa. Then he looked at French.

"My God!" he muttered.

The Professor pushed past. He, too, looked around the room, and gazed at the two bodies with an expression of blank and absolute terror. Then he fell back into Craig's arms.

"The poor girl!" he cried. "Horrible! Horrible! Horrible!"

Craig led him for a moment to one side. The Professor was overcome and almost hysterical. Quest and French were left face to face.

"Know anything about this?" Quest asked quickly.

"Not a thing," the Inspector replied. "We arrived, Mrs. Rheinholdt and I, at five minutes past twelve. There was no answer to our ring. I used my pass-key and entered. This is what I found."

Quest stood over the body of his valet for a moment. The man was obviously dead. The Inspector took his handkerchief and covered up the head. A few feet away was a heavy paper-weight.

"Killed by a blow from behind," French remarked grimly, "with that little affair. Look here!"

They glanced down at the girl. Quest's eyebrows came together quickly. There were two blue marks upon her throat where a man's thumbs might have been.

"The hands again!" he muttered.

The Inspector nodded.

"Can you make anything of it?"

"Not yet," Quest confessed. "I must think."

The Inspector glanced at him curiously.

"Where on earth have you been to?" he demanded.

"Been to?" Quest repeated.

"Look in the mirror!" French suggested.

Quest glanced at himself. His collar had given way, his tie was torn, a button and some of the cloth had been wrenched from his coat, his trousers were torn, he was covered with dust.

"I'll tell you about my trouble a little later on," he replied. "Say, can't we keep those girls out?"

They were too late. Laura and Lenora were already upon the threshold. Quest swung round towards them.

"Girls," he said, "there has been some trouble here. Go and wait upstairs, Lenora, or sit in the hall. Laura, you had better telephone to the police station, and for a doctor. That's right, isn't it, Inspector?"

"Yes!" the latter assented thoughtfully.

Lenora, white to the lips, staggered a few feet back into the hall. Laura set her teeth and lingered.

"Is that Ross?" she asked.

"It's his body," Quest replied. "He's been murdered here, he and the Salvation Army girl who was to come this morning for her cheque."

Laura turned away, half dazed.

"I'd have trusted Ross with my life," Quest continued, "but he must have been alone in the house when the girl came. Do you suppose it was the usual sort of trouble?"

Inspector French stooped down and picked up the paper-weight. Across it was stamped the name of Sanford Quest.

"This yours, Quest?"

"Of course it is," Quest answered. "Everything in the room is mine."

"The girl would fight to defend herself," the Inspector remarked slowly, "but she could never strike a man such a blow as your valet died from."

Once more he stooped and picked up a small clock. It had stopped at eleven-fifteen. He looked at it thoughtfully.

"Quest," he said, "I'll have to ask you a question."

"Why not?" Quest replied, looking quickly up.

"Where were you at eleven-fifteen?"

"On tower Number 10 of the New York Central, scrapping for my life," Quest answered grimly. "I've reason to remember it."

Something in the Inspector's steady gaze seemed to inspire the criminologist suddenly with a new idea. He came a step forward, a little frown upon his forehead.

"Say, French," he exclaimed, "you don't—you don't suspect me of this?"

French was unmoved. He looked Quest in the eyes.

"I don't know," he said.

CHAPTER VI

ON THE RACK

1.

For the moment a new element had been introduced into the horror of the little tableau. All eyes were fixed upon Quest, who had listened to the Inspector's dubious words with a supercilious smile upon his lips.

"Perhaps," he suggested, "you would like to ask me a few questions?"

"Perhaps I may feel it my duty to do so," the Inspector replied gravely. "In the first place, then, Mr. Quest, will you kindly explain the condition of your clothes?"

Quest looked down at himself quickly. More than ever he realised the significance of his dishevelled appearance.

"I travelled from number ten tower, just outside New York, on top of a freight car," he said grimly. "It wasn't a very comfortable ride."

"Perhaps you will explain what made you take it, then?" the Inspector continued.

Quest shrugged his shoulders.

"Here you are, then," he replied. "This morning I decided to make an attempt to clear up the mystery of Macdougal's disappearance. I sent on my secretary, Miss Laura, to make friends with the section boss, and Lenora and I went out by automobile a little later. We instituted a search on a new principle, and before very long we found Macdougal's body. That's one up against you, I think, Inspector."

"Very likely," the Inspector observed. "Go on, please."

"I left the two young ladies, at Miss Lenora's wish, to superintend the removal of the body. I myself had an engagement to deliver over her jewels to Mrs. Rheinholdt here at mid-day. I returned to where my automobile was waiting, started for the city and was attacked by two thugs near the section house. I got away from them, ran to the tower house to try and stop the freight, was followed by the thugs, and jumped out on to the last car from the signal arm."

There was a dead silence. Quest began quietly to dust his clothes. The Inspector stopped him.

"Don't do that," he said.

Quest paused in his task and laid down the brush.

"Any more questions?"

"Where is your automobile?"

"No idea," Quest replied. "I left it in the road. When I jumped from the freight car, I took a taxicab to the Professor's and called for him, as arranged."

"That is perfectly true," the Professor intervened. "Mr. Quest called for us, as arranged previously, at ten minutes to twelve."

The inspector nodded.

"I shall have to ask you to excuse me for a moment," he said, "while I ring up Number 10 signal tower. If Mr. Quest's story receives corroboration, the matter is at an end. Where shall I find a telephone?"

"In every room in the house," Quest answered shortly. "There is one outside in the passage."

The Inspector left the room almost immediately. The Professor crossed to Quest's side. A kindly smile parted his lips.

"My dear Mr. Quest," he exclaimed, "our friend the Inspector's head has been turned a little, beyond doubt, by these horrible happenings! Permit me to assure you, for one, that I look upon his insinuations as absurd."

"The man has gone off his head!" Laura declared angrily.

"It will be all right directly he comes back," Lenora whispered, laying her hand upon Quest's arm.

"If only some one would give me my jewels and let me go!" Mrs. Rheinholdt moaned.

The door opened and the Inspector reappeared. He was looking graver than ever.

"Quest," he announced, "your alibi is useless—in fact a little worse than useless. The operator at Number 10 has been found murdered at the back of his tower!"

Quest started.

"I ought not to have left him to those thugs," he murmured regretfully.

"There is no automobile of yours in the vicinity," the Inspector continued, "nor any news of it. I think it will be as well now, Quest, for this matter to take its obvious course. Will you, first of all, hand over her jewels to Mrs. Rheinholdt?"

Quest drew the keys of the safe from his pocket, crossed the room and swung open the safe door. For a moment afterwards he stood transfixed. His arm, half outstretched, remained motionless. Then he turned slowly around.

"The jewels have been stolen," he announced with unnatural calm.

Mrs. Rheinholdt pushed her way forward, wringing her hands.

"Stolen again?" she said. "Mr. Quest! Inspector!"

"They were there," Quest declared, "when I left the house this morning. It seems probable," he added, "that the same person who is responsible for this double tragedy has also taken the jewels."

The Inspector laid his hand heavily upon Quest's shoulder.

"It does seem as though that might be so," he assented grimly. "You will kindly consider yourself under arrest, Quest. Ladies and gentlemen, will you clear the room now, if you please? The ambulance I telephoned for is outside."

The Professor, who had been looking on as though dazed, suddenly intervened.

"Mr. French," he said earnestly, "I am convinced that you are making a great mistake. In arresting and taking away Mr. Quest, you are removing from us the one man who is likely to be able to clear up this mystery."

The Inspector pushed him gently on one side.

"You will excuse me, Professor," he said, "but this is no matter for argument. If Mr. Quest can clear himself, no one will be more glad than I."

Quest shrugged his shoulders.

"The Inspector will have his little joke," he observed drily. "It's all right, girls. Keep cool," he went on, as he saw the tears in Lenora's eyes. "Come round and see me in the Tombs, one of you."

"If I can be of any assistance," the Professor exclaimed, "I trust that you will not fail to call upon me, Mr. Quest. I repeat, Inspector," he added, "I am convinced that you are making a very grave mistake. Mrs. Rheinholdt, you must let me take you home."

She gave him her arm.

"My jewels!" she sobbed. "Just as they had been recovered, too!"

"My dear lady," the Professor reminded her, with a faint air of reproach in his tone, "I think we must remember that we are in the presence of a graver tragedy than the loss of a few jewels."...

The ambulance men came and departed with their grim burden, the room on the ground floor was locked and sealed, and the house was soon empty except for the two girls. Towards three o'clock, Lenora went out and returned with a newspaper. She opened it out upon the table and they both pored over it.—

"WELL-KNOWN CRIMINOLOGIST ARRESTED FOR DOUBLE TRAGEDY!

"Sanford Quest, the famous New York criminologist, was arrested at noon today, charged with the murder of his valet, Ross Brown, and Miss Quigg, Salvation Army canvasser. The crime seems to be mixed up in some mysterious fashion with others. John D. Martin, of signal tower Number 10, offered by Quest as an alibi, was found dead behind his tower. Quest claimed that he travelled from the signal tower to New York on a freight train, leaving his automobile behind, but neither machine nor chauffeur have been discovered.

"Justice Thorpe has refused to consider bail."

"He's a guy, that Justice Thorpe, and so's the idiot who wrote this stuff!" Laura exclaimed, thrusting the paper away from her. "I guess the Professor was dead right when he told French he was locking up the one man who could clear up the whole show."

Lenora nodded thoughtfully.

"The Professor spoke up like a man," she agreed, "but, Laura, I want to ask you something. Did you notice his servant—that man Craig?"

"Can't say I did particularly," Laura admitted.

"Twice," Lenora continued, "I thought he was going to faint. I tell you he was scared the whole of the time."

"What are you getting at, kid?" Laura demanded.

"At Craig, if I can," Lenora replied, moving towards the telephone. "Please give me the phototelesme. I am going to talk to the Professor."

Laura adjusted the mirror to the instrument and Lenora rang up. The Professor himself answered the call.

"Have you seen the three o'clock edition, Professor?" Lenora asked.

"I never read newspapers, young lady," the Professor replied.

"Let me tell you what they say about Mr. Quest!"

Lenora commenced a rambling account of what she had read in the newspaper. All the time the eyes of the two girls were fixed upon the mirror. They could see the Professor seated in his chair with two huge volumes by his side, a pile of manuscript, and a pen in his hand. They could even catch the look of sympathy on his face as he listened attentively. Suddenly Lenora almost broke off. She gripped Laura by the arm. The door of the study had been opened slowly, and Craig, carrying a bundle, paused for a moment on the threshold. He glanced nervously towards the Professor, who seemed unaware of his entrance. Then he moved stealthily towards the fireplace, stooped down and committed something to the flames. The relief on his face, as he stood up, was obvious.

"All I can do for Mr. Quest, young lady, I will," the Professor promised. "If you will forgive my saying so, you are a little over-excited just now. Take my advice and rest for a short time. Call round and see me whenever you wish."

He laid the receiver down and the reflection on the mirror faded away. Lenora started up and hastily put on her coat and hat, which were still lying on the chair.

"I am going right down to the Professor's," she announced.

"What do you think you can do there?" Laura asked.

"I am going to see if I can find out what that man burnt," she replied. "I will be back in an hour."

Laura walked with her as far as the street car, and very soon afterwards Lenora found herself knocking at the Professor's front door.

Craig admitted her almost at once. For a moment he seemed to shiver as he recognised her. The weakness, however, was only momentary. He showed her into the study with grave deference. The Professor was still immersed in his work. He greeted her kindly, and with a little sigh laid down his pen.

"Well, young lady," he said, "have you thought of something I can do?"

She took no notice of the chair to which he pointed, and rested her hand upon his shoulder.

"Professor," she begged, "go and see Mr. Quest! He is in the Tombs prison. It would be the kindest thing any one could possibly do."

The Professor glanced regretfully at his manuscript, but he did not hesitate. He rose promptly to his feet.

"If you think he would appreciate it, I will go at once," he decided.

Her face shone with gratitude.

"That is really very kind of you, Professor," she declared.

"I will send for my coat and we will go together, if you like," he suggested.

She smiled.

"I am going the other way, back to Georgia Square," she explained. "No, please don't ring. I can find my own way out."

She hurried from the room. Outside in the hall she paused, for a moment, listening with beating heart. By the side wall was a hat rack with branching pegs, from which several coats were hanging. She slipped quietly behind their shelter. Presently the Professor came out of the room.

"My coat, please, Craig," she heard him say.

Her heart sank. Craig was coming in her direction. Her discovery seemed certain. Then, as his hand was half stretched out to remove one of the garments, she heard the Professor's voice.

"I think that I shall walk, Craig. I have been so much upset today that the exercise will do me good. I will have the light coat from my bedroom."

For a moment the shock of relief was so great that she almost lost consciousness. A moment or two later she heard the Professor leave the house. Very cautiously she stole out from her hiding place. The hall was empty. She crossed it with noiseless footsteps, slipped into the study and moved stealthily to the fireplace. There was a little heap of ashes in one distinct spot. She gathered them up in her handkerchief and secreted it in her dress. Then she moved hurriedly towards the door and stepped quietly behind the curtain. She stood there listening intently. Craig was doing something in the hall. Even while she was hesitating, the door was opened. He came in and moved towards his master's table. Through a chink in the curtain she could see that he was stooping down, collecting some letters. She stole out, ran down the hall, opened the front door and hastened down the avenue. Her heart was beating quickly. The front door handle had slipped from her fingers, and it seemed to her that she could hear even now the slam with which it had swung to. At the gates she looked back. There were no signs of life. The house still bore its customary appearance, gloomy and deserted. With a sigh of relief, she hailed a taxicab and sank back into the corner.

She found Laura waiting for her, and a few minutes afterwards the two girls were examining the ashes with the aid of Quest's microscope. Among the little pile was one fragment at the sight of which they both exclaimed. It was distinctly a shred of charred muslin embroidery. Lenora pointed towards it triumphantly.

"Isn't that evidence?" she demanded. "Let's ring up Inspector French!"

Laura shook her head doubtfully.

"Not so fast," she advised. "French is a good sort in his way, but he's prejudiced just now against the boss. I'm not sure that this evidence would go far by itself."

"It's evidence enough for us to go for Craig, though! What we have got to do is to get a confession out of him, somehow!"

Laura studied her companion, for a moment, curiously.

"Taking some interest in Mr. Quest, kid, ain't you?"

Lenora looked up. Then her head suddenly sank into her hands. She knew quite well that her secret had escaped her. Laura patted her shoulder.

"That's all right, child," she said soothingly. "We'll see him through this, somehow or other."

"You don't mind?" Lenora faltered, without raising her eyes.

"Not I," she replied promptly. "I'm not looking for trouble of that sort."

Lenora raised her head. There was an immense relief in her face.

"I am so glad," she said. "I was afraid sometimes—living here with him, you know—"

Laura interrupted her with an easy laugh.

"You don't need to worry," she assured her.

Lenora rose to her feet. She was quite herself again. There was a new look of determination in her face.

"Laura," she exclaimed, "we will save Mr. Quest and we will get hold of Craig! I have a plan. Listen."

2.

Craig's surprise was real enough as he opened the back door of the Professor's house on the following morning and found Lenora standing on the threshold.

"I am very sorry, Miss Lenora," he apologised. "The front door bell must be out of order. I certainly didn't hear it ring. Mr. Ashleigh is in his study, if you wish to see him."

Lenora smiled pleasantly.

"To tell you the truth," she said, "I really do not want to see him,—at least, not just yet. I came to this door because I wanted a little talk with you."

Craig's attitude was perfect. He was mystified, but he remained respectful.

"Will you come inside?" he invited.

She shook her head.

"I am afraid," she confided, "of what I am going to say being overheard. Come with me down to the garage for a moment."

She pointed to the wooden building which stood about fifty yards away from the house. Craig hesitated.

"If you wish it, miss," he assented doubtfully. "I will get the keys."

He disappeared for a moment and came out again almost immediately afterwards with a bunch of keys in his hand. He seemed a little disturbed.

"I am doing as you wish, Miss Lenora," he said, "but there is nobody about here likely to overhear, and I have no secrets from my master."

"Perhaps not," Lenora replied, "but I have. The Professor is a dear," she added hastily, "but he is too wrapped up in his scientific work to be able to see things like men of ordinary common-sense."

"That is quite true," Craig admitted. "Mr. Ashleigh has only one idea in his life…. This way, then, if you please, miss."

He opened the door of the garage, leaving the keys in the lock, and they both passed inside. The place was gloomy and lit only by a single narrow window near the roof. The only vehicle it contained was the Professor's little car.

"You can say what you please here without the slightest fear of being overheard, miss," Craig remarked.

Lenora nodded, and breathed a prayer to herself. She was nearer the door than Craig by about half a dozen paces. Her hand groped in the little bag she was carrying and gripped something hard. She clenched her teeth for a moment. Then the automatic pistol flashed out through the gloom.

"Craig," she threatened, "if you move I shall shoot you."

It seemed as though the man were a coward. He began to tremble, his lips twitched, his eyes grew larger and rounder.

"What is it?" he faltered. "What do you want?"

"Just this," Lenora said firmly. "I suspect you to be guilty of the crime for which Sanford Quest is in prison. I am going to have you questioned. If you are innocent, you have nothing to fear. If you are guilty, there will be some one here before long who will extract the truth from you."

The man's face was an epitome of terror. Even his knees shook. Lenora felt herself grow calmer with every moment.

"I am going outside to send a message," she told him. "I shall return presently."

"Don't go," he begged suddenly. "Don't leave me!"

She turned around.

"Why not?"

He drew a step nearer. Once more the few inches of blue steel flashed out between them.

"None of your games," she warned him. "I am in earnest, and I am not afraid to shoot."

"I won't come any nearer," he promised, "but listen! I am innocent—I have done nothing wrong. If you keep me here, you will do more harm than you can dream of."

"It is for other people to decide about your innocence," Lenora said calmly. "I have nothing to do with that. If you are wise, you will stop here quietly."

"Have you said anything to Mr. Ashleigh, miss?" the man asked piteously.

"Not a word."

An expression of relief shone for a moment upon his face. Lenora pointed to a stool.

"Sit down there and wait quietly," she ordered.

He obeyed without a word. She left the place, locked the door securely, and made her way round to the other side of the garage—the side hidden from the house. Here, at the far corner, she drew a little pocket wireless from her bag and set it on the window-sill. Very slowly she sent her message,—

"I have Craig here in the Professor's garage, locked up. If our plan has succeeded, come at once. I am waiting here for you."

There was no reply. She sent the message again and again. Suddenly, during a pause, there was a little flash upon the plate. A message was coming to her. She transcribed it with beating heart:

"O.K. Coming."

The guard swung open the wicket in front of Quest's cell.

"Young woman to see you, Quest," he announced. "Ten minutes, and no loud talking, please."

Quest moved to the bars. It was Laura who stood there. She

wasted very little time in preliminaries. Having satisfied herself that the guard was out of hearing, she leaned as close as she could to Quest.

"Look here," she said, "Lenora's crazy with the idea that Craig has done these jobs—Craig, the Professor's servant, you know. We used the phototelesme yesterday afternoon and saw him burn something in the Professor's study. Lenora went up straight away and got hold of the ashes."

"Smart girl," Quest murmured, nodding approvingly. "Well?"

"There are distinct fragments," Laura continued, "of embroidered stuff such as the Salvation Army girl might have been wearing. We put them on one side, but they aren't enough evidence. Lenora's idea is that you should try and get hold of Craig and hypnotise him into a confession."

"That's all right," Quest replied, "but how am I to get hold of him?"

Laura glanced once more carelessly around to where the guard stood.

"Lenora's gone up to the Professor's again this afternoon. She is going to try and get hold of Craig and lock him in the garage. If she succeeds, she will send a message by wireless at three o'clock. It is half past two now."

"Well?" Quest exclaimed. "Well?"

"You can work this guard, if you want to," Laura went on. "I have seen you tackle much worse cases. He seems dead easy. Then let me in the cell, take my clothes and leave me here. You did it before when you were trying to hunt down those men in Chicago, and not a soul recognised you."

Quest followed the scheme in his mind quickly.

"It is all right," he decided, "but I am not at all sure that they can really hold me on the evidence they have got. If they can't, I shall be doing myself more harm than good this way."

"It's no use unless you can get hold of Craig quickly," Laura said. "He is getting the scares, as it is."

"I'll do it," Quest decided. "Call the guard, Laura."

She obeyed. The man came good-naturedly towards them.

"Well, young people, not quarrelling, I hope?" he remarked.

Quest looked at him steadfastly through the bars.

"I want you to come inside for a moment," he said.

"What for?" the man demanded.

"I want you to come inside for a moment," Quest repeated softly. "Unlock the door, please, take the key off your bunch and come inside."

The man hesitated, but all the time his fingers were fumbling with the keys. Quest's lips continued to move. The warder opened the door and entered. A few minutes later, Quest passed the key through the window to Laura, who was standing on guard.

"Come in," he whispered. "Don't step over him. He is sitting with his back to the wall, just inside."

Laura obeyed, and entered the cell. For a moment they were breathless with alarm. A passing warder looked down their avenue. Eventually, however, he turned in the other direction.

"Off with your coat and skirt like lightning, Laura," Quest ordered. "This has got to be done quickly or not at all."

Without a word, and with marvellous rapidity, the change was effected. Laura produced from her hand-bag a wig, which she pinned inside her hat and passed over to Quest. Then she flung herself on to the bed and drew the blanket up to her chin.

"How long will he stay like that?" she whispered, pointing to the warder, who was sitting on the floor with his arms folded and his eyes closed.

"Half an hour or so," Quest answered. "Don't bother about him. I shall drop the key back through the window."

A moment or two later, Quest walked deliberately down the corridor of the prison, crossed the pavement and stepped into a taxicab. He reached Georgia Square at five minutes to three. A glance up and down assured him that the house was unwatched. He let himself in with his own key and laughed softly as he caught sight of his reflection in the mirror. The house was strangely quiet and deserted, but he wasted no time in looking around. He ran quickly upstairs, paused in his sitting-room only to take a cigar from the cabinet, passed on to the bedroom, threw Laura's clothes off, and, after a few moments' hesitation, selected from the wardrobe a rough tweed suit with a thick lining and lapels. Just as he was tying his tie, the little wireless which he had laid on the table at his side began to record the message. He glanced at the clock. It was exactly three.

"I have Craig here in the Professor's garage, locked up. If our plan has succeeded, come at once. I am waiting here for you."

Quest's eyes shone for a moment with satisfaction. Then he sent off his answering message, put on a duster and slouch hat, and left the house by the side entrance. In a few moments he was in Broadway, and a quarter of an hour later a taxicab deposited him at the entrance to the Professor's house. He walked swiftly up the drive and turned towards the garage, hoping every moment to see something of Lenora. The door of the place stood open. He entered and walked around. It was empty. There was no sign of either Craig or Lenora!...

Quest, recovered from his first disappointment, stole carefully out and made a minute examination of the place. Close to the corner from which Lenora had sent her wireless message to him, he stooped and picked up a handkerchief, which from the marking he recognised at once. A few feet away, the gravel was disturbed as though by the trampling of several feet. He set his teeth. For a single moment his own danger was forgotten. A feeling which he utterly failed to recognise robbed him of his indomitable nerve. He realised with vivid but scarcely displeasing potency a weakness in the armour of his complete self-control.

"I've got to find that girl," he muttered. "Craig can go to hell!"

He turned away and approached the house. The front door stood open and he made his way at once to the library. The Professor, who was sitting at his desk surrounded by a pile of books and papers, addressed him, as he entered, without looking up.

"Where on earth have you been, Craig?" he enquired petulantly. "I have rung for you six times. Have I not told you never to leave the place without orders?"

"It is not Craig," Quest replied quietly. "It is I, Professor—Sanford Quest."

The Professor swung round in his chair and eyed his visitor in blank astonishment.

"Quest?" he exclaimed. "God bless my soul! Have they let you out already, then?"

"I came out," Quest replied grimly. "Sit down and listen to me for a moment, will you?"

"You came out?" the Professor repeated, looking a little dazed. "You mean that you escaped?"

Quest nodded.

"Perhaps I made a mistake," he admitted, "but here I am. Now listen, Professor. I know this will be painful to you, but give me your best attention for a few minutes. These young women assistants of mine have formed a theory of their own about the murder in my flat and the robbery of the jewels. Hold on to your chair, Professor. They believe that the guilty person was Craig."

The Professor's face was almost pitiful in its blank amazement. His mouth was wide open like a child's, words seemed absolutely denied to him.

"That's their theory," Quest went on. "They may be right or they may be wrong—Lenora, at any rate, has collected some shreds of evidence. They hatched a scheme between them, clever enough in its way. They locked Craig up in your garage and got me out of the Tombs in Laura's clothes. I have come straight up to find your garage open and Lenora missing."

The Professor rose to his feet, obviously making a tremendous effort to adjust his ideas.

"Craig locked up in my garage?" he murmured. "Craig guilty of those murders? Why, my dear Mr. Quest, a more harmless, a more inoffensive, peace-loving and devoted servant than John Craig never trod this earth!"

"Maybe," Quest replied, "but come out here, Mr. Ashleigh."

The Professor followed his companion out to the garage. Quest showed him the open door and the marks of footsteps around where he had picked up the handkerchief.

"Now," he said, "what has become of your man Craig, and what has become of my assistant Lenora?"

"Perhaps we had better search the house," the Professor suggested. "Craig? My dear Mr. Quest, you little know—"

"Where is he, then?" Quest interrupted.

The Professor could do nothing but look around him a little vaguely. Together they went back to the house and searched it without result. Then they returned once more to the garage.

"I am going back," Quest announced. "My only chance is the wireless. If Lenora is alive or at liberty, she will communicate with me."

"May I come, too?" the Professor asked timidly. "This matter has upset me thoroughly. I cannot stay here without Craig."

"Come, by all means," Quest assented. "I will drive you down in your car, if you like."

The Professor hurried away to get his coat and hat, and a few minutes later they started off. In Broadway, they left the car at a garage and made their way up a back street, which enabled them to enter the house at the side entrance. They passed upstairs into the sitting-room. Quest fetched the pocket wireless and laid it down on the table. The Professor examined it with interest.

"You are marvellous, my friend," he declared. "With all these resources of science at your command, it seems incredible that you should be in the position you are."

Quest nodded coolly.

"I'll get out of that all right," he asserted confidently. "The only trouble is that while I am dodging about like this I cannot devote myself properly to the task of running down this fiend of the Hands. Just one moment, Professor, while I send off a message," he continued, opening the little instrument. "Where are you, Lenora?" he signalled. "Send me word and I will fetch you. I am in my own house for the present. Let me know that you are safe."

The Professor leaned back, smoking one of Quest's excellent cigars. He was beginning to show signs of the liveliest interest.

"Quest," he said, "I wish I could induce you to dismiss this extraordinary supposition of yours concerning my servant Craig. The man has been with me for the best part of twenty years. He saved my life in South America; we have travelled in all parts of the world. He has proved himself to be exemplary, a faithful and devoted servant. I thought it absurd, Mr. Quest, when you were suspected of these crimes. I should think it even more ridiculous to associate Craig with them in any way whatever."

"Then perhaps you will tell me," Quest suggested, "where he is now, and why he has gone away? That does not look like complete innocence, does it?"

The Professor sighed.

"Appearances are nothing," he declared. "Craig is a man of highly nervous susceptibilities. The very idea of being suspected of anything so terrible would be enough to drive him almost out of his mind. I am convinced that we shall find him at home presently, with some reasonable explanation of his absence."

Quest paced the room for a few moments, moodily.

There was a certain amount of reason in the Professor's point of view.

"Anyway, I cannot stay here much longer, unless I mean to go back to the Tombs," he declared.

"Surely," the Professor suggested, "your innocence will very soon be established?"

"There is one thing which will happen, without a doubt," Quest replied. "My auto and the chauffeur will be discovered. I have insisted upon enquiries being sent out throughout the State of Connecticut. They tell me, too, that the police are hard on the scent of Red Gallagher and the other man. Unless they get wind of this and sell me purposely, their arrest will be the end of my troubles. To tell you the truth, Professor," Quest concluded, "it is not of myself I am thinking at all just now. It is Lenora."

The Professor nodded sympathetically.

"The young lady who shut Craig up in the garage, you mean? A plucky young woman she must be."

"She has a great many other good qualities besides courage," Quest declared. "Women have not counted for much with me, Professor, up till now, any more than they have done, I should think, with you, but I tell you frankly, if any one has hurt a hair of that girl's head I will have their lives, whatever the penalty may be! It is for her sake—to find her—that I broke out of prison and that I am trying to keep free. The wisest thing to do, from my own point of view, would be to give myself up. I can't bring myself to do that without knowing what has become of her."

The Professor nodded again.

"A charming and well-bred young woman she seems," he admitted. "I fear that I should only be a bungler in your profession, Mr. Quest, but if there is anything I can do to help you to discover her whereabouts, you can count upon me. Personally, I am convinced that Craig will return to me with some plausible explanation as to what has happened. In that case he will doubtless bring news of the young lady."

Quest, for the third or fourth time, moved cautiously towards the window. His expression suddenly changed. He glanced downwards, frowning slightly. An alert light flashed into his eyes.

"They're after me!" he exclaimed. "Sit still, Professor."

He darted into his room and reappeared again almost immediately. The Professor gave a gasp of astonishment at his altered appearance. His tweed suit seemed to have been turned inside out. There were no lapels now and it was buttoned up to his neck. He wore a long white apron; a peaked cap and a chin-piece of astonishing naturalness had transformed him into the semblance of a Dutch grocer's boy.

"I'm off, Professor," Quest whispered. "You shall hear from me soon. I have not been here, remember!"

He ran lightly down the steps and into the kitchen, picked up a basket, filled it haphazard with vegetables and threw a cloth over the top. Then he made his way to the front door, peered out for a moment, swung through it on to the step, and, turning round, commenced to belabour it with his fist. Two plain-clothes men stood at the end of the street. A police automobile drew up outside the gate. Inspector French, attended by a policeman, stepped out. The former looked searchingly at Quest.

"Well, my boy, what are you doing here?" he asked.

"I cannot answer get," Quest replied, in broken English. "Ten minutes already have I wasted. I have knocked at all the doors."

French smiled.

"You can hop it, Dutchie," he advised. "By-the-bye, when was that order for vegetables given?" he added, frowning for a moment.

"It is three times a week the same," Quest explained, whipping the cloth from the basket. "No word has been sent to alter anything."

The Inspector pushed him hurriedly in the direction of the street.

"You run along home," he said, "and tell your master that he had better leave off delivering goods here for the present."

Quest went off, grumbling. He walked with the peculiar waddle affected by young Dutchmen of a certain class, and was soon out of sight round the corner of the street. French opened the door with a masterkey and secured it carefully, leaving one of his men to guard it. He searched the rooms on the ground floor and finally ascended to Quest's study. The Professor was still enjoying his cigar.

"Say, where's Quest?" the Inspector asked promptly.

"Have you let him out already?" the Professor replied, in a tone of mild surprise. "I thought he was in the Tombs prison."

The Inspector pressed on without answering. Every room in the house was ransacked. Presently he came back to the room where the Professor was still sitting. His usually good-humoured face was a little clouded.

"Professor," he began—"What's that, Miles?"

A plain-clothes man from the street had come hurrying into the room.

"Say, Mr. French," he reported, "our fellows have got hold of a newsie down in the street, who was coming along way round the back and saw two men enter this house by the side entrance, half an hour ago. One he described exactly as the Professor here. The other, without a doubt, was Quest."

French turned swiftly towards the Professor.

"You hear what this man says?" he exclaimed. "Mr. Ashleigh, you're fooling me! You entered this house with Sanford Quest. You must tell us where he is hiding."

The Professor knocked the ash from his cigar and replaced it in his mouth. His clasped hands rested in front of him. There was a twinkle of something almost like mirth in his eyes as he glanced up at the Inspector.

"Mr. French," he said, "Mr. Sanford Quest is my friend. I am here in charge of his house. Believing as I do that his arrest was an egregious blunder, I shall say or do nothing likely to afford you any information."

French turned impatiently away. Suddenly a light broke in upon him, he rushed towards the door.

"That damned Dutchie!" he exclaimed.

The Professor smiled benignly.

CHAPTER VII

THE UNSEEN TERROR

1.

With a little gesture of despair, Quest turned away from the instrument which seemed suddenly to have become so terribly unresponsive, and looked across the vista of square roofs and tangled masses of telephone wires to where the lights of larger New York flared up against the sky. From his attic chamber, the roar of the City a few blocks away was always in his ears. He had forgotten in those hours of frenzied solitude to fear for his own safety. He thought only of Lenora. Under which one of those thousands of roofs was she being concealed? What was the reason for this continued silence? Perhaps they had taken her instrument away—perhaps she was being ill-used. The bare thought opened the door to a thousand grim and torturing surmises. He paced restlessly up and down the room. Inaction had never seemed to him so wearisome. From sheer craving to be doing something, he paused once more before the little instrument.

"Lenora, where are you?" he signalled. "I have taken a lodging in the Servants' Club. I am still in hiding, hoping that Craig may come here. I am very anxious about you."

Still no reply! Quest drew a chair up to the window and sat there with folded arms looking down into the street. Suddenly he sprang to his feet. The instrument quivered—there was a message at last! He took it down with a little choke of relief.

"I don't know where I am. I am terrified. I was outside the garage when I was seized from behind. The Hands held me. I was unconscious until I found myself here. I am now in an attic room with no window except the skylight, which I cannot reach. I can see nothing—hear nothing. No one has hurt me, no one comes near. Food is pushed through a door, which is locked again immediately. The house seems empty, yet I fancy that I am being watched all the time. I am terrified!"

Quest drew the instrument towards him.

"I have your message," he signalled. "Be brave! I am watching for Craig. Through him I shall reach you before long. Send me a message every now and then."

Then there was a silence.

Quest was conscious of an enormous feeling of relief and yet an almost maddening sense of helplessness. She was imprisoned by the Hands. She was in their power, and up till now they had shown themselves ruthless enough. A room with a roof window only! How could she define her whereabouts! His first impulse was to rush madly out into the street and search for her. Then his common sense intervened. His one hope was through Craig. Again he took up his vigil in front of the window. Once more his eyes swept the narrow street with its constant stream of passers-by. Each time a man stopped and entered the building, he leaned a little further forward, and at each disappointment he seemed to realise a little more completely the slenderness of the chance upon which he was staking so much. Then suddenly he found himself gripping the window-sill in a momentary thrill of rare excitement. His vigil was rewarded at last. The man for whom he was waiting was there! Quest watched him cross the street, glance furtively to the right and to the left, then enter the club. He turned back to the little wireless and his fingers worked as though inspired.

"I am on Craig's track," he signalled. "Be brave."

He waited for no reply, but opened the door and stealing softly out of the room, leaned over the banisters. His apartment was on the fourth story. The floor below was almost entirely occupied by the kitchen and other offices. The men's club room was on the second floor. From where he stood he heard the steward of the club greeting Craig. He was a big man with a hearty voice, and the sound of his words reached Quest distinctly.

"Say, Mr. Craig, you're an authority on South America, aren't you? I bought some beans in the market this morning which they told me were grown down there, and my chef don't seem to know what to make of 'em. I wonder whether you would mind stepping up and giving him your advice?"

Craig's much lower voice was inaudible but it was evident that he had consented, for the two men ascended to the third floor together. Quest watched them enter the kitchen. A moment or two later the steward was summoned by a messenger and descended alone. Quest ran quickly down the stairs and planted himself behind the kitchen door. He had hardly taken up his position before the handle was turned. He heard Craig's last words, spoken as he looked over his shoulder.

"You want to just soak them for two hours longer than any other beans in the world. That's all there is about it."

Craig appeared and the door swung back behind him. Before he could utter a cry, Quest's left hand was over his mouth and the cold muzzle of an automatic pistol was pressed to his ribs.

"Turn round and mount those stairs, Craig," Quest ordered.

The man shrunk away, trembling. The pistol pressed a little further into his side.

"Upstairs," Quest repeated firmly. "If you utter a cry I shall shoot you."

Craig turned slowly round and obeyed. He mounted the stairs

with reluctant footsteps, followed by Quest.

"Through the door to your right," the latter directed. "That's right! Now sit down in that chair facing me."

Quest closed the door carefully. Craig sat where he had been ordered, his fingers gripping the arms of the chair. In his eyes shone the furtive, terrified light of the trapped criminal.

Quest looked him over a little scornfully. It was queer that a man with apparently so little nerve should have the art and the daring to plan such exploits.

"What do you want with me?" Craig asked doggedly.

"First of all," Quest replied, "I want to know what you have done with my assistant, the girl whom you carried off from the Professor's garage."

Craig shook his head.

"I know nothing about her."

"She locked you in the garage," Quest continued, "and sent for me. When I arrived, I found the garage door open, Lenora gone and you a fugitive."

Bewilderment struggled for a moment with blank terror in Craig's expression.

"How do you know that she locked me in the garage?"

Quest smiled, stretched out his right arm and his long fingers played softly with the pocket wireless.

"In just the same way," he explained, "that I am sending her this message at the present moment—a message which she will receive and understand wherever she is hidden. Would you like to know what I am telling her?"

The man shivered. His eyes, as though fascinated, watched the little instrument.

"I am saying this, Craig," Quest continued. "Craig is here and in my power. He is sitting within a few feet of me and will not leave this room alive until he has told me your whereabouts. Keep up your courage, Lenora. You shall be free in an hour."

The trapped man looked away from the instrument into Quest's face. There was a momentary flicker of something that might have passed for courage in his tone.

"Mr. Quest," he said, "you are a wonderful man, but there are limits to your power. You can tear my tongue from my mouth but you cannot force me to speak a word."

Quest leaned a little further forward in his chair, his gaze became more concentrated.

"That is where you are wrong, Craig. That is where you make a mistake. In a very few minutes you will be telling me all the secrets of your heart."

Craig shivered, drew back a little in his chair, tried to rise and fell back again helpless.

"My God!" he cried. "Leave me alone!"

"When you have told me the truth," Quest answered, swiftly, "and you will tell me all I want to know in a few moments.... Your eyelids are getting a little heavy, Craig. Don't resist. Something which is like sleep is coming over you. You see my will has yours by the throat."

Craig seemed suddenly to collapse altogether. He fell over on one side. Every atom of colour had faded from his cheeks. Quest leaned over him with a frown. The man was in a stupor without a doubt, but it was a physical state of unconsciousness into which he had subsided. He felt his pulse, unbuttoned his coat, and listened for a moment to the beating of his heart. Then he crossed the room, fetched the pitcher of water and dashed some of its contents in Craig's face. In a few moments the man opened his eyes and regained consciousness. His appearance, however, was still ghastly.

"Where am I?" he murmured.

"You are here in my room, at the Servants' Club," Quest replied. "You are just about to tell me where I shall find Lenora."

Craig shook his head. A very weak smile of triumph flickered for a moment at the corners of his lips.

"Your torture chamber trick won't work on me!" he exclaimed. "You can never—"

The whole gamut of emotions seemed already to have spent themselves in the man's face, but at that moment there was a new element, an element of terrified curiosity in the expression of his eyes as he stared towards the door.

"Is this another trick of yours?" he muttered.

Quest, too, turned his head and sprang instantly to his feet. From underneath the door came a little puff of smoke. There was a queer sense of heat of which both men were simultaneously conscious. Down in the street arose a chorus of warning shouts, increasing momentarily in volume. Quest threw open the door and closed it again at once.

"The place is on fire," he announced briefly. "Pull yourself together, man. We shall have all we can do to get out of this."

Craig turned to the door but staggered back almost immediately.

"The stairs are going!" he shrieked. "It is the kitchen that is on fire. We are cut off! We cannot get down!"

Quest was on his hands and knees, fumbling under his truckle bed. He pulled out a crude form of fire escape, a rough sort of cradle with a rope attached.

"Know how to use this?" he asked Craig quickly. "Here, catch hold. Put your arms inside this strap."

"You are going to send me down first?" Craig exclaimed incredulously.

Quest smiled. Then he drew the rope round the table and tied it.

"You would like to have a chance of cutting the rope, wouldn't you, when I was half way down?" he asked grimly. "Now then, don't waste time. Get on to the window-sill. Don't brake too much. Off you go!"

Yard by yard, swinging a little in the air, Craig made his descent. When he arrived in the street, there were a hundred willing hands to release him. Quest drew up the rope quickly, warned by a roar of anxious voices. The walls of the room were crumbling. Volumes of smoke were now pouring in underneath the door, and through the yawning fissures of the wall. Little tongues of flame were leaping out dangerously close to the spot where he must pass. He let fall the slack of the rope and leaned from the window to watch it anxiously. Then he commenced to descend, letting himself down hand over hand, always with one eye upon that length of rope that swung below. Suddenly, as he reached the second floor, a little cry from the crowd warned him of what had happened. Tongues of flame curling out from the blazing building, had caught the rope, which was being burned through not a dozen feet away from him. He descended a little further and paused in mid-air.

A shout from the crowd reached him.

"The cables! Try the cables!"

He glanced round. Seven or eight feet away, and almost level with him was a double row of telegraph wires. Almost as he saw them the rope below him burned through and fell to the ground. He swung a little towards the side of the house, pushed himself vigorously away from it with his feet, and at the farthest point of the outward swing, jumped. His hands gripped the telegraph wires safely. Even in that tense moment he heard a little sob of relief from the people below.

Hand over hand he made his way to the nearest pole and slipped easily to the ground. The crowd immediately surged around him. Some one forced a drink into his hand. A chorus of congratulations fell upon his deafened ears. Then the coming of the fire engines, and the approach of a police automobile diverted the attention of the onlookers. Quest slipped about amongst them, searching for Craig.

"Where is the man who came down before me?" he asked a bystander.

"Talking to the police in the car over yonder," was the hoarse reply. "Say, Guv'nor, you only just made that!"

Quest pushed his way through the crowd to where Craig was speaking eagerly to Inspector French. He stopped short and stooped down. He was near enough to hear the former's words.

"Mr. French, you saw that man come down the rope and swing on to the cables? That was Quest, Sanford Quest, the man who escaped from the Tombs prison. He can't have got away yet."

Quest drew off his coat, turned it inside out, and replaced it swiftly. He coolly picked up a hat some one had lost in the crowd and pulled it over his eyes. He passed within a few feet of where Craig and the Inspector were talking.

"He was hiding in the Servants' Club," Craig continued, "he had just threatened to shoot me when the fire broke out."

"I'll send the word round," French declared. "We'll have him found, right enough."

For a single moment Quest hesitated. He had a wild impulse to take Craig by the neck and throw him back into the burning house. Then he heard French shout to his men.

"Say, boys, Sanford Quest is in the crowd here somewhere. He's the man who jumped on to the cable lines. A hundred dollars for his arrest!"

Quest turned reluctantly away. Men were rushing about in all directions looking for him. He forced a passage through the crowd and in the general confusion he passed the little line of police without difficulty. His face darkened as he looked behind at the burning block. A peculiar sense of helplessness oppressed him. His pocket wireless was by now a charred heap of ashes. His one means of communication with Lenora was gone and the only man who knew her whereabouts was safe under the protection of the police.

2.

The Professor swung round in his chair and greeted Quest with some surprise but also a little disappointment.

"No news of Craig?" he asked.

Quest sank into a chair. He was fresh from the Turkish baths and was enjoying the luxury of clean linen and the flavour of an excellent cigar.

"I got Craig all right," he replied. "He came to the Servants' Club where I was waiting for him. My luck's out, though. The place was burnt to the ground last night. I saved his life and then the brute gave me away to the police. I had to make my escape as best I could."

The Professor tapped the table peevishly.

"This is insufferable," he declared. "I have had no shaving water; my coffee was undrinkable; I can find nothing. I have a most important lecture to prepare and I cannot find any of the notes I made upon the subject."

Quest stared at the Professor for a moment and then laughed softly.

"Well," he remarked, "you are rather an egoist, Professor, aren't you?"

"Perhaps I am," the latter confessed. "Still, you must remember that the scientific world on those few occasions when I do appear in public, expects much of me. My sense of proportion may perhaps be disarranged by this knowledge. All that I can realise at the present moment, is this. You seem to have frightened away the one man in the world who is indispensable to me."

Quest smoked in silence for a moment.

"Any mail for me, Professor?" he asked, abruptly.

The Professor opened a drawer and handed him a telegram.

"Only this!"

Quest opened it and read it through. It was from the Sheriff of a small town in Connecticut:—

"The men you enquired for are both here. They have sold an automobile and seem to be spending the proceeds. Shall I arrest?"

Quest studied the message for a moment.

"Say, this is rather interesting, Professor," he remarked.

"Really?" the latter replied tartly. "You must forgive me if I cannot follow the complications of your—pardon me for saying Munchausenlike affairs. How does the arrest of these two men help you?"

"Don't you see?" Quest explained. "These are the two thugs who set upon me up at the section house. They killed the signalman, who could have been my alibi, and swiped my car, in which, as it cannot be found, French supposes that I returned to New York. With their arrest the case against me collapses. I tell you frankly, Professor," Quest continued, frowning, "I hate to leave the city without having found that girl; but I am not sure that the quickest way to set things right would not be to go down, arrest these men and bring them back here, clear myself, and then go tooth and nail for Craig."

"I agree with you most heartily," the Professor declared. "I recommend any course which will ensure the return of my man Craig."

"I cannot promise you that you will ever have Craig here again," Quest observed grimly. "I rather fancy Sing-Sing will be his next home."

"Don't be foolish, Mr. Quest," the Professor advised. "Don't let me lose confidence in you. Craig would not hurt a fly, and as to abducting your assistant—if my sense of humour were developed upon normal lines—well, I should laugh! What you have really done, you, and that young lady assistant of yours, is to terrify the poor fellow into such a state of nerves that he scarcely knows what he is doing. As a matter of fact, how do you know that that young woman has been abducted at all? Such things are most unlikely, especially in this part of the city."

"What reason do you suggest, then, for her disappearance?" Quest enquired.

"At my age," the Professor replied, drily, "I naturally know nothing of these things. But she is a young woman of considerable personal attractions—I should think it not unlikely that she is engaged in some amorous adventure."

Quest laughed derisively.

"You do not know Lenora, Mr. Ashleigh," he remarked. "However, if it interests you, I will tell you why I know she has been abducted. Only a few hours ago, I was talking to her."

The Professor turned his head swiftly towards Quest. There was a queer sort of surprise in his face.

"Talking to her?"

Quest nodded.

"Our pocket wireless!" he explained. "Lenora has even described to me the room in which she is hidden."

"And the neighbourhood also?" the Professor demanded.

"Of that she knows nothing," Quest replied. "She is in a room apparently at the top of a house and the only window is in the roof. She can see nothing, hear nothing. When I get hold of the man who put her there," Quest continued slowly, "it will be my ambition to supplement personally any punishment the law may be able to inflict."

The Professor's manner had lost all its petulance. He looked at Quest almost with admiration.

"The idea of yours is wonderful," he confessed. "I am beginning to believe in your infallibility, Mr. Quest. I am beginning to believe that on this occasion, at any rate, you will triumph over your enemies."

Quest rose to his feet.

"Well," he said, "if I can keep out of my friend French's way for a few hours longer, I think I can promise you that I shall be a free man when I return from Bethel. I'm off now, Professor. Wish me good luck!"

"My friend," the Professor replied, "I wish you the best of luck, but more than anything else in the world," he added, a little peevishly, "I hope you may bring me back my servant Craig, and leave us both in peace."

Quest stepped off the cars at Bethel a little before noon that morning. The Sheriff met him at the depot and greeted him cordially but with obvious surprise.

"Say, Mr. Quest," he exclaimed, as they turned away, "I know these men are wanted on your charge, but I thought—you'll excuse my saying so—that you were in some trouble yourself."

Quest nodded.

"I'm out of that—came out yesterday."

"Very glad to hear it," the Sheriff assured him heartily. "I never thought that they'd be able to hold you."

"They hadn't a chance," Quest admitted. "Things turned out a little awkwardly at first, but this affair is going to put me on my feet again. The moment my car is identified and Red Gallagher and his mate arrested, every scrap of evidence against me goes."

"Well, here's the garage and the man who bought the car," the Sheriff remarked, "and there's the car itself in the road. It's for you to say whether it can be identified."

Quest drew a sigh of relief.

"That's mine, right enough," he declared. "Now for the men."

"Say, I want to tell you something," the Sheriff began dubiously. "These two are real thugs. They ain't going to take it lying down."

"Where are they?" Quest demanded.

"In the worst saloon here," the Sheriff replied. "They've been there pretty well all night, drinking, and they're there again this morning, hard at it. They've both got firearms, and though I ain't exactly a nervous man, Mr. Quest—"

"You leave it to me," Quest interrupted. "This is my job and I want to take the men myself."

"You'll never do it," the Sheriff declared.

"Look here," Quest explained, "if I let you and your men go in, there will be a free fight, and as likely as not you will kill one, if not both of the men. I want them alive."

"Well, it's your show," the Sheriff admitted, stopping before a disreputable-looking building. "This is the saloon. They've turned the place upside down since they've been here. You can hear the row they're making now. Free drinks to all the toughs in the town! They're pouring the stuff down all the time."

"Well," Quest decided, "I'm going in and I'm going in unarmed. You can bring your men in later, if I call for help or if you hear any shooting."

"You're asking for trouble," the Sheriff warned him.

"I've got to do this my own way," Quest insisted. "Stand by now."

He pushed open the door of the saloon. There were a dozen men drinking around the bar and in the centre of them Red Gallagher and his mate. They seemed to be all shouting together, and the air was thick with tobacco smoke. Quest walked right up to the two men.

"Gallagher," he said, "you're my prisoner. Are you coming quietly?"

Gallagher's mate, who was half drunk, swung round and fired a wild shot in Quest's direction. The result was a general stampede. Red Gallagher alone remained motionless. Grim and dangerously silent, he held a pistol within a few inches of Quest's forehead.

"If my number's up," he exclaimed ferociously, "it won't be you who'll take me."

"I think it will," Quest answered. "Put that gun away."

Gallagher hesitated. Quest's influence over him was indomitable.

"Put it away," Quest repeated firmly. "You know you daren't use it. Your account's pretty full up, as it is."

Gallagher's hand wavered. From outside came the shouts of the Sheriff and his men, struggling to fight their way in through the little crowd who were rushing for safety. Suddenly Quest backed, jerked the pistol up with his right elbow, and with almost the same movement struck Red Gallagher under the jaw. The man went over with a crash. His mate, who had been staggering about, cursing viciously, fired another wild shot at Quest, who swayed and fell forward.

"I've done him!" the man shouted. "Get up, Red! I've done him all right! Finish yer drink. We'll get out of this!"

He bent unsteadily over Quest. Suddenly the latter sprang up, seized him by the leg and sent him sprawling. The gun fell from his hand. Quest picked it up and held it firmly out, covering both men. Gallagher was on his knees, groping for his own weapon.

"Get the handcuffs on them," Quest directed the Sheriff, who with his men had at last succeeded in forcing his way into the saloon.

The Sheriff wasted no words till the two thugs, now nerveless and cowed, were handcuffed. Then he turned to Quest. There was a note of genuine admiration in his tone.

"Mr. Quest," he declared, "you've got the biggest nerve of any man I have ever known."

The criminologist smiled.

"This sort of bully is always a coward when it comes to the pinch," he remarked.

Crouching in her chair, her pale, terror-stricken face supported between her hands, Lenora, her eyes filled with hopeless misery, gazed at the dumb instrument upon the table. Her last gleam of hope seemed to be passing. Her little friend was silent. Once more her weary fingers spelt out a final, despairing message.

"What has happened to you? I am waiting to hear all the time. Has Craig told you where I am? I am afraid!"

There was still no reply. Her head sank a little lower on to her folded arms. Even the luxury of tears seemed denied her. Fear, the fear which dwelt with her day and night, had her in its grip. Suddenly she leaped, screaming, from her place. Splinters of glass fell all around her. Her first wild thought was of release; she gazed upwards at the broken pane. Then very faintly from the street below she heard the shout of a boy's angry voice.

"You've done it now, Jimmy! You're a fine pitcher, ain't you? Lost it, that's what you've gone and done!"

The thoughts formed themselves mechanically in her mind. Her eyes sought the ball which had come crashing into the room. There was life once more in her pulses. She found a scrap of paper and a pencil in her pocket. With trembling fingers she wrote a few words:

"Police head-quarters. I am Sanford Quest's assistant, abducted and imprisoned here in the room where the ball has fallen. Help! I am going mad!"

She twisted the paper, looked around the room vainly for string, and finally tore a thin piece of ribbon from her dress. She tied the message around the ball, set her teeth, and threw it at the empty skylight. The first time she was not successful and the ball came back. The second time it passed through the centre of the opening. She heard it strike the sound portion of the glass outside, heard it rumble down the roof. A few seconds of breathless silence! Her heart almost stopped beating. Had it rested in some ledge, or fallen into the street below? Then she heard the boy's voice.

"Gee! Here's the ball come back again!"

A new light shone into the room. She seemed to be breathing a different atmosphere—the atmosphere of hope. She listened no longer with horror for a creaking upon the stairs. She walked back and forth until she was exhausted.... Curiously enough, when the end came she was asleep, crouched upon the bed and dreaming wildly. She sprang up to find Inspector French, with a policeman behind him, standing upon the threshold.

"Inspector!" she cried, rushing towards him. "Mr. French! Oh, thank God!"

Her feelings carried her away. She threw herself at his feet. She was laughing and crying and talking incoherently, all at the same time. The Inspector assisted her to a chair.

"Say, what's all this mean?" he demanded.

She told him her story, incoherently, in broken phrases. French listened with puzzled frown.

"Say, what about Quest?" he asked. "He ain't been here at all, then?"

She looked at him wonderingly.

"Of course not! Mr. Quest—"

She hesitated. The Inspector laid his hand upon her wrist. Then he realised that she was on the point of a nervous breakdown, and in no condition for interrogations.

"That'll do," he said. "I'll take care of you for a time, young lady, and I'll ask you a few questions later on. My men are searching the house. You and I will be getting on, if you can tear yourself away."

She laughed hysterically and hurried him towards the door. As they passed down the gloomy stairs she clung to his arm. The first breath of air seemed wonderful to her as they passed out into the street. It was freedom!

The plain-clothes man, who was lounging in Quest's most comfortable easy-chair and smoking one of his best cigars, suddenly laid down his paper. He moved to the window. A large, empty automobile stood in the street outside, from which the occupants had presumably just descended. He hastened towards the door, which was opened, however, before he was halfway across the room. The cigar slipped from his fingers. It was Sanford Quest who stood there, followed by the Sheriff of Bethel, two country policemen, and Red Gallagher and his mate, heavily handcuffed. Quest glanced at the cigar.

"Say, do you mind picking that up?" he exclaimed. "That carpet cost me money."

The plain-clothes man obeyed at once. Then he edged a little towards the telephone. Quest had opened his cigar cabinet.

"Glad you've left me one or two," he remarked drily.

"Say, aren't you wanted down yonder, Mr. Quest?" the man enquired.

"That's all right now," Quest told him. "I'm ringing up Inspector French myself. You'd better stand by the other fellows there and keep your eye on Red Gallagher and his mate."

"I guess Mr. Quest is all right," the Sheriff intervened. "We're ringing up headquarters ourselves, anyway."

The plain-clothes man did as he was told. Quest took up the receiver from his telephone instrument and arranged the phototelesme.

"Police-station Number One, central," he said,—"through to Mr. French's office, if you please. Mr. Quest wants to speak to him. Yes, Sanford Quest. No need to get excited!... All right. I'm through, am I?... Hullo, Inspector?"

A rare expression of joy suddenly transfigured Quest's face. He was gazing downward into the little mirror.

"You've found Lenora, then, Inspector?" he exclaimed. "Bully for you!... What do I mean? What I say! You forget that I am a scientific man, French. No end of appliances here you haven't had time to look at. I can see you sitting there, and Lenora and Laura looking as though you had them on the rack. You can drop that, French. I've got Red Gallagher and his mate, got them here with the Sheriff of Bethel. They went off with my auto and sold it. We've got that. Also, in less than five minutes my chauffeur will be here. He's been lying in a farmhouse, unconscious, since that scrap. He can tell you what time he saw me last. Bring the girls along, French—and hurry!"

Quest hung up the receiver.

"I've given Inspector French something to think about," he remarked, as he turned away. "Now, Mr. Sheriff, if you can make yourself at home for a quarter of an hour or so, French will be here and take these fellows off your hands. I've still a little more telephoning to do."

"You go right ahead," the Sheriff acquiesced.

Quest rang up the Professor. His response to the call was a little languid, and his reception of the news of Quest's successful enterprise was almost querulous.

"My friend," the Professor said, "your news gratifies me, of course. Your rehabilitation, however, was a matter of certainty. With me life has become a chaos. You can have no idea, with your independent nature, what it means to entirely rely upon the ministrations of one person and to be suddenly deprived of their help."

"No news of Craig, then?" Quest demanded.

"None at all," was the weary reply. "What about your young lady assistant?"

"She'll be here in five minutes," Quest told him. "You had better come along and hear her story. It ought to interest you."

"Dear me!" the Professor exclaimed. "I will certainly come—certainly!"

Quest set down the receiver and paced the room thoughtfully for a moment or two. Although his own troubles were almost over, the main problem before him was as yet unsolved. The affair with the Gallaghers was, after all, only an off-shoot. It was the mystery of Lenora's abduction, the mystery of the black box, which still called for the exercise of all his ingenuity.

Inspector French was as good, even better, than his word. In a surprisingly short time he entered the room, followed by Laura and Lenora. Quest gave them a hand each, but it was into Lenora's eyes that he looked. Her coming, her few words of greeting, timid though they were, brought him an immense sense of relief.

"Well, girls," he said, "both full of adventures, eh? What did they do with you in the Tombs, Laura?"

"Pshaw! What could they do?" Laura replied. "If they're guys enough to be tricked by a girl, the best thing they can do is to keep mum about it and let her go. That's about what they did to me."

Inspector French, who was standing a little aloof, regarded Laura with an air of unwilling admiration.

"That's some girl, that Miss Laura," he muttered in an undertone to Quest. "She roasted us nicely."

"I mustn't stop to hear your story, Lenora," Quest said. "You're safe—that's the great thing."

"Found her in an empty house," French reported, "out Gayson Avenue way. Now, Mr. Quest, I don't want to come the official over you too much, but if you'll kindly remember that you're an escaped prisoner—"

There was a knock at the door. A young man entered in chauffeur's livery, with his head still bandaged. Quest motioned him to come in.

"I'll just repeat my story of that morning, French," Quest said. "We went out to find Macdougal, and succeeded, as you know. Just as

I was starting for home, those two thugs set upon me. They nearly did me up. You know how I made my escape. They went off in my automobile and sold it in Bethel. I arrested them there myself this morning. Here's the Sheriff, who will bear out what I say, also that they arrived at the place in my automobile."

"Sure!" the Sheriff murmured.

"Further," Quest continued, "there's my chauffeur. He knows exactly what time it was when the tire of my car blew out, just as we were starting for New York."

"It was eleven-ten, sir," the chauffeur declared. "Mr. Quest and I both took out our watches to see if we could make New York by midday. Then one of those fellows hit me over the head and I've been laid up ever since. A man who keeps a store a little way along the road picked me up and looked after me."

Inspector French held out his hand.

"Mr. Quest," he said, "I reckon we'll have to withdraw the case against you. No hard feeling, I hope?"

"None at all," Quest replied promptly, taking his hand.

"That's all right, then," French declared. "I've brought two more men with me. Perhaps, Mr. Sheriff, you wouldn't mind escorting your prisoners around to headquarters? I'll be there before long."

"And you girls," Quest insisted, "go right to your room and rest. I'll come upstairs presently and have a talk. Look after her, Laura," he added, glancing a little anxiously at Lenora. "She has had about as much as she can bear, I think."

The two girls left the room. Quest stood upon the threshold, watching the Sheriff and his prisoners leave the house. The former turned round to wave his adieux to them.

"There's an elderly josser out here," he shouted; "seems to want to come in."

Quest leaned forward and saw the Professor.

"Come right in, Mr. Ashleigh," he invited.

The Professor promptly made his appearance. His coat was ill-brushed and in place of a hat he was wearing a tweed cap which had seen better days. His expression was almost pathetic.

"My dear Quest," he exclaimed, as he wrung his hand, "my heartiest congratulations! As you know, I always believed in your innocence. I am delighted that it has been proved."

"Come in and sit down, Mr. Ashleigh," Quest invited. "You know the Inspector."

The Professor shook hands with French, and then, feeling that his appearance required some explanation, he took off his cap and looked at it ruefully.

"I am aware," he said, "that this is not a becoming headgear, but I am lost—absolutely lost without my servant. If you would earn my undying gratitude, Mr. Quest, you would clear up the mystery about

Craig and restore him to me."

Quest was helping the Inspector to the whisky at the sideboard. He paused to light a cigar before he replied.

"I very much fear, Professor," he observed, "that you will never have Craig back again."

The Professor sank wearily into an easy-chair.

"I will take a little whisky and one of your excellent cigars, Quest," he said. "I must ask you to bear with me if I seem upset. After more than twenty years' service from one whom I have always treated as a friend, this sudden separation, to a man of my age, is somewhat trying. My small comforts are all interfered with. The business of my every-day life is completely upset. I do not allude, as you perceive, Mr. Quest, to the horrible suspicions you seem to have formed of Craig. My own theory is that you have simply frightened him to death."

"All the same," the Inspector remarked thoughtfully, "some one who is still at large committed those murders and stole those jewels. What is your theory about the jewels, Mr. Quest?"

"I haven't had time to frame one yet," the criminologist replied. "You've been keeping me too busy looking after myself. However," he added, "it's time something was done."

He took a magnifying glass from his pocket and examined very closely the whole of the front of the safe.

"No sign of finger-prints," he muttered. "The person who opened it probably wore gloves."

He fitted the combination and swung open the door. He stood there, for a moment, speechless. Something in his attitude attracted the Inspector's attention.

"What is it, Mr. Quest?" he asked eagerly.

Quest drew a little breath. Exactly facing him, in the spot where the jewels had been, was a small black box. He brought it to the table and removed the lid. Inside was a sheet of paper, which he quickly unfolded. They all three read the few lines together:—

"Pitted against the inherited cunning of the ages, you have no chance. I will take compassion upon you. Look in the right-hand drawer of your desk."

Underneath appeared the signature of the Hands. Quest moved like a dream to his cabinet and pulled open the right-hand drawer. He turned around and faced the other two men. In his hand was Mrs. Rheinholdt's necklace!

CHAPTER VIII

THE HOUSE OF MYSTERY

1.

Something in the nature of a conference was proceeding in Quest's study. The Professor was there, seated in the most comfortable easy-chair, smoking without relish one of his host's best cigars, watching with nervous impatience the closed door. Laura and Lenora were seated at the table, dressed for the street. They had the air of being prepared for some excursion. Quest, realising the Professor's highly-strung state, had left him alone for a few moments and was studying a map of New York. The latter, however, was too ill at ease to keep silent for long.

"Our friend French," he remarked, "gave you no clue, I suppose, as to the direction in which his investigations are leading him?"

Quest glanced up from the map.

"None at all. I know, however, that the house in which Lenora here was confined, is being watched closely."

The Professor glanced towards the table before which Lenora was seated.

"It seems strange," he continued, "that the young lady should have so little to tell us about her incarceration."

Lenora shivered for a moment.

"What could there be to tell," she asked, "except that it was all horrible, and that I felt things—felt dangers—which I couldn't describe."

The Professor gave vent to an impatient little exclamation.

"I am not speaking of fancies," he persisted. "You had food brought to you, for instance. Could you never see the hand which placed it inside your room? Could you hear nothing of the footsteps of the person who brought it? Could you not even surmise whether it was a man or a woman?"

Lenora answered him with an evident effort. She had barely, as yet, recovered from the shock of those awful hours.

"The person who brought me the food," she said, "came at night—never in the daytime. I never heard anything. The most I ever saw was once—I happened to be looking towards the door and I saw a pair of hands—nothing more—setting down a tray. I shrieked and called out. I think that I almost fainted. When I found courage enough to look, there was nothing there but the tray upon the floor."

"You never heard, for instance, the rustling of a gown or the sound of a footstep?" the Professor asked. "You could not even say whether your jailer were man or woman?"

Lenora shook her head.

"All that I ever heard was the opening of the door. All that I ever saw was that pair of hands. One night I fancied—but that must have been a dream!"

"You fancied what?" the Professor persisted.

"That I saw a pair of eyes glaring at me," Lenora replied, "eyes without any human body. I know that I ran round the room, calling out. When I dared to look again, there was nothing there."

The Professor sighed as he turned away.

"It is evident, I am afraid," he said, "that Miss Lenora's evidence will help no one. As an expert in these affairs, Mr. Quest, does it not seem to you that her imprisonment was just a little purposeless? There seems to have been no attempt to harm her in any way whatever, that I can see."

"Whoever took the risk of abducting her," Quest pointed out grimly, "did it for a purpose. That purpose would probably have become developed in course of time. However we look at it, Mr. Ashleigh, there was only one man who must have been anxious to get her out of the way, and that man was Craig."

The Professor's manner betrayed some excitement.

"Then will you tell me this?" he demanded. "The young lady is confident that she locked Craig up in the coach-house and that the key was on the outside of the door, a fact which would prevent the lock being picked from inside, even if such a thing were possible. The window is small, and up almost in the roof. Will you tell me how Craig escaped from the coach-house in order to carry out this abduction—all within a few minutes, mind, of his having been left there? Will you tell me that, Mr. Sanford Quest?" the Professor concluded, with a note of triumph in his tone.

"That's one of the troubles we are up against," Quest admitted. "We have to remember this, though. The brain that planned the two murders here, that stole and restored Mrs. Rheinholdt's jewels, that sends us those little billets-doux from time to time, is quite capable of finding a way out of a jerry-built garage."

The Professor sniffed. He turned once more to Lenora.

"Young lady," he said, "I will ask you this. I do not wish to seem obstinate in my refusal to accept Craig's guilt as proved, but I would like to put this simple question to you. Did Craig's demeanour during your conversation seem to you to indicate the master criminal? Did he seem to you to be possessed of supreme courage, of marvellous intelligence?"

Lenora smiled very faintly.

"I am afraid," she replied, "that this time I'll have to satisfy the Professor. He was white and trembling all the time. I thought him an arrant coward."

The Professor smiled beatifically as he glanced around. He had the air of one propounding an unanswerable problem.

"You hear what Miss Lenora says? I ask you whether a man who even knew the meaning of the word fear could have carried out these ghastly crimes?"

"I have known cases," Quest observed, "where the most cold-blooded criminals in the world have been stricken with the most deadly fear when it has come to a question of any personal danger. However," he added, "here comes our friend French. I have an idea that he has something to tell us."

They glanced expectantly towards the door as French entered. The Inspector, who was looking very spruce and well-brushed, wished them a general good-morning. His eyes rested last and longest upon Laura, who seemed, however, unconscious of his presence.

"Now, then, French," Quest began, as he returned his greeting, "take a cigar, make yourself comfortable in that chair and let us have your news. As you see, we have obeyed orders. We are all ready to follow you anywhere you say."

"It won't be to the end of the world, anyway," the Inspector remarked, as he lit his cigar. "I am going to propose a little excursion down Gayson Avenue way."

"Back to that house?" Lenora exclaimed, with a grimace.

The Inspector nodded.

"We have had those boys at the station," he went on, "and we have questioned them carefully. It seems that after they had picked up the ball, a man came out of the side entrance of the house, saw them reading Miss Lenora's message, and shouted after them. The boys had sense enough to scoot. The man ran after them, but had to give it up. Here is their description of him."

The Inspector took a piece of paper from his pocket. They all waited breathlessly.

"Had to drag this out of the boys, bit by bit," the Inspector proceeded, "but boiled down and put into reasonable language, this is what it comes to. The man was of medium height, rather thin, pale, and dressed in black clothes. He had what they call anxious eyes, and after running a short distance he put his hand to his heart, as though out of breath. One of the boys thought his nose was a little hooked, and they both remarked upon the fact that although he shouted after them, he used no swear words, but simply tried to induce them to stop. This description suggest anything to you, gentlemen?"

"Craig," Lenora said firmly.

"It is a very accurate description of Craig," Sanford Quest agreed.

The Professor looked troubled, also a little perplexed. He said nothing, however.

"Under these circumstances," the Inspector continued, "I have had the house watched, and I propose that we now search it systematically. It is very possible that something may transpire to help us. Of course, my men went through it roughly when we brought Miss Lenora away, but that wasn't anything of a search to count, if the place really has become a haunt of criminals."

"What about the ownership of the house?" Quest asked, as he took up his hat.

The Inspector nodded approvingly.

"I am making a few enquiries in that direction," he announced. "I expect to have something to report very shortly."

The Professor stood drawing on his gloves. The vague look of trouble still lingered in his face.

"Tell me again," he begged, "the name of the avenue in which this residence is situated?"

"Gayson Avenue," the inspector replied. "It's a bit out of the way, but it's not a bad neighbourhood."

The Professor repeated the address to himself softly. For a moment he stood quite still. His manner showed signs of growing anxiety. He seemed to be trying to remember something.

"The name," he admitted finally, as they moved towards the door, "suggests to me, I must confess—We are going to see the house, Inspector?"

"We are on our way there now, sir—that is, if the young ladies are willing?" he added, glancing at Laura.

"We've been waiting here with our hats on for the last half hour," Laura replied promptly. "You've stretched your ten minutes out some, Mr. French."

The Inspector manoeuvred to let the others pass on, and descended the stairs by Laura's side.

"Couldn't help it," he confided, lowering his tone a little. "Had some information come in about that house I couldn't quite size up. You're looking well this morning, Miss Laura."

"Say, who are you guying!" she replied.

"I mean it," the Inspector persisted. "That hat seems to suit you."

Laura laughed at the top of her voice.

"Say, kid," she exclaimed to Lenora, "the Inspector here's setting up as a judge of millinery!"

Lenora turned and looked at them both with an air of blank astonishment. The Inspector was a little embarrassed.

"No need to give me away like that," he muttered, as they reached the hall. "Now then, ladies and gentlemen, if you are ready."

They took their places in the automobile and drove off. As they neared the vicinity of Gayson Avenue, the Professor began to show signs of renewed uneasiness. When they drew up at last outside the house, he gave a little exclamation. His face was grave, almost haggard.

"Mr. Quest," he said, "Inspector French, I deeply regret that I have a statement to make."

They both turned quickly towards him. The Inspector smiled in a confidential manner at Laura. It was obvious that he knew what was coming.

"Some years ago," the Professor continued, "I bought this house and made a present of it to—"

"To whom?" Quest asked quickly.

"To my servant Craig," the Professor admitted with a groan.

Lenora gave a little cry. She turned triumphantly towards the Inspector.

"All recollection as to its locality had escaped me," the Professor continued sorrowfully. "I remember that it was on the anniversary of his having been with me for some fifteen years that I decided to show him some substantial mark of my appreciation. I knew that he was looking for a domicile for his father and mother, who are since both dead, and I requested a house agent to send me in a list of suitable residences. This, alas! was the one I purchased."

Quest glanced around the place.

"I think," he said, "that the Professor's statement now removes any doubt as to Craig's guilt. You are sure the house has been closely watched, Inspector?"

"Since I received certain information," French replied, "I have had half a dozen of my best men in the vicinity. I can assure you that no one has entered or left it during the last twenty-four hours."

They made their way to the piazza steps and entered by the front door. The house was an ordinary framework one of moderate size, in poor repair, and showing signs of great neglect. The rooms were barely furnished, and their first cursory search revealed no traces of habitation. There was still the broken skylight in the room which Lenora had occupied, and the bed upon which she had slept was still crumpled. French, who had been tapping the walls downstairs, called to them. They trooped down into the hall. The Inspector was standing before what appeared to be an ordinary panel.

"Look here," he said, glancing out of the corner of his eye to be sure that Laura was there, "let me show you what I have just discovered."

He felt with his thumb for a spring. In a moment or two a portion of the wall, about two feet in extent, slowly revolved, disclosing a small cupboard fitted with a telephone instrument.

"A telephone," the Inspector remarked, pointing to it, "in an unoccupied house and a concealed cupboard. What do you think of that?"

The Professor shook his head.

"Don't ask me," he groaned.

French took the receiver from its rest and called up the exchange.

"Inspector French speaking," he announced. "Kindly tell me

what is the number of the telephone from which I am speaking, and who is the subscriber?"

He listened to the reply and asked another question.

"Can you tell me when this instrument was last used?... When?... Thank you!"

The Inspector hung up the receiver.

"The subscriber's name," he told them drily, "is Brown. The number is not entered in the book, by request. The telephone was used an hour ago from a call office, and connection was established. That is to say that some one spoke from this telephone."

"Then if your men have maintained their search properly, that some one," Quest said slowly, "must be in the house at the present moment."

"Without a doubt," the Inspector agreed. "I should like to suggest," he went on, "that the two young ladies wait for us now in the automobile. If this man turns out as desperate as he has shown himself ingenious, there may be a little trouble."

They both protested vigorously. Quest shrugged his shoulders.

"They must decide for themselves," he said. "Personally, I like Lenora, who has had less experience of such adventures, to grow accustomed to danger.... With your permission, Inspector, I am going to search the front room on the first floor before we do anything else. I think that if you wait here I may be able to show you something directly."

Quest ascended the stairs and entered a wholly unfurnished room on the left-hand side. He looked for a minute contemplatively at a large but rather shallow cupboard, the door of which stood open, and tapped lightly with his forefinger upon the back part of it. Then he withdrew a few feet and, drawing out his revolver, deliberately fired into the floor, a few inches inside. There was a half stifled cry. The false back suddenly swung open and a man rushed out. Quest's revolver covered him, but there was no necessity for its use. Craig, smothered with dust, his face white as a piece of marble, even his jaw shaking with fear, was wholly unarmed. He seemed, in fact, incapable of any form of resistance. He threw himself upon his knees before Quest.

"Save me!" he begged. "Help me to get away from this house! You don't belong to the police. I'll give you every penny I have in the world to let me go!"

Quest smiled at him derisively.

"Get up," he ordered.

Very slowly Craig obeyed him. He was a pitiful-looking object, but a single look into Quest's face showed him the folly of any sort of appeal.

"Walk out of the room," Quest ordered, "in front of me—so! Now, then, turn to the right and go down the stairs."

They all gave a little cry as they saw him appear, a trembling, pitiful creature, glancing around like a trapped animal. He commenced to descend the stairs, holding tightly to the banisters. Quest remained on the landing above, his revolver in his hand. French waited in the hall below, also armed. Laura gripped Lenora's arm in excitement.

"They've got him now!" she exclaimed. "Got him, sure!"

On the fourth or fifth stair, Craig hesitated. He suddenly saw the Professor standing below. He gripped the banisters with one hand. The other he flung out in a threatening gesture.

"You've given me away to these bloodhounds!" he cried,—"you, for whom I have toiled and slaved, whom I have followed all over the world, whom I have served faithfully with the last breath of my body and the last drop of blood in my veins! You have brought them here—tracked me down! You!"

The Professor shook his head sorrowfully.

"Craig," he said, "you have been the best servant man ever had. If you are innocent of these crimes, you can clear yourself. If you are guilty, a dog's death is none too good for you."

Craig seemed to sway for a moment upon his feet. Only Lenora, from the hall, saw that he was fitting his right foot into what seemed to be a leather loop hanging from the banisters. Then a wild shout of surprise broke from the lips of all of them, followed by a moment of stupefied wonder. The whole staircase suddenly began to revolve. Craig, clinging to the banisters, disappeared. In a moment or two there was a fresh click. Another set of stairs, almost identical to the first, had taken their place.

"The cellar!" Quest shouted, as he rushed down the stairs. "Quick!"

They wrenched open the wooden door and hurried down the dark steps into the gloomy, unlit cellar. The place was crowded with packing-cases, and two large wine barrels stood in the corner. At the farther end was a door. Quest rushed for it and stood on guard. A moment later, however, he called to Laura and pressed his revolver into her hand.

"Stand here," he ordered. "Shoot him if he tries to run out. I'll search in the packing-cases. He might be dangerous."

The Professor, out of breath, was leaning against one of the pillars, his arm passed around it for support. Lenora, with Quest and French, searched hastily amongst the packing-cases. Suddenly there was a loud crack, the sound of falling masonry, followed by a scream from Laura. French, with a roar of anger, rushed towards her. She was lying on her side, already half covered by falling bricks and masonry. He dragged her away, just in time.

"My God, she's fainted!" he exclaimed.

"I haven't," Laura faltered, trying to open her eyes, "and I'm not going to, but I think my arm's broken, and my side hurts."

"The fellow's not down here, anyway," Quest declared. "Let's help her upstairs and get her out of this devil's house."

They supported her up the steps and found a chair for her in the hall. She was white almost to the lips, but she struggled bravely to keep consciousness.

"Don't you bother about me," she begged. "Don't let that blackguard go! You find him. I shall be all right."

The Inspector swung open the telephone cupboard and called for an ambulance. Then Quest, who had been examining the staircase, suddenly gave a little exclamation.

"He's done us!" he cried. "Look here, French, this is the original staircase. There's the leather loop. I know it because there was a crack on the fourth stair. When we rushed down the cellar after him, he swung the thing round again and simply walked out of the front door. Damn it, man, it's open!"

They hurried outside. French blew his whistle. One of the plain-clothes men came running up from the avenue. He was looking a little sheepish.

"What's wrong?" French demanded.

"He's gone off," was the unwilling reply. "I guess that chap's given us the slip."

"Speak up," French insisted.

"The only place," the man went on, "we hadn't our eyes glued on, was the front door. He must have come out through that. There's been a motor truck with one or two queer-looking chaps in it, at the corner of the avenue there for the last ten minutes. I'd just made up my mind to stroll round and see what it was up to when Jim, who was on the other side, shouted out. A man jumped up into it and they made off at once."

"Could he have come from this house?" French asked sternly.

"I guess, if he'd come out from the front door, he might just have done it," the man admitted.

Quest and the Inspector exchanged glances.

"He's done us!" Quest muttered,—"done us like a couple of greenhorns!"

The Inspector's rubicund countenance was white with fury. His head kept turning in the direction of Laura, to whom the Professor was busy rendering first aid.

"If I never take another job on as long as I live," he declared, "I'll have that fellow before I'm through!"

2.

The Professor roused himself from what had apparently been a very gloomy reverie.

"Well," he announced, "I must go home. It has been very kind of you, Mr. Quest, to keep me here for so long."

Quest glanced at the clock.

"Don't hurry, Mr. Ashleigh," he said. "We may get some news at any moment. French has a dozen men out on the search and he has promised to ring me up immediately he hears anything."

The Professor sighed.

"A man," he declared, "who for twenty years can deceive his master as utterly and completely as Craig has done me, who is capable of such diabolical outrages, and who, when capture stares him in the face, is capable of an escape such as he made today, is outside the laws of probability. Personally, I do not believe that I shall ever again see the face of my servant, any more than that you, Quest, will entirely solve the mystery of these murders and the theft of the Rheinholdt jewels."

Lenora, who, with her hat on, was packing a small bag at the other end of the room, glanced up for a moment.

"The man is a demon!" she exclaimed. "He would have sacrificed us all, if he could. When I think of poor Laura lying there in the hospital, crushed almost to death, so that he could save his miserable carcass, and realise that he is free, I feel—"

She stopped short. Quest looked at her and nodded.

"Don't mind hurting our feelings, Lenora," he said. "French and I are up against it all right. We're second best, at the present moment—I'll admit that—but the end hasn't come yet."

"I am sorry," she murmured. "I was led away for a moment. But, Mr. Quest," she went on piteously, "can't we do something? Laura's so brave. She tried to laugh when I left her, an hour ago, but I could see all the time that she was suffering agony. Fancy a man doing that to a woman! It makes me feel that I can't rest or sleep. I think that when I have left the hospital I shall just walk up and down the streets and watch and search."

Quest shook his head.

"That sort of thing won't do any good," he declared. "It isn't any use, Lenora, working without a plan. That's why I'm here now, waiting. I want to formulate a plan first."

"Who are we," the Professor asked drearily, "to make plans against a fiend like that? What can we do against men who have revolving staircases and trolley-loads of river pirates waiting for them? You may be a scientific criminologist, Quest, but that fellow Craig is a scientific criminal, if ever there was one."

Quest crossed the room towards his cigar cabinet, and opened it. His little start was apparent to both of them. Lenora laid down the bag which she had just lifted up. The Professor leaned forward in his chair.

"What is it, Quest?" he demanded.

Quest stretched out his hand and picked up from the top of the cigars a small black box! He laid it on the table.

"Unless I am very much mistaken," he said, "it is another communication from our mysterious friend."

"Impossible!" the Professor exclaimed hoarsely.

"How can he have been here?" Lenora cried.

Quest removed the lid from the box and drew out a circular card. Around the outside edge was a very clever pen and ink sketch of a lifebuoy, and inside the margin were several sentences of clear handwriting. In the middle was the signature—the clenched hands! Quest read the message aloud—

"In the great scheme of things, the Supreme Ruler of the Universe divided an inheritance amongst His children. To one He gave power, to another strength, to another beauty, but to His favourites He gave cunning."

They all looked at one another.

"What does it mean?" Lenora gasped.

"A lifebuoy!" the Professor murmured.

They both stared at Quest, who remained silent, chewing hard at the end of his cigar.

"Every message," he said, speaking half to himself, "has had some significance. What does this mean—a lifebuoy?"

He was silent for a moment. Then he turned suddenly to the Professor.

"What did you call those men in the motor-truck, Professor—river pirates? And a lifebuoy! Wait."

He crossed the room towards his desk and returned with a list in his hand. He ran his finger down it, stopped and glanced at the date.

"The *Durham*," he muttered, "cargo cotton, destination Southampton, sails at high tide on the 16th. Lenora, is that calendar right?"

"It's the 16th, Mr. Quest," she answered.

Quest crossed the room to the telephone.

"I want Number One Central, Exchange," he said. "Thank you! Put me through to Mr. French's office.... Hullo, French! I've got an idea. Can you come round here at once and bring an automobile? I want to get down to the docks—not where the passenger steamers start from—lower down.... Good! We'll wait."

Quest hung up the receiver.

"See here, Professor," he continued, "that fellow wouldn't dare to send this message if he wasn't pretty sure of getting off. He's made all his plans beforehand, but it's my belief we shall just get our hands upon him, after all. Lenora, you'd better get along round to the hospital. You don't come in this time. It's bad enough to have Laura laid up—can't risk you. There'll be a little trouble, too, before we're through, I'm afraid."

Lenora sighed as she picked up her bag.

"If it weren't for Laura," she said, "you'd find it pretty hard to keep me away. I think that if I could see the handcuffs put on that man, it would be the happiest moment of my life."

"We'll get him all right," Quest promised. "Remember me to Laura."

"And present my compliments, also," the Professor begged.

Lenora left them. The Professor, his spirits apparently a little improved by the prospect of action, accepted some whisky and a cigar. Presently they heard the automobile stop outside and French appeared.

"Anything doing?" he asked.

Quest showed him the card and the sailing list. The Inspector nodded.

"Say, that fellow's some sport!" he remarked admiringly. "You wouldn't believe it just to look at him. That staircase this afternoon, though, kind of teaches one not to trust to appearances. So you think he's getting a move on him, Mr. Quest?"

"I think he had a truck waiting for him at the corner of Gayson Avenue," Quest replied. "It was the machine my men went after. The men looked like river thugs, although I shouldn't have thought of it if the Professor hadn't used the word 'river pirates.' It's quite clear that they took Craig down to the river. There's only one likely ship sailing tonight and that's the *Durham*. It's my belief Craig's on her."

The Inspector glanced at the clock.

"Then we've got to make tracks," he declared, "and pretty quick, too. She'll be starting from somewhere about Number Twenty-eight dock, a long way down. Come along, gentlemen."

They hurried out to the automobile and started off for the docks. The latter part of their journey was accomplished under difficulties, for the street was packed with drays and heavy vehicles. They reached dock Number Twenty-eight at last, however, and hurried through the shed on to the wharf. There were no signs of a steamer there.

"Where's the *Durham*?" Quest asked one of the carters, who was just getting his team together.

The man pointed out to the middle of the river, where a small steamer was lying.

"There she is," he replied. "She'll be off in a few minutes. You'll hear the sirens directly, when they begin to move down."

Quest led the way quickly to the edge of the wharf. There was a small tug there, the crew of which were just making her fast for the night.

"Fifty dollars if you'll take us out to the *Durham* and catch her before she sails," Quest shouted to the man who seemed to be the captain. "What do you say?"

The man spat out a plug of tobacco from his mouth.

"I'd take you to hell for fifty dollars," he answered tersely. "Step in. We'll make it, if you look quick."

They clambered down the iron ladder and jumped on to the deck of the tug. The captain seized the wheel. The two men who formed the crew took off their coats and waistcoats.

"Give it her, Jim," the former ordered. "Now, then, here goes! We'll just miss the ferry."

They swung around and commenced their journey. Quest stood with his watch in his hand. They were getting up the anchor of the *Durham*, and from higher up the river came the screech of steamers beginning to move on their outward way.

"We'll make it all right," the captain assured them.

They were within a hundred yards of the *Durham* when Quest gave a little exclamation. From the other side of the steamer another tug shot away, turning back towards New York. Huddled up in the stern, half concealed in a tarpaulin, was a man in a plain black suit. Quest, with a little shout, recognised the man at the helm from his long brown beard.

"That's one of those fellows who was in the truck," he declared, "and that's Craig in the stern! We've got him this time. Say, Captain, it's that tug I want. Never mind about the steamer. Catch it and I'll make it a hundred dollars!"

The man swung round the wheel, but he glanced at Quest a little doubtfully.

"Say, what is this show?" he asked.

Quest opened his coat and displayed his badge. He pointed to the Inspector.

"Police job. This is Inspector French, I am Sanford Quest."

"Good enough," the man replied. "What's the bloke wanted for?"

"Murder," Quest answered shortly.

"That so?" the other remarked. "Well, you'll get him, sure! He's looking pretty scared, too. You'd better keep your eyes open, though. I don't know how many men there are on board, but that tug belongs to the toughest crew up the river. Got anything handy in the way of firearms?"

Quest nodded.

"You don't need to worry," he said. "We've automatics here, but as long as we're heading them this way, they'll know the game's up."

"We've got her!" the captain exclaimed. "There's the ferry and the first of the steamers coming down in the middle. They'll have to chuck it."

Right ahead of them, blazing with lights, a huge ferry came

churning the river up and sending great waves in their direction. On the other side, unnaturally large, loomed up the great bows of an ocean-going steamer. The tug was swung round and they ran up alongside. The man with the beard leaned over.

"Say, what's your trouble?" he demanded.

The Inspector stepped forward.

"I want that man you've got under the tarpaulin," he announced.

"Say, you ain't the river police?"

"I'm Inspector French from headquarters," was the curt reply. "The sooner you hand him over, the better for you."

"Do you hear that, O'Toole?" the other remarked, swinging round on his heel. "Get up, you blackguard!"

A man rose from underneath the oilskin. He was wearing Craig's clothes, but his face was the face of a stranger. As quick as lightning, Quest swung round in his place.

"He's fooled us again!" he exclaimed. "Head her round, Captain—back to the *Durham!*"

The sailor shook his head.

"We've lost our chance, guvnor," he pointed out, "Look!"

Quest set his teeth and gripped the Inspector's arm. The place where the *Durham* had been anchored was empty. Already, half a mile down the river, with a trail of light behind and her siren shrieking, the *Durham* was standing out seawards.

CHAPTER IX

THE INHERITED SIN

1.

"Getting kind of used to these courthouse shows, aren't you, Lenora?" Quest remarked, as they stepped from the automobile and entered the house in Georgia Square.

Lenora shrugged her shoulders. She was certainly a very different-looking person from the tired, trembling girl who had heard Macdougal sentenced not many weeks ago.

"Could anyone feel much sympathy," she asked, "with those men? Red Gallagher, as they all called him, is more like a great brute animal than a human being. I think that even if they had sentenced him to death I should have felt that it was quite the proper thing to have done."

"Too much sentiment about those things," Quest agreed, clipping the end off a cigar. "Men like that are better off the face of the earth. They did their best to send me there."

"Here's a cablegram for you!" Lenora exclaimed, bringing it over to him. "Mr. Quest, I wonder if it's from Scotland Yard!"

Quest tore it open. They read it together, Lenora standing on tiptoe to peer over his shoulder:

"Stowaway answering in every respect your description of Craig found on 'Durham.' Has been arrested, as desired, and will be taken to Hamblin House for identification by Lord Ashleigh. Reply whether you are coming over, and full details as to charge."

"Good for Scotland Yard!" Quest declared. "So they've got him, eh? All the same, that fellow's as slippery as an eel. Lenora, how should you like a trip across the ocean, eh?"

"I should love it," Lenora replied. "Do you mean it really?"

Quest nodded.

"The fellow's fooled me pretty well," he continued, "but somehow I feel that if I get my hands on him this time, they'll stay there till he stands where Red Gallagher did today. I don't feel content to let anyone else finish off the job. Got any relatives over there?"

"I have an aunt in London," Lenora told him, "the dearest old lady you ever knew. She'd give anything to have me make her a visit."

Quest moved across to his desk and took up a sailing list. He studied it for a few moments and turned back to Lenora.

"Send a cable off at once to Scotland Yard," he directed.

"Say—'Am sailing on *Lusitania* tomorrow. Hold prisoner. Charge very serious. Have full warrants.'"

Lenora wrote down the message and went to the telephone to send it off. As soon as she had finished, Quest took up his hat again.

"Come on," he invited. "The machine's outside. We'll just go and look in on the Professor and tell him the news. Poor old chap, I'm afraid he'll never be the same man again."

"He must miss Craig terribly," Lenora observed, as they took their places in the automobile, "and yet, Mr. Quest, it does seem to me a most amazing thing that a man so utterly callous and cruel as Craig must be, should have been a devoted and faithful servant to anyone through all these years."

Quest nodded.

"I am beginning to frame a theory about that. You see, all the time Craig has lived with the Professor, he has been a sort of dabbler with him in his studies. Where the Professor's gone right into a thing and understood it, Craig, you see, hasn't managed to get past the first crust. His brain wasn't educated enough for the subjects into the consideration of which the Professor may have led him. See what I'm driving at?"

"You mean that he may have been mad?" Lenora suggested.

"Something of that sort," Quest assented. "Seems to me the only feasible explanation. The Professor's a bit of a terror, you know. There are some queer stories about the way he got some of his earlier specimens in South America. Science is his god. What he has gone through in some of those foreign countries, no one knows. Quite enough to unbalance any man of ordinary nerves and temperament."

"The Professor himself is remarkably sane," Lenora observed.

"Precisely," Quest agreed, "but then, you see, his brain was big enough, to start with. It could hold all there was for it to hold. It's like pouring stuff into the wrong receptacle when a man like Craig tries to follow him. However, that's only a theory. Here we are, and the front door wide open. I wonder how our friend's feeling today."

They found the Professor on his hands and knees upon a dusty floor. Carefully arranged before him were the bones of a skeleton, each laid in some appointed place. He had a chart on either side of him, and a third one on an easel. He looked up a little impatiently at the sound of the opening of the door, but when he recognised Quest and his companion the annoyance passed from his face.

"Are we disturbing you, Mr. Ashleigh?" Quest enquired.

The Professor rose to his feet and brushed the dust from his knees.

"I shall be glad of a rest," he said simply. "You see what I am doing? I am trying to reconstruct from memory—and a little imagination, perhaps—the important part of my missing skeleton. It's a wonderful problem which those bones might have solved, if I had been able to place them fairly before the scientists of the world. Do you understand much about the human frame, Mr. Quest?"

Quest shook his head promptly.

"Still life doesn't interest me," he declared. "Bones are bones, after all, you know. I don't even care who my grandfather was, much less who my grandfather a million times removed might have been. Let's step into the study for a moment, Professor, if you don't mind," he went on. "Lenora here is a little sensitive to smell, and a spray of lavender water on some of your bones wouldn't do them any harm."

The Professor ambled amiably towards the door.

"I never notice it myself," he said. "Very likely that is because I see beyond these withered fragments into the prehistoric worlds whence they came. I sit here alone sometimes, and the curtain rolls up, and I find myself back in one of those far corners of South America, or even in a certain spot in East Africa, and I can almost fancy that time rolls back like an unwinding reel and there are no secrets into which I may not look. And then the moment passes and I remember that this dry-as-dust world is shrieking always for proofs—this extraordinary conglomeration of human animals in weird attire, with monstrous tastes and extraordinary habits, who make up what they call the civilized world. Civilized!"

They reached the study and Quest produced his cigar case.

"Can't imagine any world that existed before tobacco," he remarked cheerfully. "Help yourself, Professor. It does me good to see you human enough to enjoy a cigar!"

The Professor smiled.

"I never remember to buy any for myself," he said, "but one of yours is always a treat. Miss Lenora, I am glad to see, is completely recovered."

"I am quite well, thank you, Mr. Ashleigh," Lenora replied. "I am even forgetting that I ever had nerves. I have been in the courthouse all the morning, and I even looked curiously at your garage as we drove up."

"Very good—very good, my dear!" the Professor murmured. "At the courthouse, eh? Were those charming friends of yours from Bethel being tried, Quest?"

Quest nodded.

"Red Gallagher and his mate! Yes, they got it in the neck, too."

"Personally," the Professor exclaimed, his eyes sparkling with appreciation of his own wit, "I think that they ought to have got it round the neck! However, let us be thankful that they are disposed of. Their attack upon you, Mr. Quest, introduced rather a curious factor into our troubles. Even now I find it a little difficult to follow the workings of our friend French's mind. It seems hard to believe that he could really have imagined you guilty."

"French is all right," Quest declared. "He fell into the common error of the detective without imagination."

"What about that unhappy man Craig?" the Professor asked gloomily. "Isn't the *Durham* almost due now?"

Quest took out the cablegram from his pocket and passed it over. The Professor's fingers trembled a little as he read it. He passed it back, however, without immediate comment.

"You see, they have been cleverer over there than we were," Quest remarked.

"Perhaps," the Professor assented. "They seem, at least, to have arrested the man. Even now I can scarcely believe that it is Craig—my servant Craig—who is lying in an English prison. Do you know that his people have been servants in the Ashleigh family for some hundreds of years?"

Quest was clearly interested. "Say, I'd like to hear about that!" he exclaimed. "You know, I'm rather great on heredity, Professor. What class did he come from then? Were his people just domestic servants always?"

The Professor's face was for a moment troubled. He moved to his desk, rummaged about for a time, and finally produced an ancient volume.

"This really belongs to my brother, Lord Ashleigh," he explained. "He brought it over with him to show me some entries concerning which I was interested. It contains a history of the Hamblin estate since the days of Cromwell, and here in the back, you see, is a list of our farmers, bailiffs and domestic servants. There was a Craig who was a tenant of the first Lord Ashleigh and fought with him in the Cromwellian Wars as a trooper and since those days, so far as I can see, there has never been a time when there hasn't been a Craig in the service of our family. A fine race they seem to have been, until—"

"Until when?" Quest demanded.

The look of trouble had once more clouded the Professor's face. He shrugged his shoulders slightly.

"Until Craig's father," he admitted. "I am afraid I must admit that we come upon a bad piece of family history here. Silas Craig entered the service of my father in 1858, as under game-keeper. Here we come upon the first black mark against the name. He appears to have lived reputably for some years, and then, after a quarrel with a neighbour about some trivial matter, he deliberately murdered him, a crime for which he was tried and executed in 1867. John Craig, his only son, entered our service in 1880, and, when I left England, accompanied me as my valet."

There was a moment's silence. Quest shook his head a little reproachfully.

"Professor," he said, "you are a scientific man, you appreciate the significance of heredity, yet during all this time, when you must have seen for yourself the evidence culminating against Craig, you never mentioned this—this—damning piece of evidence."

The Professor closed the book with a sigh.

"I did not mention it, Mr. Quest," he acknowledged, "because I did not believe in Craig's guilt and I did not wish to further prejudice you against him. That is the whole and simple truth. Now tell me what you are going to do about his arrest?"

"Lenora and I are sailing tomorrow," Quest replied. "We are taking over the necessary warrants and shall bring Craig back here for trial."

The Professor smoked thoughtfully for some moments. Then he rose deliberately to his feet. He had come to a decision. He announced it calmly but irrevocably.

"I shall come with you," he announced. "I shall be glad of a visit to England, but apart from that I feel it to be my duty. I owe it to Craig to see that he has a fair chance, and I owe it to the law to see that he pays the penalty, if indeed he is guilty of these crimes. Is Miss Laura accompanying you, too?"

Quest shook his head.

"From what the surgeons tell us," he said, "it will be some weeks before she is able to travel. At the same time, I must tell you that I am glad of your decision, Professor."

"It is my duty," the latter declared. "I cannot rest in this state of uncertainty. If Craig is lost to me, the sooner I face the fact the better. At the same time I will be frank with you. Notwithstanding all this accumulated pile of evidence I feel in my heart the urgent necessity of seeing him face to face, of holding him by the shoulders and asking him whether these things are true. We have faced death together, Craig and I. We have done more than that—we have courted it. There is nothing about him I can accept from hearsay. I shall go with you to England, Mr. Quest."

2.

The Professor rose from his seat in some excitement as the carriage passed through the great gates of Hamblin Park. He acknowledged with a smile the respectful curtsey of the woman who held it open.

"You have now an opportunity, my dear Mr. Quest," he said, "of appreciating one feature of English life not entirely reproducible in your own wonderful country. I mean the home life and surroundings of our aristocracy. You see these oak trees?" he went on, with a little wave of his hand. "They were planted by my ancestors in the days of Henry the Eighth. I have been a student of tree life in South America and in the dense forests of Central Africa, but for real character, for splendour of growth and hardiness, there is nothing in the world to touch the Ashleigh oaks."

"They're some trees," the criminologist admitted.

"You notice, perhaps, the smaller ones, which seem dwarfed. Their tops were cut off by the Lord of Ashleigh on the day that Lady Jane Grey was beheaded. Queen Elizabeth heard of it and threatened to confiscate the estate. Look at the turf, my friend. Ages have gone to the making of that mossy, velvet carpet."

"Where's the house?" Quest enquired.

"A mile farther on yet. The woods part and make a natural avenue past the bend of the river there," the Professor pointed out. "Full of trout, that river, Quest. How I used to whip that stream when I was a boy!"

They swept presently round a bend in the avenue. Before them on the hill-side, surrounded by trees and with a great walled garden behind, was Hamblin House. Quest gave vent to a little exclamation of wonder as he looked at it. The older part and the whole of the west front was Elizabethan, but the Georgian architect entrusted with the task of building a great extension had carried out his work in a manner almost inspired. Lines and curves, sweeping everywhere towards the same constructive purpose, had been harmonised by the hand of time into a most surprising and effectual unity. The criminologist, notwithstanding his unemotional temperament, repeated his exclamation as he resumed his place in the carriage.

"This is where you've got us beaten," he admitted. "Our country places are like gew-gaw palaces compared to this. Makes me kind of sorry," he went on regretfully, "that I didn't bring Lenora along."

The Professor shook his head.

"You were very wise," he said. "My brother and Lady Ashleigh have recovered from the shock of poor Lena's death in a marvellous manner, I believe, but the sight of the girl might have brought it back to them. You have left her with friends, I hope, Mr. Quest?"

"She has an aunt in Hampstead," the latter explained. "I should have liked to have seen her safely there myself, but we should have been an hour or two later down here, and I tell you," he went on, his voice gathering a note almost of ferocity, "I'm wanting to get my hands on that fellow Craig! I wonder where they're holding him."

"At the local police-station, I expect," the Professor replied. "My brother is a magistrate, of course, and he would see that proper arrangements were made. There he is at the hall door."

The carriage drew up before the great front, a moment or two later. Lord Ashleigh came forward with outstretched hands, the genial smile of the welcoming host upon his lips. In his manner, however, there was a distinct note of anxiety.

"Edgar, my dear fellow," he exclaimed, "I am delighted! Welcome back to your home! Mr. Quest, I am very happy to see you here. You have heard the news, of course?"

"We have heard nothing!" the Professor replied.

"You didn't go to Scotland Yard?" Lord Ashleigh asked.

"We haven't been to London at all," Quest explained. "We got on the boat train at Plymouth, and your brother managed to induce one of the directors whom he saw on the platform to stop the train for us at Hamblin Road. We only left the boat two hours ago. There's nothing wrong with Craig, is there?"

Lord Ashleigh motioned them to follow him.

"Please come this way," he invited.

He led them across the hall—which, dimly-lit and with its stained-glass windows, was almost like the nave of a cathedral,—into the library beyond. He closed the door and turned around.

"I have bad news for you both," he announced. "Craig has escaped."

Neither the Professor nor Quest betrayed any unusual surprise. So far as the latter was concerned, his first glimpse at Lord Ashleigh's face had warned him of what was coming.

"Dear me!" the Professor murmured, sinking into an easy-chair. "This is most unexpected!"

"We'll get him again," Quest declared quickly. "Can you let us have the particulars of his escape, Lord Ashleigh? The sooner we get the hang of things, the better."

Their host turned towards the butler, who was arranging a tray upon the sideboard.

"You must permit me to offer you some refreshments after your journey," he begged. "Then I will tell you the whole story. I think you will agree, when you hear it, that no particular blame can be said to rest upon any one's shoulders. It was simply an extraordinary interposition of chance. There is tea, whisky and soda, and wine here, Mr. Quest. Edgar, I know you'll take some tea."

"English tea for me," the Professor remarked, watching the cream.

"Whisky and soda here," Quest decided.

Lord Ashleigh himself attended to the wants of his guests. Then, at his instigation, they made themselves comfortable in easy-chairs and he commenced his narration.

"You know, of course," he began, "that Craig was arrested at Liverpool in consequence of communications from the New York police. I understand that it was with great difficulty he was discovered, and it is quite clear that some one on the ship had been heavily bribed. However, he was arrested, brought to London, and then down here for purposes of identification. I would have gone to London myself, and in fact offered to do so, but on the other hand, as there are many others on the estate to whom he was well-known, I thought that it would be better to have more evidence than mine alone. Accordingly, they left London one afternoon, and I sent a dog-cart to the station to meet them. They arrived quite safely and started for here, Craig handcuffed to one of the Scotland Yard men on the back seat, and the other in front with the driver. About half a mile from the south entrance to the park, the road runs across a rather desolate strip of country with a lot of low undergrowth on one side. We have had a little trouble with poachers, as there is a sort of gipsy camp on some common land a short distance away. My head-keeper, to whom the very idea of a poacher is intolerable, was patrolling this ground himself that afternoon, and caught sight of one of these gipsy fellows setting a trap. He chased him, and more, I am sure, to frighten him than anything else, when he saw that the fellow was getting away he fired his gun, just as the dog-cart was passing. The horse shied, the wheel caught a great stone by the side of the road, and all four men were thrown out. The man to whom Craig was handcuffed was stunned, but Craig himself appears to have been unhurt. He jumped up, took the key of the handcuffs from the pocket of the officer, undid them, and slipped off into the undergrowth before either the groom or the other Scotland Yard man had recovered their senses. To cut a long story short, that was last Thursday, and up till now not a single trace of the fellow has been discovered."

Quest rose abruptly to his feet.

"I'd like to take this matter up right on the spot where Craig disappeared," he suggested. "Couldn't we do that?"

"By all means," Lord Ashleigh agreed, touching a bell. "We have several hours before we change for dinner. I will have a car round and take you to the spot."

The Professor acquiesced readily, and very soon they stepped out of the automobile on to the side of a narrow road, looking very much as it had been described. Further on, beyond a stretch of open common, they could see the smoke from the gipsy encampment. On their left-hand side was a stretch of absolutely wild country, bounded in the far distance by the grey stone wall of the park. Lord Ashleigh led the way through the thicket, talking as he went.

"Craig came along through here," he explained. "The groom and the Scotland Yard man who had been sitting by his side followed him. They searched for an hour but found no trace of him at all. Then they returned to the house to make a report and get help. I will now show you how Craig first eluded them."

He led the way along a tangled path, doubled back, plunged into a little spinney and came suddenly to a small shed.

"This is an ancient gamekeeper's shelter," he explained, "built a long time ago and almost forgotten now. What Craig did, without a doubt, was to hide in this. The Scotland Yard man who took the affair in hand found distinct traces here of recent occupation. That is how he made his first escape."

Quest nodded.

"Sure!" he murmured. "Well now, what about your more extended search?"

"I was coming to that," Lord Ashleigh replied. "As Edgar will remember, no doubt, I have always kept a few bloodhounds in my kennels, and as soon as we could get together one or two of the keepers and a few of the local constabulary, we started off again from here. The dogs brought us without a check to this shed, and started off again in this way."

They walked another half a mile, across a reedy swamp. Every now and then they had to jump across a small dyke, and once they had to make a detour to avoid an osier bed. They came at last to the river.

"Now I can show you exactly how that fellow put us off the scent here," their guide proceeded. "He seems to have picked up something, Edgar, in those South American trips of yours, for a cleverer thing I never saw. You see all these bullrushes everywhere—clouds of them, all along the river?"

"We call them tules," Quest muttered. "Well?"

"When Craig arrived here," Lord Ashleigh continued, "he must have heard the baying of the dogs in the distance and he knew that the game was up unless he could put them off the scent. He cut a quantity of these bullrushes from a place a little further behind those trees there, stepped boldly into the middle of the water, waded down to that spot where, as you see, the trees hang over, stood stock still and leaned them all around him. It was dusk when the chase reached the river bank, and I have no doubt the bullrushes presented quite a natural appearance. At any rate, although the dogs came without a check to the edge of the river, where he stepped off, they never picked the scent up again either on this side or the other. We tried them for four or five hours before we took them home. The next morning, while the place was being thoroughly searched, we came upon the spot where these bullrushes had been cut down, and we found them caught in the low boughs of a tree, drifting down the river."

The Professor's tone was filled with something almost like admiration.

"I must confess," he declared, "I never realised for a single moment that Craig was a person of such gifts. In all the small ways of life, in campaigning, camping out, dealing with natural difficulties incidental to our expeditions, I have found him invariably a person of resource, ready-witted and full of useful suggestions. But that he should be able to apply his gifts with such infinite cunning, to a suddenly conceived career of crime, I must admit amazes me."

Quest had lit a fresh cigar and was smoking vigorously.

"What astonishes me more than anything," he pronounced, as he stood looking over the desolate expanse of country, "is that when one comes face to face with the fellow he presents all the appearance of a nerveless and broken-down coward. Then all of a sudden there spring up these evidences of the most amazing, the most diabolical resource.... Who's this, Lord Ashleigh?"

The latter turned his head. An elderly man in a brown velveteen suit, with gaiters and thick boots, raised his hat respectfully.

"This is my head-keeper, Middleton," his master explained. "He was with us on the chase."

The Professor shook hands heartily with the newcomer.

"Not a day older, Middleton!" he exclaimed. "So you are the man who has given us all this trouble, eh? This gentleman and I have come over from New York on purpose to lay hands on Craig."

"I am very sorry, sir," the man replied. "I wouldn't have fired my gun if I had known what the consequences were going to be, but them poaching devils that come round here rabbiting fairly send me furious and that's a fact. It ain't that one grudges them a few rabbits, but my tame pheasants all run out here from the home wood, and I've seen feathers at the side of the road there that no fox nor stoat had nothing to do with. All the same, sir, I'm very sorry," he added, "to have been the cause of any inconvenience."

"It is rather worse than inconvenience, Middleton," the Professor said gravely. "The man who has escaped is one of the worst criminals of these days."

"He won't get far, sir," the gamekeeper remarked, with a little smile. "It's a wild bit of country, this, and I admit that men might search it for weeks without finding anything, but those gentlemen from Scotland Yard, sir, if you'll excuse my making the remark, and hoping that this gentleman," he added, looking at Quest, "is in no way connected with them—well, they don't know everything, and that's a fact."

"This gentleman is from the United States," Lord Ashleigh reminded him, "so your criticism doesn't affect him. By-the-by, Middleton, I heard this morning that you'd been airing your opinions down in the village. You seem to rather fancy yourself as a thief-catcher."

"I wouldn't go so far as that, my lord," the man replied respectfully, "but still, I hope I may say that I've as much common sense as most people. You see, sir," he went on, turning to Quest, "the spots where he could emerge from this track of country are pretty well guarded, and he'll be in a fine mess, when he does put in an appearance, to show himself upon a public road. Yet by this time I should say he must be nigh starved. Sooner or later he'll have to come out for food. I've a little scheme of my own, sir, I don't mind admitting," the man concluded, with a twinkle in his keen brown eyes. "I'm not giving it away. If I catch him for you, that's all that's wanted, I imagine, and we shan't be any the nearer to it for letting any one into my little secret."

His master smiled.

"You shall have your rise out of the police, if you can, Middleton," he observed. "It seems queer, though, to believe that the fellow's still in hiding round here."

As though by common consent, they all stood, for a moment, perfectly still, looking across the stretch of marshland with its boggy places, its scrubby plantations, its clustering masses of tall grasses and bullrushes. The grey twilight had become even more pronounced during the last few minutes. Little wreaths of white mist hung over the damp places. Everywhere was a queer silence. The very air seemed breathless. The Professor shivered and turned away.

"My nerves," he declared, "are scarcely what they were. I have listened in a primeval forest, listened for the soft rustling of a snake in the undergrowth, or the distant roar of some beast of prey. I have listened then with curiosity. I have not known fear. It seems to me, somehow, that in this place there is something different afoot. I don't like it, George—I don't like it. We will go home, if you please."

They made their way, single file, to the road and up to the house. Lord Ashleigh did his best to dispel a queer little sensation of uneasiness which seemed to have arisen in the minds of all of them.

"Come," he said, "we must put aside our disappointment for the present, and remember that after all the chances are that Craig will never make his escape alive. Let us forget him for a little while.... Mr. Quest," he added, a few minutes later, as they reached the hall, "Moreton here will show you to your room and look after you. Please let me know if you will take an aperitif. I can recommend my sherry. We dine at eight o'clock. Edgar, you know your way. The blue room, of course. I am coming up with you myself. Her ladyship back yet, Moreton?"

"Not yet, my lord."

"Lady Ashleigh," her husband explained, "has gone to the other side of the county to open a bazaar. She is looking forward to the pleasure of welcoming you at dinner-time."

Dinner, served, out of compliment to their transatlantic visitor, in the great banqueting hall, was to Quest especially a most impressive meal. They sat at a small round table lit by shaded lights, in the centre of an apartment which was large in reality, and which seemed vast by reason of the shadows which hovered around the unlit spaces. From the walls frowned down a long succession of family portraits—Ashleighs in the queer Tudor costume of Henry the Seventh; Ashleighs in chain armour, sword in hand, a charger waiting, regardless of perspective, in the near distance; Ashleighs befrilled and bewigged; Ashleighs in the Court dress of the Georges—judges, sailors, statesmen and soldiers. A collection of armour which would have gladdened the eye of many an antiquarian, was ranged along the black-panelled walls. Everything was in harmony, even the grave precision of the solemn-faced butler and the powdered hair of the two footmen. Quest, perhaps for the first time in his life, felt almost lost, hopelessly out of touch with his surroundings, an alien and a struggling figure. Nevertheless, he entertained the little party with many stories. He struggled all the time against that queer sensation of anachronism which now and then became almost oppressive.

The Professor's pleasure at finding himself once more amongst these familiar surroundings was obvious and intense. The conversation between him and his brother never flagged. There were tenants and neighbours to be asked after, matters concerning the estate on which he demanded information. Even the very servants' names he remembered.

"It was a queer turn of fate, George," he declared, as he held out before him a wonderfully chased glass filled with amber wine, "which sent you into the world a few seconds before me and made you Lord of Ashleigh and me a struggling scientific man."

"The world has benefited by it," Lord Ashleigh remarked, with more than fraternal courtesy. "We hear great things of you over here, Edgar. We hear that you have been on the point of proving most unpleasant things with regard to our origin."

"Oh! there is no doubt about that," the Professor observed. "Where we came from and where we are going to are questions which no longer afford room for the slightest doubt to the really scientific mind. What sometimes does elude us is the nature of our tendencies while we are here on earth."

"Mine, I fancy, are obvious enough," Lord Ashleigh interposed.

"Superficially, I grant it," his brother acknowledged. "As a matter of scientific fact, I recognize the probability of your actually being a person utterly different from what you appear. Man becomes what he is according to the circumstances by which he is assailed. Now your life here, George, must be a singularly uneventful one."

"Not during the last six months," Lord Ashleigh remarked, with a sigh. "Even these last few days have been exciting enough. I must confess that they have left me with a queer sort of nervousness. I find myself listening intently sometimes,—conscious, as it were, of the influence or presence of some indefinite danger."

"Very interesting," the Professor murmured. "Spiritualism, as an exact science, has always interested me very much."

Lady Ashleigh made a little grimace.

"Don't encourage George," she begged. "He is much too superstitious, as it is."

There was a brief silence. The port had been placed upon the table and coffee served. The servants, according to the custom of the house, had departed. The great apartment was empty. Even Quest was impressed by some peculiar significance in the long-drawn-out silence. He looked around him uneasily. The frowning regard of that long line of painted warriors seemed somehow to be full of menace. There was something grim, too, in the sight of those empty suits of armour.

"I may be superstitious," Lord Ashleigh said, "but there are times, especially just lately, when I seem to find a new and hateful quality in silence. What is it, I wonder? I ask you but I think I know. It is the conviction that there is some alien presence, something disturbing lurking close at hand."

He suddenly rose to his feet, pushed his chair back and walked to the window, which opened level with the ground. He threw it up and listened. The others came over and joined him. There was nothing to be heard but the distant hooting of an owl, and farther away the barking of some farmhouse dog. Lord Ashleigh stood there with straining eyes, gazing out across the park.

"There was something here," he muttered, "something which has gone. What's that? Quest, your eyes are younger than mine. Can you see anything underneath that tree?"

Quest peered out into the grey darkness.

"I fancied I saw something moving in the shadow of that oak," he muttered. "Wait."

He crossed the terrace, swung down on to the path, across a lawn, over a wire fence and into the park itself. All the time he kept his eyes fixed on a certain spot. When at last he reached the tree, there was nothing there. He looked all around him. He stood and listened for several moments. A more utterly peaceful night it would be hard to imagine. Slowly he made his way back to the house.

"I imagine we are all a little nervous tonight," he remarked. "There's nothing doing out there."

They strolled about for an hour or more, looking into different rooms, showing their guest the finest pictures, even taking him down into the wonderful cellars. They parted early, but Quest stood, for a few moments before retiring, gazing about him with an air almost of awe. His great room, as large as an apartment in an Italian palace, was lit by a dozen wax candles in silver candlesticks. His four-poster was supported by pillars of black oak, carved into strange forms, and sur-mounted by the Ashleigh coronet and coat of arms. He threw his windows open wide and stood for a moment looking out across the park, more clearly visible now by the light of the slowly rising moon. There was scarcely a breeze stirring, scarcely a sound even from the animal world. Nevertheless, Quest, too, as reluctantly he made his preparations for retiring for the night, was conscious of that queer sensation of unimagined and impalpable danger.

CHAPTER X

LOST IN LONDON

1.

Quest, notwithstanding the unusual nature of his surroundings, slept that night as only a tired and healthy man can. He was awakened the next morning by the quiet movements of a man-servant who had brought back his clothes carefully brushed and pressed. He sat up in bed and discovered a small china tea equipage by his side.

"What's this?" he enquired.

"Your tea, sir."

Quest drank half a cupful without protest.

"Your bath is ready at any time, sir."

"I'm coming right along," Quest replied, jumping out of bed.

The man held up a dressing-gown and escorted him to an unexpectedly modern bathroom at the end of the corridor. When Quest returned, his toilet articles were all laid out for him with prim precision; the window was wide open, the blinds drawn, and a soft breeze was stealing through into the room. Below him, the park, looking more beautiful than ever in the morning sunshine, stretched away to a vista of distant meadowlands and cornfields, with here and there a little farmhouse and outbuildings, gathered snugly together. The servant, who had heard him leave the bathroom, reappeared.

"Is there anything further I can do for you, sir?" he enquired.

"Nothing at all, thanks," Quest assured him. "What time's breakfast?"

"Breakfast is served at nine o'clock, sir. It is now half past eight."

The man withdrew and Quest made a brisk toilet. The nameless fears of the previous night had altogether disappeared. To his saner morning imagination, the atmosphere seemed somehow to have become cleared of that cloud of mysterious depression. He was whistling to himself from sheer light-heartedness as he turned to leave the room. Then the shock came. At the last moment he stretched out his hand to take a handkerchief from his satchel. A sudden exclamation broke from his lips. He stood for a moment as though turned to stone. Before him, on the top of the little pile of white cambric, was a small black box! With a movement of the fingers which was almost mechanical, he removed the lid and drew out the customary little scrap of paper. He smoothed it out before him on the dressing-case and read the message:—

"You will fail here as you have failed before. Better go back.

There is more danger for you in this country than you dream of."

His teeth came fiercely together and his hands were clenched. His thoughts had gone like a flash to Lenora. Was it possible that harm was intended to her? He put the idea away from him almost as soon as conceived. The thing was unimaginable. Craig was here, must be here, in the close vicinity of the house. He could have had no time to communicate with confederates in London. Lenora, at any rate, was safe. Then he glanced around the room and thought for a moment of his own danger. In the dead of the night, as he had slept, mysterious feet had stolen across his room, mysterious hands had placed those few words of half mocking warning in that simple hiding-place! It would have been just as easy, he reflected with a grim little smile, for those hands to have stretched their death-dealing fingers over the bed where he had lain asleep. He looked once more out over the park. Somehow, its sunny peace seemed to have become disturbed. The strange sense of foreboding which he, in common with the others, had carried about with him last night, had returned.

The atmosphere of the pleasant breakfast-room to which in due course he descended, was cheerful enough. Lady Ashleigh had already taken her place at the head of the table before a glittering array of silver tea and coffee equipage. The Professor, with a plate in his hand, was making an approving survey of the contents of the dishes ranged upon the sideboard.

"An English breakfast, my dear Quest," he remarked, after they had exchanged the usual greetings, "will, I am sure, appeal to you. I am not, I confess, given to the pleasures of the table, but if anything could move me to enthusiasm in dietary matters, the sight of your sideboard, my dear sister-in-law, would do so. I commend the bacon and eggs to you, Quest, or if you prefer sausages, those long, thin ones are home-made and delicious. Does Mrs. Bland still cure our hams, Julia?"

"Her daughter does," Lady Ashleigh replied, smiling. "We are almost self-supporting here. All our daily produce, of course, comes from the home farm. Tea or coffee, Mr. Quest?"

"Coffee, if you please," Quest decided, returning from his visit to the sideboard. "Is Lord Ashleigh a late riser?"

"Not by any means," his wife declared. "He very often gets up and rides in the park before breakfast. I don't know where he is this morning. He didn't even come in to see me. I think we must send up."

She touched an electric bell under her foot and a moment or two later the butler appeared.

"Go up and see how long your master will be," Lady Ashleigh directed.

"Very good, your ladyship."

The man was backing through the doorway in his usual dignified manner when he was suddenly pushed to one side. The valet who had waited upon Quest, and who was Lord Ashleigh's own servant, rushed into the room. His face was white. He had forgotten all decorum. He almost shouted to Lady Ashleigh.

"Your ladyship—the master! Something has happened! He won't move! He—he—"

They all rose to their feet. Quest groaned to himself. The black box!

"What do you mean?" Lady Ashleigh faltered. "What do you mean, Williams?"

The man shook his head. He seemed almost incapable of speech.

"Something has happened to the master!"

They all trooped out of the room and up the stairs, the Professor leading the way. They pushed open the door of Lord Ashleigh's bed-chamber. In the far corner of the large room was the four-poster, and underneath the clothes a silent figure. The Professor turned down the sheets. Then he held out his hand. His face, too, was blanched.

"Julia, don't come," he begged.

"I must know!" she almost shrieked. "I must know!"

"George is dead," the Professor said slowly.

There was a moment's awful silence, broken by a piercing scream from Lady Ashleigh. She sank down upon the sofa and the Professor leaned over her. Quest turned to the little group of frightened servants who were gathering round the doorway.

"Telephone for a doctor," he ordered, "also to the local police-station."

He, too, approached the bed and reverently lifted the covering. Lord Ashleigh was lying there, his body a little doubled up, his arms wide outstretched. On his throat were two black marks.

"Where is the valet—Williams?" Quest asked, as he turned away.

The man came forward.

"Tell us at once what you know?" Quest demanded.

"I came in, as usual, to call his lordship before I called you," the man replied. "He did not answer, but I thought, perhaps, that he was sleepy. I filled his bath, which, as you see, opens out of the room, and then came to attend on you. When you went down to breakfast, I returned to his lordship's room expecting to find him dressed. Instead of that the room was silent, the bath still unused. I spoke to him—there was no answer. Then I lifted the sheet!"

They had led Lady Ashleigh from the room. The Professor and Quest stood face to face. The former's expression, however, had lost all his amiable serenity. His face was white and pinched. He looked shrivelled up. It was as though some physical stroke had fallen upon him.

"Quest! Quest!" he almost sobbed. "My brother!—George, whom I loved like nobody else on earth! Is he really dead?"

"Absolutely!"

The Professor gripped the oak pillar of the bedstead. He seemed on the point of collapse.

"The mark of the Hands is upon his throat," Quest pointed out.

"The Hands! Oh, my God!" the Professor groaned.

"We must not eat or drink or sleep," Quest declared fiercely, "until we have brought this matter to an end. Craig must be found. This is the supreme horror of all. Pull yourself together, Mr. Ashleigh. We shall need every particle of intelligence we possess. I begin to think that we are fighting against something superhuman."

The butler made an apologetic appearance. He spoke in a hushed whisper.

"You are wanted downstairs, gentlemen. Middleton, the head-keeper, is there."

As though inspired with a common idea, both Quest and the Professor hurried out of the room and down the broad stairs. Their inspiration was a true one. The gamekeeper welcomed them with a smile of triumph. By his side, the picture of abject misery, his clothes torn and muddy, was Craig!

"I've managed this little job, sir," Middleton announced, with a smile of slow triumph.

"How did you get him?" Quest demanded.

"Little idea of my own," the gamekeeper continued. "I guessed pretty well what he'd be up to. He'd tumbled to it that the usual way off the moor was pretty well guarded, and he'd doubled back through the thin line of woods close to the house. I dug one of my poachers' pits, sir, and covered it over with a lot of loose stuff. That got him all right. When I went to look this morning I saw where he'd fallen through, and there he was, walking round and round at the bottom like a caged animal. Your servants have telephoned for the police, Mr. Ashleigh," he went on, turning to the Professor, "but I'd like you just to point out to the Scotland Yard gentleman—called us yokels, he did, when he first came down—that we've a few ideas of our own down here."

Quest suddenly whispered to the Professor. Then he turned to the keeper.

"Bring him upstairs, Middleton, for a moment," he directed. "Follow us, please."

The Professor gripped Quest's arm as they ascended the stairs.

"What is this?" he asked hoarsely. "What is it you wish to do?"

"It's just an idea of my own," Quest replied. "I rather believe in that sort of thing. I want to confront him with the result of his crime."

The Professor stopped short. His eyes were half closed.

"It is too horrible!" he muttered.

"Nothing could be too horrible for an inhuman being like this," Quest answered tersely. "I want to see whether he'll commit himself."

They passed into the bedchamber. Quest signed to the keeper to bring Craig to the side of the four-poster. Then he drew down the sheet.

"Is that your work?" he asked sternly.

Craig, up till then, had spoken no word. He had shambled to the bedside, a broken, yet in a sense, a stolid figure. The sight of the dead man, however, seemed to galvanise him into sudden and awful vitality. He threw up his arms. His eyes were horrible as they glared at those small black marks. His lips moved, helplessly at first. Then at last he spoke.

"Strangled!" he cried. "One more!"

"That is your work," the criminologist said firmly.

Craig collapsed. He would have fallen bodily to the ground if Middleton's grip had not kept him up. Quest bent over him. It was clear that he had fainted. They led him from the room.

"We'd better lock him up until the police arrive," Quest suggested. "I suppose there is a safe place somewhere?"

The Professor awoke from his stupor.

"Let me show you," he begged. "I know the way. We've a subterranean hiding-place which no criminal on this earth could escape from."

They led him down to the back part of the house, a miserable, dejected procession. Holding candles over their heads, they descended two sets of winding stone steps, passed along a gloomy corridor till they came to a heavy oak door, which Moreton, the butler, who carried the keys, opened with some difficulty. It led into a dry cellar which had the appearance of a prison cell. There was a single bench set against the wall. Quest looked around quickly.

"This place has been used before now, in the old days, for malefactors," the Professor remarked. "He'll be safe there. Craig," he added, his voice trembling, "Craig—I—I can't speak to you. How could you!"

There was no answer. Craig's face was buried in his hands. They left him there and turned the key.

2.

Quest stood, frowning, upon the pavement, gazing at the obviously empty house. He looked once more at the slip of paper which Lenora had given him. There was no possibility of any mistake:—

"Mrs. Willet,
157 Elsmere Road,

Hampstead."

This was 157 and the house was empty. After a moment's hesitation he rang the bell at the adjoining door. A woman who had been watching him from the front room, answered the summons at once.

"Can you tell me," he enquired, "what has become of the lady who used to live at 157—Mrs. Willet?"

"She's moved," was the uncompromising reply.

"Do you know where to?" Quest asked eagerly.

"West Kensington—Number 17 Princes' Court Road. There was a young lady here yesterday afternoon enquiring for her."

Quest raised his hat. It was a relief, at any rate, to have news of Lenora.

"I am very much obliged to you, madam."

"You're welcome!" was the terse reply.

Quest gave the new address to the taxi-driver and was scarcely able to restrain his impatience during the long drive. They pulled up at last before a somewhat dingy-looking house. He rang the bell, which was answered by a trim-looking little maid-servant.

"Is Mrs. Willet in?" he enquired.

The maid-servant stood on one side to let him pass. Almost at the same moment, the door of the front room opened and a pleasant-looking elderly lady appeared.

"I am Mrs. Willet," she announced.

"I am Mr. Quest," the criminologist told her quickly. "You may have heard your niece, Lenora, speak of me."

"Then perhaps you can tell me what has become of her?" Mrs. Willet observed.

"Isn't she here?"

Mrs. Willet shook her head.

"I had a telegram from her from New York to say that she was coming, but I've seen nothing of her as yet."

"You've changed your address, you know," Quest reminded her, after a moment's reflection.

"I wrote and told her," Mrs. Willet began. "After all, though," she went on thoughtfully, "I am not sure whether she could have had the letter. But if she went up to Hampstead, any one would tell her where I had moved to. There's no secret about me."

"Lenora did go up to 157 Elsmere Road yesterday," Quest told her. "They gave her your address here, as they have just given it to me."

"Then what's become of the child?" Mrs. Willet demanded.

Quest, whose brain was working quickly, scribbled upon one of his cards the address of the hotel where he had taken rooms, and passed it over.

"Why Lenora didn't come on to you here I can't imagine," he

said. "However, I'll go back to the hotel where she was to spend the night after she arrived. She may have gone back there. That's my address, Mrs. Willet. If you hear anything, I wish you'd let me know. Lenora's quite a particular friend of mine and I am a little anxious."

Mrs. Willet smiled knowingly.

"I'll let you know certainly, sir," she promised, "and glad I shall be to hear of Lenora's being comfortably settled, after that first unfortunate affair of hers. You'll excuse me a moment. I'm a little slower in my wits than you. Did you say that Lenora was at Hampstead yesterday afternoon and they told her my address?"

"That's so," Quest admitted.

The woman's face grew troubled.

"I don't like it," she said simply.

"Neither do I," Quest agreed.

"London's no place, nowadays," Mrs. Willet continued, "for girls as pretty as Lenora to be wandering about in. Such tales as there have been lately in the Sunday papers as makes one's blood run cold if one can believe them all."

"You don't have any—what we call the White Slave Traffic—over here, do you?" Quest asked quickly.

"I can't say that I've ever come across any case of it myself, sir," the old lady replied. "I was housekeeper to the Duke of Merioneth for fifty years, and where we lived we didn't hear much about London and London ways. You see, I never came to the town house. But since I retired and came up here, and took to reading the Sunday papers, I begin to be thankful that my ways have been country ways all my life."

"No need to alarm ourselves, I'm sure," Quest intervened, making his way towards the door. "Lenora is a particularly capable young lady. I feel sure she'd look after herself. I am going right back to the hotel, Mrs. Willet, and I'll let you know directly I hear anything."

"I shall be very anxious, Mr. Quest," she reminded him, earnestly, "very anxious indeed. Lenora was my sister's favourite child, and my sister—"

Quest had already opened the front door for himself and passed out. He sprang into the taxi which he had kept waiting.

"Clifford's Hotel in Payne Street," he told the man sharply.

He lit a cigar and smoked furiously all the way, throwing it on to the pavement as he hurried into the quiet private hotel which a fellow-passenger on the steamer had recommended as being suitable for Lenora's one night alone in town.

"Can you tell me if Miss Lenora Macdougal is staying here?" he asked at the office.

The woman shook her head.

"Miss Macdougal stayed here the night before last," she said, "and her luggage is waiting for orders. She left here yesterday afternoon to go to her aunt's, and promised to send for her things later on during the day. There they stand, all ready for her."

Quest followed the direction of the woman's finger. Lenora's familiar little belongings were there, standing in a corner of the hall.

"You haven't heard from her, then, since she went out yesterday afternoon?" he asked, with sinking heart.

"No, sir!"

"What time did she go?"

"Directly after an early lunch. It must have been about two o'clock."

Quest hurried away. So after all there was some foundation for this queer sense of depression which had been hovering about him for the last few days!

"Scotland Yard," he told the taxi-driver.

He thrust another cigar between his teeth but forgot to light it. He was amazed at his own sensations, conscious of fears and emotions of which he would never have believed himself capable. He gave in his card, and after a few moments' delay he was shown into the presence of one of the chiefs of the Detective Department, who greeted him warmly.

"My name is Hardaway," the latter announced. "Glad to meet you, Mr. Quest. We've heard of you over here. Take a chair."

"To tell you the truth," Quest replied, "my business is a little urgent."

"Glad to hear you've got that fellow Craig," Mr. Hardaway continued. "Ridiculous the way he managed to slip through our fingers. I understand you've got him all right now, though?"

"He is safe enough," Quest declared, "but to tell you the truth, I'm worried about another little affair."

"Go on," the other invited.

"My assistant, a young lady, Miss Lenora Macdougal, has disappeared! She and I and Professor Ashleigh left the steamer at Plymouth and travelled up in the boat train. It was stopped at Hamblin Road for the Professor and myself, and Miss Macdougal came on to London. She was staying at Clifford's Hotel in Payne Street for the night, and then going on to an aunt. Well, I've found that aunt. She was expecting the girl but the girl never appeared. I have been to the hotel where she spent the night before last, and I find that she left there at two o'clock and left word that she would send for her luggage. She didn't arrive at her aunt's, and the luggage is still uncalled for."

The Inspector was at first only politely interested. It probably occurred to him that young ladies have been known before now to disappear from their guardians for a few hours without serious results.

"Where did this aunt live?" he enquired.

"Number 17, Princes' Court Road, West Kensington," Quest replied. "She had just moved there from Elsmere Road, Hampstead. I went first to Hampstead. Lenora had been there and learnt her aunt's correct address in West Kensington. I followed on to West Kensington and found that her aunt was still awaiting her."

A new interest seemed suddenly to have crept into Hardaway's manner.

"Let me see," he said, "if she left Clifford's Hotel about two, she would have been at Hampstead about half past two. She would waste a few minutes in making enquiries, then she probably left Hampstead for West Kensington, say, at a quarter to three."

"Somewhere between those two points," Quest pointed out, "she has disappeared."

"Give me at once a description of the young lady," Mr. Hardaway demanded.

Quest drew a photograph from his pocket and passed it silently over. The official glanced at it and down at some papers which lay before him. Then he looked at the clock.

"Mr. Quest," he said, "it is just possible that your visit here has been an exceedingly opportune one."

He snatched his hat from a rack and took Quest by the arm.

"Come along with me," he continued. "We'll talk as we go."

They entered a taxi and drove off westwards.

"Mr. Quest," he went on, "for two months we have been on the track of a man and a woman whom we strongly suspect of having decoyed half a dozen perfectly respectable young women, and shipped them out to South America."

"The White Slave Traffic!" Quest gasped.

"Something of the sort," Hardaway admitted. "Well, we've been closing the net around this interesting couple, and last night I had information brought to me upon which we are acting this afternoon. We've had them watched and it seems that they were sitting in a tea place about three o'clock yesterday afternoon, when a young woman entered who was obviously a stranger to London. You see, the time fits in exactly, if your assistant decided to stop on her way to Kensington and get some tea. She asked the woman at the desk the best means of getting to West Kensington without taking a taxi-cab. Her description tallies exactly with the photograph you have shown me. The woman whom my men were watching addressed her and offered to show her the way. They left the place together. My men followed them. The house has been watched ever since and we are raiding it this afternoon. You and I will just be in time."

"You've left her there since yesterday afternoon? You've left her there all night?" Quest exclaimed. "My God!"

Hardaway touched his arm soothingly.

"Don't worry, Mr. Quest," he said. "We don't want the woman alone; we want the man, too. Now the man was away. He only visits the house occasionally, and I am given to understand that he is a member of several West End clubs. When the two women entered that house yesterday afternoon, there wasn't a soul in it except servants. The woman telephoned for the man. He never turned up last night nor this morning. He arrived at that house twenty minutes ago."

Quest drew a little breath.

"It gave me a turn," he admitted. "Say, this is a slow taxi!"

The Inspector glanced out of the window.

"If this is the young lady you're looking for," he said, "you'll be in plenty of time, never fear. What I am hoping is that we may be able to catch my fellows before they try to rush the place. You understand, with your experience, Mr. Quest, that there are two things we've got to think of. We not only want to put our hand upon the guilty persons, but we want to bring the crime home to them."

"I see that," Quest assented. "How much farther is this place?"

"We're there," Hardaway told him.

He stopped the cab and they got out. A man who seemed to be strolling aimlessly along, reading a newspaper, suddenly joined them.

"Well, Dixon?" his chief exclaimed.

The man glanced around.

"I've got three men round at the back, Mr. Hardaway," he said. "It's impossible for any one to leave the place."

"Anything fresh to tell me?"

"There are two men in the place besides the governor—butler and footman, dressed in livery. They sleep out, and only come after lunch."

Hardaway paused to consider for a moment.

"Look here," Quest suggested, "they know all you, of course, and they'll never let you in until they're forced to. I'm a stranger. Let me go. I'll get in all right."

Hardaway peered around the corner of the street.

"All right," he assented. "We shall follow you up pretty closely, though."

Quest stepped back into the taxi and gave the driver a direction. When he emerged in front of the handsome grey stone house he seemed to have become completely transformed. There was a fatuous smile upon his lips. He crossed the pavement with difficulty, stumbled up the steps, and held on to the knocker with one hand while he consulted a slip of paper. He had scarcely rung the bell before a slightly parted curtain in the front room fell together, and a moment later the door was opened by a man in the livery of a butler, but with the face and physique of a prize-fighter.

"Lady of the house," Quest demanded. "Want to see the lady of the house."

Almost immediately he was conscious of a woman standing in the hall before him. She was quietly but handsomely dressed; her hair was grey; her smile, although a little peculiar, was benevolent.

"You had better come in," she invited. "Please do not stand in the doorway."

Quest, however, who heard the footsteps of the others behind him, loitered there for a moment.

"You're the lady whose name is on this piece of paper?" he demanded. "This place is all right, eh?"

"I really do not know what you mean," the woman replied coldly, "but if you will come inside, I will talk to you in the drawing-room."

Quest, as though stumbling against the front-door, had it now wide open, and in a moment the hall seemed full. The woman shrieked. The butler suddenly sprang upon the last man to enter, and sent him spinning down the steps. Almost at that instant there was a scream from upstairs. Quest took a running jump and went up the stairs four at a time. The butler suddenly snatched the revolver from Hardaway's hand and fired blindly in front of him, missing Quest only by an inch or two.

"Don't be a fool, Karl!" the woman called out. "The game's up. Take it quietly."

Once more the shriek rang through the house. Quest rushed to the door of the room from whence it came, tried the handle and found it locked. He ran back a little way and charged it. From inside he could hear a turmoil of voices. White with rage and passion, he pushed and kicked madly. There was the sound of a shot from inside, a bullet came through the door within an inch of his head, then the crash of broken crockery and a man's groan. With a final effort Quest dashed the door in and staggered into the room. Lenora was standing in the far corner, the front of her dress torn and blood upon her lip. She held a revolver in her hand and was covering a man whose head and hands were bleeding. Around him were the debris of a broken jug.

"Mr. Quest!" she screamed. "Don't go near him—I've got him covered. I'm all right."

Quest drew a long breath. The man who stood glaring at him was well-dressed and still young. He was unarmed, however, and Quest secured him in a moment.

"The girl's mad!" he said sullenly. "No one wanted to do her any harm."

Hardaway and his men came trooping up the stairs. Quest relinquished his prisoner and went over to Lenora.

"I've been so frightened," she sobbed. "They got me in here—they told me that this was the street in which my aunt lived—and they wouldn't let me go. The woman was horrible. And this afternoon this man came. The brute!"

"He hasn't hurt you?" Quest demanded fiercely, as he passed his arm around her.

She shook her head.

"He would never have done that," she murmured. "I had my hatpin in my gown and I should have killed myself first."

Quest turned to Hardaway.

"I'll take the young lady away," he said. "You know where to find us."

Hardaway nodded and Quest supported Lenora down the stairs and into the taxi-cab, which was still waiting. She leaned back and he passed his arm around her.

"Are you faint?" he asked anxiously, as they drove towards the hotel.

"A little," she admitted, "not very. But oh! I am so thankful—so thankful!"

He leaned a little nearer towards her. She looked at him wonderingly. Suddenly the colour flushed into her cheeks.

"I couldn't have done without you, Lenora," he whispered, as he kissed her.

Lenora had almost recovered when they reached the hotel. Walking up and down they found the Professor. His face, as he came towards them, was almost pitiful. He scarcely noticed Lenora's deshabille, which was in a measure concealed by the cloak which Quest had thrown around her.

"My friend!" he exclaimed—"Mr. Quest! It is the devil incarnate against whom we fight!"

"What do you mean?" Quest demanded.

The Professor wrung his hands.

"I put him in our James the Second prison," he declared. "Why should I think of the secret passage? No one has used it for a hundred years. He found it, learnt the trick—"

"You mean," Quest cried—

"He has escaped!" the Professor broke in. "Craig has escaped again! They are searching for him high and low, but he has gone!"

Quest's arm tightened for a moment in Lenora's. It was curious how he seemed to have lost at that moment all sense of proportion. Lenora was safe—the relief of that one thought overshadowed everything else in the world.

"The fellow can't get far," he muttered.

"Who knows?" the Professor replied dolefully. "The passage—I'll show it you some day and you'll see how wonderful his escape has been—leads on to the first floor of the house. He must have got into my dressing-room, for his old clothes are there and he went away in a suit of mine. No one has seen him or knows anything about him. All that the local police can find out is that a man answering somewhat his description caught the morning train for Southampton from Hamblin Roads."

They had been standing together in a little recess of the hall. Suddenly Lenora, whose face was turned towards the entrance doors, gave a little cry. She took a quick step forward.

"Laura!" she exclaimed, wonderingly. "Why, it's Laura!"

They all turned around. A young woman had just entered the hotel, followed by a porter carrying some luggage. Her arm was in a sling and there was a bandage around her forehead. She walked, too, with the help of a stick. She recognized them at once and waved it gaily.

"Hullo, you people?" she cried. "Soon run you to earth, eh?"

They were for a moment dumbfounded; Lenora was the first to find words. "But when did you start, Laura?" she asked. "I thought you were too ill to move for weeks."

The girl smiled contemptuously.

"I left three days after you, on the *Kaiser Frederic*," she replied. "There was some trouble at Plymouth, and we came into Southampton early this morning, and here I am. But, before we go any farther, tell me about Craig?"

"We've had him," Quest confessed, "and lost him again. He escaped last night."

"Where from?" Laura asked.

"Hamblin House."

"Is that anywhere near the south coast?" the girl demanded excitedly.

"It's not far away," Quest replied quickly. "Why?"

"I'll tell you why," Laura explained. "I was as sure of it as any one could be. Craig passed me in Southampton Water this morning, being rowed out to a steamer. Not only that but he recognized me. I saw him draw back and hide his face, but somehow I couldn't believe that it was really he. I was just coming down the gangway and I nearly fell into the sea, I was so surprised."

Quest was already turning over the pages of a time-table.

"What was the steamer?" he demanded.

"I found out," Laura told him. "I tell you, I was so sure of it's being Craig that I made no end of enquiries. It was the *Barton*, bound for India, with first stop at Port Said."

"When does she sail?" Quest asked.

"Tonight—somewhere about seven," Laura replied.

Quest glanced at the clock and threw down the time-table. He turned towards the door. They all followed him.

"I'm for Southampton," he announced. "I'm going to try to get on board that steamer before she sails. Lenora, you'd better go upstairs and lie down. They'll give you a room here. Don't you stir out till I come back. Professor, what about you?"

"I shall accompany you," the Professor declared. "The discomforts of travelling without luggage are nothing compared with the importance of discovering this human fiend."

"Luggage—pshaw!" Laura exclaimed. "Who cares about that?"

"And nothing," Lenora declared firmly, as she caught at Quest's arm, "would keep me away."

"I'll telephone to Scotland Yard, in case they care to send a man down," Quest decided. "We must remember, though," he reminded them, "that it will very likely be a wild-goose chase."

"It won't be the first," Laura observed grimly, "but Craig's on board that ship all right."...

They caught a train to Southampton, where they were joined by a man from Scotland Yard. The little party drove as quickly as possible to the docks.

"Where does the *Barton* start from?" Quest asked the pier-master.

The man pointed a little way down the harbor.

"She's not in dock, sir," he said. "She's lying out yonder. You'll barely catch her, I'm afraid," he added, glancing at the clock.

They hurried to the edge of the quay.

"Look here," Quest cried, raising his voice, "I'll give a ten pound note to any one who gets me out to the *Barton* before she sails."

The little party were almost thrown into a tug, and in a few minutes they were skimming across the smooth water. Just as they reached the steamer, however, she began to move.

"Run up alongside," Quest ordered.

"She won't stop, sir," the Captain of the tug replied doubtfully. "She is an hour late, as it is."

"Do as I tell you," Quest insisted.

They raced along by the side of the great steamer. An officer came to the rail and shouted down to them.

"What do you want?"

"The Captain," Quest replied.

The Captain came down from the bridge, where he had been conferring with the pilot.

"Keep away from the side there," he shouted. "Who are you?"

"We are in search of a desperate criminal whom we believe to be on board your steamer," Quest explained. "Please take us on board."

The Captain shook his head.

"Are you from Scotland Yard?" he asked. "Have you got your warrant?"

"We are from America," Quest answered, "but we've got a Scotland Yard man with us, and a warrant, right enough."

"Any extradition papers?"

"No time to get them yet," Quest replied, "but the man's wanted for murder."

"Are you from the New York police?"

Quest shook his head.

"I am a private detective," he announced. "I am working in conjunction with the New York Police."

The Captain shook his head.

"I am over an hour late," he said, "and it's costing me fifty pounds a minute. If I take you on board, you'll have to come right along with me, unless you find the fellow before we've left your tug behind."

Quest turned around.

"Will you risk it?" he asked.

"Yes!" they all replied.

"We're coming, Captain," Quest decided.

A rope ladder was let down. The steamer began to slow.

"Can you girls manage it?" Quest asked doubtfully.

Laura smiled.

"I should say so," she replied. "I can go up that with only one arm. You watch me!"

They cheered her on board the steamer as she hobbled up. The others followed. The tug, the crew of which had been already well paid, raced along by the side. The Captain spoke once more to the pilot and came down from the bridge.

"I'm forced to go full speed ahead to cross the bar," he told Quest. "I'm sorry, but the tide's just on the turn."

They looked at one another a little blankly.

The Professor, however, beamed upon them all.

"I have always understood," he said, "that Port Said is a most interesting place."

CHAPTER XI

THE SHIP OF HORROR

Quest leaned a little forward and gazed down the line of steamer chairs. The Professor, in a borrowed overcoat and cap, was reclining at full length, studying a book on seagulls which he had found in the library. Laura and Lenora were both dozing tranquilly. Mr. Harris of Scotland Yard was deep in a volume of detective stories.

"As a pleasure cruise," Quest remarked grimly, "this little excursion seems to be a complete success."

Laura opened her eyes at once.

"Trying to get my goat again, eh?" she retorted. "I suppose that's what you're after. Going to tell me, I suppose, that it wasn't Craig I saw board this steamer?"

"We are all liable to make mistakes," Quest observed, "and I am inclined to believe that this is one of yours."

Laura's expression was a little dogged.

"If he's too clever for you and Mr. Harris," she said, "I can't help that. I only know that he came on board. My eyes are the one thing in life I do believe."

"If you'll excuse my saying so, Miss Laura," Harris ventured, leaning deferentially towards her, "there isn't a passenger on board this ship, or a servant, or one of the crew, whom we haven't seen. We've been into every stateroom, and we've even searched the hold. We've been over the ship, backwards and forwards. The Captain's own steward has been our guide, and we've conducted an extra search on our own account. Personally, I must say I have come to the same conclusion as Mr. Quest. At the present moment there is no such person as the man we are looking for, on board this steamer."

"Then he either changed on to another one," Laura declared obstinately, "or else he jumped overboard."

Harris, who was a very polite man, gazed thoughtfully seaward. Quest smiled.

"When Laura's set on a thing," he remarked, "she takes a little moving. What do you think about it, Professor?"

The Professor laid down his book, keeping his finger in the place. He had the air of a man perfectly content with himself and his surroundings.

"My friend," he said, "I boarded this steamer with only one thought in my mind—Craig. At the present moment, I feel myself compelled to plead guilty to a complete change of outlook. The horrors of the last few months seem to have passed from my brain like a dream. I lie here, I watch these white-winged birds wheeling around us, I watch the sunshine make jewels of the spray, I breathe this wonderful air, I relax my body to the slow, soothing movements of the boat, and I feel a new life stealing through me. Is Craig really on board? Was it really he whom Miss Laura here saw? At the present moment, I really do not care. I learn from the steward, who arranged my bath this morning, that we are bound for India. I am very glad to hear it. It is some time since I saw Bombay, and the thought of these long days of complete peace fills me with a most indescribable satisfaction."

Quest grunted a little as he knocked the ash from his cigar.

"Not much of the bloodhound about the Professor," he remarked. "What about you, Lenora?"

She smiled at him.

"I agree entirely with the Professor," she murmured, "except that I am not quite so sure that I appreciate the rhythmical movement of the boat as he seems to. For the rest, I have just that feeling that I would like to go on and on and forget all the horrible things that have happened, to live in a sort of dream, and wake up in a world from which Craig had vanished altogether."

"Enervating effect this voyage seems to be having upon you all," Quest grumbled. "Even Harris there looks far too well contented with life."

The detective smiled. He was young and fresh-coloured, with a shrewd but pleasant face. He glanced involuntarily at Laura as he spoke.

"Well, Mr. Quest," he said, "I didn't bring you on the steamer so I don't feel any responsibility about it, but I must confess that I am enjoying the trip. I haven't had a holiday this year."

Quest struggled to his feet and threw back the rug in his chair.

"If you all persist in turning this into a pleasure cruise," he remarked, "I suppose I'll have to alter my own point of view. Come on, Harris, you and I promised to report to the Captain this morning. I don't suppose he'll be any too pleased with us. Let's get through with it."

The two men walked down the deck together. They found the Captain alone in his room, with a chart spread out in front of him and a pair of compasses in his hand. He turned round and greeted them.

"Well?"

"No luck, sir," Quest announced. "Your steward has given us every assistance possible and we have searched the ship thoroughly. Unless he has found a hiding place unknown to your steward, and not apparent to us, the man is not on board."

The Captain frowned slightly.

"You are not suggesting that that is possible, I suppose?"

Quest did not at once reply. He was thinking of Laura's obstinacy.

"Personally," he admitted, "I should not have believed it possible.

The young lady of our party, however, who declares that she saw Craig board the steamer, is quite immovable."

The Captain rose to his feet. He was a man of medium height, strongly built, with short brown beard and keen blue eyes.

"This matter must be cleared up entirely," he declared brusquely. "If you will excuse me for a moment, I will talk to the young lady myself."

He walked firmly down the deck to where the two girls were seated, and paused in front of Laura.

"So you're the young lady," he remarked, touching his cap, "who thinks that I come to sea with criminals stowed away on my ship?"

"I don't know what your habits are, Captain," Laura replied, "but this particular criminal boarded your ship all right in Southampton Harbour."

"Anything wrong with your eyesight?" the Captain enquired blandly.

"No," Laura assured him. "I saw the man, saw him just as plainly as I see you now."

"Do you know," the Captain persisted, "that Mr. Quest and Mr. Harris have searched every nook and corner of the ship? They have had an absolutely free hand, and my own steward has been their guide. They have seen every man, boy, woman and animal amongst my crew or passengers."

"They've been fooled somehow," Laura muttered.

The Captain frowned. He was on the point of a sharp rejoinder when he met Laura's eyes. She was smiling very faintly and there was something in her expression which changed his whole point of view.

"I'll go and make a few enquiries myself," he declared. "See you at dinner-time, I hope, young ladies."

"If you keep her as steady as this," Laura promised, "there are hopes."

He disappeared along the deck, and presently re-entered his room, where Harris and Quest were waiting for him. He was fol-lowed by his steward, an under-sized man with pallid complexion and nervous manner. He closed the door behind him.

"Brown," he said, turning to the steward, "I understand you to say that you have taken these gentlemen into every corner of the ship, that you have ransacked every possible hiding-place, that you have given them every possible opportunity of searching for themselves?"

"That is quite true, sir," the man acknowledged.

"You agree with me that it is impossible for any one to remain hidden in this ship?"

"Absolutely, sir."

"You hear, gentlemen?" the Captain continued. "I really can do no more. It is perfectly clear to me that the man you are seeking is not on my ship. Your very charming young lady friend seems to think it impossible that she could have been mistaken, but as a matter of fact she was. If I might take the liberty, Mr. Quest, I would suggest that you ask her, at any rate, to keep her suspicions to herself."

"I'll see she doesn't talk," Quest promised. "Very sorry to have given you all this trouble, I'm sure."

"It's no trouble," the Captain replied, "and apart from the disagreeable nature of your business, I am delighted to have you on board. If you can forget your suspicions about this fellow Craig, I shall do my best to make your trip a pleasant one as far as Port Said, or on to India if you decide to take the trip with me."

"Very good of you, Captain, I'm sure," Quest pronounced. "We shall go on keeping our eyes open, of course, but apart from that we'll forget the fellow."

The Captain nodded.

"I am coming down to dinner tonight," he announced, "and shall hope to find you in your places. What the mischief are you hanging about for, Brown?" he asked, turning to the steward, who was standing by with a carpet-sweeper in his hand.

"Room wants cleaning out badly, sir."

The Captain glanced distastefully at the carpet-sweeper.

"Do it when I am at dinner, then," he ordered, "and take that damned thing away."

The steward obeyed promptly. Quest and Harris followed him down the deck.

"Queer-looking fellow, that," the latter remarked. "Doesn't seem quite at his ease, does he?"

"Seemed a trifle over-anxious, I thought, when he was showing us round the ship," Quest agreed.

"M-m," Harris murmured softly, "as the gentleman who wrote the volume of detective stories I am reading puts it, we'd better keep our eye on Brown."...

The Captain, who was down to dinner unusually early, rose to welcome Quest's little party and himself arranged the seats.

"You, Miss Lenora," he said, "will please sit on my left, and you, Miss Laura, on my right. Mr. Quest, will you sit on the other side of Miss Laura, and Mr. Harris two places down on my left. There is an old lady who expects to be at the table, but the steward tells me she hasn't been in yet."

They settled down into the places arranged for them. Harris was looking a little glum. Lenora and Quest exchanged a meaning glance.

"I'm not sure that I appreciate this arrangement," Harris whispered to his neighbour.

"You may be candid," Lenora replied, "but you aren't very polite, are you?"

Harris almost blushed as he realized his slip.

"I am sorry," he said, "but to tell you the truth," he added, glancing towards Quest, "I fancied that you were feeling about the same."

"We women are poor dissemblers," Lenora murmured. "Do look how angry this old woman seems."

An elderly lady, dressed in somewhat oppressive black, with a big cameo brooch at her throat and a black satin bag in her hand, was being shown by the steward to a seat by Quest's side. She acknowledged the Captain's greeting acidly.

"Good evening, Captain," she said. "I understood from the second steward that the seat on your right hand would be reserved for me. I am Mrs. Foston Rowe."

The Captain received the announcement calmly.

"Very pleased to have you at the table, madam," he replied. "As to the seating, I leave that entirely to the steward. I never interfere myself."

Laura pinched his arm, and Lenora glanced away to hide a smile. Mrs. Foston Rowe studied the menu disapprovingly.

"Hors d'oeuvres," she declared, "I never touch. No one knows how long they've been opened. Bouillon—I will have some bouillon, steward."

"In one moment, madam."

The Professor just then came ambling along towards the table.

"I fear that I am a few moments late," he remarked, as he took the chair next to Mrs. Foston Rowe. "I offer you my apologies, Captain. I congratulate you upon your library. I have discovered a most interesting book upon the habits of seagulls. It kept me engrossed until the very last moment."

"Very disagreeable habits, those I've noticed," Mrs. Foston Rowe sniffed.

"Madam," the Professor assured her, "yours is but a superficial view. For myself, I must confess that the days upon which I learn something new in life are days of happiness for me. Today is an example; I have learnt something new about seagulls, and I am hungry."

"Well, you'll have to stay hungry a long time at this table, then," Mrs. Foston Rowe snapped. "Seems to me that the service is going to be abominable."

The steward, who had just arrived, presented a cup of bouillon to Quest. The others had all been served. Quest stirred it thoughtfully.

"And as to the custom," Mrs. Foston Rowe continued, "of serving gentlemen before ladies, it is, I suppose, peculiar to this steamer."

Quest hastily laid down his spoon, raised the cup of bouillon and presented it with a little bow to his neighbour.

"Pray allow me, madam," he begged. "The steward was to blame."

Mrs. Foston Rowe did not hesitate for a moment. She broke up some toast in the bouillon and commenced to sip it.

"Your politeness will at least teach them a lesson," she said. "I am used to travel by the P. & O. and from what I have seen of this steamer—"

The spoon suddenly went clattering from her fingers. She caught at the sides of the table, there was a strange look in her face. With scarcely a murmur she fell back in her seat. Quest leaned hurriedly forward.

"Captain!" he exclaimed. "Steward! Mrs. Foston Rowe is ill."

There was a slight commotion. The Doctor came hurrying up from the other side of the salon. He bent over her and his face grew grave.

"What is it?" the Captain demanded.

The Doctor glanced at him meaningly.

"She had better be carried out," he whispered.

It was all done in a moment. There was nothing but Mrs. Foston Rowe's empty place at the table and the cup of bouillon, to remind them of what had happened.

"Was it a faint?" Lenora asked.

"We shall know directly," the Captain replied. "Better keep our places, I think. Steward, serve the dinner as usual."

The man held out his hand to withdraw the cup of bouillon, but Quest drew it towards him.

"Let it wait for a moment," he ordered.

He glanced at the Captain, who nodded back. In a few moments the Doctor reappeared. He leaned down and whispered to the Captain.

"Dead!"

The Captain gave no sign.

"Better call it heart failure," the Doctor continued. "I'll let the people know quietly. I don't in the least understand the symptoms, though."

Quest turned around.

"Doctor," he said, "I happen to have my chemical chest with me, and some special testing tubes. If you'll allow me, I'd like to examine this cup of bouillon. You might come round, too, if you will."

The Captain nodded.

"I'd better stay here for a time," he decided. "I'll follow you presently."

The service of dinner was resumed. Laura, however, sent plate after plate away. The Captain watched her anxiously.

"I can't help it," she explained. "I don't know whether you've had any talk with Mr. Quest, but we've been through some queer times lately. I guess this death business is getting on my nerves."

The Captain was startled.

"You don't for a moment connect Mrs. Foston Rowe's death

with the criminal you are in search of?" he exclaimed.

Laura sat quite still for a moment.

"The bouillon was offered first to Mr. Quest," she murmured.

The Captain called his steward.

"Where did you get the bouillon you served—that last cup especially?" he asked.

"From the pantry just as usual, sir," the man answered. "It was all served out from the same cauldron."

"Any chance of any one getting at it?"

"Quite impossible, sir!"

Laura rose to her feet.

"Sorry," she apologized, "I can't eat anything. I'm off on deck."

The Captain rose promptly.

"I'll escort you, if I may," he suggested.

Harris, too, rose from his place, after a final and regretful glance at the menu, and joined the others. The Captain, however, drew Laura's arm through his as they reached the stairs, and Harris, with a little shrug of the shoulders, made his way to Quest's stateroom. The Doctor, the Professor, Quest and Lenora were all gathered around two little tubes, which the criminologist was examining with an electric torch.

"No reaction at all," the latter muttered. "This isn't an ordinary poison, any way."

The Professor, who had been standing on one side, suddenly gave vent to a soft exclamation.

"Wait!" he whispered. "Wait! I have an idea."

He hurried off to his stateroom. The Doctor was poring over a volume of tabulated poisons. Quest was still watching his tubes. Lenora sat upon the couch. Suddenly the Professor reappeared. He was carrying a small notebook in his hand; his manner betrayed some excitement. He closed the door carefully behind him.

"I want you all," he begged, "to listen very carefully to me. You will discover the application of what I am going to read, when I am finished. Now, if you please."

They looked at him wonderingly. It was evident that the Professor was very much in earnest. He held the book a little way away from him and read slowly and distinctly.

"This," he began, "is the diary of a tour made by Craig and myself in Northern Egypt some fourteen years ago. Here is the first entry of import:—

"*Monday.* Twenty-nine miles south-east of Port Said. We have stayed for two days at a little Mongar village. I have today come to the definite conclusion that anthropoid apes were at one time denizens of this country.

"*Tuesday.* Both Craig and I have been a little uneasy today.

These Mongars into whose encampment we have found our way, are one of the strangest and fiercest of the nomad tribes. They are descended, without a doubt, from the ancient Mongolians, who invaded this country some seven hundred years before Christ. They have interbred with the Arabs to some extent, but have preserved in a marvellous way their individuality as a race. They have the narrow eyes and the thick nose base of the pure Oriental; also much of his cunning. One of their special weaknesses seems to be the invention of the most hideous forms of torture, which they apply remorselessly to their enemies."

"Pleasant sort of people," Quest muttered.

"We escaped with our lives," the Professor explained earnestly, "from these people, only on account of an incident which you will find in this next paragraph:—"

"*Wednesday.* This has been a wonderful day for as, chiefly owing to what I must place on record as an act of great bravery by Craig, my servant. Early this morning, a man-eating lion found his way into the encampment. The Mongars behaved like arrant cowards. They fled right and left, leaving the Chief's little daughter, Feerda, at the brute's mercy. Craig, who is by no means an adept in the use of firearms, chased the animal as he was making off with the child, and, more by good luck than anything else, managed to wound it mortally. He brought the child back to the encampment just as the Chief and the warriors of the tribe returned from a hunting expedition. Our position here is now absolutely secure. We are treated like gods, and, appreciating my weakness for all matters of science, the Chief has today explained to me many of the secret mysteries of the tribe. Amongst other things, he has shown me a wonderful secret poison, known only to this tribe, which they call Veedemzoo. It brings almost instant death, and is exceedingly difficult to trace. The addition of sugar causes a curious condensation and resolves it almost to a white paste. The only antidote is a substance which they use here freely, and which is exactly equivalent to our camphor."

The Professor closed his book. Quest promptly rang the bell.

"Some sugar," he ordered, turning to the steward.

They waited in absolute silence. The suggestion which the Professor's disclosure had brought to them was stupefying, even Quest's fingers, as a moment or two later he rubbed two knobs of sugar together so that the particles should fall into the tubes of bouillon, shook. The result was magical. The bouillon turned to a strange shade of grey and began slowly to thicken.

"It is the Mongar poison!" the Professor cried, with breaking voice.

They all looked at one another.

"Craig must be here amongst us," Quest muttered.

"And the bouillon," Lenora cried, clasping Quest's arm, "the bouillon was meant for you!"...

There seemed to be, somehow, amongst all of them, a curious indisposition to discuss this matter. Suddenly Lenora, who was sitting on the lounge underneath the porthole, put out her hand and picked up a card which was lying by her side. She glanced at it, at first curiously. Then she shrieked.

"A message!" she cried. "A message from the Hands! Look!"

They crowded around her. In that same familiar handwriting was scrawled across the face of the card these few words—

"To Sanford Quest.
     "You have escaped this time by a chance of fortune, not because your wits are keen, not because of your own shrewdness; simply because Fate willed it. It will not be for long."
Underneath was the drawing of the clenched hands.

"There is no longer any doubt," Lenora said calmly. "Craig is on board. He must have been on deck a few minutes ago. It was his hand which placed this card in the porthole.... Listen! What's that?"

There was a scream from the deck. They all recognised Laura's voice. Harris was out of the stateroom first but they were all on deck within ten seconds. Laura was standing with one hand clasping the rail, her hand fiercely outstretched towards the lower part of the promenade deck. Through the darkness they heard the sound of angry voices.

"What is it, Laura?" Lenora cried.

She swung round upon them.

"Craig!" she cried. "Craig! I saw his face as I sat in my chair there, talking to the Captain. I saw a man's white face—nothing else. He must have been leaning over the rail. He heard me call out and he disappeared."

The Captain came slowly out of the shadows, limping a little and followed by his steward, who was murmuring profuse apologies.

"Did you find him?" Laura demanded eagerly.

"I did not," the Captain replied, a little tersely. "I ran into Brown here and we both had a shake-up."

"But he was there—a second ago!" Laura cried out.

"I beg your pardon, miss," Brown ventured, "but the deck's closed at the end, as you can see, with sail-cloth, and I was leaning over the rail myself when you shrieked. There wasn't any one else near me, and no one can possibly have passed round the deck, as you can see plainly for yourself."

Laura stood quite still.

"What doors are there on the side?" she asked.

"The doors of my room only," the Captain replied, a little shortly. "It was Brown you saw, of course. He was standing exactly where you thought you saw Craig."

Laura walked to the end of the deck and back.

"Very well, then," she said, "you people had better get a strait-waistcoat ready for me. If I didn't see Craig there, I'm going off my head."

Quest had disappeared some seconds ago. He came thoughtfully back, a little later.

"Captain," he asked, "what shall you say if I tell you that I have proof that Craig is on board?"

The Captain glanced at Laura and restrained himself.

"I should probably say a great many things which I should regret afterwards," he replied grimly.

"Sit down and we'll tell you what has happened in my room," Quest continued.

He told the story, calmly and without remark. The Captain held his head.

"Of course, I'm convinced that I am a sane man," he said, "but this sounds more like a Munchausen story than anything I've ever heard. I suppose you people are all real? You are in earnest about this, aren't you? It isn't a gigantic joke?"

"We are in deadly earnest," the Professor pronounced gravely.

"I have been down to the pantry," Quest went on. "The porthole has been open all day. It was just possible for a man to have reached the cups of bouillon as they were prepared. That isn't the point, however. Craig is cunning and clever enough for any devilish scheme on earth, and that card proves that he is on board."

"The ship shall be searched," the Captain declared, "once more. We'll look into every crack and every cupboard."

Lenora turned away with a little shiver. It was one of her rare moments of weakness.

"You won't find him! You won't ever find him!" she murmured. "And I am afraid!"

Lenora grasped the rails of the steamer and glanced downwards at the great barge full of Arab sailors and merchandise. In the near background were the docks of Port Said. It was their first glimpse of Eastern atmosphere and colour.

"I can't tell you how happy I am," she declared to Quest, "to think that this voyage is over. Every night I have gone to bed terrified."

He smiled grimly.

"Things have been quiet enough the last few days," he said. "There's Harris on this barge. Look at Laura waving to him!"

The Scotland Yard man only glanced up at them. He was occupied in leaning over towards Laura, who was on the deck below.

"If you said the word," he called out, "I wouldn't be going back, Miss Laura. I'd stick to the ship fast enough."

She laughed at him gaily.

"Not you! You're longing for your smoky old London already. You cut it out, my friend. You're a good sort, and I hope we'll meet again some day. But—"

She shook her head at him good-humouredly. He turned away, disappointed, and waved his hand to Lenora and Quest on the upper deck.

"Coming on shore, any of you?" he enquired.

"We may when the boat moves up," Quest replied. "The Professor went off on the first barge. Here he is, coming back."

A little boat had shot out from the docks, manned by a couple of Arabs. They could see the Professor seated in the stern. He was poring over a small document which he held in his hand. He waved to them excitedly.

"He's got news!" Quest muttered.

With much shouting the boat was brought to the side of the barge. The Professor was hauled up. He stumbled blindly across towards the gangway and came up the steps with amazing speed. He came straight to Quest and Lenora and gripped the former by the arm.

"Look!" he cried. "Look!"

He held out a card. Quest read it aloud:—

"There is not one amongst you with the wit of a Mongar child. Good-bye!"
"The Hands!"

"Where did you get it?" Quest demanded.

"That's the point—the whole point!" the Professor exclaimed excitedly. "He's done us! He's landed! That paper was pushed into my hand by a tall Arab, who mumbled something and hurried off across the docks. On the landing-stage, mind!"

The Captain came and put his head out of the door.

"Mr. Quest," he said, "can you spare me a moment? You can all come, if you like."

They moved up towards him. The Captain closed the door of his cabin. He pointed to a carpet-sweeper which lay against the wall.

"Look at that," he invited.

They lifted the top. Inside were several sandwiches and a small can of tea.

"What on earth is this?" Quest demanded.

The Captain, without a word, led them into his inner room. A huge lounge stood in one corner. He lifted the valance. Underneath were some crumbs.

"You see," he pointed out, "there's room there for a man to have hidden, especially if he could crawl out on deck at night. I couldn't make out why the dickens Brown was always sweeping out my room, and I took up this thing a little time ago and looked at it. This is what I found."

"Where's Brown?" Quest asked quickly.

"I rang down for the chief steward," the Captain continued, "and ordered Brown to be sent up at once. The chief steward came himself instead. It seems Brown went off without his wages but with a huge parcel of bedding, on the first barge this morning, before any one was about."

Quest groaned as he turned away.

"Captain," he declared, "I am ashamed. He has been here all the time and we've let him slip through our fingers. Girls," he went on briskly, turning towards Laura, who had just come up, "India's off. We'll catch this barge, if there's time. Our luggage can be put on shore when the boat docks."

The Captain walked gloomily with them to the gangway.

"I shall miss you all," he told Laura.

She laughed in his face.

"If you ask me, I think you'll be glad to be rid of us."

"Not of you, Miss Laura," he insisted.

She made a little grimace.

"You're as bad as Mr. Harris," she declared. "We'll come for another trip with you some day."

They left him leaning disconsolately over the rails. The Professor and Quest sat side by side on one of the trunks which was piled up on the barge.

"Professor," Quest asked, "how long would it take us to get to this Mongar village you spoke about?"

"Two or three days, if we can get camels," the other replied. "I see you agree with me, then, as to Craig's probable destination?"

Quest nodded.

"What sort of fellows are they, any way?" he asked. "Will it be safe for us to push on alone?"

"With me," the Professor assured him, "you will be safe anywhere. I speak a little of their language. I have lived with them. They are far more civilized than some of the interior tribes."

"We'll find a comfortable hotel where we can leave the girls—" Quest began.

"You can cut that out," Laura interrupted. "I don't know about the kid here, but if you think I'm going to miss a camel ride across the desert, you're dead wrong, so that's all there is to it."

Quest glanced towards Lenora. She leaned over and took his arm.

"I simply couldn't be left behind," she pleaded. "I've had quite enough of that."

"The journey will not be an unpleasant one," the Professor declared amiably, "and the riding of a camel is an accomplishment easily acquired. So far as I am aware, too, the district which we shall have to traverse is entirely peaceable."

They disembarked and were driven to the hotel, still discussing their project. Afterwards they all wandered into the bazaars, along the narrow streets, where dusky children pulled at their clothes and ran by their side, where every now and then a brown-skinned Arab, on a slow-moving camel, made his way through the throngs of veiled Turkish women, Syrians, Arabs, and Egyptians. Laura and Lenora, at any rate, attracted by the curious novelty of the scene, forgot the heat, the street smells, and the filthy clothes of the mendicants and loafers who pressed against them. They bought strange jewellery, shawls, beads and perfumes. The Professor had disappeared for some time but rejoined them later.

"It is all arranged," he announced. "I found a dragoman whom I know. We shall have four of the best camels and a small escort ready to start tomorrow morning. Furthermore, I have news. An English-man whose description precisely tallies with Craig's, started off, only an hour ago, in the same direction. This time, at any rate, Craig cannot escape us."

"He might go on past the Mongar camp," Quest suggested.

The Professor shook his head.

"The Mongar village," he explained, "is placed practically at a cul-de-sac so far as regards further progress southwards without making a detour. It is flanked by a strip of jungle and desert on either side, in which there are no wells for many miles. We shall find Craig with the Mongars."

They made their way back to the hotel, dined in a cool, bare room, and sauntered out again into the streets. The Professor led the way to a little building, outside which a man was volubly inviting all to enter.

"You shall see one of the sights of Port Said," he promised. "This is a real Egyptian dancing girl."

They took their seats in the front row of a dimly-lit, bare-looking room. The stage was dark and empty. From some unseen place came the monotonous rhythm of a single instrument. They waited for some time in vain. At last one or two lights in front were lit, the music grew more insistent. A girl who seemed to be dressed in little more than a winding veil, glided on to the stage, swaying and moving slowly to the rhythm of the monotonous music. She danced a mea-sure which none of them except the Professor had ever seen before, coming now and then so close that they could almost feel her hot breath, and Lenora felt somehow vaguely disturbed by the glitter of her eyes. An odd perfume was shaken into the air around them from her one flowing garment, through which her limbs continually flashed. Lenora looked away.

"I don't like it," she said to Quest simply.

Suddenly Laura leaned forward.

"Look at the Professor," she whispered.

They all turned their heads. A queer change seemed to have come into the Professor's face. His teeth were gleaming between his parted lips, his head was a little thrust forward, his eyes were filled with a strange, hard light. He was a transformed being, unrecognisable, perturbing. Even while they watched, the girl floated close to where he sat and leaned towards him with a queer, mocking smile. His hand suddenly descended upon her foot. She laughed still more. There was a little exclamation from Lenora. The Professor's whole frame quivered, he snatched the anklet from the girl's ankle and bent over it. She leaned towards him, a torrent of words streaming from her lips. The Professor answered her in her own language. She listened to him in amazement. The anger passed. She held out both her hands. The Professor still argued. She shook her head. Finally he placed some gold in her palms. She patted him on the cheek, laughed into his eyes, pointed behind and resumed her dancing. The anklet remained in the Professor's hand.

"Say, we'll get out of this," Quest said. "The girls have had enough."

The Professor made no objection. He led the way, holding the anklet all the time close to his eyes, and turning it round. They none of them spoke to him, yet they were all conscious of an immense sense of relief when, after they had passed into the street, he commenced to talk in his natural voice.

"Congratulate me," he said. "I have been a collector of Assyrian gold ornaments all my life. This is the one anklet I needed to complete my collection. It has the double mark of the Pharaohs. I recognised it at once. There are a thousand like it, you would think, in the bazaars there. In reality there may be, perhaps, a dozen more in all Egypt which are genuine."

They all looked at one another. Their relief had grown too poignant for words.

"Early start tomorrow," Quest reminded them.

"Home and bed for me, this moment," Laura declared.

"The camels," the Professor assented, "will be round at daybreak."

Lenora, a few nights later, looked down from the star-strewn sky which seemed suddenly to have dropped so much nearer to them, to the shadows thrown across the desert by the dancing flames of their fire.

"It is the same world, I suppose," she murmured.

"A queer little place out of the same world," Quest agreed.

"Listen to those fellows, how they chatter!"

The camel drivers and guides were sitting together in a little group, some distance away. They had finished their supper and were chattering together now, swaying back and forth, two of them at least in a state of wild excitement.

"Whatever can they be talking about?" Laura asked. "They sound as though they were going to fight every second."

The Professor smiled.

"The last one was talking about the beauty of his fat lady friend," he remarked drily. "Just before, they were discussing whether they would be given any backsheesh in addition to their pay. We are quite off the ordinary routes here, and these fellows aren't much used to Europeans."

Laura rose to her feet.

"I'm going to get a drink," she announced.

The dragoman, who had been hovering around, bowed gravely and pointed towards the waterbottles. Lenora also rose.

"I'm coming too," she decided. "It seems a sin to think of going to sleep, though. The whole place is like a great silent sea. I suppose this isn't a dream, is it, Laura?"

"There's no dream about my thirst, any way," Laura declared.

She took the horn cup from the dragoman.

"Have some yourself, if you want to, Hassan," she invited.

Hassan bowed gravely, filled a cup and drank it off. He stood for a moment perfectly still, as though something were coming over him which he failed to understand. Then his lips parted, his eyes for a moment seemed to shoot from out of his dusky skin. He threw up his arms and fell over on his side. Laura, who had only sipped her cup, threw it from her. She, too, reeled for a moment. The Professor and Quest came running up, attracted by Lenora's shriek.

"They're poisoned!" she cried.

"The Veedemzoo!" Quest shouted. "My God! Pull yourself together, Laura. Hold up for a minute."

He dashed back to their little encampment and reappeared almost immediately. He threw Laura's head back and forced some liquid down her throat.

"It's camphor," he cried. "You'll be all right, Laura. Hold on to yourself."

He swung round to where the dragoman was lying, forced his mouth open, but it was too late—the man was dead. He returned to Laura. She stumbled to her feet. She was pale, and drops of perspiration were standing on her forehead. She was able to rise to her feet, however, without assistance.

"I am all right now," she declared.

Quest felt her pulse and her forehead. They moved back to the fire.

"We are within a dozen miles or so of the Mongar village," Quest said grimly. "Do you suppose that fellow could have been watching?"

They all talked together for a time in low voices. The Professor was inclined to scout the theory of Craig having approached them.

"You must remember," he pointed out, "that the Mongars hate these fellows. It was part of my arrangement with Hassan that they should leave us when we got in sight of the Mongar Encampment. It may have been meant for Hassan. The Mongars hate the dragomen who bring tourists in this direction at all."

They talked a little while longer and finally stole away to their tents to sleep. Outside, the camel drivers talked still, chattering away, walking now and then around Hassan's body in solemn procession. Finally, one of them who seemed to have taken the lead, broke into an impassioned stream of words. The others listened. When he had finished, there was a low murmur of fierce approval. Silent-footed, as though shod in velvet, they ran to the tethered camels, stacked the provisions once more upon their backs, lashed the guns across their own shoulders. Soon they stole away—a long, ghostly procession—into the night.

"Those fellows seem to have left off their infernal chattering all of a sudden," Quest remarked lazily from inside the tent.

The Professor made no answer. He was asleep.

CHAPTER XII

A DESERT VENGEANCE

1.

Quest was the first the next morning to open his eyes, to grope his way through the tent opening and stand for a moment alone, watching the alabaster skies. Away eastwards, the faint curve of the blood-red sun seemed to be rising out of the limitless sea of sand. The light around him was pearly, almost opalescent, fading eastwards into pink. The shadows had passed away. Though the sands were still hot beneath his feet, the silent air was deliciously cool. He turned lazily around, meaning to summon the Arab who had volunteered to take Hassan's place. His arms—he had been in the act of stretching—fell to his sides. He stared incredulously at the spot where the camels had been tethered. There were no camels, no drivers, no Arabs. There was not a soul nor an object in sight except the stark body of Hassan, which they had dragged half out of sight behind a slight knoll. High up in the sky above were two little black specks, wheeling lower and lower. Quest shivered as he suddenly realised that for the first time in his life he was looking upon the winged ghouls of the desert. Lower and lower they came. He turned away with a shiver.

The Professor was still sleeping when Quest re-entered the tent. He woke him up and beckoned him to come outside.

"Dear me!" the former exclaimed genially, as he adjusted his glasses, "I am not sure that my toilet—however, the young ladies, I imagine, are not yet astir. You did well to call me, Quest. This is the rose dawn of Egypt. I have watched it from solitudes such as you have never dreamed of. After all, we are here scarcely past the outskirts of civilisation."

"You'll find we are far enough!" Quest remarked grimly. "What do you make of this, Professor?"

He pointed to the little sandy knoll with its sparse covering of grass, deserted—with scarcely a sign, even, that it had been the resting place of the caravan. The Professor gave vent to a little exclamation.

"Our guides!" he demanded. "And the camels! What has become of them?"

"I woke you up to ask you that question?" Quest replied, "but I guess it's pretty obvious. We might have saved the money we gave for those rifles in Port Said."

The Professor hurried off towards the spot where the encampment had been made. Suddenly he stood still and pointed with his finger. In the clearer, almost crystalline light of the coming day, they saw the track of the camels in one long, unbroken line stretching away northwards.

"No river near, where they could have gone to water the camels, or anything of that sort, I suppose?" Quest asked.

The Professor smiled.

"Nothing nearer than a little stream you may have heard of in the days when you studied geography," he observed derisively,—"the Nile. I never liked the look of those fellows, Quest. They sat and talked and crooned together after Hassan's death. I felt that they were up to some mischief."

He glanced around a little helplessly. Quest took a cigar from his case, and lit it.

"To think that an old campaigner like I am," the Professor continued, in a tone of abasement, "should be placed in a position like this! There have been times when for weeks together I have slept literally with my finger upon the trigger of my rifle, when I have laid warning traps in case the natives tried to desert in the night. I have even had our pack ponies hobbled. I have learnt the secret of no end of devices. And here, with a shifty lot of Arabs picked up in the slums of Port Said, and Hassan, the dragoman, dying in that mysterious fashion, I permit myself to lie down and go to sleep! I do not even secure my rifle! Quest, I shall never forgive myself."

"No good worrying," Quest sighed. "The question is how best to get out of the mess. What's the next move, anyway?"

The Professor glanced towards the sun and took a small compass from his pocket. He pointed across the desert.

"That's exactly our route," he said, "but I reckon we still must be two days from the Mongars, and how we are going to get there ourselves, much more get the women there, without camels, I don't know. There are no wells, and I don't believe those fellows have left us a single tin of water."

"Any chance of falling in with a caravan?" Quest enquired.

"Not one in a hundred," the Professor replied gloomily. "If we were only this short distance out of Port Said, and on one of the recognised trade routes, we should probably meet half a dozen before mid-day. Here we are simply in the wilds. The way we are going leads to nowhere and finishes in an utterly uninhabitable jungle."

"Think we'd better turn round and try and bisect one of the trade routes?" Quest suggested.

The Professor shook his head.

"We should never know when we'd struck it. There are no milestones or telegraph wires. We shall have to put as brave a face on it as possible, and push on."

Laura put her head out of the tent in which the two women had slept.

"Say, where's breakfast?" she exclaimed. "I can't smell the coffee."

They turned and approached her silently. The two girls, fully dressed, came out of the tent as they approached.

"Young ladies," the Professor announced, "I regret to say that a misfortune has befallen us, a misfortune which we shall be able, without a doubt, to surmount, but which will mean a day of hardship and much inconvenience."

"Where are the camels?" Lenora asked breathlessly.

"Gone!" Quest replied.

"And the Arabs?"

"Gone with them—we are left high and dry," Quest explained. "Those fellows are as superstitious as they can be, and Hassan's death has given them the scares. They have gone back to Port Said."

"And what is worse," the Professor added, with a groan, "they have taken with them all our stores, our rifles and our water."

"How far are we from the Mongar Camp?" Lenora asked.

"About a day's tramp," Quest replied quickly. "We may reach there by nightfall."

"Then let's start walking at once, before it gets any hotter," Lenora suggested.

Quest patted her on the back. They made a close search of the tents but found that the Arabs had taken everything in the way of food and drink, except a single half filled tin of drinking water. They moistened their lips with this carefully, Quest with the camphor in his hand. They found it good, however, though lukewarm. Laura produced a packet of sweet chocolate from her pocket.

"It's some breakfast, this," she remarked, as she handed it round. "Let's get a move on."

"And if I may be permitted to make the suggestion," the Professor advised, "not too much chocolate. It is sustaining, I know, but this sweetened concoction encourages thirst, and it is thirst which we have most to—from which we may suffer most inconvenience."

"One, two, three—march!" Laura sung out. "Come on, everybody."

They started bravely enough, but by mid-day their little stock of water was gone, and their feet were sorely blistered. No one complained, however, and the Professor especially did his best to revive their spirits.

"We have come further than I had dared to hope, in the time," he announced. "Fortunately, I know the exact direction we must take. Keep up your spirits, young ladies. At any time now we may see signs of our destination."

"Makes one sad to think of the drinks we could have had," Quest muttered. "What's that?"

The whole party stopped short. Before them was a distant vision of white houses, of little stunted groves of trees, the masts of ships in the distance.

"It's Port Said!" Quest exclaimed. "What the mischief—have we turned round? Say, Professor, has your compass got the jim-jams?"

"I don't care where it is," Lenora faltered, with tears in her eyes. "I thought Port Said was a horrible place, but just now I believe it's heaven."

The Professor turned towards them and shook his head.

"Can't you see?" he pointed out. "It's a mirage—a desert mirage. They are quite common at dusk."

Lenora for a moment was hysterical, and even Laura gave a little sob. Quest set his teeth and glanced at the Professor.

"Always water near where there's a mirage, isn't there, Professor?"

"That's so," the Professor agreed. "We are coming to something, all right."

They struggled on once more. Night came and brought with it a half soothing, half torturing coolness. That vain straining of the eyes upon the horizon, at any rate, was spared to them. They slept in a fashion, but soon after dawn they were on their feet again. They were silent now, for their tongues were swollen and talk had become painful. Their walk had become a shamble, but there was one expression in their haggard faces common to all of them—the brave, dogged desire to struggle on to the last. Suddenly Quest, who had gone a little out of his way to mount a low ridge of sand-hills, waved his arm furiously. He was holding his field-glasses to his eyes. It was wonderful how that ray of hope transformed them. They hurried to where he was. He passed the glasses to the Professor.

"A caravan!" he exclaimed. "I can see the camels, and horses!"

The Professor almost snatched the glasses.

"It is quite true," he agreed. "It is a caravan crossing at right angles to our direction. Come! They will see us before long."

Lenora began to sob and Laura to laugh. Both were struggling with a tendency towards hysterics. The Professor and Quest marched grimly side by side. With every step they took the caravan became more distinct. Presently three or four horsemen detached themselves from the main body and came galloping towards them. The eyes of the little party glistened as they saw that the foremost had a water-bottle slung around his neck. He came dashing up, waving his arms.

"You lost, people?" he asked. "Want water?"

They almost snatched the bottle from him. It was like pouring life into their veins. They all, at the Professor's instigation, drank sparingly. Quest, with a great sigh of relief, lit a cigar.

"Some adventure, this!" he declared.

The Professor, who had been talking to the men in their own language, turned back towards the two girls.

"It is a caravan," he explained, "of peaceful merchants on their way to Jaffa. They are halting for us, and we shall be able, without a doubt, to arrange for water and food and a camel or two horses. The man here asks if the ladies will take the horses and ride?"

They started off gaily to where the caravan had come to a standstill. They had scarcely traversed a hundred yards, however, before the Arab who was leading Lenora's horse came to a sudden standstill. He pointed with his arm and commenced to talk in an excited fashion to his two companions. From across the desert, facing them, came a little company of horsemen, galloping fast and with the sunlight flashing upon their rifles.

"The Mongars!" the Arab cried, pointing wildly. "They attack the caravan!"

The three Arabs talked together for a moment in an excited fashion. Then, without excuse or warning, they swung the two women to the ground, leapt on their horses, and, turning northwards, galloped away. Already the crack of the rifles and little puffs of white smoke showed them where the Mongars, advancing cautiously, were commencing their attack. The Professor looked on anxiously.

"I am not at all sure," he said in an undertone to Quest, "about our position with the Mongars. Craig has a peculiar hold upon them, but as a rule they hate white men, and their blood will be up.... See! the fight is all over. Those fellows were no match for the Mongars. Most of them have fled and left the caravan."

The fight was indeed over. Four of the Mongars had galloped away in pursuit of the Arabs who had been the temporary escort of Quest and his companions. They passed about a hundred yards away, waving their arms and shouting furiously. One of them even fired a shot, which missed Quest by only a few inches.

"They say they are coming back," the Professor muttered. "Who's this? It's the Chief and—"

"Our search is over, at any rate," Quest interrupted. "It's Craig!"

They came galloping up, Craig in white linen clothes and an Arab cloak; the Chief by his side—a fine, upright man with long grey beard; behind, three Mongars, their rifles already to their shoulders. The Chief wheeled up his horse as he came within twenty paces of the little party.

"White! English!" he shouted. "Why do you seek death here?"

He waited for no reply but turned to his men. Three of them dashed forward, their rifles, which were fitted with an odd sort of bayonet, drawn back for the plunge. Quest, snatching his field-glasses from his shoulders, swung them by the strap above his head, and brought them down upon the head of his assailant. The man reeled and his rifle fell from his hand. Quest picked it up, and stood on guard. The other two Mongars swung round towards him, raising their rifles to their shoulders. Quest held Lenora to him. It seemed as though their last second had come. Suddenly Craig, who had been a little in the rear, galloped, shouting, into the line of fire.

"Stop!" he ordered. "Chief, these people are my friends. Chief, the word!"

The Chief raised his arm promptly. The men lowered their rifles, and Craig galloped back to his host's side. The Chief listened to him, nodding gravely. Presently he rode up to the little party. He saluted the Professor and talked to him in his own language. The Professor turned to the others.

"The Chief apologises for not recognising me," he announced. "It seems that Craig had told him that he had come to the desert for shelter, and he imagined at once, when he gave the order for the attack upon us, that we were his enemies. He says that we are welcome to go with him to his encampment."

Quest stood for a moment irresolute.

"Seems to me we're in a pretty fix," he muttered. "We've got to owe our lives to that fellow Craig, anyway, and how shall we be able to get him away from them, goodness only knows."

"That is for later," the Professor said gravely. "At present I think we cannot do better than accept the hospitality of the Chief. Even now the Chief is suspicious. I heard him ask Craig why, if these were his friends, he did not greet them."

Craig turned slowly towards them. It was a strange meeting. His face was thin and worn, there were hollows in his cheeks, a dull light in his sunken eyes. He had the look of the hunted animal. He spoke to them in a low tone.

"It is necessary," he told them, "that you should pretend to be my friends. The Chief has ordered two of his men to dismount. Their ponies are for the young ladies. There will be horses for you amongst the captured ones from the caravan yonder."

"So we meet at last, Craig," the Professor said sternly.

Craig raised his eyes and dropped them again. He said nothing. He turned instead once more towards Quest.

"Whatever there may be between us," he said, "your lives are mine at this moment, if I chose to take them. For the sake of the women, do as I advise. The Chief invites you to his encampment as his guests."

They all turned towards the Chief, who remained a little on the outside of the circle. The Professor raised his hat and spoke a few words in his own language, then he turned to the others.

"I have accepted the invitation of the Chief," he announced. "We had better start."

"This may not be Delmonico's," Laura remarked, a few hours later, with a little sigh of contentment, "but believe me that goat-stew and sherbet tasted better than any chicken and champagne I ever tasted."

"And I don't quite know what tobacco this is," Quest added, helping himself to one of a little pile of cigarettes which had been brought in to them, "but it tastes good."

They moved to the opening of the tent and sat looking out across the silent desert. Laura took the flap of the canvas in her hand.

"What do all these marks mean?" she asked.

"They are cabalistic signs," the Professor replied, "part of the language of the tribe. They indicate that this is the guest tent, and there are a few little maxims traced upon it, extolling the virtues of hospitality. Out in the desert there we met the Mongars as foes, and we had, I can assure you, a very narrow escape of our lives. Here, under the shelter of their encampment, it is a very different matter. We have eaten their salt."

"It's a strange position," Quest remarked moodily.

Lenora leaned forward to where a little group of Mongars were talking together.

"I wish that beautiful girl would come and let us see her again," she murmured.

"She," the Professor explained, "is the Chief's daughter, Feerda, whose life Craig saved."

"And from the way she looks at him," Laura observed, "I should say she hadn't forgotten it, either."

The Professor held up a warning finger. The girl herself had glided to their side out of the shadows. She faced the Professor. The rest of the party she seemed to ignore. She spoke very slowly and in halting English.

"My father wishes to know that you are satisfied?" she said. "You have no further wants?"

"None," the Professor assured her. "We are very grateful for this hospitality, Feerda."

"Won't you talk to us for a little time?" Lenora begged, leaning forward.

The girl made no responsive movement. She seemed, if anything, to shrink a little away. Her head was thrown back, her dark eyes were filled with dislike. She turned suddenly to the Professor and spoke to him in her own language. She pointed to the signs upon the tent, drew her finger along one of the sentences, flashed a fierce glance at them all and disappeared.

"Seems to me we are not exactly popular with the young lady," Quest remarked. "What was she saying, Professor?"

"She suspects us," the Professor said slowly, "of wishing to bring evil to Craig. She pointed to a sentence upon the tent. Roughly it means 'Gratitude is the debt of hospitality.' I am very much afraid that the young lady must have been listening to our conversation a while ago."

Lenora shivered.

"To think of any girl," she murmured, "caring for a fiend like Craig!"

Before they knew it she was there again, her eyes on fire, her tone shaking.

"You call him evil, he who saved your lives, who saved you from the swords of my soldiers!" she cried. "I wish that you had all died before you came here. I hope that you yet may die!"

She passed away into the night. The Professor looked anxiously after her.

"It is a humiliating reflection," he said, "but we are most certainly in Craig's power. Until we have been able to evolve some scheme for liberating ourselves and taking him with us, if possible, I think that we had better avoid any reference to him as much as possible. That young woman is quite capable of stirring up the whole tribe against us. The whole onus of hospitality would pass if they suspected we meant evil to Craig, and they have an ugly way of dealing with their enemies.... Ah! Listen!"

The Professor suddenly leaned forward. There was a queer change in his face. From somewhere on the other side of that soft bank of violet darkness came what seemed to be the clear, low cry of some animal.

"It is the Mongar cry of warning," he said hoarsely. "Something is going to happen."

The whole encampment was suddenly in a state of activity. The Mongars ran hither and thither, getting together their horses. The Chief, with Craig by his side, was standing on the outskirts of the camp. The cry came again, this time much louder and nearer. Soon they caught the muffled trampling of a horse's hoofs galloping across the soft sands, then the gleam of his white garments as he came suddenly into sight, in the edge of the little circle of light thrown by the fire. They saw him leap from his horse, run to the Chief, bend double in some form of salute, then commence to talk rapidly. The Chief listened with no sign of emotion, but in a moment or two he was giving rapid orders. Camels appeared from some invisible place. Men, already on horseback, were galloping hither and thither, collecting fire-arms and spare ammunition. Pack-horses were being loaded, tents rolled up and every evidence of breaking camp.

"Seems to me there's a move on," Quest muttered, as they rose to their feet. "I wonder if we are in it."

A moment or two later Craig approached them. He came with his shoulders stooped and his eyes fixed upon the ground. He scarcely raised them as he spoke.

"Word has been brought to the Chief," he announced, "that the Arab who escaped from the caravan has fallen in with an outpost of British soldiers. They have already started in pursuit of us. The

Mongars will take refuge in the jungle, where they have prepared hiding-places. We start at once."

"What about us?" the Professor enquired.

"I endeavoured," Craig continued, "to persuade the Chief to allow you to remain here, when the care of you would devolve upon the English soldiers. He and Feerda, however, have absolutely refused my request. Feerda has overheard some of your conversation, and the Chief believes that you will betray us. You will have to come along, too."

"You mean," Laura exclaimed, "that we've got to tramp into what you call the jungle, and hide there because these thieves are being chased?"

Craig glanced uneasily around.

"Young lady," he said, "you will do well to speak little here. They have long ears and quick understandings, these men. You may call them a race of robbers. They only remember that they are the descendants of an Imperial race, and what they take by the right of conquest they believe Allah sends them. You must do the bidding of the Chief."

He turned away towards where the Chief and Feerda, already on horseback, were waiting for him. Quest leaned towards the Professor.

"Why not tackle the Chief yourself?" he suggested. "Here he comes now. Craig may be speaking the truth, but, on the other hand, it's all to his interests to keep us away from the soldiers."

The Professor rose at once to his feet and stepped out to where the Chief was giving orders.

"Chief," he said, "my friends desire me to speak with you. We are worn out with our adventures. The young ladies who are with us are unused to and ill-prepared for this hard life. We beg that you will allow us to remain here and await the arrival of the English soldiers."

The Chief turned his head. There was little friendliness in his tone.

"Wise man," he replied, "I have sent you my bidding by him who is our honoured guest. I tell you frankly that I am not satisfied with the explanations I have received of your presence here."

Feerda leaned forward, her beautiful eyes flashing in the dim light.

"Ah! but I know," she cried, "they would bring harm to the master. I can read it in their hearts as I have heard it from their own lips."

"What my daughter says is truth," the Chief declared. "Back, wise man, and tell your friends that you ride with us tonight, either as guests or captives. You may take your choice."

The Professor returned to where the others were eagerly awaiting him.

"It is useless," he announced. "The girl, who is clearly enamoured of Craig, suspects us. So does the Chief. Perhaps, secretly, Craig himself is unwilling to leave us here. The Chief never changes his mind and he has spoken. We go either as his captives or his guests. I have heard it said," the Professor added grimly, "that the Mongars never keep captives longer than twenty-four hours."

They all rose at once to their feet, and a few moments later horses were brought. The little procession was already being formed in line. Craig approached them once more.

"You will mount now and ride in the middle of our caravan," he directed. "The Chief does not trust you. If you value your lives, you will do as you are bidden."

"I don't like the idea of the jungle," Lenora sighed.

"Gives me the creeps," Laura admitted, as she climbed upon her horse. "Any wild animals there, Professor?"

The Professor became more cheerful.

"The animal life of the region we are about to traverse," he observed, as they moved off, "is in some respects familiar to me. Twelve years ago I devoted some time to research a little to the westward of our present route. I will, if you choose, as we ride, give you a brief account of some of my discoveries."

The two girls exchanged glances. Quest, who had intercepted them, turned his horse and rode in between the Professor and Lenora.

"Go right ahead, Professor," he invited. "Fortunately the girls have got saddles like boxes—I think they both mean to go to sleep."

"An intelligent listener of either sex," the Professor said amiably, "will be a stimulus to my memory."

2.

"You can call this fairyland, if you want," Laura remarked, gazing around her; "I call it a nasty, damp, oozy spot."

"It seemed very beautiful when we first came," Lenora sighed, "but that was after the heat and glare of the desert. There does seem something a little unhealthy about it."

"I'm just about fed up with Mongars," Quest declared.

"We do nothing but lie about, and they won't even let us fire a gun off."

"Personally," the Professor confessed, holding up a glass bottle in front of him from which a yellow beetle was making frantic efforts to escape, "I find this little patch of country unusually interesting. The specimen which I have here—I spare you the scientific name for him—belongs to a class of beetle which has for long eluded me."

Laura regarded the specimen with disfavour.

"So far as I am concerned," she observed, "I shouldn't have cared if he'd eluded you a little longer. Don't you dare let him out, Professor."

"My dear young lady," the Professor assured her, "the insect is perfectly secure. Through the cork, as you see, I have bored a couple of holes, hoping to keep him alive until we reach Port Said, when I can prepare him as a specimen."

"Port Said!" Lenora murmured. "It sounds like heaven."

Quest motioned them to sit a little nearer.

"Well," he said, "I fancy we are all feeling about the same except the Professor, and even he wants to get some powder for his beetle. I had a moment's talk with Craig this morning, and from what he says I fancy they mean to make a move a little further in before long. It'll be all the more difficult to escape then."

"You think we could get away?" Lenora whispered eagerly.

Quest glanced cautiously around. They were surrounded by thick vegetation, but they were only a very short distance from the camp.

"Seems to me," he continued, "we shall have to try it some day or other and I'm all for trying it soon. Even if they caught us, I don't believe they'd dare to kill us, with the English soldiers so close behind. I am going to get hold of two or three rifles and some ammunition. That's easy, because they leave them about all the time. And what you girls want to do is to hide some food and get a bottle of water."

"What about Craig?" the Professor asked.

"We are going to take him along," Quest declared grimly. "He's had the devil's own luck so far, but it can't last forever. I'll see to that part of the business, if you others get ready and wait for me to give the signal…. What's that?"

They all looked around. There had been a little rustling amongst the canopy of bushes. Quest peered through and returned, frowning.

"Feerda again," he muttered. "She hangs around all the time, trying to listen to what we are saying. She couldn't have heard this, though. Now, girls, remember. When the food is about this evening, see how much you can get hold of. I know just where to find the guns and the horses. Let's separate now. The Professor and I will go on a beetle hunt."

They dispersed in various directions. It was not until late in the evening, when the Mongars had withdrawn a little to indulge in their customary orgy of crooning songs, that they were absolutely alone. Quest looked out of the tent in which they had been sitting and came back again.

"Well?"

Laura lifted her skirt and showed an unusual projection underneath.

"Lenora and I have pinned up our petticoats," she announced. "We've got plenty of food and a bottle of water."

Quest threw open the white Arab cloak which he had been wearing. He had three rifles strapped around him.

"The Professor's got the ammunition," he said, "and we've five horses tethered a hundred paces along the track we came by, just behind the second tree turning to the left. I want you all to go there now at once and take the rifles. There isn't a soul in the camp and you can carry them wrapped in this cloak. I'll join you in ten minutes."

"What about Craig?" the Professor enquired.

"I am seeing to him," Quest replied.

Lenora hesitated.

"Isn't it rather a risk?" she whispered fearfully.

Quest's face was suddenly stern.

"Craig is going back with us," he said. "I'll be careful, Lenora. Don't worry."

He strolled out of the tent and came back again.

"The coast's clear," he announced. "Off you go.... One moment," he added, "there are some papers in this little box of mine which one of you ought to take care of."

He bent hastily over the little wallet, which never left him. Suddenly a little exclamation broke from his lips. The Professor peered over his shoulder.

"What is it?"

Quest never said a word. From one of the spaces of the wallet he drew out a small black box, removed the lid and held out the card. They read it together:

"Fools, all of you! The cunning of the ages defeats your puny efforts at every turn.
"The Hands!"

Even the Professor's lips blanched a little as he read. Quest, however, seemed suddenly furious. He tore the card and the box to pieces, flung them into a corner of the tent and drew a revolver from his pocket.

"This time," he exclaimed, "we are going to make an end of the Hands! Out you go now, girls. You can leave me to finish things up."

One by one they stole along the path. Quest came out and watched them disappear. Then he gripped his revolver firmly in his hand and turned towards Craig's tent. There was something in the breathless stillness of the place, at that moment, which seemed almost a presage of coming disaster. Without knowing exactly why, Quest's fingers tightened on the butt of his weapon. Then, from the thick growth by the side of the clearing, he saw a dark shape steal out and vanish in the direction of Craig's tent. He came to a standstill, puzzled. There had been rumours of lions all day, but the Professor had been incredulous. The nature of the country, he thought, scarcely favoured the probability of their presence. Then the still, heavy air was suddenly rent by a wild scream of horror. Across the narrow opening the creature had reappeared, carrying something in its mouth, something which gave vent all the time to the most awful yells. Quest fired his revolver on chance and broke into a run. Already the Mongars, disturbed in their evening amusement, were breaking into the undergrowth in chase. Quest came to a standstill. It was from Craig's tent that the beast had issued!

He turned slowly around. If Craig had indeed paid for his crimes by so horrible a death, there was all the more reason why they should make their escape in the general confusion, and make it quickly. He retraced his steps. The sound of shouting voices grew less and less distinct. When he reached the meeting place, he found the Professor standing at the corner with the rest. His face showed signs of the most lively curiosity.

"From the commotion," he announced, "I believe that, after all, a lion has visited the camp. The cries which we have heard were distinctly the cries of a native."

Quest shook his head.

"A lion's been here all right," he said, "and he has finished our little job for us. That was Craig. I saw him come out of Craig's tent."

The Professor was dubious.

"My friend," he said, "you are mistaken. There is nothing more characteristic and distinct than the Mongar cry of fear. They seldom use it except in the face of death. That was the cry of a native Mongar. As for Craig, well, you see that tree that looks like a dwarfed aloe?"

Quest nodded.

"What about it?"

"Craig was lying there ten minutes ago. He sprang up when he heard the yells from the encampment, but I believe he is there now."

"Got the horses all right?" Quest enquired.

"Everything is waiting," the Professor replied.

"I'll have one more try, then," Quest declared.

He made his way slowly through the undergrowth to the spot which the Professor had indicated. Close to the trunk of a tree Craig was standing. Feerda was on her knees before him. She was speaking to him in broken English.

"Dear master, you shall listen to your slave. These people are your enemies. It would be all over in a few minutes. You have but to say the word. My father is eager for it. No one would ever know."

Craig patted her head. His tone was filled with the deepest despondency.

"It is impossible, Feerda," he said. "You do not understand. I cannot tell you everything. Sometimes I almost think that the best thing I could do would be to return with them to the countries you know nothing of."

"That's what you are going to do, any way," Quest declared, suddenly making his appearance. "Hands up!"

He covered Craig with his revolver, but his arm was scarcely extended before Feerda sprang at him like a little wild-cat. He gripped her with his left arm and held her away with difficulty.

"Craig," he continued, "you're coming with us. You know the way to Port Said and we want you—you know why. Untie that sash from your waist. Quickly!"

Craig obeyed. He had the stupefied air of a man who has lost for the time his volition.

"Tie it to the tree," Quest ordered. "Leave room enough."

Craig did as he was told. Then he turned and held the loose ends up. Quest lowered his revolver for a moment as he pushed Feerda toward it. Craig, with a wonderful spring, reached his side and kicked the revolver away. Before Quest could even stoop to recover it, he saw the glitter of the other's knife pressed against his chest.

"Listen," Craig declared. "I've made up my mind. I won't go back to America. I've had enough of being hunted all over the world. This time I think I'll rid myself of one of you, at any rate."

"Will you?"

The interruption was so unexpected that Craig lost his nerve. Through an opening in the trees, only a few feet away, Lenora had suddenly appeared. She, too, held a revolver; her hand was as steady as a rock.

"Drop your knife," she ordered Craig.

He obeyed without hesitation.

"Now tie the sash around the girl."

He obeyed mechanically. Feerda, who had been fiercely resisting Quest's efforts to hold her, yielded without a struggle as soon as Craig touched her. She looked at him, however, with bitter reproach.

"You would tie me here?" she murmured. "You would leave me?"

"It is Fate," Craig muttered. "I am worn out with trying to escape, Feerda. They will come soon and release you."

She opened her lips to shriek, but Quest, who had made a gag of her linen head-dress, thrust it suddenly into her mouth. He took Craig by the collar and led him to the spot where the others were waiting. They hoisted him on to a horse. Already behind them they could see the flare of the torches from the returning Mongars.

"You know the way to Port Said," Quest whispered. "See that you lead us there. There will be trouble, mind, if you don't."

Craig made no reply. He rode off in front of the little troop, covered all the time by Quest's revolver. Very soon they were out of the jungle and in the open desert. Quest looked behind him uneasily.

"To judge by the row those fellows are making," he remarked, "I should think that they've found Feerda already."

"In that case," the Professor said gravely, "let me recommend you to push on as fast as possible. We have had one escape from them, but nothing in the world can save us now that you have laid hands upon Feerda. The Chief would never forgive that."

"We've got a start, any way," Quest observed, "and these are the five best horses in the camp. Girls, a little faster. We've got to trust Craig for the direction but I believe he is right."

"So far as my instinct tells me," the Professor agreed, "I believe that we are heading in precisely the right direction."

They galloped steadily on. The moon rose higher and higher until it became almost as light as day. Often the Professor raised himself in his saddle and peered forward.

"This column of soldiers would march at night," he remarked. "I am hoping all the time that we may meet them."

Quest fell a little behind to his side, although he never left off watching Craig.

"Look behind you, Professor," he whispered.

In the far distance were a number of little black specks, growing every moment larger. Even at that moment they heard the low, long call of the Mongars.

"They are gaining on us," Quest muttered.

The two girls, white though they were, bent over their horses.

"We'll stick to it till the last moment," Quest continued, "then we'll turn and let them have it."

They raced on for another mile or more. A bullet whistled over their heads. Quest tightened his reins.

"No good," he sighed. "We'd better stay and fight it out, Professor. Stick close to me, Lenora."

They drew up and hastily dismounted. The Mongars closed in around them. A cloud had drifted in front of the moon, and in the darkness it was almost impossible to see their whereabouts. They heard the Chief's voice.

"Shoot first that dog of a Craig!"

There was a shriek. Suddenly Feerda, breaking loose from the others, raced across the little division. She flung herself from her horse.

"Tell my father that you were not faithless," she pleaded. "They shall not kill you!"

She clung to Craig's neck. The bullets were beginning to whistle around them now. All of a sudden she threw up her arms. Craig, in a fury, turned around and fired into the darkness. Then suddenly, as though on the bidding of some unspoken word, there was a queer silence. Every one was distinctly conscious of an alien sound—the soft thud of many horses' feet galloping from the right; then a sharp, English voice of command.

"Hold your fire, men. Close into the left there. Steady!"

The cloud suddenly rolled away from the moon. A long line of horsemen were immediately visible. The officer in front rode forward.

"Drop your arms and surrender," he ordered sternly.

The Mongars, who were outnumbered by twenty to one, obeyed without hesitation. Their Chief seemed unconscious, even, of what had happened. He was on his knees, bending over the body of Feerda, half supported in Craig's arms. The officer turned to Quest.

"Are you the party who left Port Said for the Mongar Camp?" he asked.

Quest nodded.

"They took us into the jungle—just escaped. They'd caught us here, though, and I'm afraid we were about finished if you hadn't come along. We are not English—we're American."

"Same thing," the officer replied, as he held out his hand. "Stack up their arms, men," he ordered, turning around. "Tie them in twos. Dennis, take the young ladies back to the commissariat camels."

The Professor drew a little sigh.

"Commissariat!" he murmured. "That sounds most inviting."

CHAPTER XIII

'NEATH IRON WHEELS

1.

Side by side they leaned over the rail of the steamer and gazed shorewards at the slowly unfolding scene before them. For some time they had all preserved an almost ecstatic silence.

"Oh, but it's good to see home again!" Laura sighed at last.

"I'm with you," Quest agreed emphatically. "It's the wrong side of the continent, perhaps, but I'm aching to set my foot on American soil again."

"This the wrong side of the continent! I should say not!" Laura exclaimed, pointing to where in the distance the buildings of the Exposition gleamed almost snow-white in the dazzling sunshine. "Why, I have never seen anything so beautiful in my life."

The Professor intervened amiably. His face, too, shone with pleasure as he gazed landwards.

"I agree with the young lady," he declared. "The blood and sinews of life may seem to throb more ponderously in New York, but there is a big life here on this western side, a great, wide-flung, pulsating life. There is room here, room to breathe."

"And it is so beautiful," Lenora murmured.

Quest glanced a little way along the deck to where a pale-faced man stood leaning upon his folded arms, gazing upon the same scene. There was no smile on Craig's face, no light of anticipation in his eyes.

"I guess there's one of us here," Quest observed, "who is none too pleased to see America again."

Lenora shivered a little. They were all grave.

"We must, I think, admit," the Professor said, "that Craig's deportment during the voyage has been everything that could be desired. He has even voluntarily carried out certain small attentions to my person which I must confess that I had greatly missed."

"That's all right," Quest agreed. "At the same time I am afraid the moment has come now to remind him that the end is drawing near."

Quest moved slowly down the deck towards Craig's side, and touched him on the arm.

"Give me your left wrist, Craig," he said quietly.

The man slunk away. There was a sudden look of horror in his white face. He started back but Quest was too quick for him. In a moment there was the click of a handcuff, the mate of which was concealed under the criminologist's cuff.

"You'd better take things quietly," the latter advised. "It will only hurt you to struggle. Step this way a little. Put your hand in your pocket, so, and no one will notice."

Craig obeyed silently. They stepped along the deck towards the rest of the party. Lenora handed her glasses to Quest.

"Do look, Mr. Quest," she begged. "There is Inspector French standing in the front row on the dock, with two enormous bunches of flowers—carnations for me, I expect, and poinsettias for Laura. They're the larger bunch."

Quest took the glasses and nodded.

"That's French, right enough," he assented. "Look at him standing straightening his tie in front of that advertisement mirror! Flowers, too! Say, he's got his eye on one of you girls. Not you, by any chance, is it, Lenora?"

Lenora laughed across at Laura, who had turned a little pink.

"I guess French has got sense enough to know I'm not that sort," the latter replied. "The double-harness stuff doesn't appeal to me, and he knows it!"

Lenora made a little grimace as she turned away.

"Well," she said, "it's brave talk."

"Almost," the Professor pointed out, "Amazonian. Yet in the ancient days even the Amazons were sometimes tamed."

"Oh, nonsense!" Laura exclaimed, turning away. "I don't see why the man wants to make himself look like a walking conservatory, though," she added under her breath.

"And I think it's sweet of him," Lenora insisted. "If there's anything I'm longing for, it's a breath of perfume from those flowers."

Slowly the great steamer drifted nearer and nearer to the dock, hats were waved from the little line of spectators, ropes were drawn taut. The Inspector was standing at the bottom of the gangway as they all passed down. He shook hands with every one vigorously. Then he presented Lenora with her carnations and Laura with the poinsettias. Lenora was enthusiastic. Even Laura murmured a few words of thanks.

"Some flowers, those poinsettias," the Inspector agreed.

Quest gripped him by the arm.

"French," he said, "I tell you I shall make your hair curl when you hear all that we've been through. Do you feel like having me start in right away, on our way to the cars?"

French withdrew his arm.

"Nothing doing," he replied. "I want to talk to Miss Laura. You can stow that criminal stuff. It'll wait all right. You've got the fellow—that's what matters."

Quest exchanged an amused glance with Lenora. The Inspector and Laura fell a little behind. The former took off his hat for a moment and fanned himself.

"Say, Miss Laura," he began, "I'm a plain man, and a poor hand at speeches. I've been saying a few nice things over to myself on the dock here for the last hour, but everything's gone right out of my head. Look here, it sums up like this. How do you feel about quitting this bunch right away and coming back to New York with me?"

"What do I want to go to New York for?" Laura demanded.

"Oh, come on, Miss Laura, you know what I mean," French replied. "We'll slip off and get married here and then take this man Craig to New York. Once get him safely in the Tombs and we'll go off on a honeymoon anywhere you say."

Laura was on the point of laughing at him. Then the unwonted seriousness of his expression appealed suddenly to her sympathy. She patted him kindly on the shoulder.

"You're a good sort, Inspector, but you've picked the wrong girl. I've run along on my own hook ever since I was born, I guess, and I can't switch my ideas over to this married stuff. You'd better get a move on and get Craig back to New York before he slips us again. I'm going to stay here with the others."

The Inspector sighed. His face had grown long, and the buoyancy had passed from his manner.

"This is some disappointment, believe me, Miss Laura," he confessed.

"Cheer up," she laughed. "You'll get over it all right."

They found the others waiting for them at the end of the great wooden shed. Quest turned to French.

"Look here, French," he said, "you know I don't want to hurry you off, but I don't know what we're going to do with this fellow about in San Francisco. We don't want to lodge two charges, and we should have to put him in jail tonight. Why don't you take him on right away? There's a Limited goes by the southern route in an hour's time."

French assented gloomily.

"That suits me," he agreed. "You'll be glad to get rid of the fellow, too," he added.

They drove straight to the depot, found two vacant seats in the train, and Quest with a little sigh of relief handed over his charge. Craig, who, though still dumb, had shown signs of intense nervousness since the landing, sank back in his corner seat, covering the upper part of his head with his hands. Suddenly Lenora, who had been chatting with French through the window, happened to glance towards Craig. She gave a little cry and stepped back.

"Look!" she exclaimed. "The eyes! Those are the eyes that haunted me all through those terrible days!"

She was suddenly white. Quest passed his arm through hers and glanced through the carriage window. In the shaded light, Craig's eyes seemed indeed to have suddenly grown in power and intensity.

They shone fiercely from underneath the hands which clasped his forehead.

"Well, that's the last you'll see of them," Quest reminded her soothingly. "Come, you're not going to break down now, Lenora. We've been through it all and there he is, safe and sound in French's keeping. There is nothing more left in the world to frighten you."

Lenora pulled herself together with an effort.

"It was silly," she confessed, "yet even now—"

"Don't you worry, Miss Lenora," French cried from out of the window. "You can take my word for it the job's finished this time. Good-bye, all of you! Good-bye, Miss Laura!"

Laura waved her hand gaily. They all stood and watched the train depart. Then they turned away from the depot.

"Now for a little holiday," Quest declared, passing Lenora's arm through his. "We'll just have a look round the city and then get down to San Diego and take a look at the Exposition there. No responsibilities, no one to look after, nothing to do but enjoy ourselves."

"Capital!" the Professor agreed, beaming upon them all. "There is a collection of fossilised remains in the museum here, the study of which will afford me the greatest pleasure and interest."

The girls laughed heartily.

"I think you and I," Quest suggested, turning to them, "will part company with the Professor!"

Quest and Lenora turned away from the window of the hotel, out of which they had been gazing for the last quarter of an hour. Stretched out before them were the lights of the Exposition, a blur of twinkling diamonds against the black garb of night. Beyond, the flashing of a light-house and a faint background of dark sea.

"It's too beautiful," Lenora sighed.

Quest stood for a moment shaking his head. The Professor with a pile of newspapers stretched out before him, was completely engrossed in their perusal. Laura, who had been sitting in an arm-chair at the further end of the apartment, was apparently deep in thought. The newspaper which she had been reading had slipped unnoticed from her fingers.

"Say, you two are no sort of people for a holiday," Quest declared. "As for you, Laura, I can't think what's come over you. You never opened your mouth at dinner-time, and you sit there now looking like nothing on earth."

"I am beginning to suspect her," Lenora chimed in. "Too bad he had to hurry away, dear!"

Laura's indignation was not altogether convincing. Quest and Lenora exchanged amused glances. The former picked up the newspaper from the floor and calmly turned out the Professor's lamp.

"Look here," he explained, "this is the first night of our holiday.

I'm going to run the party and I'm going to make the rules. No more newspapers tonight or for a fortnight. You understand? No reading, nothing but frivolity. And no love-sickness, Miss Laura."

"Love-sickness, indeed!" she repeated scornfully.

"Having arranged those minor details," Quest concluded, "on with your hats, everybody. I am going to take you out to a café where they play the best music in the city. We are going to have supper, drink one another's health, and try and forget the last few months altogether."

Lenora clapped her hands and Laura rose at once to her feet. The Professor obediently crossed the room for his hat.

"I am convinced," he said, "that our friend Quest's advice is good. We will at any rate embark upon this particular frivolity which he suggests."

2.

Quest took the dispatch which the hotel clerk handed to him one afternoon a fortnight later, and read it through without change of expression. Lenora, however, who was by his side, knew at once that it contained something startling.

"What is it?" she asked.

He passed his arm through hers and led her down the hall to where the Professor and Laura were just waiting for the lift. He beckoned them to follow him to a corner of the lounge.

"There's one thing I quite forgot, a fortnight ago," he said, slowly, "when I suggested that we should none of us look at a newspaper all the time we were in California. Have you kept to our bargain, Professor?"

"Absolutely!"

"And you, girls?"

"I've never even seen one," Lenora declared.

"Nor I," Laura echoed.

"I made a mistake," Quest confessed. "Something has happened which we ought to have known about. You had better read this message—or, wait, I'll read it aloud:—

"To Sanford Quest, Garfield Hotel, San Diego.
"Injured in wreck of Limited. Recovered consciousness to-day. Craig reported burned in wreck but think you had better come on."
"French, Samaritan Hospital, Allguez."

"When can we start?" Laura exclaimed excitedly.

Lenora clutched at Quest's arm.

"I knew it," she declared simply. "I felt perfectly certain, when they left San Francisco, that something would happen. We haven't seen the end of Craig yet."

Quest, who had been studying a time-table, glanced once more at the dispatch.

"Look here," he said, "Allguez isn't so far out of the way if we take the southern route to New York. Let's get a move on tonight."

Laura led the way to the lift. She was in a state of rare discomposure.

"To think that all the time we've been giddying round," she muttered, "that poor man has been lying in hospital! Makes one feel like a brute."

"He's been unconscious all the time," Quest reminded her.

"Might have expected to find us there when he came-to, any way," Laura insisted.

Lenora smiled faintly as she caught a glance from Quest.

"Laura's got a heart somewhere," she murmured, "only it takes an awful lot of getting at!"...

They found French, already convalescent, comfortably installed in the private ward of a small hospital in the picturesque New Mexican town. Laura almost at once established herself by his side.

"You're going to lose your job here, nurse," Quest told her, smiling.

The nurse glanced at French.

"The change seems to be doing him good, any way," she remarked. "I haven't seen him look so bright yet."

"Can you remember anything about the wreck, French?" Quest enquired.

The Inspector passed his hand wearily over his forehead.

"It seems more like a dream—or rather a nightmare—than anything," he admitted. "I was sitting opposite Craig when the crash came. I was unconscious for a time. When I came to, I was simply pinned down by the side of the car. I could see a man working hard to release me, tugging and straining with all his might. Every now and then I got a glimpse of his face. It seemed queer, but I could have sworn it was Craig. Then other people passed by. I heard the shriek of a locomotive. I could see a doctor bending over some bodies. Then it all faded away and came back again. The second time I was nearly free. The man who had been working so hard was just smashing the last bit of timber away, and again I saw his face and that time I was sure that it was Craig. Anyway, he finished the job. I suddenly felt I could move my limbs. The man stood up as though exhausted, looked at me, called to the doctor, and then he seemed to fade away. It might have been because I was unconscious myself, for I don't remember anything else until I found myself in bed."

"It would indeed," the Professor remarked, "be an interesting circumstance—an interesting psychological circumstance, if I might put it that way—if Craig, the arch-criminal, the man who has seemed to us so utterly devoid of all human feeling, should really have toiled in this manner to set free his captor."

"Interesting or not," Quest observed, "I'd like to know whether it was Craig or not. I understand there were about a dozen unrecognisable bodies found."

The nurse, who had left the room for a few minutes, returned with a small package in her hand, which she handed to French. He looked at it in a puzzled manner.

"What can that be?" he muttered, turning it over. "Addressed to me all right, but there isn't a soul knows I'm here except you people. Will you open it, Miss Laura?"

She took it from him and untied the strings. A little breathless cry escaped from her lips as she tore open the paper. A small black box was disclosed. She opened the lid with trembling fingers and drew out a scrap of paper. They all leaned over and read together:—

"You have all lost again. Why not give it up? You can never win.
"The Hands."

Lenora was perhaps the calmest. She simply nodded with the melancholy air of satisfaction of one who finds her preconceived ideas confirmed.

"I knew it!" she exclaimed softly. "I knew it at the depot. Craig's time has not come yet. He may be somewhere near us, even now."

She glanced uneasily around the ward. Quest, who had been examining the post-mark on the package, threw the papers down.

"The post-mark's all blurred out," he remarked. "There's no doubt about it, that fellow Craig has the devil's own luck, but we'll get him—we'll get him yet. I'll just take a stroll up to police head-quarters and make a few inquiries. You might come with me, Lenora, and Laura can get busy with her amateur nursing."

"I shall make inquiries," the Professor announced briskly, "concerning the local museum. There should be interesting relics hereabouts of the prehistoric Indians."

3.

A man sat on the steps of the range cook wagon, crouching as far back as possible to take advantage of its slight shelter from the burning sun. He held before him a newspaper, a certain paragraph of which he was eagerly devouring. In the distance the mail boy was already disappearing in a cloud of dust.

"FAMOUS CRIMINOLOGIST IN ALLGUEZ

"Sanford Quest and his assistants, accompanied by Professor Lord Ashleigh, arrived in Allguez a few days ago to look for John Craig, formerly servant to the scientist. Craig has not been seen since the accident to the Limited, a fortnight ago, and by many is supposed to have perished in the wreck. He was in the charge of Inspector French, and was on his way to New York to stand his trial for homicide. French was taken to the hospital, suffering from concussion of the brain, but is now convalescent."

The man read the paragraph twice. Then he set down the paper and looked steadily across the rolling prairie land. There was a queer, bitter little smile upon his lips.

"So it begins again!" he muttered.

There was a cloud of dust in the distance. The man rose to his feet, shaded his eyes with his hand and shambled round to the back of the wagon, where a long table was set out with knives and forks, hunches of bread and tin cups. He walked a little further away to the fire, and slowly stirred a pot of stew. The little party of cowboys came thundering up. There was a chorus of shouts and exclamations, whistlings and good-natured chaff, as they threw themselves from their horses. Long Jim stood slowly cracking his whip and looking down the table.

"Say, boys, I think he's fixed things up all right," he remarked. "Come on with the grub, cookie."

Silently the man filled each dish with the stew and laid it in its place. Then he retired to the background and the cowboys commenced their meal. Long Jim winked at the others as he picked up a biscuit.

"Cookie, you're no good," he called out. "The stew's rotten. Here, take this!"

He flicked the biscuit, which caught the cook on the side of the head. For a moment the man started. With his hand upon his temple he flashed a look of hatred towards his assailant. Long Jim laughed carelessly.

"Say, cookie," the latter went on, "where did you get them eyes? Guess we'll have to tame you a bit."

The meal was soon over, and Jim strolled across to where the others were saddling up. He passed his left arm through the reins of his horse and turned once more to look at Craig.

"Say, you mind you do better tonight, young fellow. Eh!"

He stopped short with a cry of pain. The horse had suddenly

started, wrenching at the reins. Jim's arm hung helplessly down from the shoulder.

"Gee, boys, he's broken it!" he groaned. "Say, this is hell!"

He swore in agony. They all crowded around him.

"What's wrong, Jim?"

"It's broken, sure!"

"Wrong, you helpless sons of loons!" Jim yelled. "Can't any of you do something?"

The cook suddenly pushed his way through the little crowd. He took Jim's shoulder firmly in one hand and his arm in the other. The cowboy howled with pain.

"Let go my arm!" he shouted. "Kill him, boys! My God, I'll make holes in you for this!"

He snatched at his gun with his other hand and the cowboys scattered a little. The cook stepped back, the gun flashed out, only to be suddenly lowered. Jim looked incredulously towards his left arm, which hung no longer helplessly by his side. He swung it backwards and forwards, and a broad grin slowly lit up his lean, brown face. He thrust the gun in his holster and held out his hand.

"Cookie, you're all right!" he exclaimed. "You've done the trick this time. Say, you're a miracle!"

The cook smiled.

"Your arm was just out of joint," he remarked. "It was rather a hard pull but it's all right now."

Jim looked around at the others.

"And to think that I might have killed him!" he exclaimed. "Cookie, you're a white boy. You'll do. We're going to like you here."

Craig watched them ride off. The bitterness had passed from his face. Slowly he began to clean up. Then he crept underneath the wagon and rested....

Evening came and with it a repetition of his labours. When everything was ready to serve, he stepped from behind the wagon and looked across the rolling stretch of open country. There was no one in sight. Softly, almost stealthily, he crept up to the wagon, fetched out from its wooden case a small violin, made his way to the further side of the wagon, sat down with his back to the wheel and began to play. His eyes were closed. Sometimes the movements of his fingers were so slow that the melody seemed to die away. Then unexpectedly he picked it up, carrying the same strain through quick, convulsive passages, lost it again, wandered as though in search of it, extemporising all the time, yet playing always with the air of a man who feels and sees the hidden things. Suddenly the bow rested motionless. A look of fear came into his face. He sprang up. The cowboys were all stealing from the other side of the wagon. They had arrived and dismounted without his hearing them. He sprang to his feet and began to stammer apologies. Long Jim's hand was laid firmly upon his shoulders.

"Say, cookie, you don't need to look so scared. You ain't done nothing wrong. Me and the boys, we like your music. Sing us another tune on that fiddle!"

"I haven't neglected anything," Craig faltered. "It's all ready to serve."

"The grub can wait," Jim replied. "Pull the bow, partner, pull the bow."

The cook looked at him for a moment incredulously. Then he realised that the cowboy was in earnest. He picked up the bow and commenced to play again. They sat around him, wondering, absolutely absorbed. No one even made a move towards the food. It was Craig who led them there at last himself, still playing. Long Jim threw his arm almost caressingly around his shoulder.

"Say, Cookie," he began, "there ain't never no questions asked concerning the past history of the men who find their way out here, just so long as they don't play the game yellow. Maybe you've fitted up a nice little hell for yourself somewhere, but we ain't none of us hankering to know the address. You're white and you're one of us and any time any guy wants to charge you rent for that little hell where you got the furniture of your conscience stored, why, you just let us settle with him, that's all. Now, one more tune, Cookie."

Craig shook his head. He had turned away to where the kettle was hissing on the range fire.

"It is time you had your food," he said.

Long Jim took up the violin and drew the bow across it. There was a chorus of execrations. Craig snatched it from him. He suddenly turned his back upon them all. He had played before as though to amuse himself. He played now with the complete, almost passionate absorption of the artist. His head was uplifted, his eyes half closed. He was no longer the menial, the fugitive from justice. He was playing himself into another world, playing amidst a silence which, considering his audience, was amazing. They crouched across the table and watched him. Long Jim stood like a figure of stone. The interruption which came was from outside.

"More of these damned tourists," Long Jim muttered. "Women, too!"

Craig had stopped playing. He turned his head slowly. Quest was in the act of dismounting from his horse. By his side was the Professor; just behind, Lenora and Laura. Long Jim greeted them with rough cordiality.

"Say, what are you folks looking for?" he demanded.

Quest pointed to Craig.

"We want that man," he announced. "This is Inspector French from New York. I am Sanford Quest."

There was a tense silence. Craig covered his face with his hands, then suddenly looked up.

"I won't come," he cried fiercely. "You've hounded me all round the world. I am innocent. I won't come."

Quest shrugged his shoulders. He took a step forward, but Long Jim, as though by accident, sauntered in the way.

"Got a warrant?" he asked tersely.

"We don't need it," Quest replied. "He's our man, right enough."

"Right this minute he's our cook," drawled Long Jim, "and we ain't exactly particular about going hungry to please a bunch of strangers. Cut it short, Mister. If you ain't got a warrant, you ain't got this man. Maybe we don't sport finger-bowls and silk socks, but we're civilised enough not to let no slim dude walk off with one of our boys without proper authority. So you can just meander along back where you come from. Ain't that right, boys?"

There was a sullen murmur of assent. Quest turned back and whispered for a moment to the Inspector. Then he turned to Long Jim.

"All right," he agreed. "The Inspector here and I will soon see to that. We'll ride back to the township. With your permission, the ladies and our elderly friend will remain for a rest."

"You're welcome to anything we've got except our cook," Jim replied, turning away....

Darkness came early and the little company grew closer and closer to the camp fire, where Craig had once more taken up the violin. The Professor had wandered off somewhere into the darkness and the girls were seated a little apart. They had been treated hospitably but coldly.

"Don't seem to cotton to us, these boys," Laura remarked.

"They don't like us," Lenora replied, "because they think we are after Craig. I wonder what Long Jim has been whispering to him, and what that paper is he has been showing Craig. Do you know how far we are from the Mexican border?"

"Not more than five or six miles, I believe," Laura replied.

Lenora rose softly to her feet and strolled to the back of the range wagon. In a few moments she reappeared, carrying a piece of paper in her hand. She stooped down.

"Craig's saddling up," she whispered. "Look what he dropped."

She held out the paper, on which was traced a roughly drawn map.

"That line's the river that marks the Mexican border," she explained. "You see where Long Jim's put the cross? That's where the bridge is. That other cross is the camp."

She pointed away southwards.

"That's the line," she continued. "Laura, where's the Professor?"

"I don't know," Laura replied. "He rode off some time ago, said he was going to meet Mr. Quest."

"If only he were here!" Lenora muttered. "I feel sure Craig means to escape. There he goes."

They saw him ride off into the darkness. Lenora ran to where her horse was tethered.

"I'm going after him," she announced. "Listen, Laura. If they arrive soon, send them after me. That's the line, as near as I can tell you," she added, pointing.

"Wait; I'm coming too!" Laura exclaimed.

Lenora shook her head.

"You must stay here and tell them about it," she insisted. "I shall be all right."

She galloped off while Laura was still undecided. Almost at that moment she heard from behind the welcome sound of horses' feet in the opposite direction and Quest alone galloped up. Laura laid her hand upon his rein.

"Where are the others?" she asked.

"French and two deputies from the township are about a mile behind," Quest replied. "They've had trouble with their horses."

"Don't get off," Laura continued quickly. "Craig has escaped, riding towards the Mexican frontier. Lenora is following him. He's gone in that direction," she added, pointing. "When you come to the river you'll have to hunt for the bridge."

Quest frowned as he gathered up his reins.

"I was afraid they'd try something of the sort," he muttered. "Tell the others where I've gone, Laura."

He galloped off into the darkness. Behind, there were some growls from the little group of cowboys, none of whom, however, attempted to interfere with him. Long Jim stood up and gazed sullenly southwards.

"Cookie'll make the bridge all right," he remarked. "If the girl catches him, she can't do anything. And that last guy'll never make it. Whoop! Here come the rest of them."

The Inspector, with two deputies, rode suddenly into the camp. The Inspector paused to speak to Laura. Long Jim's eyes sparkled as he saw them approach.

"It's old Harris and fat Andy," he whispered. "We'll have some fun with them."

The older of the two deputies approached them frowning.

"Been at your games again, Long Jim?" he began. "I hear you declined to hand over a criminal who's been sheltering on your ranch? You'll get into trouble before you've finished."

"Got the warrant?" Jim asked.

The deputy produced it. Long Jim looked at it curiously and handed it back.

"Guess the only other thing you want, then, is the man."

"Better produce him quickly," the deputy advised.

Jim turned away.

"Can't do it. He's beat it."

"You mean that you've let him go?"

"Let him go?" Jim repeated. "I ain't got no right to keep him. He took the job on at a moment's notice and he left at a moment's notice. There's some of your party after him, all right."

The deputies whispered to one another. The elder of the two turned around.

"Look here," he said to the cowboys, glancing around for Long Jim, who had disappeared, "we've had about enough of your goings-on. I reckon we'll take one of you back and see what seven days' bread and water will do towards civilising you."

There was a little mutter. The deputies stood side by side. With an almost simultaneous movement they had drawn their guns.

"Where's Long Jim?" the older one asked.

There was a sudden whirring about their heads. A lariat, thrown with unerring accuracy, had gathered them both in its coil. With a jerk they were drawn close together, their hands pinned to their side. Two cowboys quickly disarmed them. Long Jim came sauntering round from the other side of the range wagon, tightening the rope as he walked.

"Say, you've got a hell of a nerve, butting into a peaceable camp like this. We ain't broke no laws. So you're a'going to civilise us, eh? Well, Mister Harris, we can play that civilising game, too. Hey boys, all together, tie 'em up against that wagon."

A dozen willing hands secured them. The two men spluttered wildly, half in anger, half in fear of their tormentors, but in a few seconds they were secured firmly against the canvas-topped wagon.

"Now sit easy, gentlemen, sit easy. Nothing's going to hurt you." Long Jim shoved fresh cartridges into his forty-five. "That is, unless you're unlucky. Line up there, boys, one at a time now. Bud, you and Tim and Dough-head give them guys a singe, their hair's getting too long. The rest of you boys just content yourselves doing a fancy decoration on the canvas all around 'em. I'll deevote my entire attenshun to trimming them lugshuriant whiskers, Mister Harris is a-sporting. All ready now,—one, two, three, let 'em whistle!"

The two deputies gave a simultaneous yell as several bullets sung by their ears.

"Whoa, old horses," drawled Long Jim. "Flies bothering you some, eh? Sit easy, sit easy. Too dangerous hopping around that way. You might stick yourselves right in the way of one of them spitballs. Some nerve tonic this! A.X.X. Ranch brand, ready to serve at all hours, cheap at half the price. Ah ha, pretty near shaved your upper lip that time, didn't I, Mister Harris. My hand's a bit unsteady, what with all the excitement hereabouts. Say, put a stem on that chrysanthemum you're doing, Cotton-top."

The two men, racked with fury and terror, ridiculous in their trussed-up state, motionless and strained, crouched in terror while the bullets passed all around them. Inspector French tapped Long Jim on the shoulder.

"Look here," he remonstrated, "you're looking for trouble. You can't treat the representatives of the law like this."

Long Jim turned slowly around. His politeness was ominous.

"Say, you got me scared," he replied. "Am I going to be hung?"

"The law must be respected," French said firmly. "Untie those men."

Long Jim scratched his head for a moment.

"Say, Mr. Inspector," he remarked, "you're a fine man in your way but you weigh too much—that's what's the matter with you. Boys," he added, turning around, "what's the best exercise for reducing flesh?"

"Dancing," they shouted.

Long Jim grinned. He fell a little back. Suddenly he lowered his gun and shot into the ground, barely an inch from French's feet. The Inspector leaped into the air.

"Once more, boys," the cowboy went on. "Keep it up, Inspector. Jump a little higher next time. You barely cleared that one."

The bullets buried themselves in the dust around the Inspector's feet. Fuming with anger, French found himself continually forced to jump. The two deputies, forgotten for the moment, watched with something that was almost like a grin upon their faces. Laura, protesting loudly, was obliged more than once to look away to hide a smile. Jim at last slipped his gun into his holster.

"No more ammunition to waste, boys," he declared. "Untie the guys with the warrant and bring out the bottle of rye. Say," he went on, addressing the deputies as they struggled to their feet, "and you, Mr. New-Yorker, is it to be friends and a drink, or do you want a quarrel?"

The deputies were very thirsty. The perspiration was streaming down French's forehead. They all looked at one another. Laura whispered in French's ear and he nodded.

"We'll call it a drink," he decided.

The hunted man turned around with a little gasp. Before him was the rude mountain bridge, and on the other side—freedom. Scarcely a dozen lengths away was Lenora, and close behind her came Quest. He slackened speed as he walked his horse cautiously on to the planked bridge. Suddenly he gave a little cry. The frail structure, unexpectedly insecure, seemed to sway beneath his weight. Lenora, who had been riding fast, was unable to stop herself. She came on to the bridge at a half canter. Craig, who had reached the other side in safety, threw up his hands.

"Look out!" he cried. "My God!"

The bridge suddenly collapsed as though it had been made of paper. Lenora, grasping her horse, was thrown into the stream. Quest, galloping up, was only able to check himself just in time. He flung himself from his horse, and plunged into the stream. It was several moments before he was able to reach Lenora. From the opposite bank Craig watched them, glancing once or twice at the bridge. One of the wooden pillars had been sawn completely through.

"Are you hurt, dear?" Quest gasped, as he drew Lenora to the bank.

She shook her head.

"Just my side. Did Craig get away?"

Quest looked gloomily across the stream.

"Craig's in Mexico, right enough," he answered savagely, "but I am beginning to feel that I could fetch him back out of hell!"

CHAPTER XIV

TONGUES OF FLAME

1.

From the shadows of the trees on the further side of the river, Craig with strained eyes watched Quest's struggle. He saw him reach Lenora, watched him struggle to the bank with her, waited until he had lifted her on to his horse. Then he turned slowly around and faced the one country in the world where freedom was still possible for him. He looked into a wall of darkness, penetrated only at one spot by a little blaze of light. Slowly, with his arm through the bridle of his horse, he limped towards it. As he drew nearer and discovered its source, he hesitated. The light came through the uncurtained windows of a saloon, three long, yellow shafts illuminating the stunted shrubs and sandy places. Craig kept in the shadow between them and drew a little nearer. From inside he could hear the thumping of a worn piano, the twanging of a guitar, the rattle of glasses, the uproarious shouting of men, the shrill laughter of women. The tired man and the lame horse stole reluctantly a little nearer. Craig listened once more wearily. It was home he longed for so much—and rest. The very thought of the place sickened him. Even when he reached the door, he hesitated and instead of entering stood back amongst the shadows. If only he could find any other sort of shelter!

Inside, the scene was ordinary enough. There was a long bar, against which were lounging half a dozen typical Mexican cowpunchers. There was a small space cleared for dancing, at the further end of which two performers were making weird but vehement music. Three girls were dancing with cowboys, not ungracefully considering the state of the floor and the frequent discords in the music. One of them—the prettiest—stopped abruptly and pushed her partner away from her.

"You have drunk too much, José!" she exclaimed. "You cannot dance. You tread on my feet and you lean against me. I do not like it. I will dance with you another night when you are sober. Go away, please."

Her cavalier swayed for a moment on his feet. Then he looked down upon her with an evil glitter in his eyes. He was tall and thin, with a black moustache and yellow, unpleasant-looking teeth.

"So you will not dance any longer with José?" he muttered. "Very well, you shall drink with him, then. We will sit together at one of those little tables. Listen, you shall drink wine."

"I do not want to drink wine with you. All that I wish is to be left alone," the girl insisted curtly. "Go and play cards, if you want to. There is Pietro over there, and Diego. Perhaps you may win some money. They say that drunkards have all the luck."

José leered at her.

"Presently I will play cards," he said. "Presently I will win all their money and I will buy jewelry for you, Marta—stones that look like diamonds and will sparkle in your neck and in your hair."

She turned disdainfully away.

"I do not want your jewelry, José," she declared.

He caught her suddenly by the wrist.

"Perhaps this is what you want," he cried, as he stooped down to kiss her.

She swung her right hand round and struck him on the face. He staggered back for a moment. There was a red flush which showed through the tan of his cheek. Then he drew a little nearer to her, and before she could escape he had passed his long arm around her body. He drew her to the chair placed by the side of the wall. His left hand played with the knife at his belt.

"Marta, little sweetheart," he said mockingly, "you must pay for that blow. Don't be afraid," he went on, as he drew the knife across his leather breeches. "A little scratch across your cheek, so! It is but the brand of your master, a love-token from José. Steady, now, little Maverick!"

The girl struggled violently, but José was strong, such brawls were common, and those of the company who noticed at all, merely laughed at the girl's futile struggles. José's arm was already raised with the knife in his hand, when a sudden blow brought a yell of pain to his lips. The knife fell clattering to the floor. He sprang up, his eyes red with fury. A man had entered the door from behind and was standing within a few feet of him, a man with long, pale face, dark eyes, travel-stained, and with the air of a fugitive. A flood of incoherent abuse streamed from José's lips. He stooped for the knife. Marta threw herself upon him. The two cowboys who had been dancing suddenly intervened. The girls screamed.

"It was José's fault!" Marta cried. "José was mad. He would have killed me!"

Craig faced them all with sudden courage.

"As I came in," he explained, "that man had his knife raised to stab the girl. You don't allow that sort of thing, do you, here?"

The two cowboys linked their arms through José's and led him off towards the door.

"The stranger's right, José," one of them insisted. "You can't carve a girl up in company."

The girl clutched at Craig's arm.

"Sit down here, please," she begged. "Wait."

She disappeared for a moment and came back with a glass full of wine, which she set down on the table.

"Drink this," she invited. "And thank you for saving me."

Craig emptied the glass eagerly. He was beginning to be more than a little conscious of his fatigue.

"I just happened to be the first to see him," he said. "They aren't quite wild enough to allow that here, are they?"

"Quien sabe? The girls do not like me! The men do not care," she declared. "José took me by surprise, though, or I would have killed him. But who are you, and where did you come from?"

"I have just crossed the border," he replied.

She nodded understandingly.

"Were they after you?"

"Yes! with a warrant for my arrest!"

She patted his hand.

"You are safe now," she whispered. "We care that much for a United States warrant," and she snapped her slim fingers. "You shall stay with us for a time. We will take care of you."

He sighed wearily.

"If I do," he said, "there will be trouble. Wherever I go there is trouble. I have been round the world looking for peace. I shall never find it in this world."

Her eyes filled with tears. There was something hopelessly pathetic in his appearance.

"You shall find it here," she promised.

Back in the camp, a spirit of deviltry had entered once more into Long Jim and his mates. A tactless remark on the part of one of the deputies had set alight once more the smouldering fire of resentment which the cowboys had all the time felt against them. At a word from Long Jim they were taken by surprise and again tied to the wagon.

"These guys ain't got a sufficiency yet, boys. Limber up them guns again. Same order as before. Put a few more petals on them flowers, and I'll trim their eyelashes for them."

The deputies spluttered with rage and fear. Shots rained about them and the canvas of the wagon was riddled. French began to get restless.

"Look here," he said to Laura, "I can't stand this any longer. It don't seem right to have two officers of the law treated like that, any way. I guess I'll have to butt in again."

"Don't," Laura advised bluntly. "You'll get yours if you do."

A yell from one of the deputies clinched the matter. French drew his revolver and advanced into the centre of the little group.

"Say, you fellows," he exclaimed, "you've got to stop this! Those men came here on a legitimate errand and it's your duty to respect them."

Long Jim strolled up to the Inspector.

"Maybe you're right, Mr. French," he remarked, "but—"

With a swoop of his long arm he snatched French's gun away, examined it for a moment, looked at French and shook his head.

"You're too fat, Inspector," he declared sorrowfully, "still too fat. That's what's the matter with you. Another ten minutes' exercise will do you all the good in the world."

A bullet struck the dust a few inches from French's feet. Furious with rage, he found himself once more forced to resort to undignified antics. This time, however, Laura intervened. She walked straight up into the little circle and stood close to French's side, regardless of the levelled guns.

"Look here, Long Jim, or whatever your name is," she protested, "you just call your crowd off and stop this. Undo those two deputies. A joke's a joke, but this has gone far enough. If you don't untie them, I will. Take your choice and get a move on."

Long Jim scratched his chin for a moment.

"Waal," he said, "I guess that what the lady says goes. We ain't often favoured with ladies' society, boys, and I guess when we are we'd better do as we are told. Turn 'em loose, boys."

They abandoned the sport a little reluctantly. Suddenly they all paused to listen. The sound of a horse's slow footfall was heard close at hand. Presently Quest appeared out of the shadows, carrying Lenora in his arms. Laura rushed forward.

"Lenora!" she cried. "Is she hurt?"

Quest laid her tenderly upon the ground.

"We had a spill at the bridge," he explained quickly. "I don't know whether Craig loosened the supports. He got over all right, but it went down under Lenora, who was following, and I had to get her out of the river. Where's the Professor?"

The Professor came ambling down from the tent where he had been lying. He stooped at once over Lenora's still unconscious form.

"Dear me!" he exclaimed. "Dear me! Come, come!"

He passed his hand over her side and made a brief examination.

"Four ribs broken," he pronounced. "It will be a week, at any rate, before we are able to move her. Nothing more serious, so far as I can see, Mr. Quest, but she'll need rest and all the comfort we can give her."

"Say, that's too bad!" Long Jim declared. "If you've got to stay around for a time, though, you can have the tents. We boys can double up anywhere, or bunk on the ground. That's right, ain't it?" he added, turning around to the cowboys.

There was a little grunt of acquiescence. They carried Lenora to the largest of the tents and made her as comfortable as possible. She opened her eyes on the way.

"I am so sorry," she faltered. "It's just my side. It—hurts. How did I get out of the stream?"

"I fished you out," Quest whispered. "Don't talk now. We are going to make you comfortable."

She pressed his hand and closed her eyes again. The Professor returned.

"We'll make the young lady comfortable all right," he assured them cheerfully, "but there's one thing you can make up your minds to. We are here for a week at the least."

They all looked at one another. The Inspector was the only one who preserved an air of cheerfulness, and he was glancing towards Laura.

"Guess we'll have to make the best of it," he murmured.

2.

The girl drew a low stool over to Craig's side. He was sitting in a rough chair tilted back against the adobe wall of the saloon.

"As tired as ever?" she asked, laying her hand upon his for a moment.

He turned his head and looked at her.

"Always tired," he answered listlessly.

She made a little grimace.

"But you are so strange," she protested. "Over the hills there are the steam cars. They would take you to some of our beautiful cities where all is light and gaiety. You are safe here, whatever your troubles may have been. You say that you have money, and if you are lonely," she added, dropping her voice, "you need not go alone."

He patted her hand affectionately but there was something a little forced about the action.

"Child," he said, "it is so hard to make you understand. I might lose myself for a few minutes, it is true, over yonder. Perhaps, even," he added, "you might help me to forget. And then there would be the awakening. That is always the same. Sometimes at night I sleep, and when I sleep I rest, and when my eyes are opened in the morning the weight comes back and sits upon my heart, and the strength seems to pass from my limbs and the will from my brain."

Her eyes were soft and her voice shook a little as she leaned towards him. Something in his helplessness had kindled the protective spirit in her.

"Has life been so terrible for you?" she whispered. "Have you left behind—but no! you never could have been really wicked. You are not very old, are you? Why do you not stand up and be a man? If you have done wrong, then very likely people have done wrong things to you. Why should you brood over these memories? Why—... What are you looking at? Who are these people?"

The Professor, with Quest and Long Jim, suddenly appeared round the corner of the building. They walked towards Craig. He shrank back in his place.

"If these are your enemies," the girl cried fiercely, "remember that they cannot touch you here. I'll have the boys out in a minute, if they dare to try it."

Craig struggled to his feet. He made no answer. His eyes were fixed upon the Professor's. The girl passed her arm through his and dragged him into the saloon. They passed José in the doorway. He scoffed at them.

"Say, the boss will fire you, Marta, if you waste all your time with that Yankee," he muttered.

Marta drew the red rose from the bosom of her dress and placed it in Craig's buttonhole. Then she led him without a word to a seat.

"If these men try any tricks in here," she said, "there'll be trouble."

Almost at that moment they all three entered. Long Jim nodded to Craig in friendly fashion.

"It's all right, cookie," he told them. "Don't you look so scared. This is just a bit of parley-vous business, that's all."

The Professor held out a piece of paper. He handed it over to Craig.

"Craig," he announced, "this is a dispatch which I found in Allguez with my letters. It is addressed to you, but under the circumstances you will scarcely wonder that I opened it. You had better read it."

Craig accepted the cable-form and read it through slowly to himself:—

"To John Craig, c/o Professor Lord Ashleigh, Yonkers, New York:
    "Your sister died today. Her daughter Mary sails on Tuesday to join you in New York. Please meet her.
    "Compton, Solicitor, London."

Craig sat for a moment as though stunned. The girl leaned over towards him.

"Are they trying to take you on a warrant?" she whispered. "Remember you don't need to go unless you want to."

Craig shook his head.

"This is something quite different," he explained. "Leave me for a moment, Marta. I must talk to these people."

She slipped regretfully away from his side and out into the darkness. He sat with his eyes fixed upon the cablegram. Then he turned towards Quest.

"Fate seems to be too strong for me," he admitted. "Leave me alone and I promise you that I'll go at once to New York, settle Mary's future, and then make a full disclosure."

Jim touched him on the shoulder.

"Remember," he told him, "you ain't no call to leave here unless you want to. Those deputies don't go this side of the border. You're safe as long as you like to stay."

Craig nodded gratefully.

"All the same," he said, "I fear that I must go."

The Professor coughed.

"I am sure, Craig," he declared, "that you have decided wisely."

Craig looked gloomily away.

"There is nothing else for me to do," he said. "The child must be met and looked after. Besides, I am sick of it all. You may as well know the truth."

"Why not now?" Quest suggested softly.

"In New York," Craig replied, "and not before."

Quest and the Professor exchanged meaning glances.

"Very well," the former decided, turning away, "in a week from today, Craig, I shall expect you to report at the Professor's house."

They left the room together. Long Jim lingered by Craig's side.

"Those guys have been scaring you some, I guess," he remarked. "Forget 'em, cookie. They can't touch you here. Of course, if you go to New York it's your own show."

"I know that," Craig replied gloomily.

One of the girls passed her arm through Long Jim's.

"Just one dance," she whispered.

He hesitated, looking out of the window. Then he shrugged his shoulders.

"I'm tired of those guys," he remarked to Craig with a grin. "Guess I'll stay here for a bit."

Craig was left alone for a few minutes. Suddenly Marta glided in and sat by his side. Her eyes were flashing with anger.

"You know what they said, those two, as they passed out?" she whispered hoarsely. "I heard them. They are going to board the eight-thirty train tomorrow morning. The dark man turned and said to the other—'If he is not on that, we'll wait till we find him. Once we get him in New York, he's our man.'"

A little exclamation of anger broke from Craig's lips. The girl caught at his arm.

"Don't go," she begged. "Don't go. There are plenty of places near here where you can hide, where we could go together and live quite simply. I'd work for you. Take me away from this, somewhere over the hills. Don't go to New York. They are cruel, those men. They are hunting you—I can see it in their faces."

Craig shook his head sadly.

"Little girl," he said, "I should like to go with you along that valley and over the hills and forget that I had ever lived in any other world. But I can't do it. There's a child there now, on the ocean, nearer to New York every day, my sister's own child and no one to meet her. And—there are the other things. I have sinned and I must pay.... My God!"

The room suddenly rang with Marta's shriek. Through the open window by which they were sitting, an arm wrapped in a serape had suddenly hovered over them. Craig, in starting back, had just escaped the downward blow of the knife, which had buried itself in Marta's arm. She fell back, screaming.

"It's José!" she cried. "The brute! The beast!"

Craig swung to his feet, furious. Long Jim, cursing fiercely, drew his gun. At that moment the door of the saloon was thrown open. José came reeling in, his serape over his shoulder, a drunken grin on his face. He staggered towards them.

"José, you beast!" the girl called out, and fell back, fainting.

There was the sound of a revolver shot and José reeled backwards and fell with a cry across the sanded floor. Jim thrust his smoking gun into his belt and caught Craig by the arm.

"Say, we'd better get out of this, cookie!" he muttered.

They were hustled out. Apparently José was unpopular, for every one seemed only anxious to have them clear away.

"I'll get you into the camp quietly," Long Jim muttered. "You'll be safer there for the night. Then you can make that eighty-thirty in the morning."

Lenora, with her bed dragged to the opening of the tent, eagerly greeted the little party on their return. Quest at once came and sat by her side.

"Where's Laura," he asked, "and the Inspector?"

She smiled and pointed to the rising ground behind them. In the faint moonlight two forms were just visible.

"The Inspector isn't taking 'no' for an answer," Lenora remarked cheerfully, "and honestly, if you ask me, I believe that Laura is weakening a little. She pretended she didn't want to go out for a walk, and mumbled something about leaving me, but she soon changed her mind when the Inspector pressed her. They have been up there for an hour or more."

Quest smiled.

"French has got it bad," he declared, "almost as badly as I have, Lenora."

She laughed at him. Her face was a little drawn with pain but her eyes were very soft.

"I wonder if you have it very badly," she murmured.

He held her hand for a moment.

"I think you know," he said.

As they talked they heard the coyotes barking in the distance. Presently Laura and the Inspector returned.

"Nice sort of nurse I am," the former grumbled. "It's all the fault of this man. He would keep me out there talking rubbish."

"We were watching you, dear," Lenora said quietly. "Somehow it didn't seem to us that you were particularly anxious to get away."

The Inspector chuckled.

"That's one for Miss Laura," he declared, with an air of satisfaction. "Little bit hard on me generally."

"Oh! I'm all right if I'm left alone," Laura retorted, bustling around. "Come along, you folks, if we are going to have any supper tonight."

They sat round the opening before Lenora's tent till the moon was high in the heavens. Quest, who had been on the outside of the circle for some little time, suddenly rose to his feet and crossed over to the cook wagon. Long Jim, who was sitting on the steps, glanced up a little surlily.

"Who's inside there?" Quest asked.

Long Jim removed his pipe from his teeth.

"That don't sound none too civil a question for a guest," he remarked, "but if you want to know, our new Chinese cookie is there."

Quest nodded.

"Sorry if I seemed abrupt," he apologised. "You've been very good to us and I'm sure we are uncommonly obliged to you, Jim. The only reason I asked the question was that I saw a face in the door there and it gave me a start. For a moment I thought it was Craig back again."

"He's gone to New York, or going tomorrow morning," Jim replied. "I don't think he's so powerful fond of your company that he'd come round here looking for it."

Quest strolled off again and glanced at his watch as he rejoined the little group.

"Well," he said, "I think we'll turn in. Seven o'clock tomorrow morning, Inspector. Jim's sending one of the boys with us and we shall catch the Eastern Limited at the junction."

The Inspector yawned.

"This open-air life makes me sleepy," he confessed.

"To bed, all of us," Quest concluded, turning away.

3.

Quest awoke the next morning, stretched out his hand and glanced at the watch by the side of his bed. It was barely six o'clock. He turned over and dozed again, looked again at half past six, and finally, at a few minutes to seven, rose and made a hasty toilet. Then, in the act of placing his watch in his waistcoat pocket, he gave a sudden start. By its side, half covered by the handkerchief which he had thrown upon the little table, stood a small black box! For a moment he was motionless. Then he stretched out his hand, removed the lid and drew out the usual neatly folded piece of paper:—

"Even time fights you. It loses that you may lose.
 "The Hands."

Quest for a moment was puzzled. Then he hurried into the next tent, where the Professor was sleeping peacefully.

"Say, Professor, what's the time by your watch?" Quest asked, shaking him gently.

The Professor sat up and drew his chronometer from under his pillow.

"Seven o'clock," he replied, "five minutes past, maybe."

Quest nodded.

"That seems all right," he declared. "I'll explain later, Professor."

He hurried out into French's tent and found the Inspector just drawing on his shoes.

"French, what's the time?" he demanded.

"Three minutes past seven, or thereabouts," French replied, yawning. "I'm coming right along. We've lots of time. Three-quarters of an hour ought to do it, the boys say."

Quest held out a strip of paper.

"This gave me a turn," he said quietly. "I found it in a black box by the side of my bed."

French gazed at it in a puzzled manner. They walked outside to the camp, where the cowboys were finishing their breakfast.

"Say, boss," one of them called out, "you're not making that eight-thirty train to New York?"

"Why not?" Quest asked quickly. "It's only three quarters of an hour's ride, is it?"

"Maybe not," the other replied, "but as it's eight now, your chances ain't looking lively. Kind of overslept, haven't you?"

Both men glanced once more at their watches. Then Quest thrust his back with a little oath.

"Our watches have been set back!" he exclaimed. "The Hands again!"

For a moment they looked at one another, dumbfounded. Then Quest moved towards the corral.

"Say, is there any quicker way to the depot?" he enquired of the cowboys.

They heard his question indifferently.

"Fifty dollars," Quest continued, "to any one who can take me by a quicker route."

One of them rose slowly to his feet.

"Waal," he observed, "fifty dollars would come in kind of handy. Yes, I reckon I can cut off a mile or two for you."

"Fifty dollars for you, then," Quest replied, as they hurried towards the horses, "and an extra ten if we make the train."

They galloped off into the distance. The cowboys finished their breakfast and went off to their work. Laura stole out from her tent and started off in rather a shame-faced manner for a ride. Presently Lenora opened her eyes. She, too, stretched out her hand for her watch. Suddenly she sat up in bed with a little exclamation. On the table by her side was a small black box. She took off the lid with trembling fingers, drew out a scrap of paper and read:—

"Fools! Tongues of flame will cross Quest's path. He will never reach the depot alive."

Lenora glanced at Laura's empty bed. Then she staggered to the opening of the tent.

"Laura!" she cried.

There was no one there. The cowboys had all gone to their work, Laura had passed out of sight across the ridge in the distance. Lenora staggered to the cook wagon, where the Chinese cook was sitting cleaning plates.

"Listen!" she cried. "They are in danger, the three men who have gone off to the depot! If you'll ride after them, I will give you a hundred dollars. Give them this," she added, holding out the scrap of paper.

The Chinaman shook his head. He glanced at the slip of paper indifferently and went on with his work.

"No can ride, missee," he said.

Lenora looked around helplessly. The camp was empty. She staggered across towards her own horse.

"Come and help me," she ordered.

The Chinaman came unwillingly. They found her saddle but he only gazed at it in a stolid sort of fashion.

"No can fix," he said. "Missee no can ride. Better go back bed."

Lenora pushed him on one side. With a great effort she managed to reach her place in the saddle. Then she turned and, with her face to the depot, galloped away. The pain was excruciating. She could only keep herself in the saddle with an effort. Yet all the time that one sentence was ringing in her mind—"Tongues of flame!" She kept looking around anxiously. Suddenly the road dropped from a little decline.

She was conscious of a wave of heat. In the distance she could see the smoke rolling across the open. She touched her horse with the quirt. The spot which she must pass to keep on the track to the depot was scarcely a hundred yards ahead, but already the fire seemed to be running like quicksilver across the ground licking up the dry greasewood with indeed a flaming tongue. She glanced once behind, warned by the heat. The fire was closing in upon her. A puff of smoke suddenly enveloped her. She coughed. Her head began to swim and a fit of giddiness assailed her. She rocked in her saddle and the pony came to a sudden standstill, faced by the mass of rolling smoke and flame.

"Sanford!" Lenora cried. "Save me!"

The pony reared. She slipped from the saddle and fell across the track.

CHAPTER XV

"A BOLT FROM THE BLUE"

1.

There was a peculiar, almost a foreboding silence about the camp that morning when Laura returned from her early ride. The only living person to be seen was the Chinaman, sitting on a stool in front of the wagon, with a dish of potatoes between his knees.

"Say, where's every one?" Laura sung out, after she had looked into Lenora's tent and found it empty.

The Chinaman continued to peel potatoes. He took no notice of the question. Laura touched her horse with the whip and cantered over to his side. At the last moment the animal swerved a little. The Chinaman, trying to draw back hastily, let the bowl slip between his knees. He gazed at the broken pieces of the dish in dismay.

"Never mind your silly potatoes!" Laura exclaimed. "Tell me where every one's gone to, can't you?"

The Chinaman looked up at her malevolently. He rose and made a stealthy movement forward. Laura backed her horse. The purpose which had gleamed for a moment in the man's narrowed eyes seemed to fade away.

"All gone," he announced. "Cowboy gone workee. Missee gone hurry up find Mr. Quest."

Laura hesitated, puzzled. Just then the Professor came cantering in with a bundle of grass in his hand. He glanced down at the Chinaman.

"Good morning, Miss Laura!" he said. "You don't seem to be getting on with our friend here," he added in an undertone. "If you would permit me to offer you just a word of advice, it really doesn't pay to annoy these Chinese too much. They never forget. I didn't like the way that fellow was looking at you. I was watching him all the way from the rise there."

"Pshaw!" she answered. "Who cares what a Chink thinks! The fellow's an idiot. I'm worried, Professor. Lenora's gone out after Mr. Quest and the Inspector. She wasn't fit to ride a horse. I can't make out why she's attempted it."

The Professor unslung some field-glasses from his shoulder and gazed steadily southward.

"It is just possible," he said softly, "that she may have received a warning of that."

He pointed with his forefinger, and Laura peered forward. Something which seemed to be just a faint cloud hung over the horizon.

The Professor handed her his glasses.

"Why, it's a fire!" she cried.

The Professor nodded.

"Just a prairie fire," he replied,—"very dangerous, though, these dry seasons. The flames move so quickly that if you happen to be in a certain position you might easily get cut off."

Laura turned her horse round.

"Come on, Professor!" she exclaimed. "That's what it is. Lenora's gone to try and warn the others."

"She is a very brave young lady," the Professor declared, as he touched his pony with the spurs. "All the same, Miss Laura, you take my advice and leave that Chinaman alone."

They rode to the very edge of the tract of country which was temporarily enveloped with smoke and flame. Here they pulled in their horses, and the Professor looked thoughtfully through his field-glasses.

"The road straight on is the ordinary way to the depot," he said, "but, as you can see, at the bend there it is becoming almost impassable. The thing is, what did Lenora do? When she got as far as this, she must have seen that further progress was dangerous."

Laura gave a little cry and pointed with her riding-whip. About twenty yards further on, by the side of the road, was a small white object. She cantered on, swung herself from her horse and picked it up.

"Lenora's handkerchief!" she cried.

The Professor waved his arm westward.

"Here come Quest and the Inspector. They are making a circuit to avoid the fire. The cowboy with them must have shown them the way. We'd better hurry up and find out if they've seen anything of Miss Lenora."

They galloped across the rough country towards the little party, who were now clearly in sight.

"Lenora isn't with them," Laura declared anxiously, "and look—what's that?"

From the centre of one of the burning patches they saw a riderless horse gallop out, stop for a moment with his head almost between its fore-legs, shake himself furiously, and gallop blindly on again.

"It's Lenora's horse!" Laura cried. "She must have been thrown. Come!"

Laura would have turned her horse, but the Professor checked her.

"Let us wait for Quest," he advised. "They are close here."

The cowboy, riding a little behind the two others, had unlimbered his lariat, and, while they watched, swung it over his head and secured the runaway. Quest galloped up to where Laura and the Professor were waving frantically.

"Say, that's some fire!" Quest exclaimed. "Did you people come out to see it?"

"No, we came to find Lenora!" Laura answered breathlessly. "That's her horse. She started to meet you. She must be some-where—"

"Lenora?" Quest interrupted fiercely. "What do you mean?"

"When I got back to the camp," Laura continued rapidly, "there wasn't a soul there except the Chinaman. He told me that Lenora had ridden off a few minutes before to find you. We came to look for her. We found her handkerchief on the road there, and that's her horse."

Quest did not wait for another word. He jumped a rough bush of scrub on the right-hand side, galloped over the ground, which was already hot with the coming fire, and followed along down the road by which Lenora had passed. When he came to the first bend, he could hear the roar of flames in the trees. A volume of smoke almost blinded him; his horse became wholly unmanageable. He slipped from the saddle and ran on, staggering from right to left like a drunken man. About forty yards along the road, Lenora was lying in the dust. A volume of smoke rushed over her. The tree under which she had collapsed was already afire. A twig fell from it as Quest staggered up, and her skirt began to smoulder. He tore off his coat, wrapped it around her, beat out the fire which was already blazing at her feet, and snatched her into his arms. She opened her eyes for a moment.

"Where are we?" she whispered. "The fire!"

"That's all right," Quest shouted. "We'll be out of it in a moment. Hold tight to my neck."

He braced himself for a supreme effort and ran along the pathway. His feet were blistered with the heat; there was a great burn on one of his arms. At last, however, he passed out of the danger zone and staggered up to where the Professor, the Inspector and Laura were waiting.

"Say, that was a close shave," he faltered, as he laid Lenora upon the ground. "Another five minutes—well, we won't talk about it. Let's lift her on to your horse, Laura, and get back to the camp."

2.

The Professor laid down his book and gazed with an amiable smile towards Quest and Lenora.

"I fear," he remarked dolefully, "that my little treatise on the fauna of the Northern Orinoco scarcely appeals to you, Mr. Quest."

Quest, whose arm was in a sling but who was otherwise none the worse for his recent adventure, pointed out of the tent.

"Don't you believe it, Professor," he begged. "I've been listening to every word. But say, Lenora, just look at Laura and French!"

They all three peered anxiously out of the opening of the tent. Laura and the Inspector were very slowly approaching the cook wagon. Laura was carrying a large bunch of wild flowers, one of which she was in the act of fastening in French's buttonhole.

"That fellow French has got grit," Quest declared. "He sticks to it all the time. He'll win out with Laura in the end, you mark my words."

"I hope he will," Lenora said. "She's a dear girl, although she has got an idea into her head that she hates men and love-making. I think the Inspector's just the man for her."

The two had paused outside the cook wagon. Laura held out the flowers to the Chinaman.

"Can't you find me a bowl for these?" she asked.

He looked slowly up at her.

"No bowlee for flowers," he answered. "All want for eatee."

Laura leaned over and shook him by the shoulder.

"Well, I'll eatee off the ground," she said. "Give me a bowl, you slant-eyed old idiot."

"Why don't you obey the lady?" French intervened.

Very slowly the Chinaman rose to his feet, disappeared inside the cook wagon and reappeared with a basin, which he handed to Laura. She thanked him carelessly, and they passed on. From where they stood, both Quest and Lenora saw the look which for a moment flashed from the Chinaman's eyes. Lenora shivered.

"I'll be glad when we get away from here," she declared, clinging to Quest's arm. "That Chinaman hates Laura like poison, and I'm afraid of him."

Quest nodded.

"She does seem to have put his back up," he agreed. "As to going on, I think we might just as well move tomorrow. My arm's all right."

"And I'm quite well," Lenora asserted eagerly.

"We've wired for them to meet Craig," Quest said. "I only hope they don't let him slip through their fingers. I haven't much faith in his promise to turn up at the Professor's. Let's see what Laura and French have to say."

"Can't see any sense in staying on here any longer," was French's immediate decision, "so long as you two invalids feel that you can stand the journey. Besides, we're using up these fellows' hospitality."

"We'll get everything in order tonight," Laura decided, "and start first thing tomorrow."

They busied themselves for the next hour or two in making preparations. After their evening meal, the two men walked with Lenora and Laura to their tent.

"I think you girls had better go to bed," Quest suggested. "Try and get a long night's sleep."

"That's all very well," French remarked, "but it's only eight o'clock. What about a stroll, Miss Laura, just up to the ridge?"

Laura hesitated for a moment and glanced towards Lenora.

"Please go," the latter begged. "I really don't feel like going to sleep just yet."

"I'll look after Lenora," Quest promised. "You have your walk. There's the Professor sitting outside his tent. Wouldn't you like to take him with you?"

Laura glanced indignantly at him as they strolled out, and Lenora laughed softly.

"How dared you suggest such a thing!" she murmured to Quest. "Do look at them. The Inspector wants her to take his watch, and she can't quite make up her mind about it. Why, Laura's getting positively frivolous."

"Guess we'd better not watch them any longer," Quest decided. "What about a game of bezique?"

"I should love it!" Lenora assented. "You'll find the cards in that satchel."

They sat and played for half an hour by the light of a lantern. Suddenly Quest paused in the act of dealing and glanced over his shoulder.

"What the mischief was that?" he muttered.

"Sounded as though the tent flapped," Lenora replied.

Quest rose, and with the lantern in his hand walked to the other side of the tent. The flap was open, but there was no sign of any one in sight. He looked around and came back.

"Queer thing!" he exclaimed. "It sounded just as though some one had pulled the flap of the tent back. The flap's open, but there isn't a soul in sight."

"I expect it was fancy," Lenora remarked. "Still, there isn't a breath of wind, is there?"

Quest returned to his place, and they recommenced the game. Just at that moment the entrance to the tent was lifted and Laura ran in. She plumped down upon her bed with her hands on either side of her.

"If that man—" she began.

Suddenly she sprang up with a little cry which turned almost into a scream. From a look of humorous indignation, her face suddenly assumed an expression of absolute terror. She shrank away.

"There's something soft in the bed!" she shrieked. "I felt it with my hand!"

They all looked towards the cot. Quest held up the lantern. They distinctly saw a movement under the bedclothes. The Inspector, stooping down, suddenly entered the tent.

"Say, what's wrong here?" he demanded.

"There's something in Laura's bed," Quest muttered. "Here, give me the camp-stool."

He stole towards the bed, gripping the camp-stool firmly with his right hand, and slowly turning down the bedclothes with the feet of the chair. Suddenly there was a piercing scream. A huge snake, coiled and quivering for the spring, lifted its head. Even Quest seemed for the moment nerveless. Then from the doorway came the sharp report of a revolver, and the snake fell, a limp, inert thing. They all looked at the Professor as though fascinated. He came a step farther into the tent, the revolver still smoking in his hand. Standing over the snake, he deliberately fired again and again into the body.

"I think," he remarked, in his usual calm tones, "that we may consider the creature now beyond any power of doing harm. You will be interested to hear," he continued, bending over the remains of the creature, "that this is an exceedingly rare species, a sort of second cousin to the rattlesnake found only in this part of the world and fatally poisonous."

"But how could it have got there?" Lenora faltered.

The Professor shook his head gravely.

"I am afraid," he said, "that there can be no doubt about that. I saw the Chinaman whom Laura is so fond of sneaking away from this tent a few minutes ago, and I suspected some devilry. That is why I went and fetched my revolver."

There was a roar of anger from French. He snatched the weapon from the Professor's hand.

"I'll kill that yellow dog!" he shouted. "Where is he?"

He dashed across the open space towards the camp wagon. His teeth were set, and there was murder in his blazing eyes.

"Where's that Chinaman?" he yelled at the top of his voice.

The cowboys struggled to their feet. The Chinaman, who was sitting inside the cook wagon, poring over a book by the light of a lantern, recognised the note of fury in French's tone and raised his head, startled. A paroxysm of fear seized him. The very moment that French threw open the door of the wagon, he kicked the lantern across the floor and plunged at the canvas sides of the vehicle, slipping underneath until he reached the ground. French, left in darkness, groped around for a moment and then emerged. The cowboys had gathered together outside.

"Say, Mr. Inspector French," one of them demanded, "what's wrong with John Chinaman? You folks seem to have a sort of grudge against our cooks. What's the Oriental been doing, eh?"

"Tried to commit a filthy murder," French shouted. "Brought a snake and put it into the bed of one of the young women."

They hesitated no longer.

"Come on, boys," one of them cried. "We'll have to see this

matter through."

They found the spot where the Chinaman had escaped from the wagon, but even at that moment they heard the sound of a horse's hoofs and saw a flying figure in the distance.

"Said he couldn't ride!" French shouted. "Told the young lady so when she wanted him to go and warn us of the fire. Look at him now!"

"Come on, all of you," one of the cowboys yelled, as they rushed for the horse. "Bring your lariats. We'll have him, sure."

French, with his start, was the first to reach a horse. The cowboys galloped off through the shadows. Dimly visible, they now and then caught a glimpse of their quarry; sometimes he faded out of sight altogether.

"We'll have him through that patch of brush," Long Jim shouted. "He won't dare to ride the pace there."

They saw him for a moment bending low over his horse, but they did not see him slip easily from its back, roll over into the brushwood, and lie there concealed. They heard the thunder of hoofs ahead, and they galloped by. When they were out of sight, the Chinaman stole away into the darkness. Nearly an hour later, the little party caught up with the riderless horse. The language of the cowboys was picturesque.

"Spread out, boys. We'll round him up going back, if we can," Long Jim directed. "If he was spilled off, we'll get him, sure. But if the dirty coyote has tricked us and slipped off into the brush, it's good night. We'll never find him."

French's hand tightened upon his revolver, and his eyes pierced the darkness to right and to left as he rode slowly back.

"There'll be no trial if I can get the drop on him," he muttered.

Away in the distance, John Chinaman was reaching Allguez, and the little party of cowboys rode into the camp without having seen a sign of him. French was narrating his failure to the three others, when Quest in silence handed him a cablegram, a messenger had just brought.

> To Inspector French, Allguez, N.M.
>
> Very sorry. Craig gave us slip after leaving depot. Niece disappeared from address given. No clues at present. When are you returning?

French swore softly for a moment. Then he dropped into a chair, exhausted.

"This," he declared, "is our unlucky evening."

3.

The woman who had just laid the cloth for a homely evening meal, smiled across at the girl who stood at the window.

"It's all ready now directly your uncle comes home," she announced. "Say, you never seem to tire of looking out of that window."

The girl turned around with a smile. She was very young and dressed in deep mourning.

"I've never seen anything like it before, Mrs. Malony," she said. "It was quite quiet where we lived in London, and here, with the street cars and the elevated railways and the clanging of bells, there never seems to be a moment's peace."

Mrs. Malony came to the girl's side.

"Your poor uncle looks as though a little peace would do him good," she remarked.

The girl sighed.

"If only I could do something for him!" she murmured.

"He's in some kind of trouble, I think," Mrs. Malony observed. "He is not what you might call a communicative person, but it's easy to see that he is far from being happy in himself. You'll ring when you're ready, Miss Mary?"

The door was suddenly opened, and Craig entered. He was very pale and a little out of breath. Before he closed the door, he listened for a moment.

"Just as we were speaking about you, Mr. Craig," the landlady continued. "I was saying to the young lady that there was only one thing I could wish for you both, and that was that you weren't quite so worried like."

Craig seemed scarcely to hear her.

"Look across the road," he begged. "Tell me if there is a man in a blue serge suit and a bowler hat, smoking a cigar, looking across here."

Mrs. Malony and the girl both obeyed. The girl was the first to speak.

"Yes!" she announced. "He is looking straight at these windows."

Craig groaned and sank down upon a chair.

"Leave us, if you please, Mrs. Malony," he ordered. "I'll ring when I'm ready."

Mrs. Malony hesitated with the door-knob in her hand.

"I'm not wishing to say anything that might sound offensive," she observed slowly, "but if it's a case of trouble of any sort with the police, Mr. Craig—"

"That will do," Craig interrupted. "It isn't anything of the sort you think. You are not likely to suffer by having me here, Mrs.

Malony, or by looking after my niece when I have gone."

The landlady left the room silently. The girl came over to her uncle and threw her arm around his neck.

"Please don't talk about going away, uncle," she pleaded. "I have been so happy since I have been with you."

He patted her head, felt in his pocket, and drew out a little paper bag, from which he shook a bunch of violets. The girl pinned them to her frock with a little cry of pleasure.

"How kind you are to me!" she exclaimed. "You think of everything!"

He sighed.

"If I had had you for a little longer, Mary," he said, "perhaps I should have been a better man. Go to the window, please, and tell me if that man is still there."

She crossed the room with light footsteps. Presently she returned.

"He is just crossing the street," she announced. "I think that he seems to be coming here."

Craig took the girl for a minute into his arms.

"Good-bye, dear," he said. "I want you to take this paper and keep it carefully. You will be cared for always, but I must go."

"But where must you go?" she asked bewildered.

"I have an appointment at Professor Ashleigh's," he told her. "I cannot tell you anything more than that. Good-bye!"

He kissed her for a moment passionately. Then suddenly he tore himself away. She heard him run lightly down the stairs. Some instinct led her to the back window. She saw him emerge from the house and pass down the yard. Then she went to the front. The man in the blue serge suit was talking to the landlady below. She sank into a chair, puzzled and unhappy. Then she heard heavy footsteps. The door was opened. The man in the blue serge suit entered, followed by the protesting landlady.

"There's no sense in coming here to worry the young lady," Mrs. Malony declared irritably. "As for Mr. Craig, I told you that he'd gone out."

"Gone out, eh?" the man repeated, speaking in a thick, disagreeable tone. "Why, I watched him in here not ten minutes ago. Now then, young lady, guess you'd better cough up the truth. Where's this precious uncle of yours?"

"My uncle has gone out," the girl replied, drawing herself up. "He left five minutes ago."

"Sneaked out by the back way, maybe," the man sneered.

"If there was any fear of your stopping to speak to him, I should think he would," the girl retorted boldly. "My uncle is rather particular about his acquaintances."

The man laughed.

"What's that in your hand?" he demanded.

"Something my uncle gave me before he went out," the girl replied. "I haven't looked at it yet myself."

"Give it here," he ordered.

She spread it out upon the table.

"You may look at it if you choose," she agreed. "My uncle did not tell me not to show it to any one."

They read it together. The few lines seemed to be written with great care. They took, indeed, the form of a legal document, to which was affixed the seal of a notary and the name of a witness.—

I, John Craig, being about to receive the just punishment for all my sins, hereby bequeath to my niece, Mary Carlton, all monies and property belonging to me, a list of which she will find at this address. I make one condition only of my bequest and I beg my niece to fervently respect it. It is that she never of her own consent or knowledge speak to any one of the name of Ashleigh, or associate with any of that name.

John Craig.

The man folded up the paper.

"I'll take care of this," he said. "It's yours, right enough. We'll just need to borrow it for a time. Go and get your hat and coat on, miss."

"I shall not," the girl objected. "My uncle told me, if anything happened to him, that I was to remain here."

"And remain here she shall, so long as she likes," Mrs. Malony insisted. "I've given my promise, too, to look after her, and Mr. Craig knows that I am an honest woman."

"You may be that," the man replied, "but it's just as well for you both to understand this. I'm from the police, and what I say goes. No harm will come to the girl, Mrs. Malony, and she shall come back here, but for the present she is going to accompany me to headquarters. If you make any trouble, I only have to blow my whistle and I can fill your house with policemen."

"I'll go," the girl whispered.

In silence she put on her hat and coat, in silence she drove with him to the police-station, where she was shown at once into an inspector's office. The man who had brought her whispered for a moment or two with his chief and handed him the paper. Inspector French read it and whistled softly. He took up the telephone by his side.

"Say, you've something of a find here," he remarked to the plain-clothes man. "Put me through to Mr. Quest, please," he added, speaking into the receiver.

The two men whispered together. The girl stole from her place and turned over rapidly the pages of a directory which was on the round table before her. She found the "A's" quickly. Her eye fell upon the name of Ashleigh. She repeated the address to herself and glanced around. The two men were still whispering. For the moment she was forgotten. She stole on tiptoe across the room, ran down the stone steps, and hastened into the street.

4.

The Professor, who was comfortably seated in Quest's favourite easy-chair, glanced at his watch and shook his head.

"I am afraid, my friend," he said, "that Craig's nerve has failed him. A voluntary surrender was perhaps too much to hope for."

Quest smoked for a moment in silence.

"Can't understand those fellows letting him give them the slip," he muttered. "He ought to have been under close surveillance from the moment he set foot in New York. What's that?" he added, turning to the door.

His servant entered, bearing a note.

"This was left a few minutes ago, sir," he announced, "by a messenger boy. There was no answer required."

The man retired and Quest unfolded the sheet of paper. His expression suddenly changed.

"Listen!" he exclaimed.

To Sanford Quest.
Gather your people in Professor Ashleigh's library at ten o'clock tonight. I will be there and tell you my whole story.
John Craig.

The Professor sat for a moment speechless.

"Then he meant it, after all!" he exclaimed at last.

"Seems like it," Quest admitted. "I'll just telephone to French."

The Professor rose to his feet, knocked the ash from his cigar, struggled into his coat, and took up his hat. Then he waited until Quest had completed his conversation. The latter's face had grown grave and puzzled. It was obvious that he was receiving information of some importance. He put down the instrument at last with a curt word of farewell.

"Let me send a couple of men up with you, Professor," he begged. "You don't want to run any risk of having Craig there before we arrive."

The Professor smiled.

"My friend," he said, "it is seldom in my life that I have had to have recourse to physical violence, but I flatter myself that there is no man who would do me any harm. We will meet, then, at my house. You will bring the young ladies?"

"Sure!" Quest replied. "I am just sending word up to them now."

The Professor moved towards the door.

"If only this may prove to be the end!" he sighed.

Quest spent the next hour or so in restless deliberations. There were still many things which puzzled him. At about a quarter past nine Lenora and Laura arrived, dressed for their expedition. Quest threw open the window and looked out across the city. A yellowish haze which, accompanied by a sulphurous heat, had been brooding over the city all day long, had suddenly increased in density. The air was stifling.

"I'm afraid we are in for a bad thunderstorm, girls," Quest remarked.

Laura laughed.

"Who cares? The automobile's there, Mr. Quest."

"Let's go, then," he replied.

They descended into the street and drove to the Professor's house in silence. Even Laura was feeling the strain of these last hours of anxiety. On the way they picked up French and a plain-clothes man, and the whole party arrived at their destination just as the storm broke. The Professor met them in the hall. He, too, seemed to have lost to some extent his customary equanimity.

"Come this way, my friends," he invited. "If Craig keeps his word, he will be here now within a few minutes. This way."

They followed him into the library. Chairs were arranged around the table in the middle of the room, and they all sat down. The Professor took out his watch. It was five minutes to ten.

"In a few minutes," he continued solemnly, "this weight is to be lifted from the minds of all of us. I have come to the conclusion that on this occasion Craig will keep his word. I am not sure, mind, but I believe that he is in the house at this present moment. I have heard movements in the room which belonged to him. I have not interfered. I have been content to wait."

"At least he has not tried to escape," Quest remarked. "French here brought news of him. He has been living with his niece very quietly, but without any particular attempt at concealment or any signs of wishing to leave the city."

"I had that girl brought to my office," French remarked, "barely an hour ago, but she slipped away while we were talking. Say, what's that?"

They all rose quickly to their feet. In a momentary lull of the storm, they could hear distinctly a girl's shrill call from outside, followed by the clamour of angry voices.

"I bet that's the girl," French exclaimed. "She's been looking up the Professor's address in a directory."

They all hurried out into the hall. The plain-clothes man whom they had left on guard was standing there with his hand upon Craig's collar. The girl, sobbing bitterly, was clinging to his arm. Craig was making desperate efforts to escape. Directly he saw the little party issue from the library, however, the strength seemed to pass from his limbs. He remained in the clutches of his captor, limp and helpless.

"I caught the girl trying to make her way into the house," the latter explained. "She called out, and this man came running downstairs, right into my arms."

"It is quite all right," the Professor said, in a dignified tone. "You may release them both. Craig was on his way to keep an appointment here at ten o'clock. Quest, will you and the Inspector bring him in? Let us resume our places at the table."

The little procession made its way down the hall. The girl was still clinging to her uncle.

"What are they going to do to you, these people?" she sobbed. "They shan't hurt you! They shan't!"

Lenora passed her arm around the girl.

"Of course not, dear," she said soothingly. "Your uncle has come of his own free will to answer a few questions, only I think it would be better if you would let me—"

Lenora never finished her sentence. They had reached the entrance now to the library. The Professor was standing in the doorway with extended hand, motioning them to take their places at the table. Then, with no form of warning, the room seemed suddenly filled with a blaze of blue light. It came at first in a thin flash from the window to the table, became immediately multiplied a thousand times, and played round the table in sparks which suddenly expanded to sheets of leaping, curling flame. The roar of thunder shook the very foundations of the house—and then silence. For several seconds not one of them seemed to have the power of speech. An amazing thing had happened. The oak table in the middle of the room was a charred fragment, the chairs were every one blackened remnants.

"A thunderbolt!" French gasped at last.

Quest was the first to cross the room. From the table to the outside window was one charred, black line which had burnt its way through the carpet. He threw open the window. The wire whose course he had followed ended there with a little lump of queer substance. He broke it off from the end of the wire, which was absolutely brittle, and brought it into the room.

"What is it?" Lenora faltered.

"What have you got there?" French echoed.

Quest examined the strange-looking lump of metal steadily. The most curious thing about it seemed to be that it was absolutely sound and showed no signs of damage. He turned to the Professor.

"I think you are the only one who will be able to appreciate this, Professor," he remarked. "Look! It is a fragment of opotan—a distinct and wonderful specimen of opotan."

Every one looked puzzled.

"But what," Lenora enquired, "is opotan?"

"It is a new metal," Quest explained gravely, "towards which scientists have been directing a great deal of attention lately. It has the power of collecting all the electricity from the air around us. There are a dozen people, at the present moment, conducting experiments with it for the purpose of cheapening electric lights. If we had been in the room ten seconds sooner—"

He paused significantly. Then he swung round on his heel. Craig, a now pitiful objcct, his hands nervously twitching, his face ghastly, was cowering in the background.

"Your last little effort, Craig?" he demanded sternly.

Craig made no reply. The Professor, who had disappeared for a moment, came back to them.

"There is a smaller room across the hall," he said, "which will do for our purpose."

Craig suddenly turned and faced them.

"I have changed my mind," he said. "I have nothing to tell you. Do what you will with me. Take me to the Tombs, deal with me any way you choose, but I have nothing to say."

French smiled a little grimly.

"We may make you change your mind when we get you there," he remarked.

"No one will ever make me change my mind," the man replied. "This is my last word."

Quest pointed a threatening finger at him.

"Your last voluntary word, perhaps," he said, "but science is still your master, Craig. Science has brought many criminals to their doom. It shall take its turn with you. Bring him along, French, to my study. There is a way of dealing with him."

Quest felt his forehead and found it damp. There were dark rims under his eyes. Before him was Craig, with a little band around his forehead and the mirror where they could all see it. The Professor stood a little in the background. Laura and French were side by side, gazing with distended eyes at the blank mirror, and Lenora was doing her best to soothe the terrified niece. Twice Quest's teeth came together and once he almost reeled.

"It's the fight of his life," he muttered at last, "but I've got him."

Almost as he spoke, they could see Craig's resistance begin to weaken. The tenseness of his form relaxed; Quest's will was triumphing. Slowly in the mirror they saw a little picture creeping from outline into definite form, a picture of the Professor's library. Craig himself was there with mortar and trowel, and a black box in his hand.

"It's coming!" Lenora moaned.

Quest stood perfectly tense. The picture suddenly flashed into brilliant clearness. They saw Craig's features with almost lifelike detail. From the corner of that room where the Professor was standing, came a smothered groan. It was a terrifying, a paralysing moment. Even the silence seemed charged with awful things. Then suddenly, without any warning, the picture faded completely away. A cry which was almost a howl of anger broke from Quest's lips. Craig had fallen sideways from his chair. There was an ominous change in his face. Something seemed to have passed from the atmosphere of the room, some tense and nameless quality. Quest moved forward and laid his hand on Craig's heart. The girl was on her knees, crying.

"Take her away," Quest whispered to Lenora.

"What about him?" French demanded, as Lenora led the girl from the room.

"He fought too hard," Quest said gravely. "He is dead. Professor,—"

They all looked around. The spot where he had been standing was empty. The Professor had gone.

CHAPTER XVI
JUSTICE CHEATED

The first shock was over. Craig's body had been removed, and the girls had taken Mary, half stunned with grief, to their room. French and Quest were left alone.

"This is some disappointment," the former remarked gloomily.

"It is a disappointment," Quest said slowly, "which may clear the way to bigger things."

"What's in your mind now?" French enquired.

Quest shook his head.

"A turmoil. First of all, where is the Professor?"

"Must have scooted right away home," French suggested. "He was looking pretty sick all the time. Guess it must have been a powerful shock for him, and he isn't so young as he used to be."

"Give me that paper of Craig's again," Quest asked, stretching out his hand.

The Inspector produced the document from his inner pocket, and Quest, stretching it out upon his knee, read it word for word.

"Never to communicate or to have anything to do with any one of the name of Ashleigh, eh?" he remarked, as he handed it back again. "Rather a queer provision, that, French."

"I've been thinking that myself," the Inspector admitted. "Seems to be rather reversing the positions, doesn't it?"

Quest glanced at the clock.

"Well," he said, "if you're ready, Inspector, we'll be getting along."

"Where to?" French demanded.

Quest looked for a moment surprised. Just then Lenora entered the room.

"Are you going out?" she asked Quest.

He nodded.

"The Inspector and I are going to have a look for that black box," he told her.

"Won't you want me?"

He shook his head.

"I think you girls have had as much as is good for you of this sort of business," he declared grimly.

"But it's all over now," Lenora protested.

Quest buttoned up his coat and motioned to French to follow him.

"I'm not so sure," he said. "I'll 'phone if we want you, Lenora. We shall be at the Professor's."

The two men drove to the outskirts of the city almost in silence, while several of the officers followed in another taxi. The Professor's house seemed more than ever deserted as they drew up at the front door. They entered without ringing and crossed the hall towards the library. On the threshold Quest paused and held up his finger.

"Some one is in there," he whispered, stepping quickly forward. "Come!"

He threw open the door. The room was empty, yet both Quest and French were conscious of a curious conviction that it had been occupied within the last few seconds. French even shook out the curtains and swung open the doors of a bureau. There was no sign of anybody, however, nor any evidence as to how they could have left the room.

"Queer, but it seemed to me I heard some one," French muttered.

"I was sure of it," Quest replied, shaking the curtains at the back of the door.

They stood still for a moment and listened. The silence in the empty house was almost unnatural. Quest turned away with a shrug of the shoulders.

"At any rate," he said, "Craig's dying thoughts must have been truthful. Come."

He led the way to the fireplace, went down on his knees and passed his hands over the bricks. The third one he touched, shook. He tapped it—without a doubt it was hollow. With his penknife he loosened the mortar a little and drew it out easily. The back was open. Inside was the black box.

"Craig's secret at last!" French muttered hoarsely. "Bring it to the light, quick!"

They were unemotional men but the moment was supreme. The key to the mystery of these tragical weeks was there in their hands! Their eyes almost devoured those few hastily scrawled words buried with so much care:

See page 62, January number, American Medical Journal 1905.

They looked at one another. They repeated vaguely this most commonplace of messages. As the final result of their strenuous enterprise, these cryptic words seemed pitifully inadequate. Quest's face darkened. He crumpled the paper in his fingers.

"There must be some meaning in this," he muttered. "It can't be altogether a fool's game we're on. Wait."

He moved towards a table which usually stood against the wall, but which had obviously been dragged out recently into the middle of the room. It was covered with bound volumes. Quest glanced at one and exclaimed softly.

"*American Medical Journal, 1905!* French, there's something in this message, after all."

He turned over the pages rapidly. Then he came to a stop. Page 60 was there; page 62 had been neatly removed with a pair of scissors.

"The Professor!" he cried. "The Professor's been at work here!"

The two men stood looking at one another across the table. Strange thoughts were framing themselves in the brains of both of them. Then there came a startling and in its way a dramatic interlude. Through the empty house came the ringing of the electric bell from the front door, shrill and insistent. Without a moment's hesitation, Quest hurried out, and French followed him. On the door-step was another surprise. Lenora and Laura were there, the former carrying a small, black-bound volume.

"Don't be cross," she begged quickly. "We just had to come. Look! We picked this up underneath the chair where Craig was sitting. It must have slipped from his pocket. You see what is written on it? DIARY OF JOHN CRAIG."

Quest took it in his hand.

"This ought to be interesting," he remarked. "Come along in."

They passed into the library. French lingered behind for a moment and caught up with them just as they were opening the book underneath the electric lamp.

"See what I've found!" he exclaimed. "It was just by the side of the wall there. Where's that journal?"

He spread out the piece of paper—it fitted exactly into the empty space. They all read together:

"Professor Ashleigh, after being bitten by the anthropoid, rapidly developed hydrophobia of a serious nature. After treatment with a new serum the patient was relieved of the hydrophobic symptoms, but to my horror this mild-mannered, humane man seems possessed at times of all the characteristics of the brutal anthropoid—cunning, thievery, brutality. I do not know what may come of this. I hesitate to put even these words on to paper. I am doubtful as to what course, in the interests of humanity, I ought to take.
(Signed) "James Merrill, M.D.

"Editor's Note. Just as we go to press, a cable announces the terrible death of Doctor Merrill, the writer of the above notes. He was attacked by wild animals while alone in a South American jungle, and torn to pieces."

There was a queer little silence among the company. No one seemed inclined for speech. They looked at one another in dumb, wondering horror. Then Quest drew a penknife from his pocket and with a turn of his wrist forced the lock of the diary. They all watched him with fascinated eyes. It was something to escape from their thoughts. They leaned over as he spread the book out before him. Those first two sentences were almost in the light of a dedication:

"For ten years I have protected my master, Professor Edgar Ashleigh, at the cost of my peace of mind, my happiness, my reputation. This book, even though it be too late to help me, shall clear my reputation."

Quest closed the volume.

"French," he decided, "we must find the Professor. Will you have your men search the house and grounds immediately?"

The Inspector left the room like a dazed man. They could hear him giving orders outside.

"The next page," Lenora begged. "Just one page more!"

Quest hesitated for a moment. Then he turned it over. All three read again:

"Ten years of horror, struggling all the while to keep him from that other self, that thing of bestiality, to keep his horrible secret from the world, to cover up his crimes, even though their shadow should rest upon me. Now Sanford Quest has come. Will this mean discovery?"

"Another page," Lenora faltered.

"No more," Quest said. "Don't you see where it is leading us? We have the truth here. Wait!"

He strode hastily to the door. French and one of the plain-clothes men were descending the stairs.

"Well?" Quest asked breathlessly.

"The Professor is not in the house," French reported. "We are going to search the grounds."

Quest returned to the library. Lenora clung to his arm. The diary lay still upon the table.

Quest opened the volume slowly. Again they all read together:

"The evil nature is growing stronger every day. He is developing a sort of ferocious cunning to help him in his crimes. He wanders about in the dark, wearing a black velvet suit with holes for his eyes, and leaving only his hands exposed. I have watched him come into a half darkened room and one can see nothing but the hands and the eyes; sometimes if he closes his eyes, only the hands."

"Mrs. Rheinholdt!" Quest muttered. "Wait. I know where that suit is."

He hastened to a cupboard at the farther end of the room,

snatched some garments from it and vanished into the hall.

"One moment, girls," he said. "I see now how he did it. Wait. I'll show you."

They stood quite still, a little terrified. In a moment or two the door reopened. A finger turned out all the electric lights but one. Then there was nothing to be seen but a pair of white hands, which seemed to come floating towards them through the darkness—a pair of white hands and a pair of gleaming eyes. Lenora screamed wildly. Even Laura was unnerved.

"Stop that!" she cried out. "Who are you, anyway?"

The lights were suddenly turned on. Quest threw off his disguise.

"There you are," he exclaimed triumphantly. "Ingenious, but one ought to have seen through it long ago. The stroke of genius about it was that as soon as he had used a dodge once or twice and set you thinking about it, he dropped it."

The door was suddenly opened and French entered.

"Beaten!" he exclaimed tersely.

"You haven't found him?" Quest asked.

French shook his head.

"We've searched every room, every cupboard, every scrap of the cellar in the house," he announced. "We've been into every corner of the grounds, searched all the place inside and out. There's no sign of the Professor."

Quest pocketed the diary.

"You're perfectly certain that he is not in this house or anywhere upon the premises?"

"Certain sure!" French replied.

Quest shrugged his shoulders.

"Well, we'd better get back," he said. "You come, too, French. We'll sit down and figure out some scheme for finding him."

They made their way to the front door and crowded into the autos. The two men left with marked reluctance. The two girls had but one idea in their heads—to get away, and get away quickly.

"Do start, please," Lenora begged. "There's just one thing in life I want, and that is to be in my own room, to feel myself away from his world of horrible, unnatural mysteries."

"The kid has the right idea," Laura agreed. "I've had enough myself."

They were on the point of starting, the chauffeur with his hand upon the starting handle, French with the steering wheel of the police car already in his hand. And then the little party seemed suddenly turned to stone. For a few breathless seconds not one of them moved. Out into the clammy night air came the echoes of a hideous, inhuman, blood-curdling scream. Quest was the first to recover himself. He leaped from his seat and rushed back across the empty hall into the study, followed a little way behind by French and the others.

An unsuspected panel door which led into the garden, stood slightly ajar. The Professor, with his hand on the back of a chair, was staring at the fireplace, shaking as though with some horrible ague, his face distorted, his body curiously hunched-up. He seemed suddenly to have dropped his humanity, to have fallen back into the world of some strange creatures. He heard their footsteps, but he did not turn his head. His hands were stretched out in front of him as though to keep away from his sight some hateful object.

"Stop him!" he cried. "Take him away! It's Craig—his spirit! He came to me in the garage, he followed me through the grounds, he mocked at me when I hid in the tree. He's there now, kneeling before the fireplace. Why can't I kill him! He is coming! Stop him, some one!"

No one spoke or moved; no one, indeed, had the power. Then at last Quest found words.

"There is no one in the room, Professor," he said, "except us."

The sound of a human voice seemed to produce a strange effect. The Professor straightened himself, shook his head, his hands dropped to his side. He turned around and faced them. He was ghastly pale, but his smile was once more the smile of the amiable naturalist.

"My friends," he said, "forgive me. I am very old, and the events of these last few hours have unnerved me. Forgive me."

He groped for a moment and sank into a chair. Quest fetched a decanter and a glass from the sideboard, poured out some wine and held it to his lips. The Professor drank it eagerly.

"My dear friend," he exclaimed, "you have saved me! I have something to tell you, something I must tell you at once, but not here. I loathe this place. Let me come with you to your rooms."

"As you please," Quest answered calmly.

The Professor rose hastily to his feet. As he turned around, he saw French concealing something in his hands. He shivered.

"I don't need those!" he cried. "What are they? Handcuffs? Ah, no! I am only too anxious to tell you all that I know. Take care of me, Mr. Quest. Take me with you."

He gripped Quest's arm. In silence they passed from the room, in silence they took their places once more in the automobiles, in silence they drove without a pause to Quest's rooms. The Professor seemed to breathe more freely as they left the neighbourhood of his house behind. He walked up the stairs to Quest's library almost blithely. If he was aware of it, he took no notice of French and the two plain-clothes men behind. As he stepped into the room, he drew a long sigh of relief. He made his way at once to his favourite easy-chair, threw off his overcoat and leaned back.

"Quest," he pronounced, "you are the best friend I have in my life! It is you who have rid me of my great burden. Tell me—help me a little with my story—have you read that page from the *Medical Journal* which Craig has kept locked up all these years?"

"We have all read it," Quest replied.

"It was forged," the Professor declared firmly, "forged by Craig. All the years since, he has blackmailed me. I have been his servant and his tool. I have been afraid to speak. At last I am free of him. Thank God!"

"Craig, after all," French muttered.

The Professor sat with a faint, wistful smile upon the corners of his lips, looking around at all of them. His face had become like the face of a child, eager for sympathy and kindness.

"You will trust me, I know," he continued. "You will believe me. All my life I have laboured for science. I have never been selfish. I have laid up no store of gold or treasure. Knowledge has been my mistress, knowledge has been my heaven. If I had been a wise man, I would have ridden myself of this hideous burden, but I was foolish and afraid. I wanted to pursue my studies, I wanted to be left in peace, so I let that fiend prey upon my fears. But now—now I feel that the burden has rolled away. I shall tell you my story, and afterwards I will do great things yet, great things for science, great things for the world."

They listened to him, spellbound. Only Lenora stood a little apart with a faint frown upon her forehead. She touched Quest on the shoulder.

"Mr. Quest," she murmured, "he is lying!"

Quest turned his head. His lips scarcely moved.

"What do you mean?" he whispered.

"He is lying!" Lenora insisted. "I tell you there's another creature there, something we don't understand. Let me bring the Electrothought transference apparatus; let us read his mind. If I am wrong, I will go down on my knees and beg for forgiveness."

Quest nodded. Lenora hastened to the further end of the room, snatched the cloth from the instrument and wheeled down the little mirror with its coils and levers. The Professor watched her. Slowly his face changed. The benevolence faded away, his teeth for a moment showed in something which was almost a snarl.

"You believe me?" he cried, turning to Quest. "You are not going to try that horrible thing on me—Professor Lord Ashleigh? I am all broken up. I am not fit for it. Look at my hands, how they shake."

"Professor," Quest said sternly, "we are surrounded by the shadow of some terrible deeds for which as yet there is no explanation. I do not say that we mistrust you, but I ask you to submit to this test."

"I refuse!" the Professor replied harshly.

"And I insist," Quest muttered.

The Professor drew a little breath. He sat back in his chair. His face became still, his lips were drawn closely together. Lenora wheeled up the machine and with deft fingers adjusted the fittings on one side. Quest himself connected it up on the other. The Professor sat there like a figure of stone. The silence in the room was so intense that the ticking of the small clock upon the mantelpiece was clearly audible. The silent battle of wills seemed like a live and visible struggle. The very atmosphere seemed charged with the thrill and wonder of it. Never before had Quest met with resistance so complete and immovable. For the first time the thought of failure oppressed him. Even that slight slackening of his rigid concentration brought relief to the Professor. Without any knowledge as to the source of their conviction, the two girls who watched felt that the Professor was becoming dominant. And then there came a sudden queer change. The intangible triumph of the Professor's stony poise seemed to fade away. His eyes had sought the corner of the room, his lips quivered. The horror was there again, the horror they had seen before. He crouched a little back. His hands were uplifted as though to keep off some evil thing.

"Craig!" Lenora whispered. "He thinks he sees Craig again!"

Quest held up his hand. He realised that this was his moment. He leaned a little farther forward. Sternly he concentrated the whole of his will power upon his task. Almost at once there was a change. The Professor fell back in the chair. The tense self-control had passed from his features, his lips twitched. Simultaneously, the mirror for a moment was clouded,—then slowly a picture upon it gathered outline and substance. There was a jungle, strange, tall trees, and brushwood so thick that it reached to the waists of the two men who were slowly making their way through it. One was the Professor, clearly recognisable under his white sun helmet; the other a stranger to all of them. Suddenly they stopped. The latter had crept a yard or so ahead, his gun raised to his shoulder, his eyes fixed upon some possible object of pursuit. There was a sudden change in the Professor. They saw him seize his gun by the barrel and whirl it above his head. He seemed suddenly to lose his whole identity. He crouched on his haunches, almost like an animal, and sprang at the other's throat. They could almost hear the snarl from his lips as the two men went down together into the undergrowth. The picture faded away.

"Dr. Merrill!" Lenora faltered. "Then it was not wild beasts which killed him."

Almost immediately figures again appeared in the mirror. This time they saw the Professor in bed in a tent, Craig sitting by him, a violin in his hand. A native servant entered with food, which he placed by the bedside with a low obeisance. Slowly the Professor raised himself in bed. His face was distorted, his mouth curved into strange lines. With a sudden spring he seized the native servant by the throat and bore him back upon the floor. Craig passed his arm through his master's and, exerting all his strength, dragged him away. They saw the man run terrified from the room, they saw Craig soothe the Professor and finally get him back to bed. Then he seized the violin and bent a little forward, playing softly. Slowly the Professor relapsed into what seemed to be a sleep. The scene faded away, to be replaced almost immediately by another. There was a small passage which seemed to lead from the back entrance of a house; the Professor with a black mantle, Craig following him, pleading, expostulating. They saw the conservatory for a minute, and then blackness. The Professor was leaning against a marble basin. There was nothing to be seen of him but his eyes and hands. They saw him listen, for a moment or two in cold, unresponsive silence, then stretch out his hand and push Craig away. The picture glowed and faded and glowed again. Then they saw through the gloom the figure of a woman approach, a diamond necklace around her neck. They saw the hands steal out and encircle her throat—and then more darkness, silence, obscurity. The mirror was empty once more.

"Mrs. Rheinholdt's jewels!" Lenora cried. "What next? Oh! my God, what next?"

Their eyes ached with the strain but there was not one of them who could even glance away from the mirror. It was Quest's study which slowly appeared then. The Salvation Army girl was there, talking to the Professor. They saw him leave her, they saw him look back from the door, a strange, evil glance. Then the secretary entered and spoke to her. Once more the door opened. The hands were there, stretching and reaching, a paper-weight gripped in the right-hand fingers. They saw it raised above the secretary's head, they saw the other hand take the girl by the throat and push her towards the table. A wild scream broke from Lenora's lips. Quest wavered for a moment. The picture faded out.

"Oh, stop it!" Lenora begged. "Haven't we seen enough? We know the truth now. Stop!"

The criminologist made no reply. His eyes were still fixed upon the Professor, who showed some signs of returning consciousness. He was gripping at his collar. He seemed to have difficulty with his breathing. Quest suddenly braced himself. He pushed Lenora back.

"One more," he muttered. "There's something growing in his mind. I can feel it. Wait!"

Again they all turned towards the mirror. They saw the hallway of Ashleigh House, the pictures upon the walls, they could almost feel the quiet silence of night. They saw the Professor come stealing down the stairs. He was wearing the black velvet suit with the cowl in his hand. They watched him pause before a certain door, draw on the cowl and disappear. Through the opening they could see Lord Ashleigh asleep in bed, the moonlight streaming through the open window across the counterpane. They saw the Professor turn with a strange, horrible look in his face and close the door. Lenora burst into sobs.

"No more!" she begged. "No more, please!"

Suddenly, without any warning, Laura also began to sob hysterically. French mopped his forehead with his handkerchief. His face was unrecognisable. He had lost all his healthy colour, and his lips were twitching. Quest himself was as pale as death, and there were black rims under his eyes.

"We've had enough," he admitted, swaying a little on his feet. "Undo the other band, if you can, Lenora."

He leaned forward and released their victim. The whole atmosphere of the place seemed immediately to change. Lenora drew a long, convulsive breath and sank into a chair. The Professor sat up, and gazed at them all with the air of a man who had just awakened from a dream. His features relapsed, his mouth once more resolved itself into pleasant and natural lines. He smiled at them cordially.

"Have I, by any chance, slept?" he asked. "Or—"

He never finished his sentence. His eyes fell upon the mirror, the metal band lying by his side. He read the truth in the faces still turned towards him. He rose to his feet. There was another and equally sudden change in his demeanour and tone. He carried himself with the calm dignity of the scientist.

"The end of our struggle, I presume?" he said to Quest, pointing to the metal band. "You will at least admit that I have shown you fine sport?"

No one answered him. Even Quest had barely yet recovered himself. The Professor shrugged his shoulders.

"I recognise, of course," he said gravely, "that this is the end. A person *in extremis* has privileges. Will you allow me to write just a matter of twenty lines at your desk?"

Silently Quest assented. The Professor seated himself in the swing chair, drew a sheet of paper towards him, dipped the pen in the ink and began to write. Then he turned round and reached for his own small black bag which lay upon the table. Quest caught him by the wrist.

"What do you want out of that, Professor?" he enquired.

"Merely my own pen and ink," the Professor expostulated. "If there is anything I detest in the world, it is violet ink. And your pen, too, is execrable. As these are to be the last words I shall leave to a sorrowing world, I should like to write them in my own fashion. Open the bag for yourself, if you will. You can pass me the things out."

Quest opened the bag, took out a pen and a small glass bottle of ink. He handed them to the Professor, who started once more to write. Quest watched him for a moment and then turned away to French. The Professor looked over his shoulder and suddenly bared his wrist. Lenora seized her employer by the arm.

"Look!" she cried. "What is he going to do?"

Quest swung round, but he was too late. The Professor had dug the pen into his arm. He sat in his chair and laughed as they all hurried towards him. Then suddenly he sprang to his feet. Again the change came into his face which they had seen in the mirror. French dashed forward towards him. The Professor snarled, seemed about to spring, then suddenly once more stretched out his hands to show that he was helpless and handed to Quest the paper upon which he had been writing.

"You have nothing to fear from me," he exclaimed. "Here is my last message to you, Sanford Quest. Read it—read it aloud. Always remember that this was not your triumph but mine."

Quest held up the paper. They all read. The Professor's letters were carefully formed, his handwriting perfectly legible.

"You have been a clever opponent, Sanford Quest, but even now you are to be cheated. The wisdom of the ages outreaches yours, outreaches it and triumphs."

Quest looked up quickly.

"What the devil does he mean?" he muttered.

The Professor's arms shot suddenly above his head. Again that strange, animal look convulsed his features. He burst into a loud, unnatural laugh.

"Mean, you fool?" he cried, holding out his wrist, which was slowly turning black. "Poisoned! That is what it means!"

They all stared at him. Quest seized the ink bottle, revealed the false top and laid it down again with a little exclamation. Then, before they could realize it, the end came. The Professor lay, a crumpled-up heap, upon the floor. The last change of all had taken place in his face. His arms were outstretched, his face deathly white, his lips faintly curved in the half amiable, half supercilious smile of the savant who sees beyond. Quest stooped over him.

"He is dead," he declared.

Quest swung round in his chair as French entered the room, and held out his left hand.

"Glad to see you, French. Help yourself to a cigar."

"I don't know as I want to smoke this morning just at present, thank you," French replied.

Quest laid down his pen and looked up. French was fidgeting about with his hat in his hand. He was dressed more carefully than usual, but he was obviously ill at ease.

"Nothing wrong, eh?"

"No, there's nothing wrong," French admitted. "I just looked in—"

Quest waited for a moment. Then he crossed his legs and assumed a patient attitude.

"What the dickens did you look in for?" he asked.

"The fact of it is," French explained, "I should like a few words with Miss Laura."

Quest laughed shortly.

"Why on earth couldn't you say so?" he observed. "Never knew you bashful before, Inspector. She's up in the laboratory. I'll ring for some one to show you the way."

Quest touched the bell and his new secretary entered almost at once.

"Take Inspector French up into the laboratory," Quest directed. "See you later, French."

"Yes—perhaps—I hope so," the Inspector replied nervously.

Quest watched him disappear, with a puzzled smile.

Then he sat down at his desk, drew a sheet of paper towards him and began to write:

"My dear Inspector,

"I am taking this opportunity of letting you know that out of deference to the wishes of the woman I hope soon to marry, I am abandoning the hazardous and nerve-racking profession of criminology for a safer and happier career. You will have, therefore, to find help elsewhere in the future.

"With best wishes,
"Yours,
"Sanford Quest."

He left the sheet of paper upon the desk and, ringing the bell, sent for Lenora. She appeared in a few moments and came over to his side.

"What is it, Mr. Quest?" she asked.

He gave her the letter without remark. She read it through and, turning slowly around, looked at him expectantly.

"How's that seem to you?" he asked, reaching out his hand for a cigar.

"Very sensible indeed," she replied.

"It's no sort of life, this, for a married man," Quest declared. "You agree with me there, don't you, Lenora?"

"Yes!" she admitted, a little faintly.

Quest lit his cigar deliberately. Then he enclosed the letter in an envelope and addressed it to Inspector French.

"You'd better deliver this to the Inspector," he said, "in case he doesn't call round here on his way out."

He handed her the note. For a moment she looked at him, then she turned quickly away.

"He shall have it at once," she said in a low tone.

Quest watched her cross the room. She opened the door and passed out without a backward glance. Then he shrugged his shoulders, hesitated for a moment, and followed her. He heard the door of her apartment on the next floor close, however, and made his way to the laboratory. He entered the room softly and paused upon the threshold. His presence was altogether unobserved by the two people who were standing at the other end of the apartment.

"I say, Miss Laura," the Inspector was saying, "this has got to come sometime or other. Why don't you make up your mind to it? I'm no great hand at love-making, but I'm the right sort of man for you and I think you know it."

"This," Quest murmured to himself, "is where Laura boxes the Inspector's ears!"

Nothing of the sort happened, however. There was a queer, a mystifying change in Laura's expression. She was looking down at the floor. Suddenly her face was hidden in her hands. The Inspector threw his arms around her.

"That's all the answer I want," he declared.

Quest stole softly away. As he regained the door of his study, Lenora, dressed for the street, hurried out. She tried to pass him but he laid his hand upon her shoulder.

"I was just going round to Mr. French's office," she explained.

"That's all right," Quest replied. "The Inspector's here. You can leave the note upon the table. Hi, Parkins," he called out to his secretary in the next room, "get my hat and coat. Come back a moment, Lenora."

She turned into the room a little unwillingly and leaned against the table. Quest stood by her side.

"Lenora," he said quietly, "that was kind of a brutal note I told you to give to French, but I thought you'd understand."

She raised her eyes suddenly to his.

"Understand what?" she whispered.

The secretary entered the room, helped Quest on with his coat and handed him his hat.

"If you are quite ready, Lenora."

"Ready?" she exclaimed. "Where are we going?"

Quest sighed.

"Fancy having to explain all these things!" he said, taking her arm. "I just want you to understand, Lenora, that I've waited—quite long enough. Parkins," he added, turning to his secretary, "if any one calls, just say that my wife and I will be back early in the afternoon. And you'd better step upstairs to the laboratory and give my compliments to Inspector French, and say that I hope he and Miss Laura will join us at Delmonico's for luncheon at one o'clock."

"Very good, sir," the man replied.

Lenora's face was suddenly transformed. She passed her arm through Quest's. He stooped and kissed her as he led her towards the door.

"You understand now, don't you?" he whispered, smiling down at her.

"I think so," she admitted, with a little sigh of content.

THE END